American Dervish

American Dervish

a novel by

Ayad Akhtar

Little, Brown and Company
New York Boston London

Little, Brown and Company
Hachette Book Group
237 Park Avenue, New York, NY 10017
www.hachettebookgroup.com

First Edition: January 2012

Little, Brown and Company is a division of Hachette Book Group, Inc., and is celebrating its 175th anniversary in 2012. The Little, Brown name and logo are trademarks of Hachette Book Group, Inc.

The publisher is not responsible for websites (or their content) that are not owned by the publisher.

The characters and events in this book are fictitious. Any similarity to real persons, living or dead, is coincidental and not intended by the author.

Library of Congress Cataloging-in-Publication Data
Akhtar, Ayad.
American dervish : a novel / by Ayad Akhtar. — 1st ed.
p. cm.
ISBN 978-0-316-18331-4 (hc) / 978-0-316-20476-7 (large print) / 978-0-316-19899-8 (int'l ed)
1. Muslim families — Fiction. 2. Pakistanis — United States — Fiction. I. Title.
PS3601.K53A83 2012
813'.6 — dc22   2011019737
10 9 8 7 6 5 4 3 2 1

RRD-C

Printed in the United States of America

For My Mother & Marc H. Glick

And Allah said: I am with the ones
whose hearts are torn.

Hadith Qudsi

Contents

BOOK THREE: PORTRAIT OF AN ANTI-SEMITE AS A BOY

BOOK FOUR: MINA THE DERVISH

American Dervish

Prologue: 1990

I remember it all with a vividness that marks the moment as the watershed it would be:

The court was glowing, its wooden surface honey-brown beneath the overhead lights. Along the edges, players huddled with their coaches, and beyond, we were gathered, the clamoring rows upon rows of us, eager for the timeout to end.

Below, I spied the vendor approaching: a burly man, thick around the waist, with a crimson-brown ponytail dropping from beneath the back of his black-and-orange cap, our school colors. "Brats and wieners!" he cried. "Brats and wieners!"

I nodded, raising my hand. He nodded back, stopping three rows down to serve another customer first. I turned to my friends and asked them if they wanted anything.

Beer and bratwurst, each of them said.

"I don't think he's got beer, guys," I replied.

Out on the court, the players were returning to their positions for the last minute of the half. The crowd was getting to its feet.

Below, the vendor made change, then lifted the metal box to his waist and mounted the steps to settle at the edge of our row.

"You have beer?" one of my friends asked.

"Just brats and wieners."

"So two bratwurst and a beef dog," I said.

With a clipped nod, he tossed open the cover of his box and reached inside. I waved away my friends' bills, pulling out my wallet. The vendor handed me three shiny packets, soft and warm to the touch.

"Beef wiener's on top. That's nine altogether."

I handed off the brats, and paid.

Cheers erupted as our side raced down the court, driving to the basket. I unwrapped my packet only to find I wasn't holding a beef frank, but a marbled, brown-and-white pork bratwurst.

"Guys? Anyone have the beef dog?" I shouted over the crowd's noise at my friends.

Both shook their heads. They were holding bratwurst as well.

I turned back to the aisle to call out to the vendor when I stopped. What reason did I have anymore not to eat it?

None at all, I thought.

We drove to the basket again, where we were fouled. When the whistle shrieked, the roar was deafening.

I lifted the sausage to my mouth, closed my eyes, and took a bite. My heart raced as I chewed, my mouth filling with a sweet and smoky, lightly pungent taste that seemed utterly re-markable—perhaps all the more so for having been so long forbidden. I felt at once brave and ridiculous. And as I swallowed, an eerie stillness came over me.

I looked up at the ceiling.

It was still there. Not an inch closer to falling in.

After the game, I walked along the campus quad alone, the walkway's lamps glowing in the mist, white blossoms on a balmy November night. The wet air swirled and blew. I felt alive as I moved. Free along my limbs. Even giddy.

Back at the dorm, I stood before the bathroom mirror. My shoulders looked different. Not huddled, but open. Unburdened. My eyes drew my gaze, and there I saw what I was feeling: something quiet, strong, still.

I felt like I was complete.

I slept soundly that night, held in restful sleep like a baby in a mother's loving arms. When I finally heard my alarm, it was a quarter of nine. The room was awash in sunlight. It was Thursday, which meant I had Professor Edelstein's Survey of Islamic History in fifteen minutes. As I slipped into my jeans, I was startled by the bright prickle of new denim against my skin. The previous night's wonders were apparently still unfolding.

Outside, it was another unseasonably warm and windy day. After hurrying over to the Student Union for a cup of tea, I rushed to Schirmer Hall, Quran tucked under my arm, spilling hot water as I ran. I didn't like being late for Edelstein's class. I needed to be certain I would find a place near the back—close to the window he kept cracked open—where I would have the space quietly to reel and contemplate as the diminutive, magnetic Edelstein continued to take his weekly sledgehammer to what still remained of my childhood faith. And there was something else that kept me in the back of the room:

It was where Rachel sat.

Professor Edelstein looked fresh and formal in a variation on his usual pastel medley: an impeccably pressed mauve oxford, topped and tightened at the neck by a rose-pink bow tie, and suspenders matching the auburn shade of newly polished penny loafers.

He greeted me with a warm smile as I entered. "Hey, Hayat."

"Hi, Professor."

I wove my way through the desks to the corner where I usually sat, and where lovely Rachel was munching on a cookie.

"Hey."

"Hey there."

"How was the game?"

"Good."

She nodded, the corners of her lips curling coyly upward as she held my gaze. It was looks like this—her bright blue eyes sparkling—that had made me hazard the invitation to the game the night prior. I'd been wanting to ask her out on a date all semester. But when I'd finally gotten up the courage, she'd told me she had to study.

"You want some?" she asked. "It's oatmeal raisin."

"Sure."

She broke off a piece and handed it to me. "You do the reading for today?" she asked.

"Didn't need to."

"Why not?"

"I already know the chapters he wanted us to read...by heart."

"You do?" Rachel's eyes widened with surprise.

"I grew up memorizing that stuff," I explained. "It's a whole production some Muslim kids go through. You memorize the Quran...They call it being a *hafiz*."

"Really?" She was impressed.

I shrugged. "Not that I remember much of it anymore. But I happen to remember the chapters he assigned for today..."

At the front of the class, Edelstein started to speak. "I trust you've all done your reading," he began. "It's not ground we're going to cover today, but it's obviously important material. I'd like you guys to keep moving. The Quran can be slow going, and the more of it we get through this semester, the better." He paused and arranged the papers gathered before him. Rachel offered me the rest of her oatmeal cookie with a whisper: "Wanna finish?"

"Absolutely," I said, taking it.

"Today, I'd like to share some of the recent work a couple of my colleagues in Germany are doing. I wasn't able to offer you any readings on their work, because it's very much happening right now. It's at the very forefront of Islamic scholarship..." Edelstein paused again, now making eye contact with the Muslim-born students in the class—there were three of us—and added cautiously, "And what I have to share may come as a shock to some of you."

So began his lecture on the Sanaa manuscripts.

In 1972, while restoring an ancient mosque in Sanaa, Yemen, a group of workers busy overhauling the original roof found a stash of parchments and damaged books buried in the rafters. It was a grave of sorts, the kind that Muslims—forbidden from burning the Quran—use to respectfully discard damaged or worn-out copies of the holy book. The workers packed the manuscripts into potato sacks, and they were locked away until one of Edelstein's close friends—a colleague—was approached some seven years later to take a look at the documents. What he discovered was unprecedented: The parchment pages dated back to Islam's first two centuries, fragments of the oldest Qurans in existence. What was shocking, Edelstein told us, was that there were aberrations and deviations from the standard Quran that Muslims had been using for more than a thousand years. In short, Edelstein claimed, his German colleague was about to show the world that the bedrock Muslim belief in the Quran as the direct, unchanged, eternal word of God was a fiction. Muslims weren't going to be spared the fate of Christians and Jews over the past three centuries of scholarship: the Quran, like the Bible, would prove to be the historical document common sense dictated it had to be.

Up in the front row, one of the students—Ahmad, a Muslim—interrupted Edelstein's lecture, raising his hand angrily.

Edelstein paused. "Yes, Ahmad?"

"Why has your friend not published his findings yet?" Ahmad barked.

Edelstein held Ahmad's gaze for a moment before replying. And when he did, his tone was conciliatory. "My colleague is concerned about continued access to the texts if they were to make these findings known to the Yemeni authorities. They're preparing a series of articles, but are ensuring that they've had enough time to go through all fourteen thousand pages carefully, just in case they never get to see the documents again."

Now Ahmad's voice bellowed, red and bitter: "And why exactly would they be barred from seeing them again?"

There was silence. The classroom was thick with tension.

"There's no need to get upset, Ahmad. We can talk about this like scholars..."

"Scholars! What scholars make claims without documented findings? Huh?!"

"I understand this is some controversial stuff...but there's no need—"

Ahmad cut him off. "It's not controversial, Pro-*fess*-or," he said, spitting the middle syllable back at Edelstein with disgust. "It's *incendiary*." Ahmad bolted up from his desk, books in hand. "In-*sult*-ing and in-*cen*-diary!" he shouted. After a look at Sahar—the usually reticent Malaysian girl sitting to his left, her head lowered as she scratched nervously on her pad—and then another look, back at me, Ahmad stormed out of the room.

"Anyone else want to leave?" Edelstein asked, clearly affected. After a short pause, Sahar quietly gathered her things, got up, and walked out.

"That leaves you, Hayat."

"Nothing to worry about, Professor. I'm a true and tried Mutazalite."

Edelstein's face brightened with a smile. "Bless your heart."

After class, I stood and stretched, surprised again at how nimble and awake I felt.

"Where you headed?" Rachel asked.

"To the Union."

"Wanna walk? I'm going to the library."

"Sure," I said.

Outside, as we strolled beneath the shedding ash trees that lined the path to the library, Rachel remarked how surprised she was at Ahmad and Sahar walking out.

"Don't be," I said. "Saying less than that could get you killed in some circles." She looked skeptical. "Look at Rushdie," I said. The fatwa was only a year old, an event still fresh in everyone's mind.

Rachel shook her head. "I don't understand these things...So what did you mean by what you said to Edelstein?"

"About being a Mutazalite?"

"Yeah."

"A school of Muslims that don't believe in the Quran as the eternal word of God. But I was joking. I'm not a Mutazalite. They died off a thousand years ago."

She nodded. We walked a few paces. "How did you feel about the lecture?" she asked.

"What's to feel? The truth is the truth. Better to know it than not to."

"Absolutely," she said, studying me, "but it doesn't mean you can't have feelings about it, right?" Her question was softly put. There was tenderness in it.

"Honestly? It makes me feel free."

She nodded. And we walked awhile in silence.

"Do you mind if I ask you a personal question?" I finally asked.

"That depends."

"On?"

"What you want to know."

"Did you really have to study last night, or were you just saying that?"

Rachel laughed, her lips parting to reveal her small square teeth. She really was lovely. "I have an organic chemistry exam tomorrow, I told you that. That's why I'm going to the library now." She stopped and put her hand on my arm. "But I promise I'll go with you to the next game . . . Okay?"

My heart surged with sudden joy. "Okay," I said with a cough.

When we got to the library's steps, I had the urge to tell her what had happened to me the night before. "Can I ask you another personal question?"

"Shoot."

"Do you believe in God?"

For a moment, Rachel looked startled. And then she shrugged. "No. At least not the *guy-in-the-sky* type thing."

"Since when?"

"Since ever, I guess. My mom was an atheist, so I don't think I ever took it that seriously. I mean, my dad made us go to temple sometimes—Rosh Hashanah and stuff—but even then, my mom would spend the whole way there and back complaining."

"So you don't know what it's like to lose your faith."

"Not really."

I nodded. "It's freeing. *So* freeing. It's the most freeing thing that's ever happened to me...You asked me how I feel about the lecture? Hearing Edelstein talk about the Quran as just a book, a book like any other, makes me feel like going out to celebrate."

"Sounds like fun," she said, smiling. "If you wait 'til tomorrow, we can celebrate together..."

"Sounds like a plan."

Rachel lingered on the step above me just long enough for the thought to occur. And when it did, I didn't question it. I leaned in and touched my lips to hers.

Her mouth pressed against mine. I felt her hand against the back of my head, the tip of her tongue gently grazing the tip of my own.

All at once, she pulled away. She turned and hopped up the steps, then stopped at the door and shot me a quick look. "Wish me luck on my exam," she said.

"Good luck," I said.

When she was gone, I lingered, in a daze, barely able to believe my good fortune.

That night, after a day of classes and an evening of Ping-Pong at the Union, I was sitting in bed, trying to study, but thinking only of Rachel...when the phone rang. It was Mother.

"She's gone, *behta*."

I was quiet. I knew, of course, who she was talking about. A month earlier she and I had gone to Kansas City to visit Mina—not only my mother's lifelong best friend, but the person who'd had, perhaps, the greatest influence on my life—as she lay in a hospital bed, her insides ravaged with cancer.

"Did you hear me, Hayat?" Mother said.

"It's probably better, isn't it, Mom? I mean, she's not in pain anymore."

"But she's gone, Hayat," Mother moaned. "She's gone..."

I listened quietly as she cried. And then I consoled her.

Mother didn't ask me that night how I felt about Mina's passing, which was just as well. I probably wouldn't have told her what I was really feeling. Even the confession I had made to Mina while she lay on what turned out to be her deathbed, even that hadn't been enough to assuage the guilt I'd been carrying since I was twelve. If I was reluctant to share how aggrieved I was with my mother, it was because my grief was not only for Mina, but for myself as well.

Now that she was gone, how could I ever repair the harm I'd done?

The following evening, Rachel and I sat side by side at a pizzeria counter, our dinner before a movie. I didn't tell her about Mina, but somehow, she sensed something was wrong. She asked me if I was all right. I told her I was. She insisted. "You sure, Hayat?" she asked. She was looking at me with a tenderness I couldn't fathom. "Thought you wanted to celebrate," she said with a smile.

"Well...after I left you yesterday, I got some bad news."

"What?"

"My aunt died. She was like...a second mother to me."

"Oh God. I'm so sorry."

All at once, my throat was searing. I was on the verge of tears.

"Sorry," I said, looking away.

Feeling her hand on my arm, I heard her voice: "You don't have to talk about it..."

I looked back and nodded.

* * *

The movie was a comedy. It distracted me. Toward the end, Rachel pushed herself up against my side, and we held hands for a while. Afterwards, she invited me back to her room, where she lit candles and played me a song on the guitar that she'd written. It was something longing and plaintive about lost love. Only three days ago, I couldn't have imagined myself being so lucky. And yet I couldn't push away thoughts of Mina.

When Rachel finished her song, I told her it was wonderful. She could tell my mind was elsewhere.

"Still thinking about your aunt, aren't you?"

"Is it that obvious?"

She shrugged and smiled. "It's okay," she said, setting her guitar aside. "My grandma was really important to me like that. I went through a lot when she died."

"But the thing is, it's not just that she died...it's that I had something to do with it." I didn't even realize I'd said it until I was almost finished with the sentence.

Rachel looked at me, puzzled, folds appearing along her forehead.

"What happened?" she asked.

"You don't know me very well...I mean, *of course* you don't. It's just...I don't think you realize how I grew up."

"I'm not following you, Hayat."

"You're Jewish, right?"

"Yeah? So?"

"You may not like me very much if I tell you what happened..."

She shifted in her place, her back straightening. She looked away.

You barely know her, I thought. *What are you trying to prove?*

"Maybe I should leave," I said.

She didn't reply.

I didn't move. The fact was, I didn't want to leave. I wanted to stay. I wanted to tell her.

We sat in silence for a long moment, and then Rachel reached out to touch my hand.

"Tell me," she said.

BOOK ONE

Paradise Lost

1

Mina

Long before I knew Mina, I knew her story.

It was a tale Mother told so many times: How her best friend, gifted and gorgeous—something of a genius, as Mother saw it—had been frustrated at every turn, her development derailed by the small-mindedness of her family, her robust will checked by a culture that made no place for a woman. I heard about the grades Mina skipped and the classes she topped, though always somewhat to the chagrin of parents more concerned with her eventual nuptials than her report card. I heard about all the boys who loved her, and how—when she was twelve—she, too, fell in love, only to have her nose broken by her father's fist when he found a note from her sweetheart tucked into her math book. I heard about her nervous breakdowns and her troubles with food and, of course, about the trove of poems her mother set alight in the living room fireplace one night during an argument about whether or not Mina would be allowed to go to college to become a writer.

Perhaps it was that I heard it all so often without knowing the woman myself, but for the longest time, Mina Ali and her gifts and travails were like the persistent smell of curry in our halls and our rooms: an ever-presence in my life of which I made little note.

And then, one summer afternoon when I was eight, I saw a picture of her. As Mother unfolded Mina's latest letter from Pakistan, a palm-sized color glossy tumbled out. "That's your auntie Mina, *kurban*," Mother said as I picked it up. "Look how beautiful she is."

Beautiful, indeed.

The picture showed a striking woman sitting on a wicker chair before a background of green leaves and orange flowers. Most of her perfectly black hair was covered with a pale pink scarf, and both her hair and scarf framed an utterly arresting face: cheekbones highly drawn—gently accentuated with a touch of blush—oval eyes, and a small, pointed nose perched above a pair of ample lips. Her features defined a perfect harmony, promising something sheltering, something tender, but not only. For there was an intensity in her eyes that belied this intimation of maternal comfort, or at least complicated it: those eyes were black and filled with piercing light, as if her vision had long been sharpened against the grindstone of some nameless inner pain. And though she was smiling, her smile was more one concealed than offered and, like her eyes, hinted at something mysterious and elusive, something you wanted to know.

Mother posted the photo on our refrigerator door, pinned in place by the same rainbow-shaped finger magnets that also affixed my school lunch menu. (This was the menu Mother consulted each night before school to see if pork was being served the following day—and if, therefore, I'd be needing a bag lunch—and which I consulted each school morning hoping to find my favorite, beef lasagna, listed among the day's offerings.) For two years, then, barely a day went by without at least a casual glance at that photograph of Mina. And there were more than a few occasions when, finishing my glass of morning milk, or munching on string cheese after school, I lingered over it, staring at her likeness as I sometimes did at the surface of the pond at Worth Park on summer afternoons: doing my best to catch a glimpse of what was hidden in the depths.

It was a remarkable photograph, and—as I was to discover from Mina herself a couple of years later—it had an equally remarkable history. Mina's parents, counting on their daughter's beauty to attract a lucrative match, brought in a fashion photographer to take pictures of her, and the photo in question was the one that would make its way—through a matchmaker—into the hands of Hamed Suhail, the only son of a wealthy Karachi family.

Hamed fell in love with Mina the moment he saw it.

The Suhails showed up at the Ali home a week and a half later, and by the end of their meeting, the fathers had shaken hands on their children's betrothal. Mother always claimed that Mina didn't dislike Hamed, and that Mina always said she could have found happiness with him. If not for Irshad, Hamed's mother.

After the wedding, Mina moved south to Karachi to live with her in-laws, and the problems between mother-in-law and daughter-in-law began the first night Mina was there. Irshad came into her bedroom holding a string of plump, pomegranate-colored stones, a garnet necklace and family heirloom which—Irshad explained—had been handed down from mother to daughter for five generations. Herself daughterless, Irshad had always imagined she would bestow these, the only family jewels, on the wife of her only son someday.

"Try it on," Irshad urged, warmly.

Mina did. And as they both stared into the mirror, Mina

couldn't help but notice the silvery thinning of Irshad's eyes. She recognized the envy.

"You shouldn't, *Ammi*," Mina said, pulling the stones from her neck.

"I shouldn't what?"

"I don't know . . . I mean, it's so beautiful . . . are you sure you want to give it to me?"

"I'm not giving it to you *yet*," Irshad replied, abruptly. "I just wanted to see how it looked."

Bruised by Irshad's sudden shift, Mina handed the necklace back to her mother-in-law. Irshad took it and, without another word, walked out of the room.

So Irshad's enmity began. First came the snide comments offered under her breath, or in passing: about how headstrong the "new girl" was; how she ate hunched over her plate like a servant; or how, as Irshad put it, Mina looked like a "mouse." Soon to follow were changes to the household routine intended to make Mina's life more difficult: servants sent up to clean Mina's room when she was still asleep; the expunging from the family menu of the foods Mina most enjoyed; the continued flurry of mean-spirited remarks, though now no longer offered sotto voce. Mina did all she could to appease and placate her mother-in-law. But this only stoked Irshad's suspicions. For as Mina tried to ply Irshad with submissiveness, the elder woman felt the change of tack, and read it as evidence of a cunning nature. Irshad now started rumors about her daughter-in-law's "wandering eyes" and "thieving hands." She warned her son to keep Mina away from the male staff, and warned her staff to keep their valuables under lock and key. (Neither Hamed nor his father—both terrified of Irshad—did anything to address the growing conflict.) And when the pleasure of verbal abuse wore thin, Irshad resorted to the physical.

Now she slapped Mina, for leaving her dirty clothes strewn around her bedroom, or talking out of turn in front of guests. On one occasion, hearing an insult in a comment Mina made about dinner not being as spicy as usual, Irshad grabbed her daughter-in-law by the hair and dragged her from the dinner table to throw her out into the hallway.

Fourteen months into this growing nightmare, Mina conceived. To escape the abuse and bring her pregnancy to term in peace, she returned north to her family home, in the Punjab. There, three weeks early, unaccompanied by her husband—who would not join her for fear of suffering his mother's wrath—Mina gave birth to a boy. And as she lay in the hospital bed exhausted from her daylong labor, a man in a long dark coat appeared at the doorway just moments after her mother left the room to fetch a cup of tea from the canteen. He stepped inside, inquiring if she was Amina Suhail née Ali.

"I am," Mina replied.

The man approached her bedside, an envelope in hand. "Your husband has divorced you. Enclosed are the papers that make this divorce official. He has written in his own hand—you will recognize the writing—that he divorces you, he divorces you, and he divorces you. As you well know, Mrs. Suhail—I mean, Ms. Ali—this is what the law requires." He laid the envelope across her belly, gently. "You have just given birth to Hamed Suhail's son. He has chosen the name Imran for the boy. Imran will stay with you until the age of seven, at which point Mr. Hamed Suhail has the right to full, undisputed custody." The lawyer took a step back, but he wasn't finished. Mina squinted at him in disbelief. "All that I have shared with you is in accordance with the law as it stands, this date of June 15, 1976, in the land of Pakistan, and you are entitled to a custody trial by law, but I would advise you to understand, Mrs.

Suhail—I mean, Ms. Ali—that any fight will be a useless one for you, and will simply cost your family resources it does not have."

Then the lawyer turned and walked out.

Mina cried for days and nights and weeks to follow. Yet, devastated as she was by Hamed's brutality—and terrified by his menacing promise to take her son away someday—when she stared down into her infant's eyes, she nevertheless cooed to him with the name that her now-ex-husband had chosen without her:

She called the boy Imran.

I first heard that Mother wanted to bring Mina to America in the winter of 1981. I was ten. The hostages in Iran had just come home, and American flags were burning on the nightly news. It was a Saturday afternoon, teatime, and my parents were sitting across from each other at the kitchen table, silently sipping from their cups. I was sitting at the other end, my back to the glass of milk Mother had set before me. I was watching a half dozen flies butting at the window overlooking the backyard.

"You know, *kurban,* your Mina-auntie might be coming to stay with us," Mother finally said. "*Kurban?*"

I turned to her. "When?" I asked.

"The sooner, the better. Her family is driving her *crazy* back home. And that boy needs to get out of the country...or his father will take him. The truth is, they *both* need to get out."

Mother paused, glancing over at Father. He was thumbing through a fishing magazine, oblivious.

I looked back at the flies, buzzing blackly along the cold glass.

"All these flies! Where are they coming from?!" Mother suddenly shouted out. "And there's so many of them up in the attic! God only knows how they got up there!"

Father looked up from his magazine, annoyed. "You say that like we haven't heard it, like it's the first time you're saying it. It's not the first time. I'm dealing with it."

"I wasn't talking to you, Naveed."

"Then who are you talking to?" Father asked, sharply. "Because the only other person here is the boy, and I don't know what he has to do with it."

Mother stared at him, her face blank. Father's hazel-green eyes glared coldly back at her. Then he buried himself again in his fishing magazine.

Mother got up from the table and went to the fridge. "It's not going to be easy, *kurban.* Even if we could arrange it, who knows if her parents will let her come. Sometimes I wonder if they just want to keep her around so they have someone to torture. You know what her father did? He sold her books! Can you imagine? Mina without her books!"

Mother glanced at Father, then looked at me, expectant. I knew she wanted me to say something, but I didn't know what to say.

"Why did he sell her books?" I finally asked.

"Because he thinks *books* are the reason for the divorce. Books encouraged her *fast mouth* . . . that's what he always said about her intelligence. '*All it does is give her a fast mouth* . . .'" Mother sneaked another glance at Father.

He just shifted in place, turning a page in his magazine.

Mother grunted as she pulled a pitcher from the fridge. "Hayat, her intelligence has been the curse of her life. When a Muslim woman is too smart, she pays the price for it. And she pays the price not in money, *behta,* but in *abuse.*" Mother paused, waiting for Father to react. He didn't. "You know what Freud said, *behta*? That brilliant man?"

I didn't know much more about Freud than that Mother liked to tell me what he said from time to time. "He said silence *kills*. If you don't talk about things...you get all *screwed up* inside." She stole another look at Father.

Now he looked up, but not because of anything she'd said. He threw back his head and emptied the rest of his tea into his mouth. Mother slammed the fridge door shut behind him. Father set down the teacup and turned another page.

"I'm telling you these things because today you are my *behta*, my child...but one day you'll be a man. And these are things you should know..."

I looked back at the window, behind which a scarlet sun was setting beneath tufts of purple-pink clouds hanging about the horizon like clumps of cotton candy. The flies were still stabbing at the glass.

"They are *so* annoying. Where are they coming from?" Mother complained again as she poured.

Again, silence. Until I finally heard Father's voice behind me: "Here."

I turned to find him holding out the rolled-up magazine toward me. "Kill them and get it over with."

"Don't make him do that," Mother said in an odd, pleading tone. "You do it, Naveed."

Father didn't budge, still pointing the magazine at me.

I took it and turned to the window. Aiming, I swatted. The glass shook. One fly fell; the others sputtered frantically. It took me a dozen more blows to get them all. When I was finished, I looked down, where the flies lay dead on the kitchen linoleum.

"Good job," Father said, taking the magazine back. Standing, he tore the cover off and crumpled it, sticking the ball into his empty cup of tea. Then he walked out.

Mother dumped her unfinished glass of water in the sink. "Next time, you don't do what he says," she hissed at me. "You do what I say."

My parents' marriage was difficult almost from the start. They'd met and fallen in love in Lahore, while they were both in college, Mother studying psychology, Father completing medical school. They married, and Father—who topped his medical class—was offered a spot in a program that brought him to Wisconsin to train as a neurologist. Mother left school to join him—it was always her great regret that she didn't wait to finish her degree—ending up far from home, in Milwaukee's rural westerly suburbs, a stone's throw from dairy country, where the landscape was flat as a table and covered for months with snow. It was a place she didn't understand. And she was with a man who started cheating on her almost as soon as they arrived in America. In short, by the time I was ten, she'd been miserable for years.

A week or so after the episode with the flies, I awoke in my bed in the middle of the night, not sure if I was dreaming. My room glowed and pulsed with a flickering orange light. Outside, people were shouting. The roar of an engine seemed to shake the air. I got up from bed and went to the window. Through a veil of swirling flakes, I made out a chaotic sight: a car in flames, and beyond it, two bright beams of light through which figures in black came and went. It took me a moment to realize it was a fire truck. The firemen were scattered about the flames, pulling at a white hose. All at once, there was a loud hissing sound, and the white hose stiffened along uneven joints, spewing an unruly, milky foam.

I still wasn't sure if I was dreaming.

"Get back in bed," I heard behind me. I turned to see

Mother in the doorway, her eyes—like the car outside—ablaze. "One of your father's white bitches set fire to his Mercedes." She approached, coming to stand alongside me. Together, we watched the firefighters douse the flames. It didn't take long. Almost at once, the fire was out, and the car's wet, windowless carcass was giving off weak smoke.

Mother turned to me, her eyes still gleaming, though the room was now dark. "That's why I always tell you, *behta*...Don't end up with a white woman."

She led me back to bed and tucked me in with a kiss. When she was gone, I got up and went back to the window. I spied Father's tall, hulking form marching through the falling snow. He led the firefighters into the house. I crawled back into bed and fell asleep to the murmur of men's voices drifting up the stairs.

All night, I dreamt of fire.

The next morning, when I came down for breakfast, Father wasn't there.

"Where's Dad?" I asked.

"Work," Mother replied. "Had to take my car," she added with a satisfied grin as she brought two plates of *paratha*s and eggs to the table.

"*Paratha*s?" I asked. She usually only made *paratha*s on the weekends.

"Eat, sweetie. I know it's your favorite."

Mother sat down across from me, tearing a piece of the ghee-soaked fried bread I so loved, and used it to poke at her egg and release the yolk. "Another of his white *prostitutes* decided she was *sick* of his promises," Mother began. "God only knows what he promised *this* one. He gets drunk and runs his mouth, and probably doesn't remember a thing he says." Using the piece of *paratha,* she took a scoopful of the running yolk into her mouth and started to chew. "*That's* why we don't drink, *kurban,* because it *impairs* you. It makes you *foolish.*" Drops of viscous yellow-orange dotted the edges of her lips as she chewed and spoke. "Give a Muslim man a drink and watch him run after white women like a crazed fool!"

I'd been hearing about Father's mistresses since the night Mother dragged me through the streets of Milwaukee as a five-year-old, searching for Father, who we eventually found at the apartment of a woman he worked with at the hospital; I waited in the stairwell as she and Father shouted at each other on the upstairs landing. Throughout my childhood, Mother spared me little detail about her troubles with Father. And at ten, I already knew myself well enough to know that if I listened too closely to what she said, my blood would start to boil.

I kept my head down, hoping she would lose interest, but that was unlikely. She was buoyant that morning. Even her appearance—usually unkempt, her round face increasingly drawn and gaunt from bitterness, her thin brown hair often tousled well into the evening as if she'd just risen from bed— was different. She'd showered and dressed for the day as if she actually planned to leave the house. "But now he has a chance to do the *right thing,*" she said, breaking off another piece of *paratha.* "Now he'll have the chance to help someone in need. Your Mina-auntie needs someone to help her and that boy...I just lose sleep every night thinking about what she's going through. The boy is already four. They have to be thinking *now* about how to get out. Or it will be too late." She took another bite and chewed, shaking her head. "You don't humiliate your wife and child in front of the world without *consequence.* He's not sure about this, he's not sure about that. Now he doesn't have a choice. She's coming and he's not going to stop it. After last night, he *owes* me."

"Mom, I'm gonna miss my bus."

She looked up at the clock. "You have time. Five minutes. Finish your breakfast."

"I'm not hungry. I have to pack my bag. My homework."

"Finish your juice."

I got up from the table and gulped down the rest of my orange juice. Before I could leave, Mother reached out and drew me to her. "*Meri-jaan,* remember: The secret of a happy life is *respect.* Respect for yourself and respect for others. That's what I learned from my father, *behta,* who you didn't know...and he was a wise man. You could almost say he wasn't really even a Muslim man. He was more like a Jew."

"I have to get my bag ready, Mom," I whined.

"Okay, okay," she sighed. I kissed her on the cheek, then ran off to my room to pack my things for school.

2

A Still, Small Voice

Mother was right. After the episode with Father's car, she would have no trouble getting him to go along with her plan to bring Mina to Milwaukee. Now it was only Mina's parents who needed convincing. Mother spent hours on the phone with Rafiq and Rabia Ali, assuring them that their daughter would be well looked after. She would have a place to stay as long as she needed to rebuild her life, and Mother promised to care for Imran, her son, like her own child. But it turned out the assurances Mina's middle-class parents really wanted had more to do with their daughter's honor than with her lodgings. For even Western-leaning Muslims like the Alis—Mina's mother was a huge Elvis fan, and her father an avid consumer of Marlboros and Zane Grey—thought of America not primarily as a land of abundance and opportunity, but of sin, where souls went to be corrupted by the very liberty that so intoxicated the world's imagination. For people like Mina's parents, there was no more emblematic image of America's spiritual corruption than that of the American woman, eager to shed her clothes in front of strangers, emboldened by freedom to cultivate her lust for pleasure and profit. That their daughter might become one of these was the only thing the Alis wished to avoid at all costs.

Or *almost* at all costs, as Father would put it at dinner one night.

"It's a double standard," Mother complained, as Father and I munched on chicken *karahi*. "Rafiq wants his sons to come here, but not his daughter. It doesn't matter if *they* run around with white women, but God forbid *she's* found looking at a white man."

"The sons?" Father asked.

"It's the only reason he'll even consider it. If she comes, then she can sponsor her younger brothers."

Father smiled wryly. "So Rafiq is trying to figure out if the cash his sons will make him when they get to America is worth the price of turning their daughter into a whore..."

I didn't know what the word meant, but before I could ask, Mother leaped in. "Do you think you're funny? Such a word in front of your own child?"

Father glanced over at me. "The sooner he knows the way the world really works, the better."

Mother turned to me. "Cover your ears," she said.

"What?"

"I said cover your ears."

"Mom..."

"Do it, Hayat."

Reluctantly, I wiped my curry-covered hands and did as I was told, but it didn't stop me from hearing what she said to him next:

"Use language like that again in his presence, and I will have you thrown out of the house. *Thrown out,* do you hear me?"

Father waited a moment before replying. "Is that a promise?" he finally said, blankly. Then he looked away with a shrug and went on with his meal.

* * *

In the end, whatever the reasoning, Mina's parents agreed to send her to us. We learned of the news when there was a knock on our door one afternoon. I opened it to find a middle-aged man, rail-thin, with searing blue eyes and a violet-colored birth stain spilling across his nose and right cheek. He held a clipboard in one hand, a thin envelope in the other.

"Shah?"

"Yeah."

"Telegram," he said, handing me the envelope.

"What's that?"

"Cable letter. Could you just sign here?" He pushed the clipboard at me, and I signed my name.

"What kind of name is that, anyway? Shah? You Iranian or something?"

"Pakistani."

He grunted. It seemed like he wasn't sure what I was saying. He looked at me now, his head tilted, suspicious. I noticed the thin silver cross dangling from a chain around his neck. "You people hate Americans, too?" he asked.

"No."

He kept staring, and then he finally nodded. "Okay," he said, satisfied. He turned and headed off toward the tan car idling in our driveway.

At the kitchen table, Mother tore open the envelope. "Mina's cable!" she cooed, delightedly.

"What is it, Mom?"

"When they send a message with the cable. From one office to the other. From one side of the world to the other, *behta*. When I was a child, Hayat, cable was how we sent messages overseas. Now, of course, phone is easier. But cable is still

31

a *hundred* times cheaper than the phone in Pakistan." She started to read. "She bought her ticket."

"What does it say?"

COMING TO AMERICA STOP MAY 13 ARRIVAL CHICAGO STOP BRITISH AIRWAYS

She handed me the gossamer-thin sheet. Everything was printed out in capitals, including the word "stop."

"Why does it say 'stop'?"

"Costs more to have punctuation," Mother said, taking the telegram back. Then she looked up at me, her eyes wide with a sudden idea. "Let's send her one back!" she said.

"Where?"

"Western Union."

And so out we went. Mother and I headed for the mall, where we stood at the counter and filled out the form to send a telegram. If the message was ten words or less, it would only cost six dollars. Every word after that was seventy cents. I couldn't see how Mother was even going to get to ten words considering all she wanted to say was that she'd gotten Mina's telegram.

CABLE RECEIVED STOP SO EXCITED STOP INSHALLAH

Mother looked at me. "What do you think?"

Sounded fine to me.

As Mother paid at the window, I spied the messenger with the stain across his face in back, milling about. He emerged from the back room and our eyes met.

He nodded. I nodded back.

* * *

Mina came in May, just as promised. On our way to the airport to pick her up, we got caught in traffic and arrived just as the plane was supposed to have touched down. Mother was frantic. Father pulled to the curb and Mother yanked me out of the backseat. We ran inside to the airline counter to ask about the flight while Father went to park the car. When the ticket clerk announced the plane had already landed, Mother yelped. Off we went down the terminal hall to Mina's gate. But when we got there, the lounge was empty. Two stewardesses stood at the gate's counter, and Mother went over to inquire. That was when I noticed a striking woman standing against the window of another gate lounge farther on. She was small and held a large sleeping child against her body, its arms dangling at her sides like ends of a stole. When Mother returned, I pointed. "Is that her?" I asked.

"Miinnaa!" Mother cried out with joy.

As Mina turned to us, I was surprised. Though she was just as beautiful as the photograph had promised, there was something different about her as well: a confidence, a magnetism.

She smiled and I was struck.

"*Bhaj*, you made me wonder if I ended up in the wrong city!"

Mother laughed, her eyes welling with sudden tears. She took Mina by the shoulders and looked deeply into her eyes. The confident smile on Mina's lips now quivered as her own eyes filled with tears. The two women hugged, melting together. Mina's son—held between them—roused and moaned.

Sniffling, Mother pulled away. She took the boy from Mina's arms. "Hi there, sweetie...," she cooed, peering into Imran's face. "Welcome to America."

Imran laid his head on Mother's shoulder, falling back asleep.

Mina wiped her eyes, smiling. "He likes you, *bhaj!*"

"Everybody likes me."

"I wouldn't get too carried away!"

They laughed. Mina turned to me, blurting out in a bright tone: "So *this* is Hayat! He's so handsome. Like a movie star!"

Mother rolled her eyes. "And just as spoiled as one, too..."

"You're going to break some hearts, aren't you, *behta?*" She was looking right at me. Again, I felt that surprise. There was something intense and alive about her gaze that the picture had only hinted at. She was dazzling.

"What's wrong, *behta?*" she asked, playful, her hand on my head now, caressing my hair. "Cat got your tongue?"

I grinned sheepishly, nodding my reply. The cat had my tongue, indeed.

In our front yard stood three large gnarled trees, old and beautiful. They formed a row, the two trees on the outside leaning in toward the center tree, their tops converging, like three old women—Mother used to say—coming together to share their secrets. Mother had been told they'd been planted too close to the house, that we risked damage to the roof from falling limbs in the event of gale-strength winds, and she'd been advised to have them removed. But Mother loved the trees too much. She and Mina stopped at one of the trunks as Father carried Mina's bags to the house. I was holding a bag as well, but I stopped to adjust my grip.

Mina was holding Imran—who pretended to be sleeping, but was actually spying on me with one open eye—as she gazed up into the branches. "White oak," she said.

"Something like that," Mother replied. "Elm or oak or *something*."

"They're oaks, *bhaj*. White oaks. You can tell from the leaves." Mina pointed. "Pink like that in spring. We used to have one at the center of the courtyard at Station School, re-member?" Mother's chin lifted ever so slightly, and her gaze clouded over. "Remember, it had pink leaves like that?" Mina asked.

Mother nodded, moved. "I knew there was a reason I didn't want to lose them."

Mina touched the trunk. "Must be a hundred years old."

"That's what the tree man said."

At the front door, Father called out: "Green room, right?"

"Yes, Naveed," Mother called back. She turned to Mina once he'd disappeared inside. "How many times I've told him where you're staying! And then he asks me again?"

Mina chuckled.

"Go on, *kurban*," Mother said to me, "take that bag up to the green room for your auntie."

"Okay, Mom."

I hauled the bag along the walkway and into the vestibule. I climbed the steps to the first room along the upstairs hall, which we called the green room for its kelly-green carpet. We could just as well have called it the cartoon room, as its walls were adorned with four human-sized cartoon decals—Goofy, Daffy Duck, Bugs Bunny, and Snow White—that had been there when we bought the house. For weeks before Mina's arri-val, Mother talked about having the carpet replaced and walls repainted to cover up the cartoons. Father said he would take care of it, but never did.

As Mina set her things down on the bed, Mother apologized. "I was going to have it recarpeted. Naveed promised me."

"But why?"

"The color? It doesn't give you a headache?"

"It's fine. I don't want you to go to the trouble."

"It's not trouble. Now that you're here, we'll do it together. You can choose the color. And we'll cover up these stupid cartoons..."

Mina looked over at me. I was standing by the closet with her things. "What do you think, *behta?*"

Truth be told, I'd always liked the carpet's color and the cartoons as well. They were an instance of something lively in our otherwise relentlessly somber home. But I had no chance to respond. Mother leaped in, answering for me: "It doesn't matter what he thinks. What matters is what *you* think."

Just then, Imran, Mina's four-year-old, lumbered groggily into the room from the toilet, his feet inexplicably wet, his shuffling steps leaving a trail of faint, darker prints along the harlequin green shade. He looked up, his eyes widening. His face broke into a sudden smile. He stepped over to the wall, stretched his arms, and pressed himself against Daffy Duck.

Mother and Mina traded looks.

"Or we could just leave it like it is," Mina said.

Mother nodded. "Now, maybe that *would* be best."

Mina and Imran were jet-lagged. They went to bed that afternoon and slept through much of the next two days. It wasn't until midweek that we all had our first meal together. I got home from school that afternoon to find the house filled with the smells of the Lahori-style lamb chops, homemade *naan*s, and *bhindi bhuna*. Sitting at the kitchen table with my homework, I watched Mina and Mother cook into the evening, trading tales in Punjabi—which I understood, but didn't speak—laughing as they went. Mother was so happy. And there was Mina, living and breathing and hovering about at the very fridge where I'd spent almost two years staring at her photograph. There really was something miraculous about it all.

That night, the splendid feast succeeded at putting even Father in a sentimental mood. At the end of the meal, he leaned back in his seat, a soft, satiated light in his eyes. He lifted his glass of *lassi* toward Mina and her son. "It's good to have you here," he said.

Mina held his gaze, the same sly, enticing smile on her face that I recognized from the photograph. "Thank you, Naveed," she said. "You're a very generous man."

Father smarted. "Nonsense," he demurred. "Anyway, I'm not the one you should thank. It's Muneer. She would have broken my legs if I didn't agree to it...But I have to say, I'm glad I did."

"So now we know," Mother joked, "the way to your heart is through your stomach."

He flashed her a mischievous smile. "Among other things," he said.

Mother blushed, looking away.

Mina looked away, too, over at her son. "Say thank you to your Muneer-auntie and Naveed-uncle."

"Thank you, Auntie. Thank you, Uncle," Imran murmured.

"You're welcome," Mother caroled.

Father gazed warmly at the boy. "You're welcome, *kurban*," he said.

I looked at Father, confused. Hearing him use that word for Imran stung, like an insect bite on my heart.

"What?" he asked.

" '*Kurban*'?" I blurted out. "That's what you call me."

"What does it mean?" Imran asked, dully.

"It means the most important thing we have to give," Mina said, turning to me with a smile. "The sacrifice of our hearts." She reached out to brush the hair away from my eyes. "You're my *kurban*, too," she intoned, lovingly.

A few weeks into Mina's stay, I had my first experience of her deeper sense of things, what most called her intelligence, but which I think was actually something closer to a spiritual gift.

She was sitting at the dining table, reading, a shaft of afternoon sunlight draped across her body like a brilliant shawl. I had a clear view of her from my place in the living room adjacent, where I was sitting and brooding over another ice cream social that was about to begin without me.

Each year, on the Thursday of the last week of school, the Lutheran church next door to Mason Elementary—where I was attending fifth grade—transformed its adjoining lawn into a mini-fairground for what it called its annual ice cream social. There were booth games, a merry-go-round, and more than a few ice cream stands. They served turtle sundaes and banana splits and—everyone's favorite—soft serve in a cone. Mason opened up the gym as well, where, as mothers and sisters and girlfriends in sandals and pastel-colored dresses ate ice cream, boys and their fathers played shirts versus skins in a basketball game everyone talked about for months before it happened. Ever since the second grade, I'd been trying to get Mother to let me go.

"We don't go to church, Hayat. We're not Christians. We have to draw the line somewhere."

"It's not church, Mom. It's playing games and eating ice cream."

"At a church."

"Outside. At the school, too."

"The sign in front of the church says 'Lutheran Parish Ice Cream Social.'"

"Please, Mom."

"Hayat. Don't be difficult."

"Pleeaase."

"Absolutely not. And that's final."

She never budged. Though one year—at the end of fourth grade—wondering if perhaps she'd been too strict about the whole thing, Mother made a point of driving by the social as it was taking place. When she got home that afternoon, she was in a lather. "Not church, Hayat? Then why are priests walking all over? All eating ice cream like it's that holy bread of theirs? Hmm? And right in front of a cross with suffering Jesus on it. What an idea!"

That was that. There was no chance I was ever going to an ice cream social.

So there I sat in the living room that last Thursday afternoon of fifth grade, still wearing the clothes I'd worn to school that day, moping as I stared at Mina. At some point she looked up and noticed me gazing at her.

"Hayat?"

"Hi, Auntie."

"Hi, *behta*. What are you doing?"

"Nothing much."

Her brows crinkled. "What's going on, Hayat?"

"Nothing."

"Come here, sweetie."

I pushed myself to my feet and trudged over to the dining table.

"What's wrong?" she asked.

I didn't know what to say. Telling her about the social wasn't going to change anything. So what was the point?

"You're not sick, are you?" Mina asked, her hand to my forehead.

"No," I said, noticing the book before her. *The Tropic of Cancer.* The cover showed a large, gray menacing crab. *Why is she reading about cancer?* "You're not a doctor, are you, Auntie?" I asked.

Just then, Mother appeared in the doorway leading to the hall and stairs beyond. "What's the problem? Hmm? He's not still complaining about that godforsaken ice cream *social,* is he?"

"The godforsaken what?" Mina asked.

"Ice cream *social.* Some Christian silliness."

"It's not Christian," I objected.

"I said no!" Mother snapped.

"What's an ice cream social?" Mina asked.

"They sell ice cream to raise money for the church," Mother said with derision.

"That's not true. It's free," I said.

Mother shot me a warning look. "Nothing in this country is *free.* The sign in front says the proceeds go to the parish. Proceeds from what? From *free* ice cream?" She snickered. "We don't need to be giving money to Christians."

As I saw it, we gave money to Christians every day. At the mall, at the grocery store, at the post office. What was the difference?

I was about to say as much when Mother lifted her finger and pointed at me. "Hayat, I don't want to hear another word about that damn *social.*"

Then she turned and walked out.

Once she was gone, Mina took my hand, tenderly. "You really wanted to go, didn't you?"

I nodded. Mina's tone brought a sore knot to my throat.

"Hayat, let it out."

"Let what out?" I said with a cough.

"What you're feeling. If you hold it in, it stays there. If you let it out, that's the only way it can go away."

I didn't know what she was talking about. Mina leaned in and took me by the shoulders, her gaze piercing me. "Let it hurt, Hayat. Don't fight it."

"Let it hurt?"

"Don't fight the pain you're feeling. Just let it be. Let it be there. Open to it, *inside* yourself..."

"Okay," I said. I held her gaze.

I could feel the aching in my heart. I stopped resisting it. Almost at once, something inside me crumbled. My throat swelled. My face contracted. Up bubbled searing tears.

Mina took me in her arms and held me. I released, crying into her shoulder. The comfort of her embrace felt like nothing I could remember.

When the tears stopped, Mina used her sleeves to wipe my face dry.

"Better?"

I nodded. I did feel better.

"If you hold it in, it *stays* in. And then all sorts of bad things can happen to you."

"Like what?"

"The worst thing that can happen? If you hold on to the pain for too long, you start to think you are this pain." Mina studied me for a moment. "Do you understand, *behta?*"

I nodded. What she was saying made sense to me.

"And if you think you are this pain, it means you start to think that what you deserve is pain. Quran always says Allah is *al-Rahim*. Do you know what '*al-Rahim*' means?"

I shook my head. For though I'd heard the words on Mother's lips countless times, she'd never explained to me what they meant.

"It means Allah is forgiving. He forgives us. And it means that we don't deserve that pain we keep inside us. Allah loves us. He wants us to let it go..."

I was losing the logic, and she could tell. She wiped again at my face with her sleeve, speaking now with a sudden bright tone: "Isn't there something you want to do...other than watch me read my book?"

"I don't know."

"Think about it."

"Think about what?"

"If there's something you want to do right now..."

"I don't know."

"When you don't know what you want, there's an easy way to find out."

"How?"

"You make the small voice inside you speak."

I was perplexed.

"I'll show you. Close your eyes..."

I did.

"What are you hearing now?"

"Your voice."

"What else?"

I listened. There was the muffled hum of a car passing along the road outside. "A car outside," I said.

"What else?"

I turned my head to one side, listening more deeply.

"Do you hear something else?"

"No."

"Your own breath, *behta?* Do you hear that?"

I kept listening. I could hear it. Gentle and steady. Going in and out of me. I nodded.

"Keep listening to your breath," she said softly.

I paid close attention, listening. I thought I heard something hollow inside me filling and emptying with a soft, dark sound.

"Do you hear the silence, *behta?*"

"Silence?"

"At the end of your breath. When you get to the end."

I breathed and listened. She was right. At the end of each inhale, each exhale, there was quiet. I nodded.

"When you hear that silence, *behta,* just stay there. And then ask the question 'What do I want to do?' Just say that to yourself in the silence: 'What do I want to do?' "

I inhaled and exhaled, waiting for the silence at the end of my breath. It was a glowing quiet, bright and pulsing, alive.

What do I want to do? I whispered to myself.

And then I saw something: my red Schwinn Typhoon one-speed. Its bars were gleaming, clean as the day my parents had brought it home.

My eyes shot open. "I want to wash my bike!" I exclaimed.

"Good, *behta.* Go. Go and clean it. And then go for a ride. Enjoy yourself."

I bolted out the door and into the garage. I pulled my bike onto the driveway and filled a bucket with soap and water. I lathered down the bars and wheels, then doused it all with water from our garden hose. When I was done, my bike looked exactly as it had in my mind's eye: red, bright, glistening.

I hopped on and pedaled off. I was rapt. I'd completely forgotten about the ice cream social. And if the ride around the subdivision that followed was anything but routine, it wasn't because of some new and remarkable encounter along the way, but because the satisfaction I'd felt cleaning my bike now developed as I rode. I was taken with the plainest pleasures: the blur of the speckled macadam passing beneath my wheels; the breeze in my face; the pressure of the pedals against my soles. Sensation itself was enough. More than enough. I felt complete. And I couldn't remember feeling anything like it.

3

The Opening

Imran was strange. Uncommonly reclusive for a four-year-old, he was given to hours of silent play in his room surrounded by the crayons and colored pencils that appeared to be his only pleasure. I had difficulty believing he was Mina's son, and not only because he shared nothing of her exuberance or magnetism. Dark, with tiny eyes and short, sharp features crammed tightly into the middle of his face, he looked nothing like her. Mother wanted me to *take him under my wing* and treat him like the little brother I didn't have. I did my best. I played with him. I lent him my special catcher's mitt, which I lent no one. I put up with the tantrums he threw when he lost pieces in our games of checkers and chess. I read him stories—even though I didn't enjoy it—in the forts we built down in the family room out of sheets. But no matter what we did, I never seemed to have his full attention. Sooner or later, Imran would grow bored and head off to his room. More than once, I followed him there to find him lying on his bed, a coloring book open in his lap, as he mumbled to the black-and-white picture that stood propped against his bedside lamp.

Noticing me at the doorway, he would turn and say, proudly:

"That's Hamed, my dad."

Imran's picture of his father showed a well-groomed man in a white oxford shirt peering out at the viewer with a paradoxical expression I found striking for the fact that I'd already seen it on Imran's own face countless times: a pair of small eyes wide with what looked like fear, but gazing out from beneath a smooth brow that showed not a ripple of worry; and down at the bottom of the face, another conundrum: a mouth dangling open, slack-jawed, unconcerned, but with the tip of a pointed tongue tensely curled around the bottom of the top teeth, as if nervously seeking its way into the small gap there.

Almost from the moment Imran could speak, he'd been asking about his father. And, sensing there was more to know than the vague, unsettling outline of a story his mother told him— that there had once been a man who had been his father, but then he'd left, and so was his father no more—Imran turned to others for answers. Indeed, it wasn't long before each new male visitor to the house would find himself besieged by the young boy; Imran would climb up a leg and into the man's embrace. "Are you my dad?" he would ask.

When Imran was three, Mina finally decided to show her son her only photograph of her ex-husband. As she feared, the picture fueled the boy's obsession. Now, nightly, Imran refused to sleep until his mother pulled out the picture and propped it against the lamp by his bed. He would talk to the photo, asking it the questions his mother was never able to answer: Where was he? When was he coming back? It broke Mina's heart to see her son talking to a picture, and so now when she tucked him in, it was always with a promise: that she was going to find Imran a real man to be his father someday.

Weeks into their stay with us, I noticed Imran had taken to sitting every evening at the bottom stair in the front vestibule, waiting for Father's return. And once he heard the rumble of Father's car coming up the driveway, and the thrum and whir of the garage door yawning open, Imran would already be on his feet, jumping about in front of the door he was so eagerly waiting to see open. And Father would appear, dropping his briefcase to his feet as he lifted the boy aloft with a kiss to the cheek. "You're home!" Imran would squeal with glee. So began their evening jaunt through the house, like cricket groundskeepers making the rounds on a pleasant, summer evening. They checked on Mother and the dinner being prepared in the kitchen, peering over the steaming pots and into the oven, where *naan*s usually lay in neat rows, heating. They stopped at the bedroom doorways—mine, Mina's—where they would linger, Imran bouncing about in Father's embrace, to inquire about our activities and our days. Then they would disappear into my parents' room, where Father sat Imran on the bed while he changed into jeans and a sweatshirt, and where they giggled and joked and played until mealtime.

Father saw much of himself in the boy, and he wasn't the only one to think that, even at the tender age of four, Imran resembled the man more than I, his real son, did. Mother constantly pointed out resemblances in their hands and feet, their shortish fingers and toes and stubby nails that never grew very much, as well as in the narrow cast of their uncommonly light-colored eyes. Mother said there was an intensity to their gazes that pointed at a stewing intelligence she hoped Imran would find better uses for than Father had.

It was strange to see Father behaving so warmly toward the boy. The stinging I felt when I first heard Father use the term of endearment "*kurban*" for Imran would recur, and I would grow accustomed to it. But if I was able to make peace with my envy at the attention Father showered on Imran, it had everything to do with an inner compensation that helped my pain make sense:

The boy could have him, as long as I had Mina...

Every night, half an hour before bedtime, Mina would come and find me. She would lead me into her room, getting into bed, where she propped two pillows, one for each of us—sometimes a third if Imran was still awake—as we settled in. After dimming the bedside lamp and huddling in closer to set the mood, with an eager look in her eye, she would begin:

"Once upon a time..."

I loved her voice. And I loved being so close to her. My days now revolved around the anticipation of that nighttime hour, when I would lie beside her, taking in the vaguely sweet, jasmine scent she wore, listening—my eyes closed—to her breathy voice as she told bedtime tales.

If Imran was with us, Mina would begin with a story about *djinn*s. *Djinn*s were creatures described in the Quran made not of mud—like us humans—but fire, able to change form at will. Mina told us tales of *djinn*s as tall as trees, and others dressed in black robes with bells for hands, and still others that ran as fast as the wind, chasing Punjabi farmers from their fields at the crack of dawn. She told us of a *djinn* called Pichulpari—famous throughout the Punjab—who roamed the forest roads of Islamabad as a woman in a scarlet *shalwar*. Pichulpari waved in distress to passing drivers, luring kind souls to the shoulder, where she then attacked them. Some of her victims, Mina said, died of fright from their encounters. Mina even knew a man who'd seen Pichulpari with his own eyes. He'd described a woman who looked nothing like a real person: a creature with a long, lupine face and the grotesque oddity of its feet and hands affixed to its limbs backwards. Imran loved these stories. I did, too.

But I loved her tales of the Prophet more.

Most Muslim kids my age would have already known the stories of Muhammad's life that she told me. But neither of my parents was particularly religious, and I heard more tales from Mother about Father's mistresses than anything else. Deep down, Mother was a believer, but the years she'd spent with Father—who thought religion was for fools—had trained her, I think, to check her religious impulses. According to Mother, Father's antipathy for the faith came from the fact that his own mother used devoutness to abuse her children, beating them out of bed for their morning prayers, not feeding them if they didn't put in their hours of daily religious study. "But that doesn't mean he doesn't still believe in Allahmia," Mother would add, assuringly. When Mina discovered how little I actually knew about Islam, she was delighted to fill the gap.

The tale of our Prophet's childhood brought tears to her eyes no matter how many times she told it: a young Arab boy who'd lost everything a boy could lose, with a father already dead when he was brought into the world, and a mother who died when he was six. And yet, despite his misfortunes, young Muhammad was never sullen. Everywhere he went, people would remark on his good nature, his unusual poise and calm, and on the special light they saw shining in his eyes. This light, Mina said, had been put there by God shortly after young Muhammad's mother's death. One afternoon, as he was playing with a group of friends, three mysterious figures enshrouded in veils of light—they were angels—appeared and whisked him off to the top of a distant mountain. There, the first angel reached into Muhammad's breast, and cut the boy open to the belly. Young Muhammad felt no pain as he watched the angel's hand disappear inside his body and bring forth the goopy tangle of his intestines. The angel cleaned the organs with fresh snow from a magical green vase. Now the second angel approached and plunged his hand into the boy's still-open chest. He took young Muhammad's heart out and searched inside, removing a tiny black clot. This clot, Mina explained, was the seed of evil contained in all human hearts, but no longer in Muhammad's. The third angel stepped forward to put the boy back together, restoring his organs and sealing up his chest. This angel declared that the mission was complete, and young Muhammad was now returned to his playmates, none of whom, oddly, had even noticed he was gone. The whole miracle had taken place in the time it took to blink an eye.

Two years later, when Muhammad was eight, the man he now called Father, his grandfather, also died. Mina was always saying that God loved Muhammad more than anyone else, but I didn't understand how that could be the case: Why did Allah take everyone Muhammad loved away from him?

"To teach him to depend on Allah only," Mina explained.

"But why?" I asked.

"Because it is the truth, *behta*. Not a truth most can handle, but truth all the same: God is the only One we can depend on, truly."

And while I didn't doubt she might have been right, I remember thinking I didn't want to lose my parents—or Mina either—just to find out something that was true. No matter how true it was.

My favorite of Mina's stories of Muhammad's life took place in a cave. It was the tale of how he became the Prophet of Islam. Already forty, he was a married man. He was a merchant by trade, but Mina called him a *seeker of the truth* by nature. And during his travels along the trade route to Syria, Muhammad met Christian and Jewish holy men from whom he'd learned about Abraham and his teachings about the one and only true God. It was from these elder Christians and Jews, Mina claimed, that Muhammad learned to pray. And it was while praying quietly one night in a dark cave at Mount Hira, not far from his home, that Muhammad heard a voice.

"Recite," it said.

Muhammad opened his eyes and found hovering before him a blinding light in the form of a man. It was Gabriel, God's archangel. Muhammad opened his mouth to speak, but nothing came out.

"Recite!" the figure repeated, the command echoing ominously through the cave.

Muhammad tried, but still couldn't speak.

Now Gabriel pressed in closer, the cloud of light growing brighter as he did, more unbearable. Muhammad felt as if his heart were going to explode.

"Recite!" Gabriel commanded again.

"I don't know what to recite!" he finally cried out, trembling.

Gabriel now took the mortal into his arms of light. Just as Muhammad was about to faint with terror, it happened. Words blossomed on his tongue, words he didn't know were inside him. And what he spoke that night, Mina said with pride, were the first words of our great Revelation.

The Quran.

It was late August, the evening of my eleventh birthday. Mina came to get me earlier than usual from the family room. "I have something for you, *behta*," she said, eagerly. Once we were in her room, she shut the door, pulling up the shawl around her shoulders to cover her head. She stepped over to the bookcase and reached for the green book that sat by itself on the highest shelf. She brought it to her lips, kissing the cover, then turned to me. "It's time you had a Quran of your own. But before I give it to you, I want you to go and wash your hands. Respect for our holy book begins with cleanliness."

I went to the bathroom and scrubbed at my hands with soap and scalding water. When I returned to her room, my palms tingling, I found Mina standing behind a chair that faced the window, the direction in which she prayed five times a day. Mina had a long piece of white muslin in her hands.

"Sit, *behta*," she said.

As I did, Mina started to wrap my head in the cloth. Her touch was warm. It sent a shudder through me. "We cover our heads in respect for the word of God." Once she'd finished, she handed me the Quran.

"Kiss it," she whispered.

I lifted the book to my face. Its soft, green leather-bound cover was cold to my lips.

"Open to the first *surah*," she said.

"First what?"

"*Surah*. It's what we call a chapter in the Quran. A *surah*."

The book's new binding cracked as I opened it. Inside, each page was like a work of art, covered on the left with a block of black Arabic text enclosed in a golden frame; on the right was the English translation. As I turned the thick pages—heavy like vellum—they released the crisp, pleasing odor of new paper.

I found the first *surah*, a half page of verse called "The Opening."

"That's it," Mina said. "Read it to me."

I cleared my voice and began to read:

In the name of God, the Benevolent, the Merciful.
Praise be to God, Lord of the Worlds,
The Benevolent, the Merciful.
Master of the Day of Judgment,
You do we serve; You do we ask for help.
Guide us on the right path,
The path of those You favor;
Not those who earn Your wrath,
Nor those who go astray.

I stumbled through the text, tripping on the words "benevolent" and "merciful." When I'd finally gotten through the text, I was surprised to find that Mina was smiling at me. "Remember when the angel Gabriel came to the cave and made the Prophet recite?"

I remembered.

"Well, *behta,*" she explained, touching the Quran, "that is how this whole book came into being through our Prophet...*peace be upon him.*"

I remembered a question I'd been meaning to ask her for some time. "Auntie, why do you always say *'peace be upon him'*?"

"Out of respect, Hayat. The Prophet gave us all so much, so we try to give something back by always praying for the peace of His soul."

"Do you have to say it every time?"

Mina laughed. "No, *behta.* With everything in life, Hayat, it's the *intention* that matters. As long as you respect the Prophet's memory, that's the important thing." Mina leaned in to turn the page. Her arm brushed against mine, her touch whispering along my skin and echoing up my arm to the back of my neck.

Mina turned the pages, explaining that there were 114 *surah*s, each the result of a different encounter between Gabriel and Muhammad, sometimes in the cave at Hira, sometimes while Muhammad was at home with his wives, sometimes as he lay dreaming on the rock-hard cot that— Mina said—Muhammad slept on his whole life, even once he had become something like a king and could afford so much more.

Mina explained a way of dividing the Quran into thirty sections of equal length called *juz*. This was how the *hafiz* broke it up, the *hafiz*, or those who knew our holy book by heart. Mina said that becoming a *hafiz* was one of the greatest things a person could do in one's life. It meant not only securing one's own place in Janaat, but a place for one's parents as well: Janaat, our word for "Paradise": that garden in the sky that was the ultimate end of all our labors. And though I didn't know much about our faith, I knew how important Paradise was. To us Muslims, life here on earth was of no value if it did not lead to that abode of endless peace and pleasure, where rivers of milk and honey flowed, and where the famous virgin hordes awaited our arrival.

I didn't know what the word "virgin" meant, though I knew it had something to do with the uneasy fascination and shame that came over me when, say, Bo Derek floated across our TV screen jogging through a golden haze in ads for *10*; or while watching the endless parade of bikini-clad women in high heels stopping to pose for the camera on the beauty pageants that Mother—inexplicably, considering her seemingly ceaseless disdain for white women—watched religiously. I knew the word "virgin" had something to do with the lure of a woman's unclothed body, still mysterious to me, as I knew nothing more about the facts of life than that it was the name of a television show about four girls at boarding school. And compounding my confusion was the apparent paradox: Why were these bodies so forbidden to us now if they were precisely what was promised to us later in Janaat?

"Are you a *hafiz*, Auntie?" I asked.

She laughed. "I'm too lazy for that, *behta*. Learning the Quran is hard work. It takes many years, and a very special person. A *hafiz* never gives up."

Nothing seemed more remarkable to me at that moment than the mysterious *hafiz*, whoever they were.

Mina turned the pages back to the opening. "Let's read it again," she said.

"Together?"

"No, *behta*. You read it to me."

I did. My voice rattled softly in my throat and chest as I read aloud. When Mina stopped me to ask if I understood what I was saying, I realized I'd been paying no attention to what I was reading, only to the pleasure of the sounds themselves.

So I read the verses to her again.

"I understand the words, Hayat," she said, stopping me. "I want to know what they *mean*."

I was looking at her lips as she spoke, their pink, plump, ridged surface moving with her words. The side of her face was bright, lit by her bedside lamp, and the other half receded gently into shadows. She was beautiful.

"Hayat? Hayat?"

"Yes, Auntie?"

"I want you to concentrate, okay?"

"I'm sorry."

"Let's take a look at these lines again. Three words are repeated more than one time ... What are they?"

I looked down at the page. In the lamplight, the black letters pulsed against the yellow-white page; Mina's fingers—tipped with red—moved along the lines. I tried to focus, looking for the repeated words.

> In the name of God, the Benevolent, the Merciful.
> Praise be to God, Lord of the Worlds,
> The Benevolent, the Merciful.

" 'God,' 'benevolent,' 'merciful,' " I said.

"Good. Now, you already know what 'God' means. But how about these other words. Let's start with 'merciful.' What does 'merciful' mean?"

"It means nice?"

"Not only. It means something more precise than that."

I had a soft feeling about the word, something kind, something released or releasing. But I didn't know how to explain it.

"I don't know," I replied, annoyed.

"Let me help you, Hayat…When someone hits you, what do you do about it?"

"Hit them back?"

"Or?"

I thought for a moment. "You tell someone?"

She smiled. "Or?"

I didn't know.

"You can forgive them," she said. "If you forgive them, you're showing mercy." I was surprised. There was a force in the clarity of her definition. It made her seem even more remarkable to me. "And 'benevolent'?" she continued. "Do you know what that means?"

I shrugged. I didn't.

"It means doing good," she said, softly. "When you do something good, you are being benevolent." She reached out and touched the side of my face. "So what is the beginning of our Quran saying?"

"That God forgives? And He does good?"

She smiled. "That's exactly right, Hayat. And I want to tell you something else, something very special..." She leaned in, her voice lowered, her lightly British accent more pronounced than usual as she went on: "Something no one told me until I was older than you...and I don't want you to forget it. Okay?"

I nodded.

"Allah will always forgive you, no matter what you do. *No matter what you do.* All you have to do is to *ask* to be forgiven. That's what it means that He is *merciful.* And Allah is also *benevolent.* And that means He will make sure that whatever happens to you is always for the good."

"You mean that even the bad things that happen to us are for the good, right?"

"Exactly, sweetie." There was a fire in her eyes now. "This *surah* is telling us about Allah's nature, *behta.* That it is His nature to forgive us. And it is His nature always to do what is for the good. And what it means is very simple: You never have to worry. Never. You are safe. As safe as if Allah Himself were holding you in the palm of His hand." She put out her palm, its narrow, waxen surface glowing above a network of crisscrossing lines. Like the page—and her fingers on it earlier—her hand struck me as startling, vivid, breathing with life. She kissed me on the forehead again. "Allah be with you, *behta.*"

That night my nerve ends teemed and pulsed. I still recall the vividness of my cotton pajamas against my arms and legs, the fabric pressing here and there, distinct points of contact alive with pleasure. And this was only the surface. Deep inside, things were stirring as well. Even my bones seemed to be breathing. My body felt whole, one, unified, filled with air, expanding with light.

I fell asleep and dreamt all night of Mina's hands turning the yellow-white pages of my new Quran.

The next night, half an hour before bedtime, I washed up, tied the muslin Mina had given me to my head, and went to see her, my new Quran in hand. Having spent recess at school memorizing the verses we'd gone over the night before, I recited them for her now from memory.

"How wonderful, *behta!*" She was so surprised. She took me into her arms, and all at once I felt it again: that exquisite shudder running along my limbs, up my back. "I have a feeling about you," she said into my ear. "I have a feeling you might just end up a *hafiz* someday."

4

A New World

The months that followed were witness to a series of spiritual experiences that would remain singular in my life, all revolving around the Quran and my evening study hour with Mina. I would leave her room feeling lively, easily moved, my heart softened and sweet, my senses heightened. Often, I was too awake to sleep, and so I took to my desk—white muslin still bound to my head—to continue memorizing verses. After long nights like these, the mornings were not difficult, as Mother warned when she would find me at my desk past ten o'clock. If anything, these mornings were even sweeter: the trees stippled with turning leaves and bathed in a glorious light that seemed like much more than just the sun's illumination; the white clouds sculpted against blue skies, stacked like majestic monuments to the Almighty's unfathomable glory. And it wasn't only beauty that moved me in these heightened states. Even the grease-encrusted axle of the yellow school bus slowing to its morning stop at the end of my driveway could captivate me, its twisting joint—and the large, squeaking wheel that turned around it—seeming to point the inscrutable way to some rich, strange, and holy power.

At school—I was starting sixth grade—I would find myself, inexplicably, in states of eerie calm and awakeness. For hours, something as simple as the play of sunlight against the class-room's green chalkboard could occupy me completely. Not to mention the food in the cafeteria. I recall sipping from my carton of milk one lunch hour, shocked. The full, creamy, com-forting flavor seemed like a miracle. And while part of me wondered how it was I had never truly tasted milk before, an-other part of me had already concluded that these experiences had their source in my new contact with our holy Quran.

That October, during a game of touch football one after-noon recess, I ran downfield, looking back over my shoulder and up at the sky, where I expected to find the ball Andy—our quarterback—had told me in the huddle was coming my way. Instead, I saw something round and perfect, a brilliant white circle appearing behind a veil of clouds. And in the few seconds it took for Andy's uneasy spiral to leave his hands and come floating toward me—and during which I realized it was the sun I was seeing—I found myself already lost in sudden contem-plation. The ball fell through my grip. My teammates jeered. I smiled, sheepish, apologizing. But my remorse was mostly an act. My thoughts were focused on the recollection of verses I'd memorized for Mina earlier that week:

> Consider the sun and its splendor....
> And the day, that reveals it...
> And the night, in which it hides...
> Consider the sky and the One who made it...
> And the earth, spread out before you...

As I made my way back to scrimmage, I gazed over at the school building, its single story of beige bricks fanning out be-neath the rows of tall trees behind it; beyond those trees was Worth Park, and beyond that, the shopping center and movie theater and local pharmacy; and beyond that, forests and fields and who knew what else. I turned to the road lined with split-level homes. Beyond those homes were other homes, then a highway, and further homes upon homes. I looked up at the sky, its thin cloud cover against a blue ceiling hiding the way to the dark space I knew lay beyond, a vastness inhabited with glowing stars and turning globes, and—according to our science book—an ever-expanding universe.

I was suddenly awestruck by the thought of infinity. And not just of the universe I couldn't see beyond the clouds, but of the world around me as well: the countless schools and trees and homes and people in them, and the countless kids on playgrounds, how many of them wondering—just like me at that very moment—about all the endless schools and homes and trees and all the infinite stars above unfolding forever...

It was probably not the first time I'd ever been moved to awe by such musing, but it was the first time I had a word to put to my feelings, a word I'd learned from the Quran:

Majesty.

It's all God's majesty, I thought as I jogged back and took my place in the huddle.

"I don't smoke. I don't drink. But *tea* is my one vice!"

I heard Mina say it so many times, but always with a sly half grin that made it hard to believe she really had any remorse. The fact was, her tea was exceptional: bold but discreet, with a sharp, clean bite that made one sit up a little straighter, abounding with complex and subtle aftertastes that drew one—as the flavors faded—to sip again. It was the result of a preparation that bore no resemblance at all to the steeping of bags in cups of hot water that my parents called tea. Mina's was more like a stew: the loose leaves (Darjeeling or Assam, with a pinch of Earl Grey or Lady Grey thrown in depending on her mood), a crushed cardamom pod, a clove or two, a dash each of cinnamon and ginger powder, and a teaspoon and a half of sugar, all dropped into one part whole milk and one part water brought to a simmer over low heat. She stood over the concoction, attentive, turning it with a wooden spoon, moving the pot off the fire each time it approached a boil. She was waiting for the tea to turn a particular hue—a creamy, deep tan—before cutting the heat and straining the brew directly into cups she had lined along the stove. The aroma of milk and tea and sugar and spices was ample and sweet, and it always made my mouth water.

Father loved her tea so much, he wanted to learn how to make it exactly as she did. I remember the afternoon he first stood beside Mina at the stove while she coached him through the preparations. When they were done—the cups were poured—Father, Mother, and Mina sat together at the kitchen table to taste the result.

"Hmmm. It's good, Naveed," Mina said, sipping.

"Not as good as when *you* make it," Mother was quick to add.

"It's his first time, Muneer."

"First or last, I don't know. I just know it's not as good."

Father ignored her.

"Too much cinnamon," Mother said.

Mina sipped, considering the flavor. "I don't think so. I think it just needs to blend a little better. Maybe straining it into a pot to let it sit before pouring."

"But you don't do that," Father objected.

"But I'm very attentive when I stir. Very slow."

"It needs more *attention,* is what she's saying," Mother

added. Father ignored her, taking another sip. Mina turned to me, offering me her cup.

"You want to try your father's tea, *behta?*"

Mother put up her hand. "None for him."

"Why not?" I asked.

"Too young. When you're eighteen you can drink tea and coffee. Not now."

"But I've had it before."

"Since when?" Mother asked, surprised.

"I've given it to him," Mina interjected before I could respond.

"Hmm," Mother hummed, disapproving.

I looked over at Imran. He was coloring in a coloring book, and had a glass of milk before him. Just like me. "I'm old enough," I said.

"According to the laws of what universe?" Mother asked.

"Don't make a big deal, Muneer," Father said. "It's just a cup of tea."

"He's old enough to be praying. Why not a cup of tea?" Mina replied, glancing over at me with a look that made me realize what she was doing. I'd been begging her for weeks to teach me to pray.

"Old enough to pray? Well, *that* would require Mr. *Inattentive* here to teach him," Mother added flatly. In Islam, it was a father's duty to teach his son to pray.

"You, Muneer, are a total contradiction," Father replied. "All your complaining about Muslim men, and here you are, criticizing me for not being Muslim enough."

"There's no contradiction," Mother said, tapping her finger nervously against the cup. "What's wrong with Muslim men has nothing to do with *prayers*. It has to do with how they treat their women."

Father rolled his eyes and took another sip.

"I'm happy to teach him, if that's not a problem for you," Mina said to Father.

I brightened, turning to Father. But he didn't look enthused. "You've already got him obsessed with that *book*."

Like clockwork, Father's lack of enthusiasm gave Mother her lead. "Well, I think that's a wonderful idea!" she said brightly.

Mina watched Father's reaction to Mother's sudden glee. "But I really don't want to intrude..."

"You're not intruding," he said. "If Muneer thinks it's fine, go ahead. Teach him." He turned to me. "But I don't want to see you end up as a *maulvi*, Hayat."

Maulvi was another name for an imam.

Mina chuckled. "It's just *namaaz,* Naveed. I hardly think teaching him to pray is going to make him end up as a *maulvi*. Who would he become a *maulvi* for? This is not Pakistan."

"Trust me," Father replied. "There are idiots enough here for someone to lead. You just haven't met them yet. Chatha and all those stooges with their *masjid* on the South Side. Be grateful you don't know any of *them* yet." He turned to me again: "All I'm saying to you is: Don't end up as a *maulvi*."

It didn't take me long to learn the prayer and its various intricacies: the texts, the movements that went with them; how many times to repeat each part; how to sit, right foot propped under one's behind, left turned in and resting on its side; the seven points that needed to touch the ground when you prostrated yourself (both knees, both hands, the chin, the nose, the forehead); and the meaning of holding up your right index finger during the prayer's final section: another way to remind oneself that there was no God but Allah.

I was a quick study, but Mina was insistent that the forms were not what mattered. And until I learned to understand what she called prayer's "inner aspect," she wouldn't let me pray for real; I could only practice. I had to sit and listen to my breath, just as she had taught me to do that afternoon of the ice cream social. In the silence, she would make me focus on God. "Always imagine him close to you when you pray," she explained. "If you think of Him as near, then that's where you will find Him. And if you think of Him as far away, then that's where He will be."

One day Mina finally decided I was ready. Much to my surprise, Father—who actually seemed proud of me—suggested an excursion to the same South Side *masjid* about which he always complained. That way, he said, I could offer my first prayer with the congregation, just as he had done as a child. But that Sunday, when we got to the mosque, there was a sign on the door announcing flood damage in the basement prayer room; the day's worship had been cancelled. We went back home, where Father had another uncharacteristic idea: that we create our own congregation by offering prayers together as a family. Surprised as they were, Mother and Mina both thought it was a wonderful idea. So Father and I tied muslin to our heads—Imran wanted to join us, so we tied a piece to his head, too—then laid out prayer carpets in the living room. Father and I stood shoulder to shoulder, and Mother and Mina prayed shoulder to shoulder behind us. Imran sat off to one side, happy to mimic our movements.

Afterwards, Mother was teary-eyed. Father pulled out his wallet and handed me a twenty-dollar bill.

"What's that for?" I asked.

"You're a man now. A man needs to have money in his pocket," he said, clapping me on the back.

"Just because you have it doesn't mean you have to spend it," Mother interrupted.

"Let the boy be," Father retorted, though more warmly than usual.

Mina took me in her arms, cooing her congratulations: "*Behta,* I'm so proud of you!"

"Thank you, Auntie," I said.

"Did you do like I taught you? Did you imagine Allah before you as you prayed?"

I realized I'd entirely forgotten. Mina read the response in my blank expression.

"It's the only reason to pray, Hayat," she said. "To be close to Allah. If you just do forms, it's useless. Even sitting quietly on the school bus and remembering your intention to be with God—even *that* is a hundred times better than just going through the motions."

"Okay, Auntie," I said. "I won't forget again. I promise."

For Mina, faith really wasn't about the outer forms. She didn't wear a head scarf. And since her troubles with food as a girl— she would stop eating when she was unhappy, and ended up in the hospital more than once because of it—she didn't fast. But she still found a way to be true to the intention of Ramadan as she saw it: She would deprive herself of things she loved, like reading, in order to feel that quickening of the will—and the deepening of one's gratitude—that she said were the reasons we Muslims fasted. Mina was an advocate of what we Muslims called *ijtihad,* or personal interpretation. The only problem was, the so-called Gates of *Ijtihad* had been famously "closed" in the tenth century, a fact I was aware of from a footnote in the Quran Mina had given me. The note explained that personal interpretation led to innovations, and that these innovations created chaos in the matter of knowing what it meant to obey God's will. I asked Mina about it one day, and she explained to me—at teatime, with Mother at the table—that as far as she was concerned, these "gates" could never be closed, because they were the gates that led to the Lord.

"Somebody just said they were closed. I walk through them as I please," she added.

"But since when is that for *you* to decide?" Mother asked, surprised.

(I was surprised myself that Mother even knew what *ijtihad* was.)

"Who else can decide, Muneer?" Mina said with passion. "Some mullah from a thousand years ago? When we're told that the Quran says we are not equal to men, is it true? The Quran's laws are more progressive than what the Arabs had before Islam. That was the intention. To move things forward, to create more freedom. How can the rule matter when it is not true to the deeper intention?"

"So they shouldn't be able to marry four wives?"

Mina considered, a smile slowly appearing on her lips: "Or we should be able to marry four men..."

"God forbid!" Mother exclaimed with a laugh. "One is enough!"

Perhaps it was her belief in her purity of intent that made Mina think she could enroll herself in a training program for beauty salon technicians and somehow remain unsullied by the cosmetic ruses of white women. How else to explain what she was thinking when she decided to make her living here in America by learning the very outward wiles so at odds with the feminine modesty central to our Islamic faith? But perhaps it was precisely in the contradiction where the appeal lay. After all, here Mina was, now living in a world where a woman's life was truly nothing like the life she'd known. What did it mean? What was it like to be a woman in America? What were the sorts of thoughts that passed through the minds of the large-boned, blonde, and blue-eyed Amazons she saw driving their children to tennis lessons and soccer practice; who wandered the malls, their arms covered with shopping bags; who shuffled along the grocery aisles, pushing carts filled to overflow? Mina must have wondered. And perhaps it was at the local grocery—where she and Mother went weekly—while standing in line and taking in the spectacle of white women with their intriguing and unfamiliar frozen dinners, deli cheeses, Hostess snack cakes, and the forbidden bottles of wine and beer in different shades of brown and green (and of course, the shocking cuts of pork, pink like human flesh); perhaps it was there that Mina first noticed the selection of magazines showing American beauties with impossibly wide smiles, their hairstyles gorgeously tousled by the breeze of freedom that seemed to blow across every glossy cover. For it was from those photo-thick fashion journals—*Vogue* and *Harper's Bazaar* and *Cosmopolitan*—that Mina would get the idea of becoming a beauty salon professional.

But if it had truly been her intention simply to learn the beauty secrets without using them on herself, she would fail miserably. Within weeks of starting her education, the habitual Pakistani garb—the loosely fitting *shalwar* pants, *kameez* tunics, and *dupatta* head coverings—gave way to not-so-loose-fitting blouses and jeans. She had to dress appropriately for school, she explained to Mother, an excuse that only forecast further innovations in her appearance. Now she started to let her new friends at the Institute for Women & Beauty—a storefront school at the local mall—make her up not only with lipstick and blush, but mascara, foundation, and eye shadow. And even if she usually wiped all the "face paint" off before coming home, leaving only the vaguest traces for us to discern, there were a few times she hazarded the full-frontal display, stepping into the kitchen, her eyes wide with defiance. Thinking back, I can only imagine that in moments like these, Mina was casting herself as the testing adolescent, and Mother as her parent. But if Mina expected resistance, Mother gave her none. She loved the fact that Mina was exploring. Likely, it was this very permission Mina had been seeking for much of her life.

Barely two months into her training, she went all out and had her hair completely redone, coming home one evening in Sue Ellen's latest, her sensuous tresses gone, the hair on top of her head spiked with gel. (Mina—like Mother, Father, and I—was an avid watcher of *Dallas,* and a devoted admirer of the lovely, long-suffering Ewing wife played by Linda Gray.) We must have looked shocked, for Mina turned red and immediately began to explain in embarrassed tones that one of her fellow students needed someone to practice on and that no one else had volunteered. But Mina didn't need to fear. Our shock was really just astonishment. The fact was: she looked incredible. With her new do, Mina was, if possible, even more beautiful. Or I should say, beautiful in an entirely new way. Her fashionable hairstyle made her a modern woman, an American woman, an astonishing prospect to folks like us who never would have thought *we* could look like *that.*

Mother spent most of dinner commenting on what the hairstyle did to her best friend's face: the way it brought forth her bone structure; further elongated her almond eyes; created space to appreciate the fineness of her features. Father was impressed, too. At one point, he pointed at Mina's head as he addressed his wife:

"Maybe you should try something like that."

But Mother wasn't keen on the idea. At least not yet. It would be years before she would attempt anything even vaguely like Mina's modern makeover. For now, Mother's hair would remain as it was: straight, falling halfway down her back, subject only to the luxury of an occasional henna coloring or permanent to give it body. Mother was more than content to live vicariously through her best friend, whether this meant purchasing Mina a vanity case filled with the latest cosmetics for her first birthday here in America, or driving her to the mall to peruse the racks for the latest styles. Mother enjoyed these outings tremendously, but she was always sure to make it known she was just "tagging along." It was all just for Mina's sake, of course.

For once, life in our home was settling into a peaceful, lively rhythm which none of us was accustomed to by nature or experience. I'm not convinced we were prepared to be happy. After all, we were formed and informed (to various degrees) by an Eastern mythos profoundly at odds with the American notion of happily-ever-after. For though we longed for happiness, we did not expect it. This was our cultural text, the message imprinted in even the movie videos my parents rented from the local Indo-Pak grocer—the only place you could find Indian films in town—lavish tales of unconsummated love, or love consummated at the price of death. These films were so unlike anything a paying American audience could ever have taken seriously as the truth about life. Americans would only have laughed in disbelief.

How ironic, then, that such disbelief was what Mina and my parents felt for the relentlessly hopeful narratives they would sit through at the local multiplexes just then opening their doors for business in the early eighties: They couldn't see in

Hollywood's rosy pictures of life's possibilities anything other than, at best, wishful thinking and, at worst, childish distraction. As a vision of life, they couldn't have taken it any more seriously than the popcorn they ate during the show could be taken for a meal. Instead, it was to the Indian weepies that they went to experience the pathos and color that felt to them like the truth about life. These were the moving pictures that had given shape and sound to their souls, stories painted from a darker palette, limned with haunting songs and built from images of elegiac beauty that conveyed an unvarying message:

Do not expect anything other than loss, pain, sorrow.

Like the odor of *masala* lingering along our hallways, the expectation of unhappiness hovered in the air we breathed, and even though Mina's presence among us had opened a window, brightening our lives, she was from the same world as my parents. And confident as she claimed to be in Allah's ultimate goodwill toward humanity, I think she fully expected things to turn against her in the end.

It was late December. After my lesson with Mina one evening, I spent another few hours at my desk with the Quran. By midnight, I was in bed. But I wasn't sleeping. I stared up into the darkness as I quietly cycled new verses on my lips:

Have We not opened your heart
And removed your burden?
Have We not remembered you?
Truly, with hardship comes ease,
With hardship comes ease!

I heard something in the hall. I stopped and listened. It was something like a voice. I got out of bed and stepped to my door, quietly pulling it open. A thin sliver of light bled through the partly open doorway of the bathroom down the hall.

Someone must have left the light on, I thought.

I stepped out and made my way to the door. As I reached my hand to the knob, I heard a sigh from inside. I stopped and pressed my eye to the crack. In the mirror, Mina stood, naked. Her breasts hung, smooth and ample and round, tipped with large dark nipples. Her skin gleamed a taut, pale brown. I had never seen anything so perfect as her naked body, its swelling at the chest and hips, the tapering between and down along her legs. My heart stirred. Something inside me was already burning.

Her eyes were closed, her left hand pushed in between her legs. She moaned softly to herself, her right hand touching her right nipple. She moaned softly again, continuing to rub her hand between her legs, more intensely now as her lips parted and she seemed to disappear inside herself. And then, all at once, her body tensed. She pulled her hand away to reveal a dark triangle between her legs. I was shocked. And then I realized:

She was looking at me.

Abruptly, she brought her right arm across her breasts and cupped her left hand over the darkness between her legs. Then she kicked the door shut.

I went back to my room and listened. A door opened. Another shut farther down the hall. I was in turmoil. I tried to sleep, and then I finally did. I tossed and turned through the night, the verses I'd learned echoing in my mind, the perfect form of Mina's naked body—and that shocking darkness at the top of her legs—haunting my dreams.

Had it not been for the awkwardness at breakfast the following morning, I might well have wondered if I hadn't dreamt the whole thing. But when I saw her sit at the table and attend coldly to her breakfast without even a look in my direction, my shame erupted—viscous, punishing. And her arctic reply to my sole attempt at bridging the sudden gulf between us—I asked her if she wanted me to pass her the salt for her eggs—sent a shudder of remorse through me.

After breakfast, she disappeared into her room. I followed her upstairs, but she wouldn't let me in. I was desperate. "I'm sorry, Auntie," I said, crying. She held the door barely cracked, just enough for me to see one eye and part of her mouth as she whispered back with a damning hush: "Hayat. We are *not* to talk about that. Don't *ever* mention it again. To me. Or anyone else." She paused, easing the door open just a crack wider to pin me with a silvered, watery gaze.

And then she shut the door in my face.

BOOK TWO

Nathan

5

Love at First Sight

It was a silent, despairing winter that followed my discovery of Mina in the bathroom. Her cooling toward me lasted weeks, and then months; her fatigue from long, late hours at work was now the excuse she used for avoiding our Quranic study hour. Whatever time we did spend together was not the same, troubled now by a discomfort whose source we both knew too well. I wished it had never happened. I prayed to God to wipe the memory of that night from both our minds. And prayer wasn't the only magical thinking to which I resorted. After reading an article in one of Mina's magazines about how we created what happened to us in our lives with our thoughts— and, particularly, by what we chose to remember—I tried to change my memory of that night. I would lie in bed, imagining it all again: the sounds in the hall that had gotten my attention, but this time I didn't get out of bed to check; or sometimes I did, but only to find Mina in the bathroom in her pajamas, brushing her teeth, looking up at me in the mirror with a smile. As the article explained, if I could only imagine a different ending, perhaps I would forget what had really happened.

But it didn't work. The image of her perfect form was never far from my mind, drifting into consciousness like smoke from a fire that just wouldn't go out.

So I tried something else. If it had been so wrong to see her private parts, I surmised, then I would stop looking at my own. It was conclusion based on a syllogism that occurred to me without effort, and brought me curious relief:

1. Seeing her nakedness was wrong.
2. So nakedness was wrong.
3. So my nakedness was wrong.

Now I went to the bathroom, careful not to look down while fulfilling my functions. I learned to perform my ritual ablutions without peeking. And even as I showered, I was sure never to look at what was between my legs.

I redoubled my Quranic efforts. It was now that I began to strive, in earnest, to become a *hafiz*. It seemed the only surefire way to earn her love and attention once again. And I wasn't wrong. My diligence in memorizing verses wore away at her resistance to me, and by that spring—some seven *surah*s and one hundred verses later—our regular study hour was restored. Once again, she was calling me "*kurban.*" It seemed to me she'd finally forgotten what happened that December night. But I hadn't. I knew now I could lose her love. And I was prepared to do anything to make sure that it never happened again.

Late that spring—just over a year since Mina and Imran had come to stay with us—we were all sitting around the kitchen table one Thursday evening. Father, Mother, and Mina drank tea as they read and exchanged sections of the evening newspaper. Imran and I sat before an array of broken crayons, coloring pictures. At some point, Mother looked up from the paper.

"They're saying it's going to be seventy-five degrees and sunny on the weekend," she said brightly. "First day of summer weather. They're saying it's a perfect day for a barbecue."

"Is that what *they're saying?*" Father mumbled, inching the business section higher to hide behind it.

Mother turned to Mina. "We should make *shaami kabab*s and Lahori ginger marinade for the chicken. We should make it *big.* And invite *lots* and *lots* of people! To celebrate the change of seasons...What do you think, Naveed? Hmm? Saturday?"

The question dangled in silence, unanswered.

Father lowered the paper just enough to gaze over its edge. His expression was dim. "You're the one who has to prepare the food. I just put it on the grill. You want a big barbecue? Be my guest."

"But then you have to invite some people, too."

"Fine," he said, returning to his paper.

Mother wasn't convinced. "Naveed, look at me when I talk to you."

"What is it, Muneer?" Father asked, annoyed. "What do you want from me? Hmm? Why can't you just drink your tea and enjoy your life for a change?"

"Don't be patronizing."

"I'm not."

"I was asking you a question. I want you to invite people, too."

"I said okay."

"Like who?"

"I'll invite Nathan." Nathan Wolfsohn was Father's colleague and research partner at the University Medical Center, and in many ways his best friend.

"Good. Who else?"

"Who else do you want me to invite?"

"The Naqvis, the Khans, the Buledis...and why not the Chathas?"

Mother was referring to the Pakistani families scattered throughout Greater Milwaukee, people we barely spent any time with because Father hated them. He called them sheep, claiming that they gathered like herd animals as a way of avoiding the fact that they were no longer in Pakistan. Father found their ceaseless complaining about the godlessness of American life particularly tiresome. He couldn't understand what they were still doing here if they thought it was all so evil.

"Chatha?" Father asked, incredulous.

"Why not?"

"*Why not?*"

"Yes. Why not, Naveed?"

Mother was needling him. She knew Father despised Ghaleb Chatha, a Pakistani-born pharmacist and entrepreneur, the owner of a growing pharmacy chain that bore his name, and— due largely to his immense wealth—the undisputed nucleus of the local Muslim community. At Mother's insistence, we'd spent some time with the Chathas a few years prior—going to their house for dinner on a few of the religious holidays, having them over to our place once—but no mutual friendship ever developed. Father couldn't bear Chatha's religiosity, announced not only by his appearance—a skullcap, box-form Islamic beard, and a knee-length Nehru coat he never seemed to take off—but also his conversation. Chatha loved to talk about what God was going to do to American unbelievers on Judgment Day: "Allah will turn them this way and that," Chatha would joke, flipping his flattened palm back and forth like a patty in a skillet. "He'll fry them just like one of their fishes at their church Friday fish fries!" And if Chatha's disdain for unbelievers wasn't enough to turn Father against him, there was always the fact that Chatha made his wife, Najat—a college-educated woman—wear the full *burqa* in public, complete with a cloth screen that entirely covered her face.

"I know you don't like him," Mother said, backing off as Father glared at her. "But you're the one always talking about how one has to *play politics* to succeed . . . So maybe you should take your own advice and make the effort. Say whatever you want about him, but Najat is a *wonderful* person."

"Wonderful? How would you know? Do you even know what she looks like?"

"Of course I know what she looks like."

"You're one of the few," Father retorted. "Just barbaric," he muttered to himself as he went back to reading.

"Who's Chatha?" Mina asked.

"The pharmacist I was telling you about," Mother said. "The one with the divorced cousin? Remember?"

Mina didn't seem to recall.

"The one whose wife ran away with the American?"

"Oh," Mina said with a nod.

"Hypocrite is what he is," Father said.

"Whatever he is, whatever he isn't, Chatha is the hub of the community," Mother said flatly. "It's no wonder we don't have any friends from back home. We never make the effort."

"Do what you want. Call them yourselves. You don't need me."

Mother glanced at Mina, then me. She looked surprised, pleased: Father was giving unexpected ground. After a pause, she began again, her tone now oily and sweet: "But if *you* do it, Naveed . . . they'll think heaven and earth are moving. '*Dr. Shah is calling us for a barbecue? We can't miss that!*' "

"Hardly, Muneer. Those people don't like me. Or *you*, for that matter . . ."

"They may not *like* you, but they *admire* you. Everyone does. Even Chatha. You are the smartest one here. And they know it." It was odd to hear Mother flattering Father like this, but she must have known what she was doing. Father visibly softened.

"Fine," he finally relented. "I'll call them."

Mother turned to Mina, beaming. "And you, too. Get some of your friends from the salon to come." Mother was referring to the salon where Mina now worked four days a week, and where she'd already made enough money to buy herself a used Dodge sedan.

"I'll ask Adrienne."

"Is that the fat one?"

"*Bhaj*," Mina warned. "She's a good person. She only has nice things to say about you."

Mother grinned, with a carefree expression that implied that had she known Adrienne was saying nice things about her, she might not have said what she said, but she was still going to think it. "Well, ask some of your other friends there, too...not just Adrienne." Mother turned back to Father. "And be sure to invite Nathan."

Father grunted.

"Did you hear me, Naveed?"

"How could I not hear you?" Father droned. "I already said I would invite him."

"So you'll do it?"

"If I remember."

"He's such a gentle, intelligent soul! Why can't some of his influence rub off on you, Naveed?"

"Muneer...," Father said firmly.

"I'm going, I'm going," Mother said placatingly as she rose from the table and shot a look at the clock over the stove.

"Seven-thirty," she muttered to herself. "Not too late to make some calls."

And off she went.

What always struck me most about Nathan Wolfsohn was that he never seemed as small as he actually was. At barely five and a half feet, with narrow shoulders and a small head covered with curly strawberry-blond hair, Nathan should have looked dwarfed alongside Father—whose tall, wide-shouldered brawn was one of the things Mother always said had attracted her to him—but he didn't. Blessed with a warmth and expansiveness you could spy from the joyous, jagged glint in his eyes, Nathan was a man with a wider sense of things, an intangible largesse that, I believe, made him seem bigger than he was.

At only twenty-eight, Nathan was something of a medical wunderkind, a specialist in a new technology known as MRI. It had been Father's idea to approach Nathan about imaging the brains of patients on antidepressant medications, and in only a few years, their work had catapulted them to the front ranks of research neurology. Father liked to refer to the two of them as "the pioneers," a label that didn't sit well with Nathan. I remember a night at a downtown pizzeria around the corner from their lab—I was seven or eight; Mother and I had gone to join them for dinner after work—when Father used the term. Nathan was quick to correct him.

"We weren't the first to do what we're doing, Naveed."

"Technicalities, Nate. Technicalities." Father waved his comment away.

"You keep saying that, but we weren't. Not by a long shot. And you know it."

"Okay, Nate. Maybe we weren't the *first*"—Father jeered, his mouth hanging open as his unfinished retort dangled in the pause he clearly let form for effect—"but you can't doubt we've been the *best,* can you?"

"I didn't know it was a competition."

"Everything is a competition, Nate. Everything."

"How depressing. How do you get up in the morning with an attitude like that?"

Father didn't reply, a mischievous smile creeping across his face.

"Oh, no."

"What?"

"That look you've got."

"Just remembered a joke."

"What is it?"

"I don't know if you're going to like it."

"Another Jew joke."

"Maybe it is."

"Because if it is, I don't want to hear it."

"You're right. You're right."

"Okay, what is it?"

"I thought you didn't want to hear it?"

"Just get it over with, Naveed."

"So why do Jews have big noses?"

Nathan groaned. "C'mon, Naveed. That's the oldest one in the book."

"Okay. So what's the answer?"

"Because air is free?"

Father's face filled with delight. His head and trunk jittered as he gave off a joyous wheezing sound. It was an odd laugh he had, but infectious. Soon we were all laughing. Even Nathan.

They were contraries in so many ways: Nathan was from Boston, Jewish, urbane, and pleasantly gregarious; Father was from a third-world village, Muslim, rough-hewn, and sardonic. Their colleagues at the hospital called them the Odd Couple. And for good reason. The countless hours Father and Nathan spent together in the radiology lab gave them ample opportunity to hone a routine their coworkers liked to call the Show, which was mostly composed of Nathan playing the straight man to Father's often questionable silliness. Father teased Nathan constantly: He made fun of his appearance; of his New England accent; of his inability to stomach our spicy food; and yes, of the fact that he was Jewish. But the butt of most of Father's jokes was Nathan's love for all things cultural: the theater, symphonies, art museums, and above all books.

"How's Dr. Wolfsohn?" I remember Mother asking over dinner, only to have Father erupt with irritation.

"That stooge! Can you believe he spent an hour at lunch reading a novel? What a waste of brain energy!"

Father made no secret of his disdain for books. He believed his success—unlikely as it was, considering the modesty of his Pakistani-village origins—was too hard-won not to be an example to all; and this success, he claimed, was the result not of "book smarts" but "street smarts." He would loudly boast he'd never read a single book, not even in his field of specialty, a strange comment, and one which could have been taken in any variety of ways—as a pledge of his allegiance to the American tradition of making oneself through deeds and not thoughts; as a revealing instance of his mostly winning grandiosity; as a measure of a quite genuine disregard he had for books in general and for novels in particular—but whatever way it could be taken, it certainly couldn't have been a statement of fact: How do you not read a single book and end up editing or contributing to fifteen of them?

As with most of Father's shenanigans, Nathan knew exactly

how to handle it. Whenever Father offered his unlikely claim, Nathan pushed back.

"That's silly, Naveed. Your office is filled with books. I don't buy it for a second."

Sooner or later, Father would relent, but always with a wily smile, still enjoying his bending of the truth. "I've read articles, Nate. And chapters. I read what I had to"—and now he would be laughing, joyous—"but I was never stupid enough to read a whole book *cover to cover!*"

Father made the calls as promised, but only to discover that Ghaleb Chatha was holding a fund-raiser for the South Side Islamic Center that very same Saturday. Which meant most of the other Pakistani families Mother mentioned wouldn't be able to come to our barbecue either. Father was pleased at how this was all turning out.

There was one Pakistani family at our house that weekend, or at least half-Pakistani: the Buledis weren't invited to the Chathas', for while psychiatrist Sonny Buledi had been born in Karachi, he'd been mostly shunned by the local Pakistani community. His Austrian wife, Katrina, made more than a few enemies by showing up at functions in sleeveless blouses and knee-length skirts, and talking freely about the fact that she served her kids pork.

A number of our neighbors showed up; so did Adrienne, Mina's friend from the salon. Adrienne was dressed in a satin wine-red *shalwar-kameez* that she was delighted to report "made her look more full-figured than fat," though I'm not sure this was the impression she made on me. I had only ever seen her briefly—on the few occasions she'd come by to pick Mina up for outings to Red Lobster, their favorite—and there was no other way to put it than to say: She was gargantuan. The loose-falling *kurta* and the neck scarf may have made her seem not quite so outsized as her more tightly fitting Western clothes did, but if so, the effect was minimal. As for the most distinctive aspect of her heft (at least to me)—her layered neck, its bulbous folds of flesh stacked successively, like scoops of a sundae, and topped with a round, reddish head so much smaller than the rest of her—the Pakistani clothes didn't change that one bit.

Nathan was there, too.

I was standing with Father and Sonny by the grill in the middle of the lawn when he made his memorably awkward entrance. Mina and Adrienne were sitting on the back patio, their hands buried in a bowl of ground *kabab* meat between them. The patio door slammed shut with a resounding thwack, and I looked up to see Nathan on the patio, three large bottles of soda held against his body, a confused look on his face. Father noticed him and waved. Nathan made some sort of gesture resembling a nod back. He hesitated as he made his way past the two women, and, stepping off the patio, he stumbled. All at once, he was on the ground, the sodas gliding across the grass around him. Nathan got up and shot a look back at the patio. Adrienne giggled. "Sorry," Nathan said, sheepishly. He collected the bottles, then headed down toward us, his beige pants sporting fresh green stains at the knees.

"You okay there, Chief?" Father teased.

"Yeah...fine." Nathan set the bottles on the table by the grill and brushed himself off. "You might wait before opening those."

"We can handle it, Chief."

Nathan nodded. "Hey, Hayat," he said, stealing another quick glance back at the patio.

"Hi, Dr. Wolfsohn."

"Call me Nathan, Hayat." He smiled. "I've told you that before..."

"Okay."

"Nathan. This is Sonny Buledi. Sonny Buledi, Nathan Wolfsohn. Sonny is a psychiatrist at the Medical College," Father said. "Nathan and I work together at the hospital."

"Nice to meet you," Sonny said, extending a hand.

"Likewise."

"Sonny was just telling me a horror story about some of these local Pakistanis here in town," Father said, rearranging the pieces of chicken on the grill with his tongs. "They don't like Mr. Buledi very much..."

"I could live with that," Sonny said, "if it wasn't for the way they treat my children. We were at a dinner a few weeks ago for the Medical College... The Naqvis were there..."

"Anil Naqvi, the anesthesiologist," Father noted for Nathan's sake. "You know him, right?"

"I know who he is."

"And the Naqvi kids were calling Satya and Otto *zebras*. Because their mother is white and I'm Pakistani. Can you believe that?"

"Of course I believe it," Father said. "Praying all day long. Nothing to show for it. They're hypocrites."

He pronounced the final word with relish as he poked at the meat on the grill.

"What does that mean, Dad?" I asked.

"What? 'Hypocrite'?"

I nodded. I'd heard him use it so many times.

Father lifted the tongs, pointing them at me. "When a person pretends to be something they are not, that's a hypocrite. Like Chatha, pretending to be a good Muslim, but who is really just filled with poison for others."

Sonny nodded, clearly agreeing. "Speaking of poison, you know what else Otto told me? One of the Naqvi kids was talking about how to blow up a church by filling it with gasoline and lighting a match."

"*What?*" Father was incredulous.

"That's the message the Naqvis are sending their children. That churches should be destroyed because Christians are *kuffar*... When I heard Otto say that word I just exploded."

"Revolting," Father muttered under his breath.

"What does it mean?" Nathan asked, looking back from the patio.

"Unbelievers," Father responded.

"At this point, I just tell them all I'm an atheist," Sonny said. "Just to be sure they stay away. Keep them as far from me as possible."

It wasn't the first time I'd heard Sonny say he was an atheist. But that afternoon, I heard it anew, understanding—I thought—for the first time what it really meant. Not just that he didn't believe in God, but almost more important, that he thought there was nothing more to life than what we were living now. For if there was no God, then there was no afterlife. And if there was one thing I'd learned from my new studies in the Quran, it was that the penalty for not believing in the afterlife was dire:

When the Trumpet finally sounds,
It will be a terrible day for the Unbeliever.
I will visit calamity on him!
For he who thought and planned,
Woe to him!
Inflated with pride, he said:
"This Quran is nothing but magic,

Nothing but a tale told by a mortal!"
I will throw him into Hell's Fire!
And what will make you see what this Fire is?
It leaves nothing and spares nothing.
Burning to black mortal skin!

As I stood there looking at Sonny, I felt moved. There was nothing in his round, pleasing face—or in the warm, intelligent eyes peering over his glasses' wire frames—to explain how such a likable man could have come to such an extraordinary and unfortunate conclusion.

"How long do you grill the thighs?" Sonny asked Father.

"Now *there's* a worthy topic...Depends on the heat. But in this case, maybe four minutes each side. Not too long. You want to make sure you don't dry them out." Father picked at the chicken again with his tongs. "Still pink at the bone. Another couple of minutes." Father glanced over at Nathan. "What's going on over there, Chief? You look confused."

"Confused?" Nathan asked, looking abruptly away from the patio. "No...just enjoying the afternoon."

"Enjoying the afternoon?" Father repeated, perplexed. He looked over at the patio himself now, where Adrienne was giggling as she talked to Mina, stealing looks our way.

Father turned to Nathan with a wry smile. "Sneaky," he teased.

"What are you talking about, Naveed?"

"No need to get touchy. There's nothing wrong with it."

"Wrong with what? I don't know what you're talking about."

"Nate. I wasn't born yesterday. I don't blame you...she's a pearl."

"Who?"

"Who do you think?" Father said sarcastically, shaking his head. "Her name's Mina. She's Muneer's best friend from childhood. I've told you about her. She's the one who's been living with us."

"Oh," Nathan responded, blankly.

"She is a beauty. That's for sure," Sonny added.

"Yes, she is," Father replied with sudden, uncharacteristic softness. He was looking down at the grill now. "She reminds me of my sister sometimes," he said quietly.

"Huma?" Nathan inquired, with sudden concern.

Father nodded. I was surprised Nathan knew the name of the sister Father had lost to pneumonia when they were both in their late teens. He'd only spoken of her to me once. Losing her, Mother used to say, was the one thing he never got over and probably never would.

Father lifted his tongs abruptly and pointed them playfully at Nathan. "That woman wastes almost as much time staring at paper as you do. The two of you will get along...how do they say it? Famously?"

"Staring at paper?" Sonny asked.

"Naveed's got a thing about reading," Nathan answered. "That's what he calls reading—staring at paper. I don't know how he gets away with it. I mean, the man was first in his class in medical school..."

"Not by reading."

"Then what?"

"Chief. When you need to get something done, you figure out a way."

Nathan's eyes lit up with a thought. "You cheated?"

"Absolutely *not*."

"Then?"

"Let's just say...I got other people to read *for* me..."

Nathan and Sonny laughed.

"Staring at paper," Sonny muttered to himself as he shook his head.

"Am I right? Or am I right? Sonny?" Father was smiling, broadly.

"For the record, I don't think you're right. But that's not really your point, is it?"

"Good man! Smart man!" Father said, now pointing his tongs at Sonny. He turned to me. "Can you hand me that plate, *behta?*"

I gave him the long serving tray that lay on the table beside me. He started picking the pieces of chicken off the grill.

"The point is, Nate, you and Mina could actually enjoy wasting your time *together.*"

"Which is actually the recipe for domestic bliss, in my opinion," Sonny added.

"Something I wouldn't know too much about," Father joked. He glanced at the patio. "They're looking over here. Go over. Talk to her. Now's your chance."

"Maybe later," Nathan said. "She looks busy."

"She *is* busy. Busy with the *kabab*s that you should go and get from her. Tell her I was asking for them. There's your excuse."

Nathan laid a long look on Father.

"Go. Go on..."

"You're something else, Naveed," Nathan said, shaking his head. Then he headed off in Mina's direction. I watched him as he went up to her and put out his hand. She held her own hands up with a shrug, both covered with the ground meat she and Adrienne had been fashioning into *kabab*s. Just then Adrienne got up, bringing over the very *kabab*s Nathan was supposed to have asked Mina for. With Adrienne gone, Nathan asked her another question. She laughed. Nathan pulled up a folding chair and sat down beside her.

My heart was pounding.

"Hey, Hayat!" I heard. It was Otto—Sonny's round, freckled son—huffing over to the grill. "Satya's gonna take us *ninja* exploring. Wanna come?"

"Go on, *kurban,*" Father said. "Play with your friends."

I looked back at the patio. Mina twirled her head to one side. Nathan was talking. I turned my back on both of them and followed as Otto waddled away.

Satya Buledi was only a year older than me, but he was big for his age, tall, broad across the shoulders—he looked like he was already in high school—and with a striking head of straw-blond hair that gleamed appealingly against the darker, caramel hue of his skin. The girls apparently loved him.

Satya was into comic books, *Daredevil* in particular, where he'd recently discovered *ninja*s. *Ninja*s, he explained, were not like samurai. They were spies and assassins, and they didn't fight out in the open or follow the rules of war. The most important thing, he said, pulling a napkin from his pocket, was that *ninja*s covered their faces. That way, no one could ever know who they really were. Satya tied the napkin to his face. Now we were all going to become *ninja*s together, he said, but *ninja*s who fought for the good. He asked me if there were any wrongs in the neighborhood that needed righting. I hadn't a clue, though I did tell him about the empty house at the end of the block that the neighborhood kids said was haunted. So we tied napkins to our faces and snuck through a succession of backyards to the home in question, though once we got there, Satya was disappointed to see through its windows only empty rooms filled with debris and dust.

"You said it was haunted."

"I said some of the kids said it was."

"Why doesn't anyone live here?"

I shrugged. I had no idea.

"Well, whatever happened here—and it must have been something—it's too late to fix now."

Satya led us along bushes and across more yards, and had us slinking up on neighbors' windows. There were lots of housewives preparing meals or lemonade in their kitchens, and a smaller number of husbands with their sons watching baseball in their family rooms. But that was about it.

On our way back up the road, Satya disappeared behind the Kuhlmanns' house, a green-and-white split-level that stood across the street. He climbed up a tree, and—peering in at one of the bedroom windows—finally looked like he'd found something worthwhile.

"Hayat, you gotta check this out."

"What's wrong?"

"Nothing's wrong..."

"So what is it?"

"A girl, and some guy. They're making out."

"That's Gina. And her boyfriend."

"No kidding. You gotta see this."

"I wanna see it, too," Otto whined.

"Stop eating so many Doritos, then," Satya snapped. "Maybe then you'll lose enough weight to climb a tree."

"I'm not too fat to..."

Satya interrupted him: "Stay down and watch the kid, Otto. Hayat, you come up here..."

I looked over at Otto with a shrug, then reached out and grabbed the trunk, pulling myself up along the knobs.

"Make sure your *ninja* mask doesn't fall off, Hayat," Satya said.

Imran moaned down below that he wanted to climb, too.

"You can't climb the tree by yourself," Otto said to him. "You're too small."

I pulled myself up into the tangle of branches, finding the footing that led me to the branch where Satya was perched. In the window directly facing us, Gina was sitting on her bed with her boyfriend, kissing.

"She looks cute," Satya said.

"She is," I said.

I didn't know Gina well—she was three years older than me—but she'd lived across the street from us for almost two years now, and for most of that time, she'd been going out with the stocky, curly-haired boy sitting on her bed. I didn't know his name—Gina didn't talk to me, or any of the younger neighborhood boys—but I knew they were together because I used to see him walk her home from school. My own school, Mason Elementary, got out before the junior high did, and there were more than a few times when I would be out on the front lawn and see them appear at the end of the street, Gina with her books pressed to her chest, that boy by her side, slowly pushing his bike along. And there were also times when, passing through the living room—which had a clear view of Gina's garage—I would find the two of them standing in the empty bay, kissing.

One afternoon, as I watched at the living room window, Mother came up behind me. "Look at *that,*" she said with disgust, "the training of a white woman...How old is she?"

"I don't know...Fourteen?"

"*Fourteen?*"

"I think."

"*Fourteen,*" she repeated, "and look at her."

Gina's boyfriend was caressing her hair now as he stared

into her eyes, the two of them looking lost in dreamy oblivion, enveloped in a sweet and perfect mist.

Mother continued, sharply: "Already *using* herself, *using* her body to get men. It's shameless. They're like animals...No...They're *worse* than animals. Even animals have some self-respect." Then she turned to me abruptly. "Go to your room. You don't need to be staring at prostitutes. You'll end up like your father. Go...go!"

Back in the tree, Satya had inched his way farther out onto the branch, trying to get a better view. Gina's boyfriend was now reaching beneath her pink sweater as he pecked at her lips. "Check it out," Satya said. "He's going to second base on her."

"Second base?"

"First base is kissing. Second's up the shirt. Third's down the pants. A home run's all the way."

I had no idea what he was talking about. "All the way?" I asked.

"Sex? You know what sex is, right?"

I stared at Satya, not knowing what to say. All I knew was that I'd heard the word.

He smiled. "Don't tell me you don't know what sex is?"

In the window, Gina's boyfriend had lifted her sweater to reveal her smooth, flat belly and a white bra above it.

"What's going on in there?" Otto asked in a whining voice, peering up at us.

"Shut up," Satya hissed. I watched him, his eyes wide with wonder over the napkin he still wore over his nose and mouth. I wondered if that's what my eyes looked like when Mother caught me at the window. *Staring at prostitutes,* she'd called it.

Satya realized I was looking at him. "What is it?" he asked.

"Nothing," I said.

"I don't know what you're looking at me for. You're missing the real action."

"I don't want the *real action.*"

"What's wrong with you?"

I pulled the napkin from my face and started to climb back down the tree.

"Where are you going?"

"Home," I said with disgust.

Back at the house, Mina and Nathan were still sitting on the patio. Even at twenty yards, I was struck by her. She looked different. Sharper. Even more magnetic than usual. Her face held my gaze, and I felt a stinging tug in my stomach, an urgency. She was separate from me, and I needed to close that gap, to seize her somehow, to make her my own.

I didn't understand it.

I stepped up onto the patio, heading for the kitchen, but as I passed their chairs, Mina reached out, pulling me to her. I felt her legs close in and hold me in place. She lifted her lips to my cheek for a kiss. "He's like my second son...," she purred, radiant. Her *dupatta* scarf was draped loosely around her head, its translucent silk gleaming in the late afternoon sun. "And if I have my way he'll end up a bibliophile just like the two of us."

"Already on his way—aren't you, Hayat?" Nathan asked with a lazy smile. He had a dazed, goofy look I found almost as unsettling as Mina's newly arresting beauty. "With a little luck, you'll keep the tradition going and end up as a thorn in your dad's side," Nathan added with a laugh. Mina laughed, too.

"Wouldn't be the worst thing in the world, would it?" Nathan continued. "If anyone can get him to read a book someday, it'll be his own son. Don't you think?"

"I doubt *that,*" Mina said, her eyes sparkling.

Something was happening, but I couldn't tell what it was. There was a charge in the air, like a cloud of whirling gnats between them.

Mina went on: about how smart I was; how I'd begun to memorize the Quran; what a good surrogate brother I'd been for Imran. Not only was she talking about me, but I was standing locked between her legs, her arms about my waist... and yet she seemed more separate from me than ever. "I have to go to the bathroom, Auntie," I finally said, pulling myself free.

"Okay, *kurban,*" she said.

I went through the patio door, making a point of slamming it shut behind me. But when I looked back through the window, neither of them seemed to notice.

They were already laughing about something else.

6

The Dervish

That week, the phone rang every night about half an hour after dinner. Mother would come bounding into the kitchen to grab it. "Hi, Dr. Wolfsohn...," she would coo, "sorry, I meant...*Nathan*...I'm fine, *Nathan*. How are you?...Of *course*. I'll get her..." Then Mother would put her palm over the mouthpiece and yell out: "Meen! For you! Dr. Wolfsohn!" And soon enough, Mina would appear at her side, hovering on her tiptoes as she took the phone and chirped into the receiver: "Hi, Nathan." But before the conversation went any further, she would turn to me—I was usually still doing the dishes— and inquire, always tenderly: "*Behta,* is it okay if I use the phone for a little while...alone?"

I would nod and head off to my room.

More than once that week, I emerged an hour or so later— after homework and some verses—hoping to bypass any unfinished dishes in the sink on my way down to the family room for some television. Invariably, I'd find Mother perched at the stairs, barring the way. And over her shoulder, down on the couch at the family room's far end, I would see Mina curled up on the corner cushion, the phone cradled lovingly against her face.

"Don't be nosy," Mother would scold.

"I'm not."

"Go finish the dishes."

"Fine," I would say.

There was no need to be nosy. Mina's peals of joyous laughter—easy to hear, even over the sound of running water as I finished up at the sink—and her dreamy gait as she came up the stairs after her calls were over left no doubt about what was happening:

She was smitten.

On Thursday night, as I sat at my desk, I heard Mina screaming at someone downstairs. I came to my doorway and saw her crying as she stormed into her room and slammed the door shut. Mother would later tell me Mina's parents had called. They'd learned of a divorced Pakistani, a dentist in South Carolina, who was looking for a wife. Without mentioning it to their daughter, the Alis had sent the man Mina's picture. Now he wanted to meet her.

Mina lost it. She told her parents that not only was she not interested, but there was no chance she would ever even consider another arranged marriage after what had happened with Hamed.

Her father started screaming. She screamed back. And then he hung up on her.

The next morning, as I readied for school, Mina was still in bed. This was odd. She was usually up early, helping Mother with breakfast, getting Imran ready for nursery school. When I left for the bus that morning, her bedroom door was shut, and when I got home that afternoon, Mother complained that Mina hadn't come out all day. At teatime she finally emerged, shuffling along the hall and down into the kitchen, where Mother was pouring tea. Mina looked drawn, downcast, her eyes wide and sunken into darkened, cavelike sockets.

"Hi, Auntie," I said, trying to be cheery.

"Hi, *behta*," she mumbled.

"Can I come see you tonight?" Since the weekend—and the subsequent nightly calls from Nathan—we'd had no time together with the Quran.

"Don't make your auntie's life difficult, Hayat," Mother said abruptly.

"It's fine, *bhaj*," Mina said with a faint smile.

"Let's go," Mother said to her friend brusquely, as she handed Mina her tea and took her by the hand.

Mina smiled at me again. "Come and see me later, *behta*," she said as Mother led her out.

At bedtime, I went to see her, Quran in hand.

"Is it okay if we do a story tonight instead of *diniyaat?*" she asked with a whisper. She pointed: Imran was lying on his bed, sleeping.

"Sure, Auntie," I whispered back.

Mina threw open the covers, inviting me inside. She asked me what story I wanted to hear. Something new, I said. She took a moment to think, and then her eyes lit up.

"I'm going to tell you about a dervish. That's someone who gives up everything for Allah."

"Gurvish?"

"Dervish. With a *d*, not a *g*."

"Dervish," I repeated, nodding. But an image had already been born from the word incorrectly heard: Mr. Gurvitz, the old janitor at my elementary school, a bald, skinny man who doddered, hunched, along the halls trailing a trash can on wheels.

"So I want to tell you about a dervish who was wandering the world by foot. He wandered and wandered, thinking only of Allah all day long. He'd given everything up in search of God, *behta,* to the point that he was depending completely on the kindness of strangers for his meals, sleeping at night on the open road, under the open sky—"

"He's a homeless guy," I said.

"Not just homeless, Hayat. I'm talking about a Sufi. A Sufi dervish. Whose whole life is devoted to Allah. It was his choice to give everything up."

What she was saying made no sense to me. "Auntie, why would anybody *choose* to be homeless?"

"Because by giving everything up, his home, his family, his job, nothing is in the way anymore. Nothing between himself and God."

Mina could tell I wasn't following.

"What is special for you, *behta?* Is there something you would never want to lose?"

"You, Auntie."

She smiled. "That's so sweet, Hayat." She ran her fingers along my forehead. "You love being with me...in this moment..."

"So much, Auntie. So much."

"You don't want it to end, right?"

"Never."

"It's the same with our dervish. He feels this kind of love with Allah. He doesn't *ever* want it to end. Just like you and me right now. Everything else, television, school, chores...those would take you away from me right now, right?"

I nodded.

"So that's what the dervish does, gets rid of his television and his school and his chores. Everything that takes him away from Allah's love."

"I understand, Auntie."

"But in this story, the dervish gave up everything, but he still felt sad and confused. He still felt he was holding on to something that took him away from God's love."

"What?"

"He didn't know. And he was asking himself that question over and over. For years he wandered and searched and prayed for an answer. And he couldn't figure out what it was...

"Then one day, the dervish lost hope. After looking for so long, he was so tired. He sat down on the side of the road. Exhausted. With no idea what to do anymore..."

I was still seeing Gurvitz in my mind's eye. And I saw him now, in tattered clothes, defeated, sitting beside an empty road.

"Just as he was sitting there, two men came walking along, eating oranges. They came closer and saw the old dervish, and one of them said: 'What a filthy old man.' And the other said: 'Look how he's staring at our oranges. With greedy eyes!' They laughed. And as they passed the dervish, they tossed the orange peels at him: 'Here, old man, eat the peels if you're so hungry!'

"Now, *behta*. If that happened to you or me, we would get angry. We would get up and say something, or throw the peels back at the men. But not this dervish. He didn't get angry. Instead, he got up and took both of them into his arms.

" 'Thank you, brothers! Thank you for giving me the *answer!*' The men were confused. 'What answer?' they asked. 'The answer I've been waiting for my whole life!' the dervish said."

Mina paused.

"It's a difficult story, *behta*. I know. But I think you can understand it...

"What the dervish found was true humility. He realized he was no better, no worse than the ground itself, the ground that takes the discarded orange peels of the world. In fact, he realized he was the same as that ground, the same as those peels, as those men, as everything else. He was the same as everything created by Allah's hand.

"What was in his way before? He thought he was different. But now he saw he was *not* different. He and Allah, and everything Allah created, it was all One."

I didn't understand what she was saying at the time. But I would never forget it.

Saturday night, our doorbell rang an hour before dinner. Mother came hurrying out of the kitchen. "Get the door, Hayat," she said, pulling her cooking apron from her waist as she headed for the stairs. I was in the living room with Imran playing chess, or at least trying to.

"Take your time and think about it," I said to Imran as I stood up. "You're close to checkmate."

Imran stared at the board for a moment, then threw his arm across it, scattering all the pieces. "I win!" he cried out.

"You didn't win," I shot back. "You don't know the rules, so you don't even know what it means to win. And after what you just did, you won't ever win, because I'll never play with you again!"

Imran squealed now, tossing the board into the air. He threw himself onto his back and started to kick and scream.

The doorbell rang again.

"What's going on down there?!" Mother shouted, peering out from the upstairs bathroom. Mina's face appeared over her shoulder.

"What happened?" Mina shouted out to her son in Urdu.

"Nothing!" I shouted back.

"Stop making trouble, Hayat," Mother said, sharply. "Go see who's at the door!"

"Yeah, I wonder," I muttered to myself. Mina and Mother had been in a frenzy all afternoon in anticipation of our dinner guest, Nathan. I opened the front door.

"Hey, Hayat!" Nathan said brightly. He was wearing a brown sport coat, a yellow buttondown oxford, and khakis. Everything was perfectly pressed, and he looked like he'd just come from a haircut. He was patting at his forehead with a handkerchief.

"Hi, Dr. Wolfsohn," I mumbled back. Nathan reached down and picked up a box lying at his feet.

"How's life treating you, Hayat?" he asked as he stepped inside.

"Fine."

Behind us, Imran dashed past, racing up the steps. He was crying.

"Everything okay?" Nathan asked.

"Don't ask me," I answered with a shrug. "The kid's always crying about something."

Nathan nodded. "Well, can't be easy for him to be in a new country..."

"It isn't that new. He's been here awhile."

"I guess...so, um, Hayat, where's your dad? He's been pestering me all week for these." Nathan indicated the box he was holding.

"Out back. In the garden."

"Mind if I go ahead and set this down?" Nathan stepped into the living room, looking about. He turned to me, nodding at the armchair. "You think it's okay if I put it over there?"

"Sure," I said.

As he made his way to the chair, his foot caught under the edge of the pink-and-red Persian carpet that covered much of our living room floor. He tripped, and the box flew from his grip. The films inside spilled everywhere. It was just like when he'd dropped the soda at the barbecue, I thought.

"Shit!" he cried out, and then shot me a look of concern. "Sorry about the language. I didn't mean..."

"That's okay," I said.

Nathan and I started collecting the spilled scans. Each showed four oval images of the human brain, and though each oval was somehow differently shaded, they all looked the same. There were literally thousands of them. I couldn't understand what he and Father spent so much time looking at.

Nathan stuffed the films into the box and got to his feet. "Thanks for helping," he said as he pulled out a handkerchief and wiped his face; he was covered in sweat. "Where is everybody?"

"Upstairs."

He sat down on the couch. He patted at his face again, now lifting his arm to sniff at his armpit. Realizing I was watching him, he lowered his arm and smiled weakly. "Is it hot in here, or is it just me?"

"I guess it's hot," I said.

"Yeah, it is. Isn't it?" He looked about the room, distracted. All at once, he turned to me, exclaiming: "Oh! I just remembered...I got you something!" He fished in his coat pocket, pulling out a slender golden package. "Here. Open it."

I took it and tore off the gold gift wrap. It was a book. *The Call of the Wild.*

"Jack London," he said, "was one of my favorites when I was your age."

I leafed through its pages, stopping at an illustration of a dog against a barren landscape.

"It's a special edition. You probably don't know what that is yet, but if you take good care of it, someday it'll be worth a lot of money...Doesn't mean you can't read it, though. I mean, that's the whole point, right? To read it?"

"Thanks, Dr. Wolfsohn."

"My pleasure, Hayat...Remember, I told you, you could call me Nathan?"

"Sorry...Nathan."

"It's okay," he said. "I hope you enjoy it."

"What do you have there, *behta?*" It was Mother's voice. I turned to look. She was standing in the living room doorway, transformed. Only minutes before, she'd rushed from the kitchen, her hair tied back in a messy bun, in a blouse and slacks beneath a kitchen apron covered with curry stains; and here she was now in a baby-blue *shalwar-kameez* covered with sequins, a turquoise-and-silver scarf draped around her neck, her brown-black hair loose and tumbling in a shapely wave about her shoulders. She was lovely.

"Just something I found for him at the bookstore around the corner from my place. I know how much he loves books. That was one of my favorites when I was his age."

"You shouldn't have," Mother said, approaching. The sweet scent of her sandalwood fragrance drifted in along with her. Mother took the book from me, thumbing at its pages, though appearing to pay little attention to what was on them. To me it seemed she was more interested in the fact that both Nathan and I were looking at her. "God, this is so *wonderful!*" she said in a honeyed tone.

"It isn't much," Nathan replied. "I hope he likes it."

"And you're modest, too!" Mother added with a theatrical nod. She turned to me. "Did you *thank* Dr. Wolfsohn, *behta?*"

"Oh, of course he did," Nathan interjected. "And... Muneer, please call me Nathan."

Mother smiled.

Nathan reached into his other coat pocket, pulling out a smaller package wrapped in the same golden paper.

"What's *that?*" Mother asked.

"For Imran," he said.

"How *thoughtful,*" she said, her eyes softening. Now, as she spoke, her head bobbed subtly side to side in typical Indo-Pak style. "Sooo *thought*-ful. Sooo, sooo *thought*-ful..." Abruptly, she turned back to the hallway and yelled out: "Imran, *behta!* Come here, honey! Dr. Wolfsohn has a present for you!"

The boy appeared at the top of the stairs, whimpering. "Look what Dr. Wolfsohn got you, *kurban,*" Mother said, holding out the small package. Imran didn't budge. "C'mon, sweetie," she coaxed.

"Hayat is there," he whined.

Mother looked at me. "What did you do to him?"

"Nothing."

Mina emerged from the bathroom, coming up behind her son at the top of the stairs. She was dressed in yellow and gold, a cream-colored shawl draped loosely around her head. She began making her way down the steps with Imran, her hands on his shoulders. I glanced over at Nathan. He looked enchanted.

"Imran, *behta*—what did Hayat do so wrong?" Mother asked.

"I didn't do anything," I snapped. "He doesn't want to learn the rules and then he acts like a brat about it."

"Hayat, he's a child," Mina said, descending the stairs. "Let him play in his own way."

"His own way is not *chess,*" I shot back. "If he wants to do that, he can play it by himself. He doesn't need me."

Mother turned to me sharply. "What did you say?"

"I said it's not *chess*. I said I don't want to play with him if he doesn't want to play by the rules."

Imran and Mina were standing in the doorway now, and Imran had a satisfied smirk on his face. Mother glared at me, chewing on her lip. "Don't talk back to your elders! Make yourself useful. Go outside and tell your father Dr. Wolfsohn is here!" She turned to Nathan, her tone abruptly softening: "I mean *Nathan,* of course..."

Outside, the lawn was covered with long shadows. The sun was setting. I stopped and looked up at the sky. Red and orange clouds burned, strange and wonderful, against the dark blue of approaching night.

I was halfway down the backyard when I suddenly heard Mother's frantic voice crying out behind me: "Naveed! Naveed!" She was standing at the patio door. "Come quickly! Come now!"

Down at the garden, Father's form appeared from behind a row of waist-high tomato plants. His arms dangled at his sides, tipped with yellow gardening gloves.

"Come quickly! Quick!" she cried out again, then turned and disappeared inside.

Father stepped over the fence, pulling off the gloves. He started up the lawn with an unhurried jog. "God only knows what she wants now," he grumbled as he passed me. "You coming?"

Back in the living room, we found Nathan splayed on the armchair, his hand over his eye. Mina was leaned over him, her face almost as red as the bright scarlet stain along the edge of her cream-colored shawl.

"What the hell happened to you?" Father asked.

"Dr. Wolfsohn got Imran a toy car..."

"Muneer, please..."

"Sorry, *Nathan*...and Imran threw it at his face."

"He hit me in the eye," Nathan said calmly. "But I think I'm fine."

"Then what the hell are you lying down for? Like you're dying..."

"I'm not *dying,* Naveed."

"Where's the toy car?" Father asked Mina.

She handed Father a small red matchbox racer. "Nate got it for him as a gift."

Father sat on the chair's armrest, leaning in to inspect. "Let me see," he said, pulling Nathan's hand away from his face. His eye was shut, and a steady trickle of blood poured out along the eyelid's corner.

"Open it, Nathan," Father prodded. Nathan's eye popped wide open. "Can you see?"

"Just fine."

"Can you move it?"

Nathan's eyeball darted about in its socket. He blinked a few times. "Yeah, fine," Nathan said.

Father took hold of Nathan's head, turning it and peering closer to study the cut. "You're fine," he said. "But just by a hair. It's a nasty cut. But the eye is fine."

"Thank God," Mother said, releasing a sigh of relief. "So his eye is okay?"

"Fine. Just clean it and put on a Band-Aid." Father stood. "Where's the boy?" he asked Mina.

"Upstairs."

"I'm going to have a talk with him," Father said as he headed out.

Mother was glowering at me. "Next time you irritate the boy like that, I'll fix you for good."

I didn't say anything. I just walked out.

Up in my room, I pulled out my Quran. Smarting, I opened it to the *surah* I'd begun memorizing that day:

> Oh, the striking of the Last Hour!
> What is the striking of the Last Hour?
> And what can make you see what the striking of
>   the Last Hour will be?
> A Day when men will swarm like moths,
> And mountains become as strands of wool...
> He whose weight of good is heavy on the scale
> Will have a good life.
> Whereas he whose weight is light on the scale
> Will be devoured by the abyss.
> And what can make you see what the abyss will
>   be?
> A blazing fire!

I read the lines to myself again and again. The words calmed me. The events downstairs began to fade. How trivial it all seemed in the light shed by the recollection of God's fire. I remembered the view of the sky outside, burning and majestic. I felt a shudder of fear and awe. And I felt relief that I had been reminded of the only thing that mattered.

If others don't want to know, let them burn. But don't you ever forget.

7

Jews and Us

Dinner that night was not an easy affair. The mood at the table was heavy. Mina was withdrawn. But Nathan was doing all he could to amuse and engage her. I thought he looked ridiculous, his left eye partly covered with a Band-Aid, twitching and blinking as he spoke and ate. And though Mina was trying to enjoy the attention, her mind was clearly elsewhere. At some point, Father rolled out his standard Nathan-mocking fare to lighten things up, but even Father's own amusement— he was always the first to laugh (and heartily) at his own jokes—seemed dimmed by the leaden mood.

After dinner, Mina and Nathan went into the living room together. No sooner had they sat down than Imran started another tantrum. He wailed at the top of his lungs for his mother, his cries piercing, like sounds of pain. Mina didn't hold out very long before going upstairs to calm him down. Half an hour later, she returned to say good night. She and Nathan got up and went to the front door. I went upstairs to my room and watched out the window as they made their way down the driveway. Standing by his car in the moonlight, Nathan leaned toward her. She put her arm around him, her hand finding the back of his head. They held each other for a long moment.

It hurt me to watch.

* * *

That evening was a preview of coming attractions: Mina and Nathan's courtship was under way, and Imran's troublemaking would be the unvarying obstacle. With my summer vacation now started, Mother charged me with getting the boy out of the house for Nathan's visits. I did what I could. The first time I got lucky. On my way to the baseball diamond behind the Fahls' house—my preferred summer-afternoon destination, where there was always a game in progress—I ran into Denise and Mandy Robinson, identical twins with curly brown hair and close-set eyes. They thought the boy was "cute as a button." They were headed to the Gartner tree house, a sprawling complex of tiny rooms connected by ladders and ropes that I'd told Imran about many times. He was eager to see it; I was eager to get rid of him. That afternoon went well—Imran loved playing with the girls. And afterwards, the Robinson twins brought him to the baseball diamond when they were all done. Unfortunately, my luck would not repeat itself, and those first couple of weeks I ended up having to bring him along to the baseball games. Try as I did to make Imran just sit and watch, he never cooperated. He distracted and pestered us until someone gave him a mitt and let him stand in the middle of the outfield, where, of course, he couldn't catch a ball. Even if it was tossed to him from three yards away.

My afternoon babysitting excursions didn't really solve the problem anyway. Just as often as not, when I got home with the boy, Nathan would still be there, and the expected tantrum was sure to bring his visit to an abrupt end. Then Father had an idea: Sundays. It was his day off, and he figured if he took Imran out for the day—to the zoo, or fishing (in which case I usually went along, too)—that would allow Mina and Nathan at least one full, worry-free afternoon each week. It worked perfectly.

In mid-June, four Sundays into their courtship, Nathan took his chances for the first time and stayed into the evening. He joined Mina and Mother in greeting us as we returned from a day on the lake, our cooler filled with the day's fishing haul. Father pulled out the trophy of our catch—a one-pound green-and-black crappie—and held it up, bragging to everyone that the boy had caught it. (He hadn't; Father had.) Nathan offered his hearty and heartfelt praise and, back inside the house, treated Imran to a surprise basket full of new toys. They played together for an hour after dinner, and Imran was on his best behavior. He didn't hurl any of his new toys at Nathan's face; he didn't whine or wail when Mina put him to bed and came back downstairs to spend more time with Nathan.

Encouraged, that week Nathan came over after work on Wednesday. But it was too much too soon, and Imran responded with an amazing fit of petty rage. He screamed so loudly, and for so long, I wondered how it was possible for anything—man or beast—to make so much noise. Two days later, on Friday afternoon, Mother pulled me aside and asked me to watch the boy again. Nathan was coming over that night.

"Mom? Why don't they just meet outside the house? Why does he always have to come over here?"

"Stop complaining."

"I'm not complaining."

"Then what are you doing?"

"I'm asking."

"Asking what?"

"Why don't they see each other somewhere else? So Imran doesn't know..."

Mother's reply was dismissive, as if she thought I should have known the answer to this already: "Because your Mina-auntie is a Muslim woman, and Muslims *don't* date."

"But they are dating."

Mother frowned.

"Aren't they?" I asked.

Mother shook her head. Then paused and nodded. Then she shook her head again. "Not exactly," she finally said. And she went on to explain that she'd promised Mina's parents to safeguard their daughter's honor, and that though she was *encouraging* the relationship with Nathan, she'd imposed a strict limit on it as well: She never left the couple alone; she had to be present whenever they were together. According to Mother, this meant it wasn't *real* dating.

"When they go to her room, they leave the door open. I check every ten minutes. If they want to watch something on TV, I sit here in the kitchen, listening. Last Sunday...when they wanted to go to Red Lobster? Do you think I let them go alone? Is that what you think?"

"I don't know."

"I did *not*. I went with them. They sat in the booth. Mina didn't want me to be able to hear their conversation, so I sat on the other side, watching every move they made. Nobody in their right mind would call this *dating*. Hmm?"

I guessed she had a point.

It was late June.

Mother stopped in one night to check on me before heading to bed. As she peered in at the door, I turned over in bed, hoping she would notice I was still awake.

She stepped inside, whispering: "What's wrong, *meri-jaan?*"

"I don't know."

"Up late reading?"

"No."

"So what's wrong?"

"Not sleepy, I guess."

"You want your *ammi* to come give you some attention?"

I nodded.

"Aww," she purred as she came and sat down next to me. She reached out and ran her fingers along my forehead. For a long, quiet moment, we stared into each other's eyes.

"Is everything okay with Mina-Auntie?" I finally asked.

"She's good, *behta*—a little confused, but good..."

"Why is she confused?"

"Things are getting serious."

"Things?"

"For once, your father did an honorable thing. He told Nathan he should figure out his intentions. Things can't go on like this forever. After all, Mina is an Eastern girl..." Mother paused, shaking her head ever so slightly, a wistful wetness in her eyes. "You know what that sweet man said?"

"No."

"That he considered himself lucky she's been so open with him. He didn't expect she would agree to see him the way she has. And he's grateful. He's such a sensitive man. So *intelligent*. I really don't know why he is so close to your father. What do they say? Opposites attract? Like Dr. Jekyll and Mr. Hyde..."

"That's supposed to be the same person."

"Hmm?"

"Dr. Jekyll and Mr. Hyde are the same person...I think."

"Don't be cheeky. My point is, Nathan is a good man. That's what matters. That's what I keep telling her. And a good man is hard to find. I mean, she doesn't need to be told that. She's seen it firsthand in her own life. And she sees it here in this house, every day." Mother was still running her fingers along my forehead. "She's worried because he's *Jewish*. I mean, of course there's Imran, too. Who keeps telling her he doesn't want a *white father*. But that's nonsense. She can't make a decision about something like that because of what a five-year-old is saying." Mother paused, drawing her hand away as she looked off. "Now she's fixated on the fact that the man's a Jew and what will people back home say and what will their children be, Muslim or Jewish. I keep telling her she shouldn't be worried about that kind of thing. But she is *so* headstrong. Just *fixated.*" She chuckled, adding, almost more to herself than me, "Dr. Freud would have written quite a case study about your Mina-auntie." Now Mother turned to me again, a sudden light in her eyes. "I keep telling her the fact that Nathan's Jewish is a *good thing*. They understand how to respect women, *behta*. They understand how to let a woman be a woman, to let her take care of them. They understand how to give a woman attention. I told Mina-Auntie that he will give her a life she can never dream of with a Muslim man. Muslim men are terrified of women…all of them." She leaned in, kissing me on the nose, her face just inches from mine, her soulful eyes swollen with abounding love. "That's why I'm bringing you up differently, so that you learn how to respect a woman. That's the truth, *kurban:* I'm bringing you up like a little Jew."

What Mother said that night about Jews I'd heard before. She said these sorts of things about *them*—as she liked to refer to those of Jewish faith—often enough: how they were smart; how they understood the nature of money; how they never let their own kind down; how they honored the place of the mother; how they loved books; how sensitive their men were; how their souls were more potent; and what a special breed they were, which was why everyone else envied them, etc., etc., repeating without exception the litany of clichés familiar to us all, which she heard first not as clichés, but as praise from the lips of her father, who instilled in his children a belief that Jews were *the* special people, blessed by God above others, difficult to bear at times, perhaps—like spoilt children in general—but with much to teach us all.

I never met my grandfather—he died soon after I was born—but I heard a lot about his respect for Jews, respect which stemmed from his experience living in their midst as a student in England in the years after the Second World War. As Mother told it, he'd been particularly impressed by what he called the Jewish respect for *real* learning, not the rote memorization and mindless regurgitation of tradition he saw as common to Muslims. Among the tightly knit London communities of Jews who had fled the horrors of Hitler's Final Solution, my grandfather discovered a group of people who, though they had every reason to harden themselves—for survival's sake—against any self-doubt or self-questioning, on the contrary debated all kinds of issues, especially religious ones. He spent a great deal of time with one family in particular, the Goldenbergs, who lived next door and befriended the then-young man from Pakistan studying to be a barrister. Years later, my grandfather would regale his children with tales of the Goldenbergs, how they and their guests used to kiss books, even ones that weren't holy; how they would joyously sing their ritual songs before and after dinner; and how openly they would discuss everything from the meanings of their customs to recent developments in science and their implications for what was taught in the Torah. This intellectual curiosity was shared by many of the Jews my grandfather came to know while living in London's slums, an engagement with ideas that did not prevent the Goldenbergs or any of their friends from offering prayers or invoking God at meals or keeping to their worship. My grandfather discovered from his contact with these London Jews that thinking did not have to weaken one's bond to tradition, but could actually strengthen it. It was not what he learned in his own religious upbringing at Punjabi mosques, where he, like so many good Sunnis, was taught that pursuing knowledge for its own sake was the sure sign one had fallen from the straight path leading to God.

But whereas my grandfather's respect for the Jewish culture was specific to certain qualities of mind he believed to be authentic enlargements of life, Mother's admiration for things Semitic was considerably more quirky. Case in point: There was the time she discovered the only kosher butcher shop in town. It was on the North Side, a thirty-minute journey if traffic was good, and we'd passed it by chance one day. She stopped the car to peer through the window, oddly intrigued— even enchanted—by the sight of Jews, young and old, chopping and buying meat. The next day she was back to purchase lamb chops she cooked for us that night, announcing to Father and me that the meat was "not only holier, but *better,* too." (Holier, she could claim, because Jews slaughtered their animals as we Muslims did, by bleeding them to death as an imam or rabbi stood over the animal and spoke God's name.) And so despite the considerably longer drive, we began eschewing the packaged cuts at the local grocer for Yakov's Kosher Meats, and it wasn't simply the sanctity (or quality) of the meat that made up for the inconvenience. At Yakov's, Mother enjoyed herself perhaps more than a patron ever did at a butcher shop. She would linger, speaking to Yakov Brustein and his two sons about everything from the weather to the meaning of Yom Kippur.

I remember the latter conversation vividly, for it lasted more than a half hour, and in its wake, Mother decided the Jewish Day of Atonement was as fine an idea as there had ever been about a holiday, and that everyone, Jewish or not, should also be celebrating it. Which meant, of course, that *we* should be celebrating it. That fall, she kept me home from school on the appointed day, but we didn't really atone for our sins, unless you consider heading for the mall and enjoying plain slices at the pizzeria atonement. After pizza, we made our way to the department store to buy me a new pair of corduroy pants, the same pants, incidentally, that I wore to school the next day with a note folded into a back pocket explaining that I had been kept home for a religious holiday. Mrs. Ike, my third-grade teacher—a woman whose Nordic facial physiognomy was as forbidding and severe as her soul was gentle and joyous—asked me with innocent curiosity what holiday it had been.

"Yom Kippur," I replied, feeling a curious relish.

Mrs. Ike was confused. "But you're Moslem, aren't you?"

I hesitated. Somehow, I don't think it had fully dawned on me—though it would, and forcefully so, in the coming months—that you couldn't be Muslim and Jewish at the same time.

"Yeah. We're Muslims," I said.

"That's what I thought your mother told me," Mrs. Ike added, still confused. And then she continued, with a bright tone and a sudden smile intended to make clear she was not judging, just interested: "I didn't realize Jews and Moslems celebrated the same holidays. That's so neat. You learn something new every day, now, don't you?"

* * *

Yet Mother's mostly amusing penchant for all things Jewish was not the whole story about our relation to the Semites. For while my family's feelings toward those of the Jewish persuasion was different than that of many Muslims I've known in that there was a lighter side to it, the more pervasive, darker strain of Muslim anti-Semitism was something I was exposed to many times, and with particularly memorable—even decisive—intensity one December night when I was nine.

My parents had been invited to a dinner at the Chatha house (Ghaleb Chatha, the affluent pharmacy owner whom Mother was always trying to get Father to befriend). There'd been heavy snow that evening, and I recall sitting in the bay window of the Chathas' palatial living room peering out at a sky that seemed to be breaking apart into tiny white pieces and drifting down everywhere.

"Is it still snowing, *behta?*" Chatha asked me as he returned from the hall. He was a tall, gaunt, ashen-brown man whose acne-scarred face was framed by a white curtain of a beard, a thick, manicured strip running from ear to ear. His arms were long and so were his thin, wrinkled fingers. As he patted me on the head, I nodded, perplexed he'd asked me a question for which the response was right there in the window before him. He smiled, then returned to his place in an armchair at the center of the room, where the men were gathered. Father was there; Chatha; Sonny Buledi, the psychiatrist with the Austrian wife (this was back before Sonny had taken to calling himself an atheist and made himself persona non grata in the local Pakistani community); and two others I didn't know: a portly engineer named Majid; and a bald, skinny, nervously intense man named Dawood. The men were sitting separate from the women, who were in the kitchen. I was the only boy there that night. Satya and Otto Buledi were with their mother, who hadn't come along.

"Where's the family tonight?" Dawood asked Sonny. "Why didn't you bring them?"

"They're in Austria," Sonny replied. "With my wife's family."

"Why aren't you with them?" Dawood asked.

"Work. But I'll be going next week."

"For Christmas?"

Sonny looked hesitant.

Chatha looked over. "Buledi-*sahib,* don't tell me you've started celebrating *Christmas?*" he asked, pointedly. His accent was odd, its thick, mannered, British overlay deforming—but not at all concealing—the Punjabi click and lilt underneath.

"I don't *celebrate* it," Sonny said, defensive.

"But you let your kids celebrate it."

"It's a cultural holiday, as I see it. A chance for the kids to spend time with their mother's family."

"Cultural holiday," Dawood said with a nod. "I like that. I think that's completely right. Not a religious holiday at all anymore. They've taken it and turned it into something else completely. Merchandise. Capitalism." Dawood glanced at Chatha. "That's the real purpose of Christmas now."

Chatha nodded, agreeing. "They don't even think about their prophet anymore. Just about buying and selling things. *Retailing...*"

"You know, it reminds me of a book I read," Dawood said. "By a chap named Max Weber. You should take a look at it, Dr. Buledi."

"Not *The Protestant Ethic and the Spirit of Capitalism?*" Sonny asked, surprised.

"Exactly!" Dawood exclaimed with a delighted clap. And

then, all at once, he was frowning. "You mean *The Christian Ethic*...don't you?"

"It's called *The Protestant Ethic*..."

Majid chimed in from his place across from Sonny and Father, who were sitting side by side on the couch, "It's the same thing. Protestant just means Christian."

"Not quite," Sonny replied. "There are different kinds of Christians. Protestants are one kind."

"They're all the *wrong* kind," Chatha offered, flatly.

Sonny looked over at him, as if wanting to respond. But he held his tongue.

Dawood continued in the pause, enthusiastically: "So you know about this Max Weber, Dr. Buledi?! The fellow is impressive. He really tells it like it is!" Dawood turned to the others. "You'd never find a Muslim like him, someone who could stand up against his own people and tell the truth behind all the lies." Dawood gesticulated with glee. "Weber shows how Christians created capitalism! He shows you that capitalism is their *real* religion! He even says it! That it's all a conspiracy! Everything is an excuse to make money!"

"That's stretching things, Dawood," Sonny corrected. "It's not really what he's saying."

"It's what I read. And trust me: I was paying attention."

"Be that as it may," Sonny said with a shake of his head. Up until now, he, like everyone else, had been speaking the usual English-and-Urdu hybrid that most in our community spoke—but now he spoke only English, and his tone was cold, academic, with a hint of disdain: "Weber is talking about how a certain mind-set, a certain Protestant way of thinking and being, had the effect of making people invest their money instead of spend it." He spoke slowly, as if uncertain those he was talking to would understand. "One of the differences between Protestants and Catholics, Weber says, is that Protestants just don't give their money away to the Church the way the Catholics do. And they also don't seem to want to spend money on themselves. So what ended up happening was that Protestants would make money and just continue to save it. And over time, they built larger and larger pools of money. Of *capital*. Which they had to put somewhere. So they would invest it. And this, Weber is saying, is how capitalism really started."

Dawood was staring off with a troubled look, as if trying to square what Sonny was suggesting with his own understanding of what he, obviously, hadn't read with nearly as much attention or comprehension. Dawood was about to speak when Chatha interrupted:

"Your Mr. Vebb is wrong."

"Not Vebb. Weber," Sonny corrected, then repeated for emphasis: "*Vay-bar.*"

"Whatever. I don't care how many books he writes. He can't change the truth: Capitalism has nothing to do with Christianity. Pools of accumulating money, you say? Where do you think those came from first?"

"I told you what Weber thinks," Sonny said. "I'm not saying I agree or disagree. I was just clarifying his point."

"I don't care about him, Doctor-*sahib*. I care about you: Where do *you* think the first pools of accumulating money came from?"

"I don't know what you're driving at, Ghaleb. You obviously know what you want to say. So just say it."

Chatha nodded, granting Sonny's point. "From interest. That's where."

Sonny shrugged. "Okay. And?"

"Who started the idea of interest?"

"I don't know."

"Everyone knows—except you and your dear Mr. Vebb, apparently—that interest is a *Jewish* invention. They are the ones who started that sin." Chatha's tone was imperious, as if he expected his pronouncement to render further discussion unnecessary. Dawood was studying Chatha, considering the thought. Father shifted in place, clearly irritated.

"So Ghaleb...," Father started. "When you just bought that pharmacy in Birch Grove, did you pay cash?"

"Of course not," Chatha answered.

"You took out a loan?"

"What do you think, Naveed?"

"And it's an *interest* loan...?"

"The only kind you can get in this country, brother."

"So let me get this right," Father continued. "You're benefiting from the *sin* of interest. Doesn't that make you as much of a sinner as your so-called Jews?"

"You ask me the question like you think I never asked this myself."

"So what's your answer?"

"Those of us living here, among the *jahil*s, we have to live with their rules..."

"*Jahil*s?" Sonny muttered to himself. Even with as little as I knew about Islam at the time, I knew the word referred to those who didn't believe.

"Sounds a bit easy..." Father went on: "Doesn't it make you a hypocrite?" His relish in saying that word was clear.

"No need to get nasty, Naveed-*bhai*."

"I'm just asking you a question, *maulvi-sahib*."

Chatha snickered. "For us, here, we have to live with the rules...When there's no other way to make your living, you do what you have to do. Family is first in our faith. You have to care for your family. That is what the Quran says. There is room for flexibility in our tradition."

"Family is first for any sane human being, Ghaleb," Father responded sharply. "Faith or not...And anyway, we're not talking about that. Your family is taken care of. We're talking about prosperity. That's what you're after. You don't need to take the interest loan to take care of your family. You would do fine without the loan. Without the new pharmacies. You could save your money and wait until you have enough in the bank to buy a new location without the loan." Father paused. "But that would mean being less aggressive than you want to be."

"Or the tax advantages," Chatha added. "The competition is fierce here. We will never succeed in changing the system if we don't participate. But when we are established, and that day will come, *inshallah,* then we can talk about banks that offer no-interest loans."

"Dance with the devil until then? Is that the plan?" Father asked.

Before Chatha had a chance to reply, Sonny started in: "So maybe we should be more grateful to the Jews," he said. "After all, Chatha-*sahib,* your master plan seems to require their invention of interest."

There was a long, tense pause.

Majid, who hadn't said much yet, offered this apparent non sequitur with visible agitation: "I pray to Allah that damn Carter loses the election!" After another short pause, he continued: "Those Jews chewed him up and spit him out. And we've done nothing but pay the price! Can you believe that *idiot?* Promising us a few hundred million when those Jews are twisting his arm to pour billions into their defense? General Zia was right to call the offer peanuts. That's what it is!

Peanuts! And Carter and his fat brother can keep those peanuts for themselves as far as I'm concerned."

"I don't know why it would be any different with Reagan," Dawood replied.

"It *has* to be different," said Majid. "He's a Republican. Nixon was a friend to Pakistan."

"Maybe he'll be a friend. Maybe he won't," Dawood said, looking over at Chatha again.

"Pakistan is one thing. Israel is another," Chatha stated with finality.

"But they need Pakistan!" Majid added in an oddly pleading tone: "Without Pakistan, they lose Afghanistan to Russia. And then they lose Pakistan! And then Iran!" He was pointing now, emphatically. "And the Americans won't like how the map looks after that!"

"Frankly," Sonny began, "they would probably prefer Iran to be Russian than run by the Ayatollah."

"I don't care about Iran! I care about *our* people!" Majid exclaimed. "We have to take care of our own business first! Then we take care of the other business. Pakistan is going to fall to pieces if the Americans don't help us. But those goddamn Jews don't want them to help us!"

Sonny looked at him, confused. "Why are you attributing the lack of support for Pakistan to Jews?"

Majid glared at Sonny, disbelieving. "Because they hate us! That's why! We're like them. The only other religious country in the world. We were created for Muslims, just like they were created for Jews. But they want to be the *only* ones!"

"Pakistan will be fine," Chatha responded confidently. "Pakistan is not the issue. The real problem is Israel. We will never have peace in this world as long as they're living on that land. They bring difficulty for others everywhere they go—it's their curse. But for that there's only one solution. And we'll have to wait another hundred years before anyone has the guts to try that again."

"Try *what* again?" Sonny asked suspiciously.

"Killing them all," Chatha replied, adding—after a pause—with the same matter-of-fact tone: "Like Hitler."

"Hitler?" Sonny asked. He looked over at Father, appalled.

Father seemed less appalled than exasperated.

Just then—as if on cue—a delightful cataract of female laughter erupted in the kitchen, where the women were gathered.

"If you knew the words of your own holy book, Dr. Buledi," Chatha began, "then you would know that Hitler was just doing what the Quran predicted and what Allah warned them about."

"What are you talking about?"

"Don't act so offended."

"Don't act offended? I am offended."

"Well...," Chatha said smugly as he rose from his armchair, "that's a matter of your politics. It has nothing to do with the truth." Chatha stepped to the bookshelf along the far wall, where he reached for a copy of the Quran sitting on the highest shelf. "*This* is what I am talking about," he said as he kissed the cover and held up the book. "The *Truth*." He opened the book, muttering an invocation as he searched its pages. "There it is," he said, stepping to the couch. He handed Sonny the book, his index finger pointing at a block of text. "Read the underlined verses. Here"—he turned the page—"and here..."

Sonny took the book from him with a skeptical look. There was an uncomfortable silence as he started to read and as Chatha sat back down in his armchair. Another wave of women's laughter washed in from the kitchen. And suddenly, there was a woman standing in the doorway.

Chatha looked over. "Yes, Najat?" he asked.

Najat was his wife. The woman I'd only ever met behind a face-covering veil, which she wasn't wearing now.

"Can we interest you men in a little *kawa?*" she asked, playfully.

She had a sweet, round face, with a wide and appealing smile. But seeing her gave me an odd feeling, as if the unpermitted face now revealed was somehow unreal, and that the gray-black hanging canvas mask that showed nothing of the woman was, in fact, her true face.

All the men wanted *kawa,* some with milk, others with sugar as well; only Father requested it the way Kashmiris—inventors of the lightly astringent, green-tea-and-spice brew—served it: with a pinch of salt.

Orders taken, Mrs. Chatha disappeared into the kitchen.

Back at the couch, Sonny turned the page, still reading. He shook his head. "It doesn't mean what you think it means," he said confidently as he looked up and gave the book back to Chatha.

Chatha ignored the gesture, turning to Dawood. "Read it to us, brother."

Dawood hesitated. He looked embarrassed.

"Go ahead," Chatha encouraged. "Do us the honor. Take it. Read it."

Dawood leaned forward and took the book from Sonny. "Which lines?" he asked.

"The underlined ones," Chatha answered.

Dawood straightened in his chair. He cleared his throat and began to read:

> Disgrace and humiliation were stamped on the
> children of Israel.

They earned the burden of God's wrath.
And all because they denied what God revealed.
They killed His messengers. They rebelled.
They did what was wrong.

Dawood turned the page. Chatha was looking at Sonny. Sonny looked away, unable—or unwilling—to hold Chatha's gray, unblinking gaze. Dawood continued:

Evil is the pride for which they sold their own
        souls,
And rejected what God has revealed,
Jealous of others whom God chooses to favor.
They have earned the burden of God's wrath.
        Over and over.

Hearing these words, Chatha excitedly raised his hand, stopping Dawood. "'They have earned the burden of God's wrath. Over and over.' That is what is written. *That* is the truth!" Chatha pointed at Sonny, putting exaggerated emphasis on certain words as he continued: "And *that* is the *curse* that has been *following* them *ever since*. It is *why* they were put in *ghettos*. *Why* there was a *Holocaust*. And *why* they will *lose* their *precious Israel*."

Majid grunted, like a farm animal anticipating feeding. Dawood was nodding.

"They are destined to suffer," Chatha added with force.

I remembered the only Jewish friend I had ever had, Jason Blum. A wave of worry went through me.

"Why only those verses, Ghaleb?" Sonny challenged, removing his glasses with disdain, wiping at the lenses with a handkerchief he produced from his shirt pocket. "Why not have him read sixty-two as well?"

"Sixty-two?" Chatha asked, confused.

"Maybe it's *you* who needs to know your own holy book a little better," Sonny said, replacing the glasses on his face. "Dawood, please do us the honor of reading verse sixty-two."

Father looked at Sonny, impressed.

"Dawood. Please. Verse sixty-two. It's one that Chatha-*sahib* did *not* underline." Sonny gave Chatha an icy look. Dawood glanced over at Chatha. "You don't need his permission, Dawood," Sonny said, abruptly. "You're a grown man. Just read it."

"Go ahead, Dawood," Father said. "What's it say?"

Dawood turned back the page, clearing his throat again:

It is true: The faithful, those who follow the
Jewish faith, the Christians, the Sabians—all
who believe in God and the Last Day and do
right—these shall find reward with the Lord.
They will not fear. They will not grieve.

There was a short silence. Sonny was looking at Chatha. "Explain that," he said. "Reconcile *that,* my dear *maulvi-sahib.*"

"Reconcile?" Chatha asked.

"C'mon, man!" Sonny exploded. "God condemns them in verse sixty-one, which you choose to underline, and then follows it with accepting them in the next?! That's an outright contradiction and unless you can explain it, it renders both verses utterly meaningless..."

Dawood and Majid traded alarmed looks. Both turned to Chatha, expectant. But Chatha didn't look worried. "The answer is simple," he began. "And if you knew the Quran at all, you wouldn't ask such a question. You wouldn't pit one verse against the next like a riddle to be resolved! There is no contradiction! The Quran is perfect and complete."

"What's the answer, Ghaleb?" Sonny insisted.

"Doctor-*sahib*," Chatha said with disdain, "our dear Allah would accept them, every single one of them, if only they would behave. But they *don't* behave. They *don't* obey. And as long as they don't, they will pay. If they were to behave righteously, they would be accepted with open arms. But this is the tragedy of the Jew: That he will never learn. Not until he's roasting in hellfire!"

I thought again of Jason Blum...

Until his parents took him out of school two months into fourth grade, Jason had been my new best friend. With an open, welcoming face—something about his wide-set eyes and broad toothy smile made you feel like you could trust him— he exuded uncommon confidence for a fourth grader. He was the smartest kid in class, and the best dressed: in a Polo or Lacoste shirt, his colored corduroys always matching, the same eternally gleaming Stan Smith tennis shoes on his feet.

Jason's country club attire was less an indicator of his family's lifestyle—they were Jewish, and would never have been accepted as members at Indian Hills, the local country club— and more a product of his passion for tennis. He was all the rage in the under-ten category of the local USTA. One evening in his bedroom, our vision blurred by a solid afternoon spent in front of the television playing Atari, he pulled the state ranking booklet from his bookshelf.

"Check it out," he said, opening to a page.

There he was. In a murky black-and-white shot, unsmiling but unmistakable, the number-one-ranking holder. Under his picture was listed a name I didn't recognize: Yitzhak Blum.

"Is that your name?" I asked.

"Yeah. It was my grandfather's name. He died in the Holocaust," he said blankly. "But everyone calls me Jason. I like Jason better."

"How do you say your real name?"

He pronounced it, and the gutturals he spoke sounded not unlike sounds my own parents made at home when they talked to each other in Punjabi. I repeated it back to him. "Exactly. That's really good, Hayat," he said, impressed. "But I like Jason better."

He couldn't have been half as impressed as I was. I'd never met anyone who had his picture in a book before. He shut it and returned it to the shelf, then said matter-of-factly: "I'm Jewish. That's why my grandfather was killed in the Holocaust. You know what the Holocaust is, right?"

I nodded. "Isn't that when Hitler killed everybody?"

"It's when he killed the Jews. He hated us."

"Oh," I replied. I felt silly. I realized that Mother had explained this to me when she wouldn't let me watch the miniseries that had created such a stir the previous year. *He's gonna think you're an idiot,* I thought.

"What are you?" he asked.

"Muslim," I replied.

He nodded, picking up a racket in the corner. I watched him, my awe only growing, as he swung it. Here before me was my first Jewish friend, tennis champ and classroom math brain, an example, I thought, of exactly why Mother said Jews were so special. If I had ever had any doubt about Mother's claims, Jason put them to rest. "My mom says you guys are special," I said with admiration.

"Who?"

"Jews."

"Oh." Jason shrugged. "Guess we are," he added. And then,

with a sudden thought, he pointed at me. "Moslem...so that means you don't go to church, you go to a mosque, right?"

I nodded. "But we don't go much. Only like on holidays and stuff."

Jason nodded. "So we're the only ones at Mason who don't go to church?"

"You don't go to church?" I asked.

"Not on your life. You couldn't get me in a church if you paid me. The Christians think we killed Jesus. My dad says they're crazy. He says *they're* the ones who killed Jesus themselves, and then they blamed us for it."

I knew the basics of the story Muslims told about Jesus, a story Mina would tell me in great detail a few years later: that Jesus never actually died, but was saved by God at the last minute. I also knew that we Muslims considered Jesus a prophet, but not the Son of God. I mentioned both details to Jason.

"I don't know about all that...All I know is, my dad says the guy was loony. He'd be in a hospital for crazy people if he was alive today. My dad says the guy was looking to get killed. He says Jesus had a death wish."

I nodded. I didn't really know much about the whole thing. And it sounded to me like Jason did.

A week after he said those things to me about Jesus at his house, he would apparently repeat them at school. I wasn't there to hear it, but I was present for the aftermath.

It was morning recess and I couldn't find him. After combing the playground—the kickball diamonds and tetherball posts—I found myself at the edge of the school grounds, where I noticed a group of boys gathered around a tree, cheering. Through an opening in the curtain that the boys' backs formed, I spied Jason. He was leaned against the tree.

"Jason!" I shouted. He didn't hear me.

As I made my way toward them, one of the boys stepped away from the tree, zipping himself up. Another stepped forward. The new boy pulled his pants down to his knees and began to pee. Someone moved and I saw Jason clearly. His hands were tied to the tree. And the boy was peeing on him.

"Jew! Jew! Jew! Jew!" they started jeering.

"You're the one with the *death wish!*" one of them shouted.

"Stop it!" I yelled. I sprinted ahead, throwing myself at them. "Stop it! Stop it!"

Hands grabbed at my windbreaker, pulling it over my head. The boys shoved me back and forth between them, weak blows slapping against my back. I heard the hiss of the playground supervisor's whistle, and everyone went scurrying off. I pulled the jacket from my head and saw Jason. He was crumpled against the tree, drenched in urine, weeping.

I went over and started to untie him. "Are you okay?" I asked.

He just shook his head. He wouldn't even look up at me.

That afternoon, I was sent to the principal's office to report the perpetrators. The boys were suspended, and I would become a pariah for weeks for having squealed for the sake of a Jew.

Jason's parents would end up pulling him from school. I would never see him again.

The *kawa* tea came, wheeled in on a trolley by Najat and a couple of the other wives. Sonny rose as the women started serving. He made his apologies to Najat, shook hands with Father, then left—and without a word to Chatha. Amidst the ensuing (and uneasy) tinkle of stirring spoons and the slurping sips, the men's discussion drifted back to the subject of Carter and Reagan. Chatha tried to provoke Father into picking up the discussion about Jews again. Father wasn't interested. He kept to himself.

On the way out to the car that night, my parents got into an argument. Father was angry that Mother had made him come to the dinner. He got into the driver's seat and slammed the door, and Mother—who didn't want to have to sit next to him—made me sit in front. As we drove back through the continuing snowstorm, the car's headlights rushing forward into the thick, insistent swirl of falling flakes, Father simmered in silence. He said nothing about the argument that had taken place among the men. Not to Mother. Not to me. And I sat next to him, worried.

I was worried that if what Chatha had said about Jews was right, then Jason's troubles had only just begun...

8

Independence Day

W hen do the fireworks start?" Nathan asked Mother.

We were sitting in folding chairs at the edge of the local high school football field, one of the few points of local elevation, and thus a privileged perch from which to watch the municipal fireworks. We came every year with our Tupperware containers filled with Pakistani food and *lassi,* and this year Nathan had joined us as well.

"When it gets dark," Father replied, taking a bite of a *samosa.* "What? You've never seen fireworks before?"

"I have, Naveed. I was just wondering. I mean, the sun's already setting."

"They'll start when they start, Nate."

"Fair enough." Nathan looked in the direction of the goalpost, where Imran was playing with a new action figure Nathan had given him that evening back at the house. "I think he likes that figure I got him," he said to Mina.

"Looks like it," she replied with a high-pitched, singsong tone. She handed him a plastic plate heaped with white rice and ground beef curry. "You want some *lassi,* Nate?" she asked.

"Do I ever."

Mina flashed him a wide grin.

I'd been noticing more and more that there was something

different about Mina when Nathan was around, something stilted and performed. Something false. I couldn't understand what it was about him that made her like this.

Mina held out a cup. Mother poured the yogurt drink into it, humming a tune to herself.

"What do you keep humming?" Mina asked.

"That song on the radio all day."

"'America the Beautiful,'" Nathan said.

"What?" Mother asked.

"It's called 'America the Beautiful.' That's what you're humming."

"I like it," Mother said. Mina handed Nathan the *lassi,* then served another small plate of food and rose to her feet.

"Where are you going?" Nathan asked.

"I'm going to get Imran to eat something." She walked over to her son and sat down next to him. As soon as he saw the food, Imran started whining.

Mother stopped humming. "Not good," she muttered as she watched Mina with her son. Imran was slapping at his mother's arm, to bat the plate away. He finally upended it, the food spilling on the grass. She got up and made her way back to us, empty plate in hand.

"*Bhaj?* Can you give me a couple *gulab jamun*s?"

"That's for dessert."

"He said he'll eat that. I just want him to eat something."

"You should be firmer with him. He leads you around by the nose."

Mina stiffened. "What do you suggest?" she asked coldly.

"*Make* him eat." Mother made no move for the dessert bin.

"That's what I'm *trying* to do," Mina replied, irritated. "Please just give me a few *gulab jamun*s."

"You know where they are. Take them yourself."

Mina stared at Mother, incredulous.

"I'll get them for you, Meen," Nathan offered, setting his plate down on the blanket. Mina ignored him as she kneeled and snatched the oblong container, tearing open the plastic lid and picking out two golden, syrupy balls.

She stood again and walked back over to her son.

"Always creating trouble, Muneer," Father said as he chewed. "Let her bring up her own child."

Mother turned to him, her eyebrows arched. "See those blondes over there?" She gestured at a group of girls in shorts playing Frisbee farther out on the field. "Why don't you offer them some of your *sage counsel?* Maybe they'll get you drunk in return? Hmm? Who knows, maybe you'll even get lucky. You would like that, I'm sure."

"That's enough, Muneer," Father said firmly.

Mother pursed her lips. She turned to Nathan now. "She's creating a monster..."

Nathan didn't reply. He smiled weakly, looking down at his plate.

When Mina returned, she took up a plate for herself, serving herself a small portion of rice and beef. No one spoke as she ate.

The aluminum joints of Father's folding chair released with a groan as he rose. "Good food, ladies. As always," he said as he walked off.

I watched to see if he was going to go over to the blondes. Instead, he went to the parking lot, where he pulled open our car trunk and stood there.

Mother watched Mina as she ate. Mina ignored her.

When Mina was done, she set her plate down. Mother reached out for the dessert bin, opened it, and pulled out a sticky *gulab jamun* ball, which she set down on Mina's plate.

Mina looked up, her gaze locking in with Mother's. They stared at each other for a moment, their expressions completely blank...

And then they burst out laughing.

"You can be such a pain, *bhaj,* you know that?"

"You're not the first to say it," Mother said with a smile.

"I don't think you're a pain, Muneer," Nathan added, clearly relieved.

"You don't know me that well, Nathan. Just wait. You'll find out."

He laughed. Then he looked over at Imran. "I'm gonna go check up on him," Nathan said, rising, his plate of unfinished food in hand.

He walked over to the goalpost and sat down beside Imran. As Nathan tried to get the boy to eat, Imran marched his action figure through Nathan's food. Nathan watched, seeming amused, and soon enough they were playing together, each taking turns at marching the figure across Nathan's plate.

I looked over at the parking lot again. Father was still standing there, staring down into the open trunk. I couldn't figure out what he was doing there. All at once, he slammed it shut.

"We had fun," Nathan said as he plopped back into his chair. "I even got him to eat a little."

"Eat what?" Mina asked, looking surprised, her eyes filled with tenderness. "You were playing with the food."

"Well, I guess that's what he wanted to do before eating it."

It was true. Imran was sitting quietly by the goalpost, discreetly eating with his fingers from the plate Nathan had left behind.

Now Father was crossing the lawn back toward us. Mother eyed him suspiciously as he took a seat again. "Muneer, can I have some *gulab jamun?*"

She handed him the Tupperware bin.

"People forget he's just a kid," Nathan said, addressing no one in particular. "He's been through a lot. All things considered, I think he's doing pretty darn well."

Mina gazed at him, a crease cutting deeply across her forehead. She looked like she was going to cry.

"You okay, Meen?" Nathan asked gently.

She lowered her head, nodding. She sniffled once, rubbed her nose. And then, suddenly, she was smiling. It was odd. "I just remembered that thing you told me yesterday, Nate...," she said, chuckling to herself. The same fake singsong tone was back.

I looked at Nathan. His half smile looked fake to me as well.

"What thing?" he asked.

"About Emerson? Having a headache? Remember?"

"That?"

"It was good," she said, sitting up in her chair and sniffling again. "Tell it again. Naveed will like it."

"Like what?" Father asked, eager.

"Nathan's joke."

"Nathan has a joke?" Father bit off a piece of his dessert with his question. His eyes had a watery, unfocused look. And his words had a light—but unmistakable—lisp.

He glanced at me, feeling my gaze.

Nathan continued: "Well, I was just telling Mina yesterday that there's this writer named Emerson..."

"A *writer?*" Father interrupted, still chewing. "And you're calling this a joke? I hate it already."

"Well, you didn't let me finish."

"I'm not stopping you... But after an opening like that, I don't have high hopes."

"Okay," Nathan began. "So there was this writer who once

said: 'Why is it a man can't sit down to think in this country without someone asking him if he's got a headache?'"

There was a pause as we waited for the rest.

Mina laughed. Nathan didn't go on. I was confused.

"And?" Father asked.

"That's it. 'Why can't a man sit down to think without someone asking if he has a headache?' That's the joke."

Mother smiled, releasing breath, as if trying to get a laugh going.

Father wore a blank stare. "You call that a joke?"

"Well, I wouldn't necessarily have called it a joke per se," Nathan said, turning to Mina, "though I understand, Meen, why you called it one."

"Nate," Father said. "That's not a joke. Period."

"Naveed," Mother interrupted, with a hint of a censoring tone.

"What?" Father whined, like a boy bristling at his mother's reprimand. "She said Nate had a joke I was going to like. I just want to hear something funny! I want to laugh! Is that a crime?"

Mother looked away. "Drunk, as usual," she mumbled.

Father turned to Nathan. "I thought at least you might have a good Polack joke or something. Everyone has one of *those...*"

"You have Polack jokes, Naveed?" Nathan asked with disbelief.

"I have Sikh jokes. Pretty much the same thing."

"Really?"

Mother explained: "For Punjabis, Sikhs are like what Polish people are here. Everybody makes fun of them."

"Well, as a matter of fact," Nathan said, "I do have a good Polish joke."

"You do?" Mina asked. She didn't sound pleased.

"I don't know about *good*," Father interjected. His eyes were brimming with glee. "After the last one, *I'll* be the judge of that."

Nathan nodded. "So did you ever hear about the Polack who studied for five days?"

Father stared at his colleague, deadpan. Nathan glanced at Mina—who was clearly annoyed—then back at Father. "He was scheduled to take a urine test."

"Now *that's* a joke!" Father roared. He laughed and laughed, his eyes filling with water.

Mina shook her head.

"What is it, Meen?" Nathan asked.

Before Mina could reply, Father started in keenly: "Here's a good one about Sikhs. There's a job interview for a detective's position, and three guys show up. A Jew, a Roman, and a Sikh. The chief decides he's going to ask his candidates one question, the same question, and make his decision based on their answers. So, one by one they're called into the chief's office. First the Jew comes, and the chief asks him to sit down. 'Who killed Jesus Christ?' The Jew answers: 'The Romans killed him.' The chief says 'Thank you.' When the Jew leaves, the Roman comes in, and the chief asks him the same question: 'Who killed Jesus Christ?' The Roman says 'The Jews killed him.' 'Thank you,' says the chief. Finally, the Sikh comes in, and the chief asks him the same question. But instead of answering right away, the Sikh asks, 'Chief, do you think I could have some time to think about it?' The chief tells him that's fine, that he should get back to him with an answer by tomorrow. When the Sikh goes home that night, his wife asks him how the interview went. 'Great, honey,' he tells her. 'I got the job, and I'm already investigating a murder!' "

"Haaaaah!" Nathan exclaimed, letting loose a hearty, vigorous laugh. Mother laughed as well. Father chuckled, enjoying the success of his joke, at least with the two of them. I wasn't laughing—I didn't understand the joke—and neither was Mina. She wore a dour look, her mood completely transformed. She was looking at Nathan like she didn't recognize him.

"The Jews didn't kill Christ, Naveed," Mina said sternly.

"It's a joke," Father said.

Mina offered a dismissive shrug. Nathan's cheeks were ruddy from laughter. "I'm not so sure about that, Meen," he said sweetly. "Supposedly, we *did* have a chance to save him and we didn't. We asked for Barabbas instead. Though I'm not sure that amounts to us having killed the man."

"Barabbas?" Mina asked, an edge in her voice. "I don't know who that is."

"He was the other prisoner. Pontius Pilate asked the Jews which one they wanted to free. And they chose Barabbas. And that meant Jesus was the one who got crucified."

Mina clearly had no idea what he was talking about.

"More food, anyone?" Mother asked. Nobody responded.

Nathan turned to Father. "But as far as the criminal investigation goes, Naveed, I think my kinsman was right on that count. The Romans are definitely the ones who did the deed."

"For the record," Mina stated sharply, "Hazrat Isa never died. The whole thing is a misunderstanding."

"Isa?" Nathan asked.

"That's what we call Jesus. I thought you would know that by now."

"He never died? What do you mean?" It looked to me like Nathan thought she was joking.

I felt a scarlet blush—it was anger—push to my face.

"When Hazrat Isa was in the prison cell," Mina continued, her voice charged, "before they were going to take him to be crucified, he prayed to Allah to spare him. And when the guard came to fetch him, he found no one in the cell. Isa was gone. Saved by Allah."

Nathan turned to Father, perplexed.

Father shrugged. He looked out at the field, where Imran was now chasing fireflies by the bleachers.

Mina glared at both of them. "Allah answered Isa's prayer and took him up to heaven directly. And when the guard came out to tell the others that Isa was gone, they seized *him*. Because the guard now looked exactly like Isa: Allah transformed the guard's face so the others would mistake him for Isa."

She had told me a much longer version of this tale during one of our story hours, complete with Isa's dialogue with Allah, in which Isa—in his holding cell—pleaded with our Lord to spare him the pain of death.

"That's why he has to come back," Mina said confidently.

"*Who* has to come back?" Nathan asked, incredulous.

"Who do you think?" Mina was indignant. The hint of violence in her replies had me rapt. "Isa...or Jesus, as you call him. He has to come back because he hasn't died. He has to come and live a normal human life. To complete his life and die like a normal person. And when he comes back, he will be a Muslim. And his death will mark the beginning of the end of the world."

Nathan stared at her, speechless. "You *believe* that?"

"No more than you believe Jesus died on the cross," she spit back at him.

"Well, I don't know that I believe that."

"So what do you believe?! Do you believe *anything?!?*"

Around us, heads turned to look. Nathan's face was blank with shock.

"When are they going to start this thing?" Mother said, looking up at the black-brown sky. Nobody answered. She pulled open a garbage bag and started dumping things inside.

"Religion, my friends," Father said as he stood, taking up a pair of plastic cups before Mother could throw them out, "is a topic for fools. And this conversation is the living proof."

Father got up and walked off to join Imran by the bleachers.

"I don't see what you're so upset about, Meen," Nathan finally said.

I was staring at him now, noticing the pallor of his creamy, lightly freckled skin.

"I don't know about all this," she muttered.

"All what?" Nathan asked. When Mina hesitated, Nathan prodded. "All what?" he asked again.

"Nothing," Mina replied, quietly.

"No, it's something . . . All what?"

Mina paused, and when she spoke, it wasn't with an answer to his question: "If you're interested in Islam . . ."

"I am. You know that."

Mina looked at him, suddenly weary, resigned, hopeless.

Nathan finally noticed me staring at him. I held his gaze with defiance. Then I looked away.

Out on the lawn, Father and Imran were creeping about, hunched, trying to catch fireflies with the plastic cups. It was just then that the first streak of light appeared, exploding against the night sky. The modest crowd responded to the golden, glittering trails with a chorus of oohs and aahs.

"It's so beautiful," Mother sang out, throwing a glance over her shoulder at Nathan and Mina. They were holding hands. Or rather, Nathan's hand was resting on Mina's, which sat leaden, unmoving on the folding chair's armrest. Her face wore the same dead expression. Again, I noticed the paleness of Nathan's face in the brown night. There was something sickly about it. I felt uneasy. And then I realized I didn't have to feel that way: It wasn't my white skin. I didn't have white skin. He did.

Nathan made efforts to appease Mina through the show, but she was unresponsive. And by the time the final flurry of Chinese stars and peony shells and roman candles was under way, Mina was already on her feet, headed back to the parking lot. We packed up and walked to the car, where we found her waiting, silent, her eyes lowered to avoid our gazes.

"Meen...," Nathan pleaded. "Talk to me." That, she wasn't going to do. Mina didn't speak a word to anyone the entire way home.

Back at the house, Mina disappeared inside without a goodnight. Nathan was panicked. "I don't understand," he said to Father. I was unloading things from the trunk. He and Father were standing by his car in the driveway.

"Probably just that time of month, Nate," Father said with a laugh.

"It's not funny, Naveed. I'm worried. I think I may have really offended her."

"With that stuff about Jesus?"

"I guess."

"Are you serious?! We're talking about *Jesus!* Who even knows if that guy lived? How stupid can you get? Arguing about nonsense like that?" Father turned to look at me.

I looked away.

What could possibly matter more? I thought. Mina had explained it all to me clearly: Isa had never died. That was why he was coming back, this time as a Muslim. And his return to earth, she'd said, would mark the end of time and the beginning of the Day of Judgment. That miraculous day when every soul that had ever lived would rise from its grave to account for itself.

"Naveed, please. Obviously she takes it very seriously—and something I said offended her."

"If she's offended by that, then she *needs* offending... That'll teach you to talk about religion. Stay away from it. You know what everybody always says? Don't discuss religion or politics. Especially with a Muslim."

"I don't know why she thinks I'm not interested in Islam. I'm reading the Quran every day."

Father laughed.

"Naveed. Stop it."

"Okay, okay, Nate..."

As they made their way down to Nathan's car, I reached into the trunk for the remaining folding chairs. One of the aluminum legs was caught on the canvas covering the spare tire. I tugged, pulling the leg free. The canvas cover ripped open.

Cradled there in the tire's hub was a bottle with a golden label, half-filled with wheat-colored water. I set the chairs down and reached for the bottle. I held it to the lightbulb in the corner.

Something inside me sank. WHISKEY, the label read.

I looked back at Father. He and Nathan were shaking hands. I reached back into the trunk and pulled the canvas closed again. My heart racing, I hurried into the open garage, the bottle hidden under my shirt. I noticed the pile of plastic tarps in the corner that Father used to collect leaves in the fall.

I looked back to see Nathan's car pulling away and Father heading up the driveway.

I stuffed the bottle underneath the tarps. The bulge it formed looked conspicuous to me. I kicked at it a few times.

"Is this all?" Father asked as he turned to me. He was holding the rest of the folding chairs.

"Yeah," I replied, hurrying back to the car.

Father stepped away. I slammed the trunk shut. I followed him into the garage, watching as he leaned the chairs along the far wall. He looked distracted, disoriented, like he was struggling with his balance.

Mother's right, I thought. *He's a drunk.*

But as he joined me at the garage's open mouth, even my anger couldn't blind me to the quiet ease in his gaze, the pleasing softness in his smile. He put his hand on my shoulder and held it there, tenderly.

"Look at that...all those fireflies," he said as he looked out at the lawn. Pinpoints of bright yellow-white light pulsed and throbbed, careening along the bushes, disappearing into the grass. Father watched for a long moment, silent. Then he turned to me. In the darkness, the corners of his eyes gleamed, wet with feeling. "That's my childhood. Right there. Fields and fields of fireflies. We used to catch them in the village. I never showed you how to do it, did I?"

"No," I mumbled.

"Let me show you now," he said brightly. He turned and headed back into the garage to inspect the shelves. "I just need to find some cups for us to use." I watched him with apprehension as he rummaged. He was about to approach the pile of discarded tarps when I blurted out:

"Dad. I don't want to."

He turned to me. "C'mon, *kurban.*"

"I'm tired, Dad."

"It will be fun."

Now I was firm, even disapproving. "I don't want to," I said.

He looked hurt. "Fine," he said. He lingered in place for a moment. "Fine with me," he repeated, curtly now. "Just make sure you shut the garage," he said as he walked out.

9

The Hypocrites

W hat I did next I can't explain.

Once Father was gone, I went back to the tarps and pulled
the bottle out. Grabbing a hand spade from the shelf covered
with gardening tools, I walked out of the garage into the
backyard. At the end of the lawn, to the right, was Father's
vegetable garden. To the left was a grove of birches. I headed
for the trees.

The night sky was heavy and brown, and the air was thick
with the cries of crickets. As I got to the trees, a branch
snapped and something brushed against my head. I looked up.
Large white wings beat without noise, then soared across our
roof to the oaks on the other side. I dropped to my knees and
pulled at the earth with the spade. The ground was soft, and it
didn't take me long to dig a hole just bigger than the bottle.

I undid the bottle's cap, sniffing at the mouth. The putrid,
smoky odor made no sense. It was unfathomable that anyone
would want to drink this. I poured the rest of the whiskey into
the hole, then laid the bottle inside. I stood up and jumped,
coming down on the glass. It took me three tries, and then it
finally cracked. I jumped again, and the bottle broke apart into
shards. Kneeling, I poured dirt back into the hole. When I was
finished, I stood up. I held my open palms before me, as we

Muslims did to address Allah with our prayers. And I looked up at the sky.

Forgive him, I whispered.

Mentioned in a footnote in the Quran Mina had given me was the tradition that anyone caught drinking alcohol was subject to forty lashes, and that whoever wasn't caught—thereby escaping this earthly punishment—had far worse to expect in the hereafter: seventy years in hellfire. Just for a single drink.

Seventy years!

And the Quran left little to the imagination when it came to hellfire. We were told of pits and abysses filled with fire; homes of flame, with fire columns and fire for roofs; rooms of fire furnished with blazing couches and blazing beds; flaming garments fit to sinners' bodies, shoes and hats so hot they roasted wrongdoers' feet and boiled their brains. There was fire as food and molten drinks that torched the guts; springs of boiling water poured from flaming buckets, and eyeballs broiled in disbelievers' sockets; there were faces shorn of lips to smile with saws of flame; fire-blackened skin that sloughed off endlessly to reveal fresh skin to burn underneath. And finally, there was the fire itself, nothing at all like the fire we knew but seventy times hotter, fueled as it was not by wood or coal but an endless store of sinners...

For two days, I obsessed over what Father had ahead of him. The whiskey he drank from that bottle alone promised him more than two centuries of these tortures. Two hundred years! And that was just the bottle I knew about. How many more were there in his past? How many more would there be in the future? And what other misdeeds—his various mistresses, say—did he stand to be punished for?

Three days after burying the bottle, I went back to the

birch trees. I knelt, my eyes closed, at the small hump of dirt. Hunched and bent about my aching heart, I saw Father waving at me through the endless flames. I begged God to forgive him, to turn him away from his sins. I heard Father's cries of pain as the fires burned him. I imagined reaching in to pull him free. But even in my imagination, I couldn't. The fires were too hot. I was powerless.

There has to be something I can do, I thought. *There has to be...*

But of course there was!

I was already doing it!

I put my head to the ground, thanking God. I got up and wiped my eyes. I went back to the house, up to my room, where I shut the door. At my desk, I opened the Quran and picked up memorizing where I'd left off. This was what I'd realized in the birch grove: All I had to do was finish becoming a *hafiz*. When I was done, both my parents would be saved. That's what Mina had said. Every *hafiz* earned not only his own place in Paradise, but his parents' as well.

No matter how many drinks, no matter how many mistresses, Father would be saved.

The week that followed was witness to a formidable feat: I got through an entire *juz* of our holy book, over two hundred verses. I shared my astonishing progress with Mina. We sat in the dining room—where I'd found her reading a book—and she followed along in my Quran, checking for mistakes as I went through the new verses. I only missed a single line. She was stunned.

"My God, *behta*," she said. "How long did that take you?"

"Three days."

"Three days?" she asked, shaking her head.

"Yes, Auntie."

"My God," she repeated. "You have a gift, *behta*...So which *surah* is next?"

"I don't know."

"Have you done *Surah Ya Sin* yet?" she asked.

I shook my head.

"Do it next. It's the heart of the Quran. What we read when someone dies...to help them into the next life." Mina turned the Quran's pages. "There it is," she said as she pushed the book across the table to me.

"What are you doing, Auntie?"

"What, *behta?*"

"It's not respectful. You should pick up the book and hand it to me."

Mina looked startled for a moment, as if smarting from my comment. Then she nodded.

"You're right," she said. She picked up the Quran and brought it to her lips, kissing the cover. "There...," she said, handing it to me now, open to a page that read "*Surah Ya Sin.*"

I settled back into my chair, murmuring the verses to myself.

Mina stopped me. "What are you doing?"

"Memorizing."

"But don't just start with memorizing. *Read* it first. See what it means."

"Okay."

"You're not just memorizing words. Words don't matter if you don't know what they mean."

"Okay, Auntie," I said.

"Don't just say *okay*, Hayat. I want to know that you understand what I'm saying."

"Intention is what matters, Auntie."

"That's right, *behta*. That's what I'm saying..."

She went back to reading her book. I went back to my Quran. At some point, I realized Mina was looking at me.

"*Behta?* What would you think if Dr. Wolfsohn became your uncle?"

I didn't understand. "How could he be my uncle?" I asked.

"We're thinking of getting married."

"Married?"

I felt my heart drop into a dark hole inside me.

"But he's not Muslim," I said.

"He's going to convert, Hayat. He's going to become one of us." She was beaming.

"Why?" I asked coldly.

Her smile dimmed. "I don't understand what you're asking, Hayat."

She seemed suddenly unsure of herself. I looked down and marked my place on the page. Then I shut the Quran. "Why does he want to become a Muslim?" I asked again.

"Why do you think?" she asked. "Because he sees it's a wonderful way of life. What other reason?"

I stared at her without a reply.

Just then the phone rang.

"Hmm? What other reason could there be?" she repeated, defensive.

I continued to stare at her. She didn't move. The ringing stopped.

She looked away from me.

And then the ringing started again. "Let me see who that is," Mina said, getting up and going to the kitchen.

It was Nathan. She didn't say his name, but I could tell from her voice. "I'll call you back," she said tenderly.

I watched her disappear down the steps into the family room. She'd left her book behind, a thin, old hardcover, not unlike the one Nathan had given me. I wondered what it was, and I wondered if he had written something inside as he'd done in mine.

I reached across and picked it up, opening to the title page. *"Heart of Darkness,"* it read. There was no message written inside, only an address inscribed in a corner of one of the blank pages:

Mina Suhail
Dawes Lines Rd 14
Karachi, Pakistan

I shut the book's cover and set it down.

That evening, I sat with Mother in the family room, and she explained to me what was happening. She and Mina had both come to the conclusion that Mina's parents were not going to accept Nathan unless he became a Muslim.

I was dumbfounded. The idea hadn't even been his own!

"Does he really believe?" I asked.

"He believes in his love for Mina-Auntie," Mother replied, her eyes liquid with reverie.

"But does he *believe?*" I repeated, insistent.

Mother looked confused. "What's wrong with you, Hayat? Are you hungry or something?"

"I want to know if he really believes."

"Believes what?"

If, in my growing religious fervor, I'd been somewhat unclear about my mother's relationship to our faith, purposely turning a blind eye to all the outward signs of her lack of interest or commitment, that question made it clear to me just how ridiculous it was that she called herself a Muslim. "In the Prophet? In the Last Day? In Allah?"

"How should I know?" she said, casually shrugging off my pointed tone. "What matters is what the man is *doing*...He is making a wonderful *sacrifice*. For goodness' sake, he's abandoning his own people because of his love for your auntie. Do you know that his father is a Holocaust survivor? What do you think *he* will say about this? But what his father says doesn't matter to the man. He is in love with your auntie." Mother paused for effect, as if to impress upon me now the true importance of Nathan's decision. "What has your Father sacrificed for my sake? Hmm? Tell me! Not even one night's pleasure with one of his white *prostitutes*..."

I knew where this was headed. I wanted nothing to do with it.

"Hayat, are you listening to me?"

I looked up. "I thought Mina-Auntie's last name was Ali," I said abruptly.

Mother looked at me, confused—it seemed—not only by the question, but by its timing. "It is her last name."

"What's Suhail?"

"That was Hamed's name. Her first husband." And Mother paused. "Her *first* husband," she repeated to herself, smiling. "How wonderful," she said, turning to me again, "now she'll have a second!"

They're hypocrites, I thought. *All of them.*

My resolve early that winter not to look directly on my lower parts had become a reflex. It had been months since I'd looked at myself there. But the following Saturday, I would have to break my own interdiction.

I awoke after sunrise, the curtains on my windows barely showing light. Something was wrong. I felt pain between my legs, like an aching hole. I got out of bed and pulled my pajamas down. My soft penis was covered with dried, flaking skin. And the front of my pajama bottom was crusty, hardened, the inside of its surface covered with a whitish film.

I headed to the bathroom, where I picked at the skin on my penis. The pieces peeled off with ease. I couldn't understand the pain. *Maybe I'm sick,* I thought. But somehow I knew that wasn't it.

I washed myself between my legs.

Back in my room, I put on another pajama bottom, hiding the one I'd worn under the bed. I went to my prayer rug in the corner of the room. Facing east, I lifted my hands to my ears...

"Allah hu akbar..."

...and began the morning prayer.

I had difficulty praying, at least as Mina had instructed me. I couldn't keep the thought of God close to me, not with the aching in my loins, and the nagging sense that something wasn't right.

When I was done, I slipped back into bed, but I couldn't sleep. At some point, I realized Mother was standing in the doorway, staring at me. "You're up, *kurban?*" she asked, crossing from her place at the jamb to my bedside.

I considered telling her about the pain. "I did my *fajr* prayers," I said instead.

She shook her head. "You put me to shame, Hayat. Either that, or you'll end up making me a better Muslim." She lingered over me, looking lost.

"I'm going to be a *hafiz,* Mom. You don't have to worry about that. Then you'll go to heaven, too."

"Oh, *behta.* You have such a good heart," she said, sniffling. "I love you so much."

"I love you too, Mom."

Hearing this, Mother sat down beside me, her hands to her face. She started to cry.

I reached out and touched her back. Now she crumpled onto the bed, sobbing in my arms. When her tears had run their course, she pulled away and looked at me.

"You're going to be a good Muslim. But you'll treat women right, won't you, *behta?* You'll be the exception…a good Muslim man who has respect for a woman, no?"

"Yes, Mom."

"And you'll give her a chance to be a woman. You'll give her the chance to take care of you, a chance to love you…"

I didn't understand what she was saying, but I was emphatic: "Yes, Mom. I will. I promise."

She nodded, looking unrelieved. "What do you say to a man who pays no attention to you? Or your feelings? What can you tell such a man?"

Her tone was insistent. Pleading. But I didn't know what to answer. She went on, her voice faltering with another surge of emotion:

"This morning we were together, *behta*…And he won't speak to me. Not a *word*. I want him to talk about himself, tell me what he's thinking, feeling…Anything. But he won't do it." Her darting eyes stilled, settling on a thought. "It's his mother, you know. What a horrible woman. You're so lucky you weren't cursed with a monster like that. It's one thing you can never overcome, *kurban,* a terrible mother. And then when his sister died, the woman only got worse. Sitting on a prayer rug morning, noon, and night. She wasn't even a mother, really, when you think about it. It destroyed him. There are so many things he is missing. Missing *pieces.* That's why I'm working so hard to give you the pieces he doesn't have. So you can have a wonderful relationship with a wonderful woman someday. Having a good partner is the greatest blessing in life. The Prophet said it! And so did Freud! Your father has a wonderful partner and he doesn't even know it!"

She looked up at the ceiling as she continued: "What he really wants, truly...I will never know. I mean, this morning we had *such* a beautiful moment together." She turned to me, her eyes suddenly glistening. "When you grow up, *kurban,* you'll understand the kinds of things a man and woman can share. Beautiful things. We were sharing such a beautiful moment together. All I wanted was to know how he was feeling! That's all! And if he didn't want to say anything, he should just tell me. But no! Instead he finds a way to hurt me. He's a cruel man. All he had to do was *not* say anything instead of what he said..."

I was confused. I thought she was upset because he hadn't spoken when she wanted him to. Now she was complaining that he *had* spoken and shouldn't have.

"When you grow up, sweetie, and when you're with a woman, a good woman, be sure you learn this lesson: Never talk to her about *other* women. She should be the only woman for you. And even if you are thinking about another woman, for whatever reason, don't tell her about it. Keep it to yourself. It's cruel and cowardly to do anything else."

She paused, her gaze narrowing as she looked into me deeply.

"He doesn't like my mouth, he told me. Not the way he likes the mouths of his white prostitutes. Free hearts, free minds, free mouths, he said. Not like Eastern women, who are heavy and dark and *mentally imprisoned,*" she said, mocking his delivery. "What the filthy man really means is that they'll put their mouths anywhere, like animals. So he can put his mouth anywhere. Like an animal. That's what they want and that's what they like. It's *disgusting*." She paused, her own mouth contorted with pain. "If that's what he wants, so be it. But he'll never get *me* to do it."

I didn't understand. Where did Father want to put his mouth?

She went on: "Listen to me, Hayat. Listen to me and never forget what I'm telling you. If you give yourself to filth and garbage, you will become filth and garbage. You will become the sum of what you desire. Your desires make you what you are." I was still trying to figure out where Father wanted to put his mouth, and as I heard her say "filth and garbage," an image popped into my mind: Father, with a white woman by his side, both of them leaned over a heap of garbage, picking at pieces of trash with their teeth.

"Promise me, *behta*. Promise me you won't end up like him. That you won't live your life like him. That you won't do things that you know you shouldn't do. Promise me, *kurban*. Promise."

"I promise," I said.

Mother started to cry again, now burying her face in my pillow. Her sobbing shook the mattress. I held her tightly. When she finally stopped—my neck and arm dripping wet from her tears—we fell asleep in each other's arms.

That afternoon, Nathan showed up looking like he'd heard about my reaction to his decision to convert: He was wearing a white knit skullcap, he hadn't shaved, and when he greeted me, it was with his hand held over his heart and a quiet "*Salaam alaikum.*" Somehow, his complexion looked different to me now than it had on the night of July Fourth. In his skullcap, with the reddish stubble growing in along his chin and cheeks, Nathan looked swarthier. Healthy. More like one of us.

Mother took Imran to the grocery store, leaving me with Mina and Nathan. Mina made three cups of tea, one for each of us, and told me I could have mine only on the condition that I didn't tell Mother about it.

That was fine with me.

"You want sugar, Hayat?" Nathan asked.

"Sure."

Nathan dropped a spoonful in my cup. Then turned to Mina: "Meen?"

"Sure, Nate. But after you."

"No. Tell me how much." Nathan's spoon was showing a small half teaspoon's worth.

"That's good."

"A little more?" he asked with a smile. Mina held his gaze, smiling as well.

"Just a bit," she replied coyly. Nathan dipped the spoon into the small sugar jar again, then dropped it in Mina's cup of tea.

"There you go," Nathan said with a flourish.

"Thank you, Nate."

"Don't thank me...Just return the favor," he said, pushing the jar across to her. He was performing. So was she. But I wasn't sure who for.

"How much?" she asked.

"One is good."

Mina held his gaze, dropping the spoon into his cup and stirring.

Nathan didn't break eye contact as he lifted the cup to his lips and sipped.

"Mmm. Perfect. You're so *sweet,* Meen. You know that?"

Mina chuckled. "Nate, that was a terrible pun."

"It's not a pun. It's the truth. You are sweet. The sweetest thing I know."

Now Mina sipped, still holding his gaze. "You're the one who's sweet."

"No, you are."

"No, *you* are."

"No, *you* are..."

"Okay. We're both sweet."

I found it hard to believe that it took them so long to notice me glaring. But as soon as they did, they shifted in their chairs. Nathan cleared his throat.

"How's your tea, Hayat?" he asked.

"Good."

"So listen, Hayat. I was thinking, there's a story I want to tell you."

"What is it?"

"About Abraham."

"Hazrat Ibrahim, *behta*," Mina added. Nathan looked over at Mina.

"Right, Ibrahim as he's called in the Quran...I wanted to tell you a little bit about the man that the Prophet, *peace be upon him,* respected so much. He used to call Ibrahim the true father of Islam."

I turned to Mina when he said this. She nodded.

So Nathan proceeded with his story of Ibrahim, the man he described as the one destined to bring the truth of the one and only God to the world. He told the story I would later read in the Quran: Ibrahim, son of a builder of idols, who, even as a young boy, thought the statues his father made were ridiculous. He couldn't understand why people expected a piece of stone or wood to help or harm them. The statues never ate the offerings worshippers laid before them; they couldn't move or talk. Why did anyone believe these idols had any power at all?

One day, young Ibrahim went up into the mountains. And

it was here Allah would reveal the truth to him. While staring at the sky, Ibrahim realized that some people worshipped stars and others the moon and others still the sun, but that there was only One who had created all these things that appeared and disappeared. And Ibrahim realized this One was God, the one and only Lord of the Universe. And in that very moment, Ibrahim heard the heavens say his name:

"O Ibrahim!"

And he knew it was the Lord speaking to him.

Ibrahim fell on the ground, crying out: "I submit to you, Lord of the Universe!"

Ibrahim went back to his people to share the truth with them. He reasoned and debated and bore witness to the miracle he'd experienced. No one listened. His enraged father threatened to stone him if he rejected the idols. But Ibrahim didn't relent. He went to the riverfront altars, where the idols had been gathered for a religious holiday, the food offerings laid out before them. "Can you eat this food?" Ibrahim yelled at the statues. They kept silent. "What is the matter with you that you don't speak?" he mocked.

And then he raised his ax and smashed the false gods.

Ibrahim was arrested. The people decided to burn him alive for what he'd done. They dug a deep pit and filled it with fire, then threw Ibrahim inside. But the flames didn't burn him, for Allah had decreed that the fire be only coolness and safety for him. And so Ibrahim sat in the flames and did not burn, and when he emerged, the people were amazed. He told the king the truth of our Lord, and finally people started to follow him. And so it was that Ibrahim became the first prophet of Islam.

I kept looking over at Mina as Nathan told his tale. She nodded all the way. When he was finished with the story, he had this to say: "Ibrahim had two sons, Hayat. Did you know that? One of them was named Isaac..."

"And the other was Ismail," I said, completing his sentence.

"Right, Ishmael...So from Isaac's sons came the Jews, and from Ishmael's sons came the Muslims. That means all of us here at this table are children of Abraham."

Mina was watching him, proud. She reached out and took his hand, pressing tightly.

He smiled at her, then at me.

I wasn't sure what to make of it all, but I smiled back.

Nathan was staying for dinner. Which meant when Mother got home from the store—looking almost as miserable and beat up as she had that morning while crying in my bed—the task of babysitting Imran fell on me. I took him down into the family room, where we built a tent from bedsheets taped together and held up at various points with poles pilfered from the mudroom's mops and brooms. I called this motley construction our castle keep. We transferred enough of our things inside—toys (for him), a Quran (for me), and a chess board and pillows (for both of us)—to have no foreseeable reason to ever leave again.

We started with a game of chess. I'd since relented on my vow to never play with him again, and he'd been doing his best to abide by rules that, in fairness to him, could not have been easy for a five-year-old to learn. But he was working at it. Like his mother, Imran was intelligent, and now that he actually wanted to learn, he was playing better chess than anyone could have expected for his age.

Imran had already heard my basics of chess strategy many times, the three rules I'd learned in Mr. Marshak's third-grade chess club: get your pieces out; protect your pieces once they're in play; control the center of the board. We went through the rules again that afternoon before beginning a new game, and a few minutes into it, I asked him if he remembered them. He repeated the first two rules back to me, but couldn't recall the last. So I went over it again. And when, after another move, I asked him to repeat what I'd taught him, he still couldn't remember the last rule.

"You don't have a very good memory, do you?" I sniped.

He looked confused. I leaned forward and took hold of his arms. "Control. The. Center. Of. The. Board."

"Control the center of the board."

"Repeat it," I said.

He did. But it wasn't enough for me. "Don't forget it," I said, still holding his arms.

"I won't, *bhaiya*," he replied, starting to whine. I'd been ignoring the fact that he'd recently been calling me "brother," but the fact was, he was starting to feel like a little brother after all.

"You want me to play with you, right?"

"Yes," he whimpered.

"Then don't whine, *bhai*."

He nodded, his eyes lighting up to hear me use the word.

I held on, tighter.

"I want you to remember something else, too," I said, grave. "Look around you. Do you see this? Do you see the sheets? The castle keep? Do you see all this?"

He nodded, alarmed.

"We are in our castle keep. We are here, inside it. It is around us. I want you to remember this moment *right now*. I want you to remember and never forget it for the rest of your life." I repeated it over and over. He kept saying he wouldn't forget. Something in me finally satisfied, I let him go.

Mina appeared at the entrance. "How beautiful," she said. "Can I join you boys?"

166

"Is it okay?" I asked Imran. He thought for a second, then nodded, and Mina came crawling in on all fours.

"Where's Nathan?" I asked.

"He went home, *behta*," she said as she took up one of Imran's *Star Wars* figures and began to play with her son. Imran took the figure from her hand and showed her how to hold it. "Like this," he explained, frustrated, "not like that." Mina looked at me, shrugging. She couldn't really tell the difference.

Drifting down from the kitchen was a vaguely unpleasant, slightly ammoniac odor.

"What's that smell?" I asked.

"Your mom's cooking kidneys, Lahori style," Mina said with eagerness.

"Smells like rubber."

"Maybe. But they don't taste like that."

"Never had them."

Mina's expression contracted with disbelief. "I don't believe that, *behta*. You must have had them. They're your father's favorite meal."

"So why is she cooking them?"

"What do you mean, *behta*?"

"If they're Dad's favorite, why is she cooking them?"

"She wanted to do something nice for your father."

"Why?" I asked, sharply.

"Why?" Mina looked surprised at my question.

"Forget about it," I said, crawling out of the tent.

If Mother's intention had been to please her husband, she succeeded. He sighed with pleasure, shoveling kidneys and *chapatti* into his mouth, looking over at his wife between bites. "Just like in Lahore, Muneer. Just like back home."

She was glowing. He took another bite, shaking his head. "Magic...just magic."

"I'm glad you like them, Naveed," Mother said.

Father swallowed the morsel in his mouth. "What would I do without you?"

Mother shrugged, seeming both eager and embarrassed by the directness of the question. Father was relishing the moment.

"I'll tell you what," he said, brightly. "I would lose myself. That's what would happen." Father turned to Mina. "This woman keeps me honest."

"That's a good thing," Mina said.

"And not only that...," he said, mischief in his eye as he reached out and touched Mother's arm.

She blushed, looking down with a schoolgirl giggle.

Was I dreaming? That morning, she'd sobbed in my arms over Father and his mouth—a conundrum that still eluded me—yet here she was now, blushing and grinning and giggling as if nothing had ever happened.

Father looked over at me, chewing. "How do you like them?"

"They smell like rubber. And they taste like it, too."

"All the better for me. I'll have them for breakfast tomorrow," he said in a strange high-pitched voice, as if playing some comic character. He just sounded silly to me.

"Take them," I said, pushing the plate away.

Mother reached for the bread basket to take a *chapatti*. "Here," she said. "Finish this with your yogurt and then you can go."

"I don't like kidneys either," Imran added.

For once, Mina wasn't accommodating. "You finish your food, Imran. Everything on your plate. No discussion." Her tone was firm.

Imran stared at her, and then looked over at Father, who leaned in over his plate and started to coo. "Mmm, so good," Father hummed, licking his lips. Imran started to laugh as he watched Father push another morsel into his mouth and begin to chew with exaggerated zeal. "Mmm," he continued, pointing at everyone's plate, "I'm going to finish *these* and finish *those*...and I'll have those, too. I'll have them *all!*" he growled with a gravelly faux-monster grumble. And as he reached out for Imran's plate, the boy leaned forward and tossed a bite into his own mouth, chewing through a wide smile.

Mother giggled some more. Mina laughed, too.

I wanted to pinch myself.

As we wrapped up dinner, Mina told my parents she was going to take care of the dishes. So Mother and Father got up and did something else they never did:

They went for a walk together.

After loading the dishwasher and wiping down the table, Mina whisked me up to her room, where she lavished on Imran and me the tale of the Prophet's night journey to Paradise. She recounted the trip made on the back of a magical horse called the Burak, a creature with an eagle's wings and a lion's head who, with a single bound, flew the Prophet from Arabia to Sinai to see where Moses spoke to God, and with another bound landed at the spot in Bethlehem where Jesus was born, and finally to Jerusalem, where a gleaming ladder descended from the heavens.

The Burak—with the Prophet on its back—climbed its hundred rungs, ascending into Paradise.

Through gates of emerald and pearl, the Prophet rode the Burak through heaven, beholding every splendor it had to offer, the palaces of gold set into the clouds, the fountains and

rivers of milk and honey and wine that inspired without in-
toxicating, the hordes of virgins and praising angels and each
and every one of the Almighty's human prophets. Muhammad greeted them all, and they prayed together in a diamond
mosque. Then he climbed again on the Burak and they flew
farther and farther upward, through veils of light upon light,
to the limit of creation itself. Finally, they came to the place
where the Burak would go no farther.

Here the Prophet looked up and saw a tree as large as the
universe. This was Sidrat al-Muntaha, the farthest tree of the
farthest boundary. Now the Burak left him. No one, not even
Gabriel, had ever ventured so far. This was where Allah lived.

Our Prophet stepped forward and entered the Lord's presence.

"Almighty God," Muhammad said, "let me see You."

And all at once, he saw nothing but the Lord. He looked to
the right and saw nothing but the Lord, and to the left and
saw nothing but the Lord, and to the front, and the back, and
above...and everywhere he looked, he saw nothing but the
Lord. What the Lord looked like Muhammad would never say,
other than that His beauty was so great he would have preferred to stand there gazing at Him forever. But the Lord told
him: "You are a Messenger, and if you stay here, you will not
communicate My Message. Go back to the world. But when
you want to see Me as you see Me now, make your prayers,
and I will appear before you."

"That's why we pray, *behta,*" Mina explained. "To know
Allah in the same way that Muhammad did when he took his
night journey."

I asked her what Muhammad himself looked like.

Mina took a long time to reply. "I never met him, *behta.* But
I had a teacher in high school, a great man, Dr. Khan. He met

the Prophet, *peace be upon him,* in a dream. He said he was a handsome man, with long eyelashes and thick black hair. He said he had a full beard and a beautiful smile that showed a gap between his two front teeth."

"But how do you know if that's how he looked? It was just a dream..."

"Dreams are very important, *behta.* In Islam, we believe they can show you things that are more real than what we see when we're awake. And when the Prophet visits someone in a dream, it's a very important sign."

"Of what, Auntie?"

"Of great holiness. It means the Prophet is watching over you."

Story hour had not calmed me. I left Mina's room still agitated, wondering why it was God lived so impossibly far from us all. Instead of heading for my bedroom, I went downstairs to the kitchen, where Mother was fiddling with the trash. She looked up and saw me. "Here," she said blankly, handing me the bag. "Take it out for pickup."

I took it, lingering at the counter. She stood at the sink, washing her hands and humming to herself. I wanted her to look at me again. She finally did. "What is it, Hayat? I'm not in the mood for your humors this evening. Go, already!"

Outside, it was a heavy, hot July night. The lawn was awash with insects. Flickering fireflies, roaring crickets. Something was hurting inside. Something raw. I trudged along the front lawn, headed for the garbage cans at the end of the driveway.

What's wrong with you? I wondered.

As I got to the cans, I stopped. The pain inside was throbbing, insistent. It seemed there was something I had to do, but I didn't know what.

I remembered what Mina had taught me. I closed my eyes and breathed.

In and out. In and out.

Beneath the crickets, beneath the wind in the trees, despite the stench of trash.

I listened for the silence. And then I heard something. It was a voice, firm, cold, convincing:

You can't even take out the garbage. You're useless.

I opened my eyes. At the end of the street, a pair of tiny lights was slowly growing. As a car's black form began to show, the engine's tinny wail deepened into a rough and noisy rumble. The car was moving with unusual speed, and as it approached, the sound it made was painful to hear. It was a sound to be heard and heeded.

I stepped out into the road, staring into the headlights.

The horn blasted. The trash fell from my grip. Behind the windshield, eyes flashed wide with alarm. The engine roared as the car careened, swerving away, missing me by barely a yard.

All at once, blood was exploding through my veins.

The car disappeared down the road, horn still blaring. My heart was pounding; my knees felt like they were going to fall out from under me. I picked up the trash and stumbled back to the cans. Opening a lid, I dumped the bag inside. Then I sat down on the pavement. I looked back at the house. The lights were on upstairs, behind Mina's closed blinds.

Above me, the white oaks swayed, their branches groaning beneath the chatter of windswept leaves. I thought of Sidrat al-Muntaha, the tree that marked the place where God lived.

Why so far away? I wondered. *Why?*

I stared up at the trees, their twisting branches silhouetted against a turbid night. Far above, behind the murky cover of thick, low-hanging clouds, there was a bright spot: the hidden moon lighting its patch of sky, its glow strong enough to limn the forms of racing, roiling clouds beneath it. *Don't waste your time,* I thought. *Go back and read your Quran.* I pushed myself to my feet and started up the driveway. But the truth was: I didn't want to go back. Not to read Quran or for any other reason.

I didn't want to go home.

BOOK THREE

Portrait of an Anti-Semite as a Boy

10

The Mosque on Molaskey Hill

How vivid was my melancholy as the summer progressed! Nothing gave me solace. Not spending time with Mina. Not reading the Quran. Gone were the days when I was moved to awe at the sight of the sky. God's glory was nothing to me, and in its place was a new and growing torment: my recollection of Mina's naked body. The image I thought I'd taught myself to forget would return, unbidden—her breasts; the thick, dark triangle at the top of her legs—and hours of confusion and unrest would ensue. I made fresh attempts to suppress the mental picture. To no avail. The more I resisted, the more persistent it proved. And now this image of Mina was making my short, soft penis grow long and hard. I had no idea what was going on. And I didn't know who to talk to.

One afternoon early that August, I took that photograph of Mina down from the refrigerator. I don't know why I had the thought I did, but it occurred to me that if, each time I found myself thinking of Mina's naked body, I had the picture to look at instead, it would distract me. For a few days, it worked. But then something curious started to happen. When I looked at the photograph, I would feel the stir and tumult that my recollection of her nakedness brought about.

More than once, I had the urge to touch myself as I held and looked at that picture of her. I would lay my hands between my legs through my shorts or jeans, or through my pajamas. I never touched myself directly. But even so, the pleasure was intense. And it would fill me with a blazing fullness.

One night I lost myself. Mina's picture before me, my hands between my legs, I disappeared into pleasure. Before I knew it, my loins shuddered and convulsed, releasing something thick and wet inside my underwear. Horrified, I unbuttoned and saw myself hard and straight, covered with gobs of milky substance. It had a strong, acrid smell, like bleach.

You knew it was something wrong, a voice inside me spoke.

My sudden shame was sharp, overwhelming. *I'll never do it again,* I thought.

The second week of August, Nathan took a trip home alone to discuss his conversion with his parents. His father had lost much of his family in the Holocaust and, though an atheist, still deeply identified with his Jewish culture. Nathan expected his father might be shocked, perhaps even violently so. Which is why he thought it best to head home and to tell his parents on his own, and to wait to introduce them to Mina on a separate visit.

He left midweek and was back on the weekend. Mina spent most of those few days on the phone with him. She was worried, though she would have little reason to be. Things with his parents would turn out just fine. Nathan's father had no objection to his son's plans, but he did have a warning:

No one will ever see you as anything other than a Jew, he told his son.

"He's wrong about that," Mother said to me one morning, cheerfully in the thick of parsing all the details. "It's what's different about us—once you're a Muslim, *that's* who you are. And it doesn't matter what you were or where you come from—it's a *true* democracy. Where everyone gets to vote."

"He's not voting, Mom. There's no election. He's just becoming a Muslim."

Mother's expression flattened. "Don't be a smart aleck, Hayat. You know what I mean."

She was right. I did. I just wasn't sure she really knew what she meant. For, if politics was—as in our yearly classroom election—about getting people to like you, then Nathan's interest in Islam really was more like politics than religion after all. More than either Mina or Mother realized.

Mina doted on Imran even more than usual while Nathan was away. Her agenda was clear: She was trying to get her son to soften to the thought of Nathan as his father. Mother called the whole situation with Imran an "absurdity." As she saw it, all Mina had to do was marry the man and force Imran to get used to it. "'*He* doesn't want a white father...,' Mother mocked. "Who in God's name cares what *he* wants? '*Why can't I have a father like Naveed-Uncle?*' The boy looks at your father and thinks that's what a father should look like. What he doesn't see... it's not the color *outside* that matters, but *inside*... And we all know your father is black on the inside! Black as pitch!" Mother paused, gathering herself. The halcyon days occasioned by her meal of Lahori-style kidneys had apparently not lasted very long. "I keep telling her... he's a *child*. Ignore him. But she doesn't. And then she starts to think: *If that's what he's saying, what will her family say...* Who *cares?!* What did *they* ever give up to make her happy? Nothing! Beating her for reading books, for God's sake. That's what they did! For someone so advanced, so intelligent, your auntie worries *too* much about what others think..." Mother sighed, considering. A subtle smile crept across her face. "*Kurban,* if I get this to work out, *I'm* the one who should be given that Nobel, not Sadat..."

By Sunday, Nathan was back. It was the day Father had agreed to accompany him to the South Side Islamic Center so that Nathan could introduce himself to the imam. Father asked me if I wanted to come along. I was ecstatic. Father almost never took me to the mosque. Of course I wanted to go, I told him.

Nathan showed up at the house late that morning wearing the same skullcap he'd worn the day he'd told his tale of Ibrahim. Father had never seen him in a *topi* skullcap before, and made no attempt to hide his surprise as we all stood in the vestibule before heading out.

"What the hell is wrong with you, Nate? Why are you wearing that thing on your head?"

"We're going to the mosque, Naveed."

"So?"

"I want to be respectful."

"I think he looks handsome," Mina said, proudly. "Don't you think, *bhaj?*"

"I *love* the *topi*," Mother said. She was holding Imran. "And the beard, too. It makes him look dignified."

Father rolled his eyes. "He already knows what I think of that growth on his face. But it's even worse with the *topi*. The man looks like a damn imam. You're a doctor, Nate. Not a *maulvi*."

"Not yet," Mina replied with a smile.

"God forbid," Father moaned.

Nathan pointed at me. "*He's* wearing one," he said.

Father shook his head. "He's a child, Nate. He doesn't know any better..."

Nathan looked at me, holding my gaze with a smile.

I looked away.

"Let's get going," Father said, pulling his keys from his pocket. "I can't believe I let you talk me into this. I really can't believe it."

"It's 'cause you love me, Naveed," Nathan said, playfully.

"It's true," Father said, suddenly serious. "I do."

For years, local Muslims had made do on religious holidays with impromptu prayer rooms hastily prepared in the banquet wings of area hotels. Adnan Souhef—a portly chemist from Jordan with enough religious education to pass for an imam—serviced the community's need to congregate by renting the rooms out and getting them ready for worship the night before either of the biannual Eid festivals: covering coffee-stained carpets with white sheets—bleached and ironed—on which worshippers could pray; erecting a *mihrab* (prayer niche) to indicate the direction of Mecca; raising a curtain to separate the sexes; and finally, installing the PA system that allowed the women on the other side of that curtain to hear the *khutbah* (sermon) that Souhef would deliver before the prayer. For ten years, this was the routine; ten years, for that's how long it took Souhef to raise enough money not to have to make do any longer.

By 1980, Souhef and his consortium of local Muslim-American professionals had enough saved to fund the purchase of a permanent home. And so it was that, for the price of a quarter of a million dollars, the Molaskey Schoolhouse—an abandoned glory in the middle of a Polish neighborhood on the South Side—would become our first Islamic Center.

Named for the hill on which it was perched, the Molaskey Schoolhouse stood four stories tall, a solid stone-and-brick block of a building complete with rounded towers and conical roofs. It looked more like a fort than a mosque. Overlooking the southbound highway, its Romanesque Revival façade (complete with Gothic gables) was dark with years of exhaust from passing cars. Empty of the children who'd once passed along its hallways and played on its lots—and whose presence would have softened the austere, forbidding impression—the Islamic Center gave off a sinister, even haunted air.

"There it is," Father said as he turned off the highway and merged onto the steeply canted Molaskey Street.

"How funny," Nathan said. "I've seen it from the highway a thousand times. I always thought it was abandoned."

"Would be better for us all if it was," Father said. We climbed another twenty yards, then turned into a parking lot filled with cars. "There he is," Father said in a joking tone.

"Who?" Nathan asked.

Father pointed over at the front steps as he pulled into an empty spot. "The king clown himself . . . or king *crook,* I should say." He was pointing at Imam Souhef, who was standing on the stairs and smoking a cigarette.

"Who is that?"

"Imaaam Souhaaaif." Father drew out the syllables for mocking effect, throwing the car into park.

"Why are you calling him a crook?"

"Did you ever meet a man of God who loved God half as much as he loved money?"

Nathan was peering out the window, intrigued.

"You hear me, Nate?"

"I heard you . . . To be honest—yes, Naveed. I have met men of God who love God more than money."

"In books," Father snickered.

"No. When I was a kid. My dad had a close friend who was

a rabbi. He was a good man. Genuinely. A *really* good man. People in his synagogue adored him."

"Well, go back there, Nate! Go back!" Father said, pushing at Nathan playfully. "I don't know what you're doing here..."

Nathan shook his head as he popped open the passenger-side door. He paused before getting out. "Naveed, I need to make a good impression on these people. I'm probably gonna need this guy in some way..."

Father waved Nathan off. "Don't worry. I'll be on my best behavior..."

"Thanks."

"Just don't come complaining when he bleeds you dry for consulting services and fees."

"Fees? For what?"

"Your conversion. Your this. Your that. And God only knows what else."

From the front steps, Souhef watched us as we made our way toward him. He was a sight to behold: his girth filling out the shimmering, silk-woven robe that flowed and billowed about his imposing frame; his unusually long, gray-black beard, its tapered tip swaying in the blistering August breeze; and on his head, the white skullcap that gleamed, like a solar panel, flat and bright in the midday sun. Father had known Souhef a long time—the two of them had been among the first of our kind to move into the area—and I'd heard more than an earful about the man over the years. For her part, Mother never took anything Father said about Souhef seriously. She couldn't understand why Father even bothered to offer an opinion about an imam. After all, a man who drank and cheated on his wife couldn't claim to have any *credibility,* she liked to say. As for my own feelings about Souhef, on the rare occasions that I ever saw him, I was drawn to the man. He had a command-

ing presence, and though his sermons could be terrifying—
filled with Islamic fire and brimstone, and delivered with decisive and pitiless passion—I always recalled his very palpable
warmth. To many of the Muslims in our community, Souhef
was a guardian angel. He presided over births and marriages
and deaths, made midnight house calls in cases of spiritual
crisis and domestic conflict, and even interceded with local authorities in matters as unremarkable as a Muslim boy who'd
been barred from gym class for refusing to shower publicly in
the locker room.

But despite Souhef's very obvious devotion to our community, Father didn't like him. He conceded the man was
committed, but to his pocketbook, Father liked to say. As
proof, he told the story of Souhef's first approaching him ten
years earlier, when the Islamic Center was nothing more than
a proposal scratched out in Souhef's hand on a piece of paper.
Souhef asked Father for a donation. Father declined. A few
months later, Souhef came back to ask for money again, but
now saying it was on behalf of a Palestinian immigrant in dire
straits. Souhef told Father a tale about a man who'd escaped
torture at the hands of Israelis and was fighting to stay in this
country. Father was moved and pulled out his checkbook.

"Who do I write the check to?"

"To me," Souhef replied.

"To you?"

"Brother Shah, don't doubt me. He's a poor man. He doesn't
know about banks and checks and things like that. He'll get
the money. As Allah is my witness."

Father was still skeptical, but he wrote a check for a thousand dollars anyway.

Over the next few weeks and months, Father asked Souhef
for news about the Palestinian. He was perplexed that he'd

never heard from the man, not a call to thank him, not a note. Souhef was always evasive. Until, one day, he told Father that the Palestinian had been picked up by immigration and deported. That was the only confirmation Father needed: He'd long since concluded that the Palestinian had been Souhef's ruse to get Father to cough up cash. From that day on, Father wanted nothing more to do with him.

"How are those brains doing, Doctor?" Souhef asked playfully as we approached the mosque steps. He stood above us, a cigarette between his lips, glancing at Nathan, then back at Father.

"Fine, Adnan," Father replied, curtly.

"*Mashallah,*" Souhef responded, laying his right hand—which was bandaged—against his heart. I was surprised at the warmth of his gesture; I wondered if he had noticed Father's coldness, or if he was just ignoring it. "So tell me, Naveed—are you any closer to discovering the secret of life?"

"Didn't know there was one."

"There is, brother. There is," Souhef replied with a wry smile, drawing on his cigarette.

"Guess we'll have to wait until we can lay you out and figure out what's going on in that brain of yours, Adnan."

"Won't be worth your while. Nothing up there but air. Air and homesickness," Souhef said, his mouth leaking smoke. He glanced at me, smiling.

I smiled back.

Just then, three men passed us. They climbed the steps, each placing his right hand on his heart to greet the imam: "*Assalamulaikum,* Imam."

"*Valaikum-salaam,*" Souhef replied with a short nod.

The men stopped as they got to the top of the stairs, looking back at Nathan. Nathan nodded. "*Assalamulaikum,*" he said.

Surprised, the men broke into bright smiles. "*Valaikum-salaam*," they replied, lingering at the door. One of them nodded again, reiterating his greeting. Nathan repeated his own. The men nodded some more and finally went inside.

I noticed Souhef studying Nathan intently.

Father cleared his throat. "Adnan...I'd like you to meet my colleague at the lab, Nathan Wolfsohn. Nathan...Adnan Souhef, the imam here at the Islamic Center."

"Pleasure to meet you, sir," Nathan replied, nervously offering his hand. The imam showed his bandaged hand. "Excuse me, brother," he said, putting his hand to his heart instead.

"What happened to your hand, Adnan?" Father asked.

"I was fixing the sink. I hurt it."

"Are you okay?"

"A nasty cut, Naveed. But it's fine. It actually served as inspiration for me. For today's *khutbah*..."

There was an awkward pause as Father didn't respond.

Souhef turned to Nathan. "So what brings you to us, brother?"

"I have an interest in Islam," Nathan began stiffly, as if repeating something he'd rehearsed. "I have interest in your way, sir...in the way of submission as I understand it."

Father looked out at the parking lot, embarrassed. My gaze followed his. On the lot, the rows of parked cars shimmered and shook in the waves of heat coming up from the hot asphalt. The bitter odor of softening tar filled the air. "More people every time I'm here, Adnan," Father said, turning back to Souhef. "You've got a good racket going..."

"Racket?"

"You know...operation."

Souhef stared at Father without replying. Father stared back. The tension between them was palpable.

"If Allah is pleased, brother, then we are, too," Souhef responded remotely, his lips closing around the filter of his cigarette as he pulled in more smoke. I noticed that though I was covered in sweat—and so were Nathan and Father—there wasn't a sign of perspiration anywhere on the imam, not his face, not his hands. Souhef finally turned away from Father, exhaling. "Brother Nathan. Is your interest in our way curiosity or something more? I hope you don't mind if I ask..."

"No, I don't mind, Imam," Nathan replied, still nervous. "Umm—actually, to be honest, it started as curiosity. But the more I've learned about Islam...the more personal my interest has become."

"I see."

"I hope it's okay if I'm here," Nathan added.

Souhef smiled. "Of course, you're welcome to join us, brother. Just be sure to remove your shoes downstairs. Naveed will show you...and please take a place at the back of the room for the prayer." Souhef took a final drag, smoking the cigarette down to its filter. "What's your tradition, brother?"

"Well...I was born into the Jewish faith."

I noticed a sudden feline glint in Souhef's eye. "People of the book," he said.

"Thank you, Imam," Nathan said.

Souhef continued: "We all come from Ibrahim. Our Jewish brothers from Isaac. Muslims from Ishmail..."

Nathan glanced over at me.

"You know our Quran, brother, don't you?" Souhef asked.

"I do, Imam. I've been learning."

"Allah's greatest miracle."

"Indeed."

"The very sounds of reality itself," Souhef added in an impressive tone. "The great song of the atoms and molecules crying out Allah's praise."

"The music of the spheres," Nathan added eagerly.

Father rolled his eyes.

Souhef nodded, smiling, and tossed the filter to the steps. He looked as if he were about to go inside when he paused. A gaunt man in an ash-gray suit was making his way from among the cars toward us. It was Ghaleb Chatha. I hadn't seen him since that December night more than two years earlier, when he'd explained the curse on the Jews. He looked different: his beard was thick and full now, covering most of his pockmarked face, and his gray, lifeless eyes were bigger than I remembered.

"Brother Chatha," Souhef said warmly. Chatha stopped alongside Father, pressing his eyelids shut and offering the imam a slow, deliberate nod. He turned to Father, repeating the gesture, but with noticeably less warmth.

"Naveed. Good to see you here."

"Good to see you, too, Ghaleb," Father replied, without much conviction.

"To what should we attribute this honor?" Chatha asked. There was something mocking about his tone.

"To my friend," Father replied, turning to Nathan.

"I'm Nathan. Nathan Wolfsohn. Colleague and friend of Naveed's."

"Ghaleb Chatha, nice to meet you." Chatha greeted Nathan as he had the others, with a hand to his heart and a gentle pressing shut of his eyelids.

"Brother Chatha," Souhef began, "Nathan is here with us today because he is thinking of coming to the faith."

Chatha's blank stare brightened with surprise. He turned to Father. "Good work, Naveed," he said, impressed.

"Nothing to do with me, Ghaleb. If I had my way..."

Nathan threw Father a sharp look. Father took notice, and paused.

"I'm listening," Chatha said. "If you had your way...?"

"Well...we would be out on the water fishing right now..."

Chatha's surprise had already passed, giving way again to that blank, almost lifeless gaze. "Then it was Allah's will that you didn't have your way today. And so you have your friend here to thank for that..." Chatha looked at Nathan and smiled. "Welcome," he said.

Nathan brought his right hand to his heart and—like Chatha—pressed his eyelids shut.

Chatha looked down at me, noticing I was watching him. He smiled, his lips parting to reveal small teeth. "Pleased to see the boy here," he said to Father.

This time, Father didn't reply.

"Whatever your beliefs may be," Chatha continued, "it's so important to be teaching the boy about our way of life."

Again Father said nothing. Another group of men, about half a dozen of them, approached the steps. They muttered *salaam*s to us all as they climbed to the entrance, gazing back at Nathan, intrigued.

"If you'll excuse me, brothers," Souhef said, "I have to see about getting the sound system ready for the *khutbah*."

Nathan responded with a short, self-conscious bow.

"I'll join you, Imam," Chatha added. "I still have to perform my *wudu*."

The two men went up the steps—Souhef gliding with a grace that belied his heft—and at the top, Chatha opened the door for him. Souhef disappeared inside. Chatha followed. Once they were gone, Nathan turned to Father with a startled smile.

"I don't know what you're so happy about," Father grunted.

"That imam. He is so self-possessed. And kind. Not like the other guy."

"They're two peas from the same pod," Father said. "And as for Souhef being kind..."

"He was kind to me..."

"Let's just say that he's smart. You've no idea what they'll be saying about him if he can get you to convert. That Chatha will pour the money down his throat like champagne on New Year's Day."

Nathan wiped his sweat-covered forehead. "You're such a cynic, Naveed. You really have to work on that."

"Don't worry about me. You get yourself ready. We're heading into the Middle Ages." Father nodded, indicating the group of women in head scarves gathered at the door to an entrance at the other end of the schoolhouse marked WOMEN. Through the waves of rising heat, their sheeted forms hovered, like specters in a mirage. There were about a half dozen of them, all looking at us.

"What are they looking at?" Nathan asked.

"What do you think, Nate?" Father answered.

"Me?"

Father nodded.

Nathan smiled and waved. Spooked, the women turned away, floating to the doorway and disappearing inside.

Father clapped Nathan on the back. "Like I said, Nate. The Middle Ages."

Downstairs, the chanting was under way:

Allah hu akbar, Allah hu akbar, Allah hu
  akbar...
la illah ilallah...

We were in the shoe closet—an alcove outside the prayer room whose walls were covered with shelves of shoes—and the rumble of men's chanting voices came through the prayer room's double doors:

> *Allah hu akbar, Allah hu akbar, Allah hu*
> *akbar...*
> *la illah ilallah...*

Nathan stared at the closed doors, listening as he removed his docksiders. Behind us, a pair of young men hurried down the staircase and quickly slipped off their shoes. They pushed open the double doors, and the droning chant sharpened, its song clearer, more forceful:

> *Allah hu akbar, Allah hu akbar, Allah hu*
> *akbar...*
> *la illah ilallah...*

Nathan turned to Father, wonder in his voice. "What are they doing?"

"*Dhikr*. They do it before the prayer."

"It's beautiful," Nathan said.

Father nodded, peering into the room, a hint of moisture collecting at the corners of his eyes. "Yes, it is," he said.

The *dhikr*—or "remembrance"—was what I recalled most vividly from the few times I'd been to a mosque. Before the services, congregants assembled in the prayer room, and by the time there were six of them gathered, the chanting would begin, a simple hypnotic tune that cycled between two deep notes...

*Allah hu akbar, Allah hu akbar, Allah hu
     akbar...*

...until the final syllables trilled along an arpeggio of higher
pitches...

     ...la illah ilallah...

...only to end with a return to the chant's first note, completing the circle, and beginning it anew.

The chant would gain breadth and volume as worshippers
arrived and joined the choir. And as the numbers grew—from a
handful to dozens, or even hundreds on a religious holiday—an
ample sound would take shape, hovering over us—ringed and
round, magical—like the angels the Quran claimed watched
over all our human actions. There was something vast and ineffable about this bellowing in praise of the greatness of the one
and only God, a vivid, sensate beauty—I felt it against my ears,
along my back, inside my ribs—capable of bringing tears even
to the eyes of a person as hardened toward his faith as Father.

The prayer room was filled with a hundred men, their seated
bodies swaying in unison as they sang. The room itself—dark
and capacious, cavelike, a sometime basement cafeteria transformed now into a Muslim prayer room—seemed to bulge and
tremble with the holy song. Nathan looked over at me, shaking his head lightly in disbelief. "It's so beautiful," he muttered
again. I nodded. Seeing Nathan so moved by the *dhikr,* I felt
something in me soften.

I smiled. He smiled back, friendship in his eyes.

Father took a deep breath, murmuring to himself as he led
Nathan to a place at the back of the room. I went over to the
shelf where copies of the Quran were kept. There was only one

left. I took it, then made my way to an empty spot near the center of the room. Holding the Quran to my chest, I joined in:

Allah hu akbar, Allah hu akbar, Allah hu
akbar...
la illah ilallah...

Eager, I swayed as I chanted. But there wasn't much *dhikr* left that afternoon. By the time Father had taken his place beside me, Imam Souhef was already settling in by the *mihrab*. Father laid his hand on my knee. When he did, I realized: Mine was the only voice still singing.

Souhef hoisted himself onto the raised platform from which he delivered his sermons. Sitting cross-legged, he untied the bandage wrapped around his right hand, then fiddled with the microphone on the stand before him.

"Testing, testing. Can you hear me?" his voice blared, rough and tinny over the loudspeakers mounted on stands. Grunts and murmurs of assent rippled through the room. Someone coughed. Souhef adjusted the mike again, releasing a painful flare of feedback. "Excuse me, brothers," he said, playing with the cord, and adding with a chuckle, "And sisters, too." (The women two flights up, crowded into a considerably smaller prayer room—listening to his voice over loudspeakers—had, no doubt, heard the feedback as well.)

His palms open and raised before him, Souhef offered the brief invocation. Finished, he looked into the Quran open in his lap and began to speak:

"Brothers and sisters, please, if you have a copy of our holy Quran, open it to *Surah Al-Baqara,* 'The Cow.' Verses forty and forty-one."

The rustling of paper erupted in the room as those with

books searched for the pages. Souhef waited, his eyes trained on a distant horizon, or perhaps—I thought—on the new-comer, Nathan, who was sitting quietly against the back wall. Finally, there was silence again. Souhef looked down at the page, his eyes narrowed and gleaming, like polished blades. He began reading, his voice loud and lofty:

> O Bani Israel!
> Remember how I favored you.
> Fulfill your promise to Me. I will fulfill my prom-
>   ise to you.
> Of Me alone stand in awe!
> Believe in what I have given. Confirm the truth
>   you know. Be not the first to deny.
> Do not give away My revelations for a trifling
>   sum.
> Of Me alone be aware!

An uneasy swell rose from the crowd. "Bani Israel" was the Quran's way of referring to Jews. Father looked at me, a crease appearing on his forehead. He looked back at Nathan. I tried to do the same, but my view of the back wall was obscured by Ghaleb Chatha, who I was surprised to find sitting directly be-hind me.

Souhef continued, casually now, as if pleased that his declamatory reading had gotten our attention:

"Yesterday, my fellow Muslims, I hurt myself. While fixing my sink in the kitchen, I was using a wrench to open the pipe. The wrench slipped in my hand. My wrist slammed on the cor-ner of the cabinet. There was blood. It was very painful..." Souhef held up the back of his right hand, which showed a long, ugly gash dark with dried blood. "The first thought I had when I felt my pain yesterday was about my son. He was singing in the next room, making noise on a cushion with a toy. The first thought I had when I hurt myself was that it was *his fault*. That his singing made me lose my concentration or something like that...And this was why I was now in pain...So I shouted at him. I told him to shut up!"

Souhef was pointing at us, but he turned his finger and pointed it back at himself.

"Of course, I was wrong. My injury had nothing to do with my son. He was just playing, singing a song, being happy. If the wrench slipped, if I hit myself, how could it be his fault? It was not. But I *felt* it was. And I have no doubt everyone here has experienced a moment like this sometime in their life..."

Nods, grunts of fulsome recognition followed.

"I thought about that moment for the rest of the day. About my feeling of pain. About the moment of injustice with my son. And I want to share some of the things I realized." Souhef paused again, now shifting in place. "Let me describe what happened again, what happened in me in that moment, so we understand it better: Brothers and sisters, the pain I felt in that moment when the wrench slipped, this pain felt unjust to me. In that moment, I felt I was a victim. A victim of something I didn't deserve. And in that moment, my feeling of injustice made me look for someone to blame. But the only thing I could find was my son...because he was the only one around. He had been singing, playing drums on his cushion. I heard this noise in the moment of my pain. And I thought that my pain was the fault of the noise he was making. I blamed him. I shouted at him. I told him to shut up."

Souhef gazed down at his son—who was sitting in the front row—and smiled warmly. "You must be asking yourselves: Why is our imam so obsessed with this event? So he made the mistake of yelling at his son? We all make these mistakes. It was wrong. We know it is wrong. We don't need our imam to tell us...

"But brothers and sisters, please be patient as we investigate this moment, as we look more deeply into it.

"When I hurt myself with the wrench, I felt there was injustice in that pain. I wanted to know who was the cause of this injustice. But that is a false question. The real question is different: Why did I feel that this pain was unjust? After all, the wrench just slipped! It was an accident! There is no question of justice here!

"The soul has its own logic, brothers and sisters. And we must listen very deeply to this logic if we are to understand anything about what Allah wills for us.

"Because that moment was painful to me, I felt it was unjust. And it is a simple fact of my nature—of human nature—that I do not want to feel pain. Any pain. And it doesn't stop there: Not only do I not want to feel pain...I feel I *deserve* not to feel pain. I feel I deserve better than pain, nice things like kindness, happiness, peace, pleasure...but not pain...

"Here is the real question, brothers and sisters: Why do I feel this? Why do I feel I do not deserve pain? Isn't *this* the question? Isn't *this* why I asked myself who was to blame? Because I felt I was too good for pain? No? Maybe? Or maybe there is another reason?"

His voice grew louder with each question. This, and the insistent, percussive stress of certain words, announced a transformation those of us who had heard his *khutbah*s before knew to expect.

"Wasn't it my *love* that caused me to ask this?!" he hollered now, the tinny boom of his amplified voice echoing around us, demanding our reply.

"Wasn't it?!"

I felt something in my stomach, a gnawing and irritation, like fear.

"Isn't it LOVE?! Love for ourselves...love of myself...love of yourself...isn't *this* what makes us all think we don't deserve pain? Isn't it this self-love that makes us think we deserve better?!"

Again he paused. I stole a sidelong look along the row of men to my right. One was fighting not to fall asleep. Another was playing with a frayed thread on the carpet. I looked to my left, at Father. The worry on his face when Souhef had mentioned Bani Israel was gone. He yawned, bored.

Souhef was leaning into the microphone now, his lips touching it as he addressed us in a gentler, intimate tone:

"My dear brothers and sisters, let's be patient with this question. Let's think on it deeply. You feel pain...and you think, when you feel this pain, that you don't deserve to feel it. Now think of your children. Think of how much you love each of them, how deeply you want them to be happy. Think about when *they* are in pain. How does it make you feel? Isn't it the same feeling? Don't you think that they deserve better than unhappiness? And isn't this because of your love for them?

"So you see, brothers and sisters. It *is* love. Love of oneself that causes this feeling of injustice when we feel pain...

"You may be wondering: Why does our imam read us verses from *Al-Baqara* and then explain to us about the bruise on the back of his hand? You might be saying: What, dear Imam, is the connection here?

"Trust me when I tell you...this experience has everything to do with *Al-Baqara*. Everything!

"Let me read these verses to you again." The imam lowered his gaze to the page open in his lap.

O Bani Israel!
Remember how I favored you.
Fulfill your promise to Me. I will fulfill my prom-
    ise to you.
Of Me alone stand in awe!
Believe in what I have given. Confirm the truth
    you know. Be not the first to deny.
Do not give away My revelations for a trifling
    sum.
Of Me alone be aware!

Souhef looked up from the page. "What the Almighty is saying to Bani Israel is this: *'Remember the blessings I gave you.
But don't put those blessings first. Put Me first.'* Blessings come
from our Lord, but we must not honor the blessings before we
honor their source.

Of Me alone stand in awe!
Of Me alone be aware!

"Why, brothers and sisters, is Allah so concerned that Bani
Israel understand this? Why only tell the Jews this? Why does
our Lord say 'Bani Israel'? Why does He not say: 'O hu-
mankind?'"

Beside me, Father shifted in place as he kept looking to the
back of the room. I leaned forward, trying to ignore the distraction, to listen more deeply. The imam went on:

"For a very simple reason, brothers and sisters: We all know
Bani Israel was the Almighty's chosen people. They were the
people He LOVED more than any other for a very long
time"—Souhef paused for effect, then continued with a sudden
angry sneer—"until He grew *sick and tired of their betrayals!*"

The anger in Souhef's voice quickened everyone's attention. Alongside me, faces tilted, eyes cleared, gazes were now rapt. "I don't need to tell you, my dear Muslims, I don't need to tell you about the time Hazrat Musa, whom they call Moses, went to the top of Sinai and stayed for forty days and nights to bring back the Almighty's Law! I don't need to tell you what Bani Israel did when he was gone! You already know what they did! They chose the golden calf! They sang and danced and abased themselves before *gold!!*"

Suddenly, Souhef was virtually screaming: "And even *then!!* When the Almighty made them *repent* and he *forgave* them!! Were they *happy?* Instead of being grateful, they said: *'Show us your God, Moses!! Show us so we can believe in Him!! Because we cannot believe a God we don't see face to face!!'* And what did Allah do? He sent a vision that *blinded* them!! A light so bright they fell down and *cried* like *children!!*

"*'Please forgive us,'* they whined. *'Please forgive us,'*" Souhef mocked, making a ridiculous face. "And what did the All-Merciful do? Of course he forgave them. Were they grateful?" Souhef shook his head. "Of course *not.* All they did was continue to abuse our Lord and His pure love." Souhef stopped, still shaking his head as he scanned the crowd, picking out faces he now addressed directly: "Brothers and sisters. Listen to me: When they were hungry in the desert, the Almighty sent them bread from heaven, and quails, but they refused to enter Jerusalem when they were told. And then the Almighty made Musa bring out water and springs from the rocks with his staff, and they drank. All twelve tribes of them! But even then they were not happy. They complained that life was better for them under Pharaoh. *'Take us back to Egypt,'* they said. *'Take us back to Pharaoh.'* They dared to say this! After all that Allah did to deliver them! *'Take us back to Egypt... We had things better there. We had food and homes, and we didn't have to wait for heaven to rain bread.'*

"Can you believe it, brothers and sisters? What will these people not do for their own well-being?! For their own comfort?! Even betray the Lord who loves them…betray him over and over—and why?!" Souhef paused. Then he leaned forward, his teeth sounding against the microphone, and he hissed: "Because they *love* themselves. They love themselves more than the Almighty! They put themselves first! They believe they deserve better than others! Better than what they are given! They believe they deserve whatever they want! They have shown it time and time again as we know from examples in the Quran—and of course, as we see now in the world today with the situation in Palestine…"

A sudden hubbub of disgruntled sounds erupted: moans and whispers, coughs, joints cracking, and the rustling of shirtsleeves and slacks as the congregation grew uneasy. There was nothing to set Muslim blood boiling like the thought of the Palestinian brethren displaced from their homeland by Jews. And though neither of my parents—nor Mina—spoke much about it at home, as I felt the rising temperature around me, my own blood started to boil, too.

Father shot another nervous look at the back wall where Nathan was sitting. He turned to me, but before he could say anything, Souhef, now riding the mounting crest of the congregation's unruly discontent, shouted out:

"We all know that Bani Israel believes it deserves the best of everything!! They are never satisfied!! They take and take!! That was then and always will be their undoing!!"

Father took my hand and rose. I didn't want to get up. The imam noticed Father and looked directly at him. "Do not misunderstand me, brother: Loathsome as the Jew is to you and me, and to the great Almighty, you must not confuse my message: I do not mean to say that *you* cannot also end up like Bani Israel. This is the real point. Putting ourselves first, believing that we deserve better than Allah gives us"—Souhef was still staring at Father, and his gaze seemed to fix him in place—"then we, too, risk losing our Lord's favor. Just as Allah turned away from Bani Israel, who were once His favorites, Allah could do the same to *you*... and if you lose His love and gain His wrath, it will all be for one reason—for the same reason that I yelled at my own son: Self-love!"

Behind us, there was commotion. I turned to look, but found Chatha's gaze boring into me, gray and unblinking.

Souhef continued:

"Self-love! That same self-love that made me think, yesterday, that I was too good for pain. When I believed I did not deserve the pain of the wrench against my hand. When I blamed and yelled at my son... in that moment, I, too, was a *Jew!*"

The commotion in back grew. By now, Father had pulled me to my feet.

Nathan was standing, his face flushed, his lips snarled, his eyes wild with anger. "This is disgusting!" he yelled. His trembling voice bellowed through the prayer room. "Disgusting! This is not Islam!" He pointed at the imam. "This is not Islam! This is hatred!"

All at once, the crowd was on its feet, everyone moving to the back. Father hurried ahead, pushing through the congregation, yanking me along behind him as we wove our way between the clumps of men. By the time we got to the double doors, Nathan was being shoved out of the room.

"Nathan!" Father shouted as the doors shut, blocking Nathan out.

I looked back at Souhef. He was sitting comfortably, at ease on his platform, watching the strife unfold before him like a pasha at a beheading.

"Hayat! What are you doing? Let's go!" Father said. My shoulder hurt as he tugged, pulling me through the doors and into the shoe closet. There, Nathan was standing, stuffed into the corner, his back up against the shelves, his feet foundering on piles of shoes. Three men were pressing in; one of them kept pushing Nathan back into the corner every time he tried to step forward. "You like Jews?" the young man yapped, stabbing at Nathan's chest with his finger. "Is that it? You like Jews? You a Jew? You a Jew? Huh? Jew?"

"Leave me alone!" Nathan shouted, batting away the young man's hand, his feet stumbling as they searched for purchase.

"He looks like a Jew," another man said. "Look at his nose," he added.

Father rushed in, forcing himself between Nathan and the men. "What the hell's wrong with you people?!" he shouted, pushing the men away. "This is a better man than any of you will ever be!"

Father turned, shoving Nathan toward the staircase forcefully. Then he reached down to grab our shoes.

Behind us, the double doors were now open. Men were gathered in the wide doorway to watch the scene unfolding in the shoe closet. Chatha stood in front, staring at us, his cadaverous gaze brightened by the mayhem. From behind the curtain of gathered spectators, Souhef's voice continued to ring out with verses:

> For Disbelievers, warn them or not, it makes no
>   difference.
> They will not believe!

Allah has sealed their hearts and ears. And veiled
   their eyes.
Great will be their punishment!

Nathan clambered up the stairs, step by step, stumbling as
he went. He looked back once, his face pale and frozen, his
eyes wide with fear.

"Hayat! Hayat! Hayat!" Father was shouting to get my attention. "Get your shoes!" I reached down for my sneakers.
He grabbed me, and I scrabbled up the steps behind him in my
socks, shoes dangling from both our hands. Behind us, the men
were now crowding in at the bottom of the stairs. Chatha was
wearing a grin as he watched us go. At the first-floor landing, I
looked up. There were dozens of women standing in the stairwell, their head-scarf-framed faces sticking out over the railing
as it receded—in a spiral—to the top floor. Nathan was already
out the front door, making his way across the black asphalt in
his bare feet.

"Filthy Jew," I heard a woman's voice say as we slipped out.

11

The Turn

Father bore left with the shape of the highway, driving at the sun, and all at once the dashboard was ablaze with a silver sheen. Squinting, Nathan looked away from the glare. He rolled down the passenger-side window, and the roar of passing cars broke the tense silence.

"You want to leave that open?" Father asked. "I can turn off the air-conditioning?"

Nathan didn't answer; he didn't even seem to register that he'd been spoken to. He was staring out the window, his expression hard against the steady gust blowing inside.

Father turned to check his blind spot, stealing a glance at Nathan as he changed lanes. "Nate?"

Without responding, Nathan rolled up the window.

Father glanced again at his friend. "I don't understand the mind-set," he said. "I really don't."

Again, Nathan said nothing. He was staring straight ahead now, his expression stony, his eyes pressed virtually shut against the silver sheen of the dashboard's glare.

Father continued, tentative: "What is the mind-set of a person who sits around all day thinking about being hit by a wrench? And what kind of idiots does he take us for? Does he actually expect us to take this stuff seriously?"

Nathan didn't stir. But he was listening. So was I.

"Nate," Father went on, looking over at Nathan again, "I've known the man for ten years now, and I'll tell you...I have never heard a worthwhile word come out of his mouth."

There was a long pause.

"Can I ask you a question?" Nathan finally asked.

"Of course."

"What would you have done if I wasn't there?"

"If you weren't there?" Father repeated, confused.

"Would you have stayed through the sermon? Would you have stayed for the prayer when the sermon was over...if I wasn't there?"

"If you weren't there? If *you* weren't there, *I* wouldn't have been there in the first place, Nate," Father said with a chuckle.

"I'm serious."

"I am, too," Father said. "Are you forgetting that I told you this was a bad idea? I told you again and again. But you insisted."

"And you thought it was a bad idea *why,* exactly?" Nathan's tone was suddenly pointed. "Because you knew that something like this might happen?"

"I didn't want you to go because these people are idiots! Plain and simple! They have nothing better to do with their time than to insult our intelligence. The last time I suffered through one of Souhef's stupid *khutbah*s, that same numbskull went on about how many years in hell we would have to spend for telling a lie, and how many years for dishonoring our parents, and how many years for turning our backs on the Afghani brothers fighting the Soviets. He had it all worked out. Seventy years for this. Seven hundred for that. All eternity for something else. It was silly! And you should have seen their faces!

Sitting there in front of him like he's the sun coming up in the morning! Eating up all of this rubbish and taking it for knowledge!"

I smarted. Father was the one person with the least excuse to be so blithe about hellfire.

"All well and good, Naveed," Nathan said, agitated. "But that's not what I asked you. I asked you if you had any idea something like that might happen?"

This time, Father didn't reply.

"Answer me, Naveed!" Nathan exploded with a shriek.

Father looked at Nathan, then back at the road. "I didn't think *this* would happen ... but I did cringe when you told him you were Jewish. I thought—"

Nathan cut him off, his voice trembling: "That sermon was not intended for me. He would have delivered it whether I was there or not. Just give me a straight answer. It's important for me to know: If you'd been there without me, would you have stayed like the rest of them?"

"I think you're forgetting: I *defended* you." Father's reply sounded at once wounded and defiant.

Nathan held Father's gaze for a long moment before turning away with a nod. He sighed, and all at once, his hard expression broke. He looked exhausted. "I'm not denying that," he said. "I'm just saying it's probably not the first time you've ever heard things like that, is it?"

"It's not," Father said, solemn.

"I'm such an idiot. My father warned me about this. He's said his whole life that no matter who we try to be, no matter who we become, we're always Jews." Nathan's voice was filled with emotion. He turned to me with a pained, searching look. I forced a smile. I could see the sudden disappointment in his eyes. He looked away.

"What he did was wrong, Nate...but you didn't have to get up and start yelling at him."

"I don't understand how you can say that, Naveed."

"You don't understand?"

"Maybe I do," Nathan said, dismissive. "Maybe I do. And maybe that's the whole point."

"What are you talking about?"

"Somebody has to say something!" Nathan barked, his teeth clenched, as if he were trying to hold in the emotion. "If nobody says anything, people think these things are acceptable. You have to speak out. If I didn't get up and say something—were *you* going to?"

"There's a time and a place."

"There's never a convenient time or place. There just isn't. If you don't speak up when it happens, then you've *lost* your chance. And if you don't say anything, you're no better than anyone else sitting in that room. And neither am I. What is *he* going to think?" Nathan indicated me with a nod. "What's he going to think if he doesn't see his father speaking out?"

Father replied after a pause, his tone grave: "Nate. I trust you like no one in my life. I've told you things I don't tell anyone. Why? Because you're the only one I know who can really listen. Listen and not judge..."

Nathan looked at Father for a long moment, his arm against the silvered dashboard, his eyes still burning.

"So, listen to me now," Father continued. "I understand you're getting emotional. But I want to remind you, *I* was the one who warned you about Souhef. I've been warning you about this Islam stuff all along—"

Nathan erupted: "Warned me? You told me he would be after my money! You didn't tell me he was a hatemonger and an anti-Semite!"

Father was silent.

Nathan sat back, disgusted. "The way he has those people beholden to him. It's revolting and immoral. And it has nothing to do with real Islam. Nothing at all."

Who does he think he is? I thought to myself. *He's not even a Muslim yet.*

I sat back and plugged my ears. I looked out the window, humming to myself to drown out any sound of their discussion. I didn't want to hear anything more they had to say.

Back home, I was the first one out of the car and into the house. Mina was in the kitchen, looking lovely in a brown *shalwar-kameez* and crimson *dupatta*. She was eager and aglow, her eyes brimming with anticipation. "How was it, *behta?*" she asked.

"Fine," I said.

"Did Nathan talk to the imam?"

I nodded.

"Good," she said, looking pleased. "And how was the prayer?"

I hesitated for a second, realizing I didn't want to tell her we hadn't prayed. "Fine," I said with a smile.

"That's nice, *behta.*" She looked over at the front door. "Where is he?"

I shrugged, suddenly elated. I leaned in to touch my lips to Mina's cheek.

"That's so sweet, *behta.*"

"I love you, Auntie."

"I love you, too, Hayat."

And then I left her there—her smile still brimming—and went up to my room.

* * *

Upstairs, I sat down at my desk with my Quran, and opened to *Al-Baqara,* the chapter from which Souhef had read to us that day. It began with a series of warnings to those who denied the truth of the Prophet's message, those he called the deniers and the hypocrites. The footnotes told the story of Muhammad's flight from Mecca in the year AD 622 and his relocation to the city of Medina, where there was a large and prosperous Jewish community. These Jews were the ones being warned at the outset of *Al-Baqara,* for even though the Prophet created a constitution that guaranteed Jews equal rights, they were not happy. It was bad enough they refused the truth of our Prophet's teachings, but then they conspired against him, making alliances with his enemies, some even plotting to kill him. It was for this, the footnotes explained, that Muhammad eventually turned against the Jews of Medina.

The verses from *Al-Baqara* that Souhef had quoted in his sermon were originally addressed to these Medina Jews who denied the Quran and believed that they—and not Muslims— were the only ones with true knowledge about the Lord. The verses offered ample proof of Souhef's contention, chronicling Moses's own troubles with his followers, a people chosen by Allah, but who would lose His love because of their selfishness. And it was in *Al-Baqara* that I found the curse Chatha shared at the December dinner at his house two years earlier.

At my open window, I heard voices. Then sniffling. I got up to look. Nathan's loafers poked out from beneath the front porch eaves. I could tell Mina was talking to him, but I couldn't make out her words. And then I distinctly heard the sound of his sobbing.

I went downstairs into the living room. There, through the

window, I saw them. Nathan's head was buried in Mina's lap, and he was clutching at her waist, crying. It felt like something I should not be seeing, but I couldn't look away. I'd never seen a grown man cry, except on television. And as Mina caressed his hair, and as Nathan's grip on her waist tightened—his thin fingers blanching as he wiggled and pressed and held her close—I wondered what he had to be crying about. If anything, he had only reason to be happy. He was going to be a Muslim. All Souhef had done was to give him reasons—better ones than the one he really had—for becoming one of us. After all, he would no longer be one of Allah's despised Jews. Which meant he wouldn't have to suffer under Allah's curse anymore. It was extraordinary news. But was he happy about it? Of course not. He was ungrateful. Just as Souhef had said Jews were. So ungrateful that it made him blind to the very truth he had heard that afternoon and that could have saved him. What I was seeing before me, I thought, was the very reason that Allah had turned his back on Bani Israel.

The Quran is right, I thought. *They will never change.*

Father, Mother, Imran, and I were gathered in the kitchen for dinner when Mina finally came inside from the front porch. And though she had every appearance of disappointment—downcast eyes, a shuffling step, mumbled replies to Mother's questions about her wanting dinner—she looked oddly satisfied. She had that same arresting bloom about her I remembered from the first afternoon she met Nathan. She muttered an apology about dinner, avoiding eye contact with all of us, especially—I thought—with Imran. And as she headed for the stairs, Mother asked if she should set a place for Nathan.

Mina stopped, shook her head. And then she was gone.

Mother lingered at the counter for a moment, troubled. She looked at Father.

"Go," he said. "I'll take care of dinner."

Mother nodded, and followed Mina out.

After dinner, Mother left the dishes for me. She and Father stood out on the patio, talking. I was finishing up, wiping down the counter, when they came back inside. Father went downstairs to join Imran for television in the family room. Mother lingered with me in the kitchen. She told me Father had explained to her what had happened that afternoon. But now she wanted to hear my version.

I told her Souhef had read to us from *Al-Baqara*.

She asked me to get the Quran and show her. So I did.

She sat at the dining table, poring over the pages where I pointed out the citations. She shook her head to herself as she read. Finally, she looked up at me, asking: "What did he say in his *khutbah*? What did Souhef say exactly about Bani Israel?"

"He said they love themselves, not Allah. He said they're selfish. He said we should never be like them." This was very different than what Mother usually said about Jews. It felt good to correct her.

She held my gaze, her expression dark. Then she looked away. From the family room downstairs, the computerized melody of the *CHiPs* opening theme drifted up into the kitchen. "The man is already having second thoughts about converting," she said quietly. "He's already asked the poor woman if she'll still have him if he *doesn't* become a Muslim." She brought her hand to her forehead to run it along the deep ridges there. "I have worked *so hard* for this...and if it doesn't happen—" She stopped herself, looking completely helpless. "Why today, Hayat?" she asked, pleading. "Why today of all days?"

I waited before replying. "It was Allah's will," I finally said, quietly.

The response surprised her. She held my gaze for a long moment, then offered a gentle, reluctant nod.

Downstairs, Father was sitting on the couch, Imran straddled on his knee. He turned to me, patting at the place beside him. "C'mon, *behta*. It just started."

I didn't move.

"You don't want to watch?" he asked.

"No."

"I thought you liked *CHiPs*."

"I love *CHiPs*, Dad!" Imran interjected. I'd never heard him call my father that. It was jarring.

"I'm going to build a castle keep," I replied. "Up in my room." I knew this would get Imran's attention.

"Can I come, too?" he asked, turning to me.

"Why don't we see a little *CHiPs?*" Father said, rubbing him tenderly on the back. "Then you go up to play with Hayat, okay?"

Imran nodded, eager, melting into Father's chest as the commercial ended and the show resumed.

On my way to my room, I slowed as I approached Mina's door. Behind it, Mother's voice came through clearly: "What does it matter?! It doesn't matter! Let him stay like he is...You stay like you are! These things don't matter!" Mother's impassioned pleas were followed by a long silence.

I moved on.

At the end of the hall, I opened the linen closet, pulling out sheets. I went into my room and draped them over my desk chair and desk, then used stacks of books to fix the corners in place. I turned out the lights and climbed inside. The tent's space was small, but it comforted me. Like the graves of the *hafiz*, I thought, which Mina had once explained to me were kept warm and comfortable through the long string of centuries until—on that last day of creation—everyone would rise from the dead to face the Final Judgment.

"Can I come inside, too?" I heard.

It was Imran. He was holding up the ends of one of the sheets as he peered in. I'd fallen asleep.

"Sure," I mumbled, turning over.

He crawled in alongside me. We lay side by side, staring up at the canopy of sheets, brushed by the moonlight coming through the windows. After a long silence, I spoke: "My dad is *my* dad, Imran. Not yours."

He didn't say anything.

"Did you hear me?" I asked.

Imran turned onto his side to face me. "He's my dad, too...," he said softly.

"No he's not. Maybe he's *like* a dad to you. But he's not your *real* dad. He's *my* dad."

"He said it."

"He said *what?*"

"He's my dad, too."

"No, he didn't. Maybe he said he loves you just like he was your dad ..."

I paused.

"And that's nice for you. But he didn't say he *was* your dad. He wouldn't do that, because it's not true. And he's not a liar."

Imran's eyes glistened with worry. "Share him with me," he whispered.

"I already share him with you. But he's not your real dad."

"Why not?"

"Because he's not married to your mom."

"She can marry him."

"No she can't. My dad's *already* married. To *my* mom."

"He can marry her, too."

"Who?"

"Your mom."

"No. I said he's already married to my mom. So he can't marry yours."

"My mom can marry him," he said, "and your mom, too. And then he can be my dad and your dad. He's a Muslim."

I was surprised. The boy's mind was quick.

"You can't do that in America. And we live in America. *This* is your home. In America, if you have more than one wife, they put you in jail."

"Why?"

"For polygamy."

"What's that?"

"When you marry more than one woman. You can't do that here, except in Utah."

"What's that?"

"It's one of the states."

He looked confused.

"It's a place in America," I explained. "It's just not here."

"You-taa?" he repeated.

"Yeah. You can do polygamy in Utah, because that's where Mormons are."

"What are Mormons?"

"People with a lot of wives. And there's a big lake there full of salt and worms."

Imran looked at me, puzzled. "Can we go fishing?"

"No," I said. "We're in our castle keep."

My response sounded ominous, even to me.

Imran didn't say anything. "I'm going to sleep," I finally said, turning away.

"Please, Hayat. Please share him with me," Imran pleaded as he pressed himself against me, his small hands tightly gripping my waist. "Please let him be my dad, too. Please let's go to *You-taa*."

"Stop it, Imran," I snapped. "Don't be stupid. It's not up to me anyway. Or you. We're just kids. Nobody's going to Utah just because you or I want to."

"Why not?"

"Because we have a house here."

"We can get a new one."

"My dad's got a job. I've got school. We can't just leave like that."

"Please," Imran cried, clinging to me. I turned, pulling him off. I looked into his face. His small, sharp eyes simmered with yearning.

"No," I said. "Anyway, you'll have a dad soon. Nathan's gonna be your dad."

"He can't be," Imran said, turning abruptly away.

"He will be. All your mom has to do is marry him."

"No!"

"Why not?"

"He's *white*. He's not my real dad."

"I didn't say he was your real dad." Imran didn't reply. "My dad wouldn't be your real dad either."

There was silence.

"Anyway," I said, "it doesn't matter if he's white or if he's a Jew or anything else. It doesn't matter what you think. She's going to do whatever she wants..."

"*Chew?*" he asked.

"What?"

"What's a *chew?*"

"*Jew,*" I said, correcting him.

"What's that?" he asked.

"A Jew is the kind of person Allah hates the most in the world," I said.

Imran's expression emptied with shock. I sensed his fear. It made me want to go on. "Jews are the people who used to live in Egypt a long time ago," I continued. "Before the pyramids... You know what the pyramids are, right?"

Imran shook his head.

"Anyway, it doesn't matter. All that matters is that a long time ago, the Jews were very special. Allah loved them a lot. He loved them more than all other kinds of people. But then something happened."

"What?"

"They didn't behave. They didn't do what they were told." I paused, staring intently at the boy. "When Allah told them to do things, they didn't listen. Instead of doing what Allah wanted, they did what *they* wanted. And then they even made fun of Allah behind his back..."

"Why?"

"Because they are selfish. And Allah realized this. And He started to hate them. And soon, Allah hated them more than all the other people He created. More than animals. More than pigs, even."

Imran's eyes widened with alarm. "Pigs?!"

I knew the effect saying this would have on him. More than alcohol, more than naked white women, more than gambling, the pig was the ultimate taboo in Islam, the summary image of everything unholy to us.

"Imran," I continued, gravely, "when I say Jews are what Allah hates the most, I mean it. On the Day of Judgment, at the

end of time, the sun will come down to the earth this high..."
I pointed at the sheeted canopy above us. "On that day Allah
will talk to every single person and ask him what good he did
in his life and what bad he did...and the people who did more
bad things will be standing on the left side of Allah"—I paused,
sticking out my tongue—"and a *huge tongue* will come and
swallow all these bad people away into hell. And you know
who the first people will be that this tongue will swallow into
hell?"

Imran shook his head.

"The Jews," I said with finality. "The Jews will be first to go
into the fire. You remember when your mom told us all about
hell, right? About the fires...where bad people burn forever
and ever...?"

Imran nodded. His eyes were filling with tears.

"Don't cry," I said. "There's no reason to cry. *You* have
nothing to be afraid of. You're a Muslim, and if you learn your
namaaz and you learn your holy book, you'll never go to hell.
Do you hear me? That tongue won't wash you into hell. If
you're a Muslim, you'll be saved."

Tears rolled down his cheeks: "But I don't want Nathan for
a dad," he pleaded.

"If you're a good boy and you pray to Allah, maybe he'll listen ..."

"Really?"

"Maybe," I offered, noncommittal, "or maybe not."

The next morning, I woke up in pain, my bones sore from a
night on the floor. I smelled ghee, heard sounds in the kitchen.
It took me a moment to remember that I'd fallen asleep holding
Imran in my arms as he cried. Now he was gone.

Downstairs, Mother was standing at the stove. She was surprised to find me still dressed in the previous day's clothes. "Didn't you change last night?" she asked. I told her I'd built a castle keep and fallen asleep inside it with Imran. "I'm such a bad mother," she said. "I didn't even check on you. Shame on me."

I sat down at the kitchen table and started on a plate of fresh *paratha*s. Mother stood over me, watching me eat. She looked angry.

"Mom? Are you okay?" I asked, chewing.

She shrugged. "You would think that last night was a night he should have stayed home. After everything that happened yesterday. You would think that, no? A time when his *presence* was needed? His *support?*" She looked away, seeming to hold in tears. "But if you thought that, you thought wrong! Instead, he gets a call and off he goes running. Chasing *white flesh*. What is it with *Eastern men?* You would think he could *desist* for one night? There's a crisis in the house? So you stay with your family? No? Of course not! The first thing he does is run off with a prostitute! Is that normal?"

My head was lowered. I was avoiding her gaze.

"Hayat," she snapped.

"Hmm?"

"Is there something wrong with me for thinking that this is not *normal* behavior?!"

I shook my head. "No," I said. And then I added: "He's sick."

"*Kurban,* you don't even know half of it," she said, sliding into the chair beside me. "I woke up this morning only to discover he was *still* gone. The man *never came home.* Who knows what happened to him? Maybe he's dead, for all we know! So I call him at the hospital. I don't tell them it's me. I have them page him. After ten minutes, he finally comes to the phone. When he realizes it's me, he starts yelling! In front of his own staff! It's just the *height* of indecency. Not only are you off running around with women when your own family needs you—on top of that, your wife calls you to find out if you're still alive, and you scream indecencies at her in front of your colleagues! You should have heard the things he said! What a *savage!*"

That was when the phone rang.

Mother looked over at the red receiver with dread. "It's probably him. God only knows where he's calling from." She turned to me. "You pick it up. If it's him, tell him I'm not here."

"Where are you?"

"What do you mean?"

"If he asks me where you are..."

"I don't know. Make up something...the post office."

I got up and answered the phone. "Hello?" I said.

"Hi there!" a woman's voice shot out brightly. "Can I speak to—uh—Mun...Mau ...Maureen?"

"You mean Muneer?"

"Now, I guess I do. Is that your mother, young man?"

From upstairs, I heard an eruption of muffled shouts and cries. The woman on the other end was still talking, but the commotion distracted me. It was Mina's voice, shouting. There was banging, and more chaos. And then a loud thud.

I stepped out of the kitchen and into the hall with the receiver to my ear.

"Hello? Excuse me, son...are you still there?"

"What's going on?" Mother said, looking over at me. I was standing at the bottom of the stairs.

"Is that her there? I'd love to have a word with her about your homeowner's insurance..."

219

Just then, Mina's bedroom door flew open, slamming against the wall. Imran's fulsome wailing burst forth from within, seeming to hurl Mina from the room. She looked large, so much larger than usual. She turned to look at me. Her electric gaze was terrifying.

The next thing I knew, she seemed to be flying down the steps, the scarlet shawl around her neck like a cape billowing behind her. "You evil child!" she screeched, headed right for me. My left leg was already wet with my own urine as she tore the phone from my hand. My face exploded with pain. "How could you say those things?! How could you?!" she screamed, hitting me with the receiver. I retreated, my hands raised to protect my face. She hit me again, hard enough to crack the phone's plastic casing.

"Stop it! Stop it!" Mother screamed, trying to pull Mina away.

Mina had beaten me back to the steps leading down to the family room.

"Stop it! Stop it!" Mother kept screaming.

She grabbed Mina by the hair and pulled. Mina's head flew back and her mouth flew open with a rending shriek: "Aaahhi-iiyyyaaa!" As she fell back, her elbow flew out and swiped me across the face. All at once my feet were lost and there was no ground. I didn't realize I was falling until my shoulder slammed into something hard. Tumbling sidewise, I rolled end over end. I reached out to stop myself, and something cracked.

From above, Mother raced down the steps and fell to her knees. Her hands were all over my face; her fingers were covered with my blood. "Hayat! Are you okay?!" she screamed. "Are you okay?"

I was dazed. My head hurt a little, but other than that, I felt fine. "I'm okay," I said.

Up above, Mina was standing at the top of the stairs, Imran at her side. She wore a look of horror.

Mother turned to her: "*What the hell do you think you're doing?!*" she screamed.

Mina shook her head, backing away from the landing as Mother stormed up the steps.

"*Bhaj...*"

Mother cut her off viciously. "If you EVER touch him again!" Her voice bellowed: "If you EVER so much as RAISE YOUR VOICE at my son...I will KILL YOU!" Mina backed away, stumbling as her son tried to hide behind her thigh.

"*Bhaj*...I'm sorry!" Mina squawked. "He was saying things to Imran...horrible things ..."

Mother wasn't listening. She grabbed Mina's collar and slapped her across the face with an open palm. "Don't you *ever* touch"—and again, now with the back of her hand—"my son!"

She hit Mina again and again.

I looked down at my right arm. It looked strange. Bent at the wrist, my hand canted away, like a leaf dangling from a broken stem. Without thinking, I reached out with my other hand and snapped it back into place.

Then there was pain. Only pain. Everywhere. I had never experienced anything like it.

I screamed. I kept screaming.

Upstairs, Mother froze and turned.

Behind her, Mina crumpled to a heap on the kitchen floor, covered in her scarlet shawl.

I could tell now that the pain was in my arm, not in the rest of my body, which was recoiling from the onslaught. My mind reeled, stunned at the agony, the inscrutable injustice of what I was feeling. I screamed again, but it didn't do any good. It seemed incomprehensible to me that I should feel such pain. My mind flashed to Souhef, and I heard his voice inside me:

Who are you not to deserve this pain?

"Haaayyyaaaat!!!" Mother cried out as she appeared at the top of the steps.

That was the last thing I remembered before I blacked out.

12

Fever Dreams

The fracture was bad. The chips of my shattered wrist had to be surgically aligned, and since the orthopedist had an immediate window, Father and Nathan—who Father had called when we got to the hospital—decided it was best to do it right away.

I spent the hours before the surgery in a haze. What I mostly remember is pain: an explosive, electric suffering that steadied—once the painkillers kicked in—into a throbbing, burning ache along the bone. But even with the sedatives, the pain was unbearable. Its pulsing, pendulumlike rhythm waxed and waned and waxed again. I'd never felt time's passing so palpably, the flux and flow of my anguish defining each moment as distinct from the next, now as pain, now as relief. And through it all, the temptation to feel that I was being treated unjustly persisted, like a foul odor I fought to ignore. I thought, instead, of Souhef.

Who are you to think you deserve anything better? I heard him say. *This pain is Allah's will for you.*

The words gave me comfort and strength. As I watched Nathan hover about—he'd shown up right after Father's call, consulting with the doctors, comforting Mother—I told myself: *I can accept my pain. I'm not like you.*

* * *

I woke up in a dark hospital room, the walls flickering blue and white with the changing images on the TV quietly humming in the corner. Mother was sitting beside me in an armchair. It took me a moment to realize where I was. Then I remembered:

The fall. My wrist. The emergency room.

I looked down at my arm, covered now to the elbow in a plaster cast. It didn't seem like it was a part of me. I tried to move it. The pain was swift and searing.

Hearing me moan, Mother got up and pressed in, holding me tightly. It only made the pain worse.

"Don't, Mom. It hurts..."

"Okay, *kurban*," Mother said, starting to cry.

I closed my eyes. The sharp pain faded, giving way to a dull ache. I felt wearied. By the flickering walls. By my aching arm. By Mother's face, slick with tears.

"I'm tired," I moaned.

"Go back to sleep. Get your rest," she said. "I love you, Hayat. I love you more than life itself."

I shut my eyes and felt her lips on my forehead. When she pulled away, I turned and waited for sleep to take me.

When I awoke again, the room was dissolving into light. Before me was a tray of food. Mother and Father stood to my right. At the foot of the bed was a large, bald, potbellied man with a stethoscope around his neck. I had the odd impression that he was surrounded in a soft white glow.

"How's the patient feeling?" the man asked in a chipper tone.

"Fine."

"Hayat, you remember Dr. Gold?" Father asked, sharply. I remembered the man from the previous day, but I wasn't sure who he was exactly. My hesitation irritated Father. "He's your surgeon. He's fixed your wrist."

"You're a brave young man," Dr. Gold said. "A model patient. I'm sure your parents are very proud of you."

"Oh, we are," Mother quickly added.

"So how's the old bod feeling?" Gold asked.

I was confused.

"The arm?" he prompted. "How's it treating you?"

I looked down at the cast. My arm was aching, but I was getting used to the pain. What was new was a coarse, irritating itch along the skin beneath the cast.

"It itches," I said, scratching at the cast's edges.

"Well, you'll have to get used to that, son," Gold said. "It can itch like hell under there. Especially with the new stuff we've got on you...But you're a tough kid. I could tell that from the way you handled everybody moving that arm around last night. Won't be the end of the world...Now, tell me: You still feeling pain?"

"Little bit."

Gold nodded, assessing my response. Then he looked down and made a note on the chart he was holding. "We'll up the dosage on the painkillers just a touch. No need for him to be in any pain at all..."

"How much longer do you want to keep him here?" Mother asked.

"No more than another couple of days. Maybe even just 'til tomorrow. Let's see what the X-rays show."

I looked over at the side table, on which a large bouquet of yellow roses stood. They were giving off the same soft light as the doctor. I stared, intrigued. And the longer I did, the more deeply the roses seemed to recede, disappearing into this diaphanous glow.

"Those are from your auntie. She's so worried for you...," Mother said, trailing off. She stole an almost fearful glance at Father, then stepped between us, reaching her hand out to check my forehead. "He's still a little hot," she said.

"We're on top of it," Gold said. "Fever's down. This is normal post-op stuff."

"So he's fine?"

"Couldn't be better—all things considered, of course." Gold laughed, then turned to me. "So listen, son. We're going to do another X-ray—maybe later today. We'll be sure to go gently, but I just want you to know, okay?"

I nodded. Dr. Gold turned to my parents. "Nothing to worry about. I'll check back in on him later today."

"Hayat. Thank Dr. Gold," Mother said.

"Thank you, Dr. Gold."

"No problem, young man. Get some rest," he said, patting me on the leg. Then he shook hands with Father and walked out.

Everywhere I looked, things were fading into a transparent haze. Even Mother and Father both seemed to be vanishing behind the peculiar and pleasing light.

Father cleared his throat: "So, Hayat..."

"Naveed, please," Mother interrupted.

"What is it?" he snapped. "You don't have any idea what I'm going to say..."

"Don't I?" Mother snapped back. "Not like you haven't been pestering me day and night about it? You're *itching* to get at him. And I'm saying: Now is not the time."

Father ignored her. "That man who just operated on you, Hayat...Dr. Gold? You know that he's Jewish?" Father pointed at me as he spoke. "Hmm? So next time you want to go around bad-mouthing Jews, make sure you tell those same people that a Jew fixed your arm. And if he hadn't, you'd never throw another ball with that hand. Or write with it!"

"What's wrong with you, Naveed?" Mother asked. "Are you drunk?"

Father glared at her, disgusted. He looked back at me. "One more thing for you and your mother to think about...," he said, his voice trembling. "If I *ever* see you with that book again, I will fix you. You can trust me on that."

I wanted to ask him what book, but before I could, Mother started shoving him toward the door. "Get back!" she shouted. "Get out! Will you?!" Finally, she pushed him out of the room.

I turned away from the door, my gaze settling on the armchair to my left, where Mother had been sitting the previous night. It was brown and beige, its upholstery worn on the headrest. It, too, was gently held in the same translucence. No matter where I looked, things appeared to be disappearing into this gossamer-thin light, a luminosity nothing at all like the hard, brisk brightness of the morning sun bleeding through the mostly drawn curtains, and nothing like the fainter whitish-blue overlay of the fluorescent ceiling beams. It did not even seem like a light that illuminated, but rather was like a thing itself. I kept gazing around me: at the sheets on my bed; at the blank, gray-white cinder-block walls; at the flowers and the dark brown surface of the table on which they stood. The effect was not only visual, for there was silence in this light, too. And in this glowing, illuminated silence each thing appeared distinctly for what it was. A chair. A table. A flower. A sheet. And each thing held my attention simply, completely. I remembered something Mina had once told me: That God's light was everywhere; one simply had to learn to see it. And she'd shown me a verse in the Quran to explain what she meant:

> God is the Light of the heavens and the earth.
> His Light like a lamp within a niche, of glass like a
>   brilliant star,
> Lit from a blessed tree, an olive tree, not from the
>   east nor from the west,
> Whose oil would burn and glow even without fire.
> Light upon Light!
> God guides to His Light whom He wills...

This is Allah's *Light,* I thought, looking around. *And He is guiding me to see It.*

That night I had a dream. I was running from a woman in a torn *burqa*. She wailed and howled as she chased me. And then I heard a deep voice: "Come with me," it said. I turned and saw the Prophet. He was just as Mina described him: warm, wide eyes rimmed with thick eyelashes, a full beard, and a gap between his front two teeth as he smiled at me.

"Come," he said again as he took my hand.

Muhammad led me to a white mosque in the mountains. Inside, the mosque was filled with figures. I couldn't tell if they were statues, or people magically frozen in place. The Prophet led me to the front of the prayer room and told me I would be leading the prayer. I sang out the call to prayer, and all the figures started to move. Amazed, I turned to the Prophet and asked: "How did they come to life?"

"Who?" he asked. I pointed at the figures now taking their place, shoulder to shoulder, for the prayer. There were only men.

"This is your *ummah*," he said. I knew from the Quran that the word meant "my fellow Muslims," but it wasn't an answer to my question. The Prophet turned away from me now, closing his eyes as he prepared for the prayer.

Silence fell through the mosque as we prayed. I moved; the Prophet moved; the figures moved in unison behind us. The prayer went on and on. At some point, I realized it would never end.

I walked out of the mosque and left them praying.

Outside, the sun was shining, bright and strong. I looked down and noticed my arm was covered with a golden cast. There was a name signed across it: Yitzhak.

I woke up.

My room was dark. Cold air soughed through the ceiling vents. I felt something inside me, a gnawing, an itch—but nothing like the itching on my arm—that my mind tried to reach. Mina had said it was a great blessing to see the Prophet in a dream, but there didn't seem to be any blessing in mine. Instead of staying and praying with him, I'd left.

Something about the figures bothered me as well. I kept thinking of Nathan's story of Ibrahim and the idols that couldn't talk or move. I turned in place, trying to doze off again. I remembered Dr. Gold. And then the golden cast from my dream signed "Yitzhak." I remembered that was Jason Blum's name.

Why does Allah hate them so much? I wondered. It didn't make sense to me.

I lay there, troubled, for what could have been minutes, or could have been hours. At some point, still only half-asleep, I heard the door hinges creak. I cracked open my eyes. A woman in white stood in the doorway. I didn't realize she was a nurse until she'd stepped inside. I shut my eyes. She approached quietly, a sweet lilac scent floating in behind her soft-soled steps. She stood beside me for a long moment, and then the door hinges yawned open again.

"What are you doing in here?" a man whispered. I stole a peek. It was Father.

"I just wanted to see him," the nurse whispered back. "He's beautiful."

"Julie," Father said.

"I just want to see what he looks like. Is that too much to ask?"

"Fine," he said after a short pause. "Just don't wake him."

"I won't."

The door closed. Julie sat down in the bedside armchair. I pretended to rouse, as if awakened by the sound of the armchair cushions taking her weight. Squinting, I feigned surprise. "Who are you?" I asked.

She didn't answer. She just kept looking at me with her long, wide-set, yellow-brown eyes. Her hair was blond beneath her nurse's cap, and her lips were thin and bright red. She looked somehow familiar to me, though I didn't know why.

She lifted her hand and ran her finger across her eyebrow. Her nails were tipped with the same bright shade as her lips.

"You have beautiful eyelashes," she finally said.

"Thanks."

"I'm Julie," she said. She got up from her chair and stood above me. She raised her hand. I closed my eyes. And I felt her finger along my forehead.

"Your father loves you, you know that?" she said. "You know how much he loves you, right, Hayat?"

I opened my eyes and shook my head.

"He loves you more than anything else in the world," she added quietly. She pressed in and kissed me on the forehead.

"Don't tell your dad you met me. Okay?"

"Why not?" I asked.

She looked away, considering. "I'm not the nurse on duty. I don't want to get in any trouble."

"Okay," I said.

"Look at him," Mother said, pointing as we pulled up the driveway. Imran was hopping about with joy on the front lawn; Mina stood by the walkway farther on. "He looks so happy to see his *bhai-jaan*." As the car came to a stop, Imran pulled open the back door and tried to hug me. "Be careful, sweetie," Mother told him. "His arm is still broken."

"Broken," he repeated with a troubled frown.

"But he's going to be all better," Mother said. "That's why he was in the hospital." Imran nodded, trying to smile. I climbed out of the car and put my free arm around him.

"I love you, *bhai-jaan*," he said, holding me tightly.

"He missed you, *behta*," Mina said. "So much. He asked about you all the time." Mina looked odd to me. Her face was covered with a layer of skin-colored paste. It looked like she was wearing a mask.

"How are you feeling, *behta*?" she asked.

"I'm okay," I said.

"I cooked your favorite for lunch."

"*Paratha*s?"

She looked at me deeply, and all at once, she started to cry. I suddenly felt like crying, too. "*Paratha*s were the least I could do," she said as she took me into her arms. "I'm sorry, *behta*. I never meant to hurt you."

"Auntie," I said into her ear. "I had a dream with the Prophet, peace be upon him."

She pulled away, surprised. "You did? When?"

"At the hospital. He looked just like how you said he would. He even had the gap between his teeth."

"My God, Hayat, what a blessing...," she said, her hand on my head.

"Okay, okay...enough of that," Father interjected from behind the trunk. "Everybody's hungry. Let's get lunch."

I smiled at her. She smiled back.

"C'mon, c'mon," Father pressed as he marched past us for the front door. "What are we waiting for? Let's get going."

"You'll tell me later," Mina said to me quietly once he'd gone inside. "Your father doesn't want to hear us talking about that...so you'll tell me later, okay?"

At lunch there was an argument. The phone rang as we were eating. Mina was sitting closest to it, but she refused to get it. Finally Father did; it was Nathan.

"No, no, Nate...you're not interrupting. We're just having some lunch. She's right here. I'll put her on."

Father held out the phone to Mina.

She shook her head.

Father's face darkened. He put his palm over the mouthpiece. "What are you doing, Mina?" he asked with a hint of aggression. He didn't look entirely surprised.

"Naveed," Mina pleaded. "Please."

"Please? What...You won't speak to him?"

"Naveed, please," Mina insisted. She looked away, resuming her lunch.

"Unbelievable. Just unbelievable," Father muttered as he brought the phone back up to his ear. "She's in the middle of lunch, Nate. I'll have her call you back. Okay?...I will. Don't worry...'Bye."

Father slammed the phone back into its holder on the wall.

"He doesn't understand," Father said after a long pause.

"Not now, Naveed," Mother said, commanding.

Father turned to her sharply, suddenly seething. "I'm going to say this once and only once. Don't you *ever* tell me what to do or when to do it. Do you understand?"

Mother recoiled, shocked at his tone.

"Bhaj," Mina interjected. "It's okay...let me handle this." Mina turned to Father. "Nathan understands. He just doesn't want to accept it."

"Well, help him accept it."

"And how do you propose I do that?"

"By talking to him."

"I don't see the point. We've talked enough." Her tone was cold. Dismissive.

"Don't see the point? Two days ago this is a man you were going to marry. Now you don't see the point of *speaking to him?* What did he do to deserve that?"

"Nothing."

"So tell him that."

"I did. I told him it has nothing to do with him. It's me. But he doesn't want to accept it."

"Who would?!" Father exclaimed, throwing up his hands in frustration. "None of it makes any sense."

She wasn't going to marry him? It was the first I was hearing of this. An effervescence bubbled up inside me.

"It won't work," Mina said. "It *can't* work."

Father bit his lip, nodding slowly. "Because he's Jewish?"

"Not only."

"Not only?!"

"I said not only."

"What else?" Father asked as he angrily crumpled up his napkin. "Huh? What else?" His lower lip was glistening with saliva.

Mina held his gaze, then calmly looked down at her plate and broke off a piece of bread, using it to scoop a morsel of meat into her mouth.

"What else, I said!" Father shouted. He looked over at me, glaring, and my sudden happiness gave way to alarm as the conflict grew.

"Why are you raising your voice?!" Mother burst out. "Everyone is worried! You're not the only one. One would think *you* were the one calling off a marriage!"

Father turned to Mother, and for a second, I thought he was going to hit her. "That is an option I should have taken more seriously." He stood up abruptly, addressing Mina. "For my sake, for the sake of the hospitality I've extended you—at least you could have the dignity to tell the man that you won't speak to him because he's a *Jew*. Please tell him you would rather have him wiped off the face of the planet like every other mindless Muslim than say another word to him!"

Father held her gaze. And though Mina was clearly reluctant, Father's insistence forced a response. "He'll never be one of us," she said quietly. "And I'm the only one who doesn't care. But that doesn't matter anymore. It doesn't matter that I don't care. I'm not the one that matters."

"Who matters?" Father asked, glancing at me again.

"Everybody else," Mina replied. Father looked away. After a long silence, Mina added: "I think it's best I leave."

Father exploded: "Did I say that? Is that what I said? You've been here more than a year! I welcomed you. You've been my family! Muneer's never been so happy! I've never been so happy! Neither has the boy! This house has been your house! I gave you my brother!..."

There was a pause.

"If only he had been your brother," Mina muttered to herself, but still loud enough for us to hear.

Father stood frozen, his face suddenly wearing a pained, vulnerable look.

Mina held his gaze. "I'm sorry, Naveed," she finally said.

The phone rang intermittently through the afternoon and evening that followed. No one picked it up. Finally, Mother took it off the hook.

Father wasn't home for dinner. Mother put together a couple of plates of leftovers for Imran and me, and sat us before the television before disappearing upstairs into the dining room to continue a discussion with Mina that had lasted most of the day already. I didn't see Mina again until that night, when she came into my room to tuck me in. She looked exhausted. "Tell me your dream, *behta*," she said with a weary smile as she settled in beside me.

I told her about the woman in the veil chasing me and how the Prophet saved me by taking me to a mosque in the mountains where he asked me to lead the prayer. Beyond this, I didn't know what to say. I didn't want to tell her about the figures coming to life, or about the fact that I'd gotten bored and left.

"What else happened?" she asked.

"Nothing, really," I said.

"It's a sign, *behta*," she said after a pause. "You're only the second person I've ever known to see the Prophet in a dream."

"A sign?"

"You've been chosen. You're going to be a leader. A leader of our people," she said flatly. I nodded. I knew she wouldn't have said this if I had told her the rest.

Mina reached out and touched my cast. Her eyes had sunk

AYAD AKHTAR

deep into the dark circles that were opening around them; the paste on her face was fading, and underneath it, the skin around her left eye was blue-black and swollen from where Mother had hit her. She looked so sad. "I can't tell you how sorry I am about this."

"You already said you were sorry, Auntie."

"I know. And I really am." She paused. "How is your arm feeling?"

"Okay."

"Do you still have pain?"

I nodded. The dull ache along the bone was a constant.

"I feel terrible about it." She paused again. "I'm sorry I didn't come to see you in the hospital."

"You sent me those flowers."

Mina smiled. "You liked them?"

"They were beautiful," I said.

I remembered how they had looked in that special light I'd seen after the operation. I wanted to tell her about that light. But before I could, Mina started to speak:

"I want you to know something, Hayat...What you told Imran was wrong. It was wrong for me to do what I did. It was wrong for me to hit you. But it was wrong for you to say what you said. It's not what is written in the Quran."

"Yes it is, Auntie...it says it in—"

She cut me off: "You're too young to understand some things. It was my mistake not being careful." Her tone was brusque, impatient. "The Quran says many things. And some you will not understand until you're older."

I looked away.

"Look at me when I am speaking to you, Hayat," Mina insisted, her finger leading my chin back to face her. It occurred to me that this—and not the dream of the Prophet—was the whole reason she had come to talk to me in the first place. "Nathan never did anything to you. He was only good to you, to me, to Imran. To this family. As far as you knew, he had a good heart. He had good *intentions*. He did not deserve to be treated the way he was treated. He did not deserve for you to say those things about him."

I didn't know how to respond. I was feeling at once ashamed and defiant. I knew looking away from her would make her think she was right.

"I want you to think about it," she said. "Okay, *behta?*"

I didn't say anything.

"Did you hear me, *behta?*" she repeated.

She can't make me speak, I thought as I stared into her face.

13

Acts of Faith

I would regret most what I did next.

Though Mina had been so insistent about not speaking to Nathan again, her resolve would not endure. I overheard her talking to Mother about seeing him. And a day later, I saw her on the phone, the cord stretched across the kitchen and out the window, where she sat on the patio, hunched over the receiver into which she tenderly spoke. I knew it was Nathan. And as I stood in the back of the kitchen, watching her through the window, something dark and obscure moved through me, like black dye suffusing my veins. I went upstairs to my bookshelf and grabbed the book Nathan had given me earlier that summer. I went out to the garage and threw it into the trash. But seeing that book heaped on the stinking pile of white twist-tie trash bags didn't make me feel like I wanted. I felt helpless.

And then I had an idea.

I went back inside and went upstairs to Mina's room. My eyes couldn't move quickly enough along her shelves. And then I found it. The thin tome without a label along its spine. I searched for the page where I recalled seeing the address with Mina's name from when she was married to Hamed.

There it was.

I took the book into my room and sat at my desk. My right

arm still in a cast, I copied the address with my left hand. It took a while. As I walked back to Mina's room to return the book to its place, the blackness in my blood moving, the idea was changing. A letter wouldn't work. It would be too easy to figure out it was me. And then I suddenly remembered the day Mina had sent word of her flight.

A telegram.

I went back to my room thinking: *Ten words or less.*

At my desk drawer, I rummaged for the remains of the twenty dollars Father had given me a year ago. I'd spent nine of it, all on candy, and still had something shy of eleven dollars left. I put on my sneakers and went out again to the garage. I had some difficulty getting onto my bike and finding my balance with my cast, but once I did, I pedaled off.

In the twenty or so minutes it took to ride to the mall, I came to a conclusion. I couldn't call him a Jew. It would be too easy to guess that I had been the one who'd sent the message. Instead, I would call him a *kafr*. The word the Quran used so often: "Unbeliever."

I set my bike along the bushes outside the mall entrance. Inside, the Western Union was empty. I walked up to the window. Sitting before me was the man with searing blue eyes and the violet stain across his face who'd brought us Mina's telegram. He was peeling an orange. He looked up.

"How can I help you?" he asked blankly. I couldn't tell if he remembered me.

"I need to send a telegram."

"Overseas?"

"Yes."

"Here," he said, wiping his hands on his sleeve and then pushing a form through the small opening at the bottom of the window. "Fill it out and bring it back. Flat rate of six dollars for ten words or less. Every word after that is another seventy cents. Punctuation counts."

"Okay."

I moved off to the side and started to fill out the form. I wrote out the message carefully, taking the time to make sure all the letters were legible:

MINA MARRYING A *KAFR* STOP HIS NAME IS NATHAN

When I was finished with that, I pulled out the piece of paper with the Karachi address on it and filled out the space for the addressee:

Hamed Suhail
Dawes Lines Rd 14
Karachi, Pakistan

There was another box under it for the sender's information. I hadn't thought of this. I considered making up a name and an address, but then I realized I didn't know any addresses other than those in the part of town where we lived.

Something inside me was whispering this wasn't going to work.

I looked over at the window and saw the man staring at me as he chewed. "You need help?" he asked.

"No."

"What's the problem?"

"Nothing. Just thinking."

He nodded and turned away, disappearing. I heard a radio, the static giving way to the faint sound of someone talking.

I looked about the office. There were torn scraps and crumpled forms littered on the linoleum, piles of dust pushed into the corners. At the end of the counter on the opposite wall was a yellow pages.

Addresses, I thought.

I went over to the phone book. Opening it at random, I scanned the page, a red-and-blue advertisement for a Chevrolet dealership catching my eye:

Seastrom Chevrolet
2710 Nebraska Avenue
Milwaukee WI 53215

I copied the address onto the form, but I still didn't have a name to put to it. I read the message I'd written out again.

Kafr.

I suddenly saw Sonny Buledi in my mind's eye. The only true *kafr* I knew.

I wrote his name in. "Sonny Buledi." And then I walked back to the window.

The man with the stain on his face was standing in the open doorway leading to a back office, listening. A strident voice was coming over the radio, speaking of the Lord and Jesus. Then he noticed me. "Done?" he asked, approaching.

It wasn't until he was reaching for the form that I felt my first hint of regret. The drabness of the office, the crying out of the voice on the radio, the stain on the man's face . . . I suddenly wanted nothing to do with any of it. As the man took hold of the paper, my grip lingered. He pulled. For a moment I thought it might tear. And then I let it go.

He didn't seem to notice anything was amiss.

"Six dollars for this," he said, reading it over. "With tax, six thirty-one." I counted out seven dollars, pushing the bills through the opening. "What's that mean?" he asked, pointing at the message.

"What?"

"*Kafr?*"

"It means...uh—" I stopped. I wasn't sure if I should go on.

"Yeah?"

"Someone who doesn't believe in God."

The man snickered to himself, disgusted. He looked at me, a frigid light in his blue eyes, and for a moment I felt relieved at the thought that he was going to tell me he couldn't send it.

"People like that?" he finally said. "They'll find out soon enough. When the fires of hell open up and they don't know what hit 'em." He looked at me—holding up my form—and faintly smiled. "I'll get this off for you. Right away."

What followed didn't take long to unfold.

I have a vague recollection of a ruckus that night, a commotion that woke me briefly. The following morning I found Mother sitting at the kitchen table, grave.

"You won't believe it, *behta*," she said. "Hamed knows about Nathan. And he's threatening to take the child back." Mother shook her head. "I mean, I don't think there's any way he can do it...at least not while she's here in this country..." She looked away. "Oh God," she sighed.

I was shocked. This was not at all what I had in mind.

"That man called her parents and told them. And then they called *here* in the middle of the night. 'Who is Nathan? What is going on?' Of course she didn't tell them. Of course, she lied. She said there was no one named Nathan...You know what her father said? That if she ever married a *kafr*, they would have nothing more to do with her." Mother paused. "Actually, he said more than that. He said he would come and break every bone in her body. And he's broken a few of them before." She paused again, getting up. "Well, now it's over for sure. That's that. I don't know what I was thinking. A fool for fantasy. That's what I am, *behta*. Always have been." She stopped and pointed at me, suddenly. "And it's something I see in you. Something you have to know about yourself. Fantasies are for fools, Hayat! *Fools!* Don't be a fool!" She turned away, a perplexed look on her face as she continued, mostly to herself now: "Sonny Buledi? Of all people? Why? How did he even know where to send it?"

Mother wasn't looking at me. If she had been, she would have noticed that I was starting to feel very uncomfortable.

"Where is Mina-Auntie now?" I asked after a long pause.

"Your father took her to see a lawyer this morning. She was in hysterics...you can understand. That bloody man threatened to take her son!" Mother shook her head again, still dumbstruck. "Sonny Buledi...What was he thinking?"

Mother went to the stove to start breakfast. As she cooked eggs, she repeated the same few details of the story, her telling inflected now with self-recrimination, now with anger, and now with her incredulity that any of these things could have come to pass. As I heard it again and again—that Mina might lose Imran, that her father was going to break her bones—it made me dizzy.

What had I done?

Mother tossed a plate of eggs and toast before me but I couldn't eat. She wasn't having any of it. "Things are bad enough right now. Don't make them more difficult for me, Hayat."

I ate a few bites. I popped the yolk on my eggs. I moved the food around and made a mess on my plate. She finally let me go.

Upstairs in my room, I got down on my knees.

"Please don't let anyone take Imran from her, Allahmia. Please. I'll do anything for you. Anything at all. I'll learn the Quran faster. I'll become a *maulvi*. Whatever you want. Whatever it is. Anything. Anything at all. Just please don't let her lose Imran. Please don't have her father break all her bones. Please, please, please..."

As I prayed, I saw pictures in my mind's eye of the man with the stain across his face, chewing, and the office itself, its floor littered with torn and crumpled forms. I relived again and again the moment I held on to the form, imagining now that I hadn't let it go. What I would have given for it to have been torn into two!

Finally, exhausted from my desperate pleas, I went to my bed. But not to sleep. I took the Quran with me. It was the only thing I thought Allah would want: For me to pick up where I'd left off.

As Mother predicted, the lawyer Mina saw that morning told her she had nothing to worry about. At least as long as she was in this country. Mother promised her that she could stay with us as long as she wanted or needed.

I didn't see Mina until that evening. And when I did, I could barely bring myself to look at her. I wanted to tell her what I'd done, but she seemed so unapproachable. There was something forbidding and fierce about her I'd never seen before. Her full, almond-shaped eyes had tapered to slim chinks, and the lines on her forehead—and along the sides of her nose and at the corners of her eyes—were deep and dark. She was even moving differently, with briskness and efficiency, not the sort of shuffling about that had accompanied her earlier discouragements. There was none of the dreaminess in her gaze that often made

it seem her mind had drifted off to some other, infinitely better place. With me, she was cold. And she would be for days
to come. At first, I thought she knew. And then I realized she
was acting like that with everyone. Something inside her had
changed.

I dreamt every night that week of the Western Union office and
the man with the stain across his face. The thought of what
I'd done—the pain of it—was never out of my mind for long. I
was so worried about what would happen to Mina and Imran.
I felt helpless. And the fact that my helplessness was my own
doing bred a new form of shame. Now, I saw clearly how I
had kept myself from Imran. I didn't understand why. I should
have been grateful to have him, I thought. So I took to calling him my brother, as he had long done with me. We played
more than ever. I deferred to his humors. I gave him my things.
But even as I embraced every opportunity to repair the damage I thought I'd done him, I just couldn't forget the telegram.
It was like plaque on my teeth that no toothbrush could scrub
away.
    At week's end, on Friday, Mother and Mina put on their
traditional Pakistani garb for a function at the Chathas' to
which we'd all been invited. Father was convinced the invitation couldn't be taken as anything other than a provocation,
considering the events at the Islamic Center. He even suspected
worse: After speaking to Sonny Buledi—who vigorously denied
having anything to do with the matter—Father had concluded
the telegram could only have been sent by someone from that
"crowd of wolves in sheep's clothing," as he now called them.
He couldn't understand how Mother would even think of going to the event.
    "We need to get out," she said. "*She* needs to get out. We

need to be with people of our own kind. And you should be coming with us."

"Absolutely not," Father said.

"Fine," Mother replied, coldly. "We'll go without you."

Father ordered cheese pizzas and mozzarella sticks from a local pizzeria for me and Imran. Father kept getting up and leaving the room and coming back as Imran and I ate, sitting through reruns of *Three's Company*.

After the show, Imran fell asleep on the couch. Father seemed to have disappeared.

I went up to my room. I opened my desk drawer. Buried under some paper was Mina's picture. I pulled it out. Her face was perfect, the very shape of a nameless feeling inside me that seemed to define all I wanted, a feeling that was now tinged with a roiling regret.

I put the picture back and picked up my Quran. But I couldn't keep my mind on the verses.

I closed my eyes and prayed.

"Please, dear Allahmia. Save Imran from that man. Save Mina from her father. I will do whatever you want me to do. I will give up whatever you want me to give up..."

I heard something. I looked over to find the door to my room yawning open. There was Father.

His hulking form appeared against the black hall, his face barely brushed by the light coming from my desk lamp, the only visible illumination. But despite the darkness, I could see his eyes. They were smoldering.

"What are you doing?" he asked. His voice was strained. His words were slurred.

"Reading Quran," I replied.

"Did you forget what I told you in the hospital?"

It was only then that I realized the book he'd mentioned in the hospital room was the Quran.

"Give it to me," he said, approaching.

I pulled back, drawing it closer. My heart was racing.

"I said give it to me!" he commanded. He was standing above me now, his hand open before me.

"Why?" I finally blurted. My voice—loud, defiant—surprised me.

He stared down at me, his jaw tightening. All at once, his closed fist was coming down at my face. I ducked. He hit the back of my neck. And then he hit me again. I tumbled from the chair.

Father had my Quran in his grip now, his right hand around its cover, his fist closed around a clump of its pages. "This goddamn thing...," he said through his teeth, his arms and shoulders tensing as he pulled and pulled. Finally, he rent the pages from the binding.

He growled as he tossed the cover down and set about ripping the pages free. He pulled and tore, pages and pieces of pages falling to his feet. He tore and tore and before long the carpet was covered with paper. And now Father danced and ground the pages underfoot. He had a wild look in his eye as he stepped madly on the pieces of our holy book. He turned to me, still dancing. "You want your Quran?!" he yelled. "That's your *fucking* Quran!" I'd never heard him use that word. It sounded awkward in his mouth, like something he didn't know how to say. "What you do when you are eighteen is your choice! Until then—if I ever see you with a Quran, I will do exactly what this *fucking* book says about thieves! I will *cut off* your *fucking* hands! Both of them!" He was pointing at me, scowling. "Do you understand?"

I was crying now. My breath was not my own. It kept getting caught in my throat, my chest and neck seizing with contractions I couldn't control.

"Do you understand?!" he screamed.

I tried to nod, but my involuntary wheezing made it difficult to do even that.

"I SAID DO YOU UNDERSTAND?!"

"Ye...e...es...," I cried, finally forcing the sounds out.

"Good," he said, his chest heaving. I looked over at the doorway. Imran was standing there, staring at me.

"We're not finished yet," Father said, headed for my bed. He tore the covers off, then snatched free the fitted sheet underneath. He dropped it to the floor and started kicking the paper onto it. Imran watched, fascinated, as Father worked himself back into a fury, throwing one foot out and now the next, teetering, a look of ever-new surprise on his face, as if he couldn't bring himself to believe it was just paper he was kicking.

The torn pages finally all gathered on the sheet, he pulled the sheet's corners together into his fist and threw the drooping bundle over his shoulder. He turned to me. "Let's go, Hayat!" he shouted. "Now!"

I got to my feet. I still couldn't control my breathing.

"Whe...where...are...we...go...ing?" I asked with difficulty.

"Just go!"

Imran followed as Father marched me down the stairs and into the kitchen. He pulled at the drawer by the telephone and grabbed a lighter lying in there. He pointed at the patio door. "Outside, Hayat! Now!"

It was a dry night. The faintest hint of autumn's coming chill was in the air. At the end of the sloping lawn, above the cover of trees whose silhouette was barely sketched against a black sky, the paper-thin wisp of a crescent moon dangled over the horizon. Father pushed me along. I was still wheezing. I turned and looked back at the house. Imran was watching at the patio door window.

Father made his way to the back of the yard, behind the vegetable garden. He tossed the bundle onto a clearing in the grass covered with ash, where he burned brush in spring and summer, and leaves in the fall. *"Noo....ooo!"* I cried out, realizing what he was going to do.

Father pulled the lighter from his pocket, leaned down, and took up a handful of the torn pages of the Quran into his fist. His thumb snapped at the lighter's switch, producing a thin, long flame. He flashed me a treacherous smile as he held the flame to the pages and waited. It wasn't until the paper actually caught fire that I realized I was surprised. I had expected the pages not to burn.

"Just paper," Father said, as if reading my thoughts. "Couldn't save my sister. And it can't save itself." He dropped the burning pages onto the pile.

The fire slowly took, the flames growing. Tears poured up through me, thick and hot. The fire danced and swam against my wet gaze.

Father was quiet.

"You...are...go...ing...to...go...to...hell...," I said through my tears.

"Good," he said.

"Go...goo...good?"

He didn't answer.

The torn pages wrinkled and turned black in the fire. The black pieces broke apart and lifted on the rising heat. Like flakes of dark snow going the wrong way, they disappeared against the night sky. "If you say anything about this to your mother," Father warned, "I swear to you I will break your *other* arm."

I watched the pages burn. *You didn't stop him*, I thought. And then I remembered what Mina said about intention. That it was all that counted.

I looked away from the fire. I hadn't stopped him. But I didn't have to watch.

BOOK FOUR

Mina the Dervish

14

Sunil the Absurd

The night Father burned my Quran was the night Mina first met Chatha's cousin Sunil. He was in a corner of the room where the men were sitting when Mina noticed him: small, dark, not particularly handsome, but she could tell he was in pain. And it was the way he held himself in that pain—with dignity, nobility, even (or so she would say)—that impressed her.

Sunil had reason to be in pain. His wife had left him for a white American, taking their only son and moving halfway across the country to Florida. (Sunil lived in Kansas City.) He'd since succumbed to paralyzing depression; his ophthalmology practice suffered; he'd been forced to sell it. And now, here he was, midway through his life, sleeping in his first cousin's guest room.

Mina noticed him on her own, but it wasn't until he came up in the dinner conversation among the women that her interest was really piqued. Chatha's wife, Najat, mentioned Sunil's divorce and his difficulties, but by way of complaint: He'd been living with them for months and maybe it was time, she said, for him to take his life into his own hands. Mina weighed in, surprised at Najat's harshness. Divorce, she said, was something you could never understand if you hadn't experienced it.

But as no one at the table expected to experience divorce, they weren't interested in discussing it. Abruptly, Najat changed the subject. And all at once, Mina found herself stewing at the end of the table, her passions inflamed, her heart softened toward the man whose very visible suffering she believed she understood only too well.

Later that night, Mina struck up a conversation with him. She saw him step out onto the front veranda for a cigarette, and she slipped away from the ladies to join him. They spoke for almost half an hour about their divorces. When Mina returned to the kitchen, she did something she had to have known would set things in motion. Najat was preparing the desserts. Mina took a bowl and scooped a hefty portion of *kheer* into it. Then, she walked right into the living room, where the men were gathered, and handed the bowl to Sunil.

In front of everyone.

Sunil sat up, awkwardly taking the bowl and the teaspoon from her. "Thank you," he said.

"You're welcome," Mina replied with a smile.

"Your father's not too happy about your Islamiat," Mother said to me a full five days after Father's Friday-night explosion. "So tone it down for now...just a little."

I stared at her, blank. I knew Father had said something to her that weekend. I'd heard them arguing on Saturday in the bedroom, and heard Father shout my name. And here she was—on Wednesday—talking about me *toning it down* with a scrunch of her face and a tamping gesture with her right hand as if she were asking me to lower the volume on the stereo. "I mean, no one's telling you to stop. But *go easy*... "

"Fine," I said.

She took my reticence as a provocation. "I know how much

you love it," she began, annoyed. "But sometimes things just are the way they are. When there's someone who pays the bills, others have to go along. It's the way of the world. When you grow up, *inshallah,* it will be different for you. But for now, our hands are tied. So just keep that Quran safely tucked away in your closet when he's around. Hmm?"

Of course, she didn't know there was no Quran to keep safely tucked away. And after Father's threat to break my other arm, I wasn't about to tell her.

"Okay," I said.

"Good boy," she said. "And one more thing: No discussion of Nathan. Don't bring him up. Don't mention his name. For *any* reason...okay?"

Only a few weeks earlier, I would have been overjoyed to hear her ask this of me. Now, I only felt my shame and regret.

"Okay, Hayat?" Mother insisted.

"Okay," I said.

Mina found me in her room that afternoon, standing at her bookshelf, perusing her Quran. "What are you doing, *behta?*" she asked.

"Checking your Quran, Auntie."

"But you have one, too."

I hesitated. "I wanted to see yours."

"But you have the same one, sweetie."

I was quiet. I wanted to tell her what had happened. It felt like a way to close the awful distance I felt between us.

"Dad burned it."

"He what?"

"He told me he didn't want me to read it. Then he caught me. And he burned it."

Mina's hand went to her mouth. "My God...," she muttered. She looked away. I had expected her to be outraged. But she just looked worried. "Come here, Hayat," she said, sitting on the bed and patting at the place beside her.

I sat next to her.

"*Behta*," she began. "Your father asked me not to participate in your religious study anymore. He made me promise and...I have to honor his promise. I am his guest, after all."

I was silent. I looked down at the Quran in my hands, remembering my first Quranic lesson—here in this room—the night my body had come alive in her presence and in the presence of the holy words she taught me to understand. That was the night Mina first told me about the *hafiz*, the night I'd gone to sleep brimming with hope and well-being, a night I now recalled with sadness. How long ago it seemed. Everything had changed. Mina didn't love me the way she did back then. And I knew it was all my own doing.

"I don't want you to think that I agree with him, sweetie," Mina continued as she wiped my tears away with her fingers. "I have to honor his will. It's his house. You understand, don't you? *Behta?* Hmm?"

I didn't know what I understood, but I nodded.

Father was increasingly in a bad way. Sometime in mid-September—once it was clear things were really over with Mina—Nathan took a leave of absence and went back to Boston to be with his parents. Two weeks later, he still hadn't returned. And then, without a call or any other warning, Father got a letter from him. Nathan had been offered a position at Mass. General and was taking it. He wanted to stay out east.

Father was desperate. As he saw it, he wasn't only losing his best friend, but also the partnership that had made them both successful. Father wasn't certain he could go on with the work without Nathan. He did all he could to get his colleague to reconsider. He even floated the idea of moving us all to Boston so they could continue their research together. But Nathan wasn't interested. The whole reason for the move, he told Father, was to cut his ties. He'd never been so heartbroken in his life—indeed, he'd never truly understood before what it meant for one's heart to *break*—and he needed to move on. Father pined and despaired. I started to notice he was disappearing into the garage after dinner each night. When he returned, he smelled of whiskey. His mood, usually already foul, would worsen. He erupted without warning. My parents now fought as they never had. They cursed and slammed doors and threatened to leave each other. More than once, Father walked out, car keys in hand, and didn't come back until the next day. Or even later.

One night after dinner Mother and Mina were talking over tea. I was sitting at the end of the table. Father had been gone an entire day and night, and Mother was complaining. After listening for a while, Mina stopped her. "I'm the problem, *bhaj*. I have to leave."

Mother was quiet.

I looked at Mother, surprised she wasn't saying anything.

"But you can't go, Auntie," I finally blurted out.

Mina turned to me. "*Behta,* your auntie has to live her own life now." She said it drily; her tone left no room for debate.

"He hasn't called yet, has he?" Mother asked after another long pause.

Mina shook her head. "But they've been asking."

I suddenly worried they were talking about Hamed. "Who?" I asked.

Mother turned to me, sharply. "Mind your own business, Hayat... Take your milk and go somewhere else."

* * *

Two days later, the phone rang. I picked it up. But before I could speak, I heard Mother's voice on the line. (She'd gotten it upstairs.) It was Ghaleb Chatha calling. I stayed on and listened. After chilly greetings, Chatha got to his point: He wanted permission for Sunil to contact Mina. The intent would of course be matrimonial, he explained.

Mother told him curtly it was fine.

Chatha's response to her was just as curt. "Muneer. I appreciate the fact that you approve. But I really should speak with the man of the house."

There was a pause.

"He has no say on the matter. I'm the one you need to speak with." Mother's tone was acerbic.

"All the same . . . Is Dr. Naveed-*sahib* there?"

"He's not."

"Would you have him call me, please?"

"Not likely, Ghaleb," Mother replied. "There's no love lost for you as far as Naveed goes."

"Then I should speak with her parents directly."

"Suit yourself."

There was another pause.

"Do you have the number, Muneer?"

"You'll have to speak to Mina about that."

"Well, I would prefer not to. If you could get the number and call Najat with it . . ."

"Fine," Mother said. There was a click. She'd hung up the phone.

Mother had no intention of following through with Chatha's request—"I won't be bossed around by that beard on a stick," she complained that night—but Mina would force her to.

Two days later, sometime before sunrise, our phone's tinny toll shattered the sleeping quiet, ringing and ringing. Someone finally picked up. After a brief silence, Mother's bedroom door flew open and she scurried down the hall to Mina's room.

"Call from Pakistan!" Mother hissed. "Your parents!"

"Is everything okay?" Mina asked, alarmed.

"I think Chatha called," Mother said through the door.

Mother was right. Chatha had called her parents in Pakistan and secured the permission he wanted, by way of a proposition: He would not only waive the dowry but he would also foot the bill for the entire wedding, including the Alis' airfare to America to attend it. Rafiq, Mina's father, was overjoyed. And he was calling the house now to persuade his daughter not to squander this second chance at a "normal life." He must have been pleasantly surprised to find his daughter wouldn't need persuading.

My first interaction with Sunil was over the phone. He and Mina had been speaking regularly for about a week when I picked up the phone one afternoon. From the other end came a peculiar, high-pitched drawl:

"Hulloo?"

"Hello?"

"This is Sunil? I'm loooking for Mina Alee?"

"Who?"

"Minaa?

"Mina?"

"Yesss?"

The voice was strange. It spoke with the same unvarying lilt, elongating sounds for no apparent reason, making every phrase sound like it was a question, even when it wasn't.

"Who's calling?"

"Sunil?" He paused. "Is this Haayat?"

"Mmm-hmm."

"I've heard about yoouu? I'm looking forward to meeting you?"

I couldn't understand why he was speaking like this.

"I would like to taaalk to your auntie Mina?"

"Okay. I'll get her."

"Thaank you, *behta?*"

I looked down into the family room, where Mina was sitting on the couch, her hand already on the receiver.

"It's for you, Auntie."

"Sunil?"

"Yes."

"Okay, sweetie," she said.

I was grateful to Allah that things looked to be turning out right. Mother explained that if Sunil and Mina married, then Mina would have no difficulty staying here in America, and Imran would be safe. And so it was with gratitude and renewed devotion that I now began to pray regularly, certain not to miss even a single one of the five daily prayers. But since I wasn't able to be seen praying at home, I concocted a new way to worship. Taking my lead from Mina's insistence on intention, I shed the traditional verses and movements of our *namaaz*. Instead, I would sit quietly at the appointed prayer times, my eyes closed, imagining I was in the presence of Allah Himself. Sometimes I thought of Him as a cloud in the sky; sometimes as the golden throne on which I imagined He sat; sometimes as simply an enormous white light. Whatever the image, I would imagine Him close to me. And then I would wait, listening to my breath, until the silence came. And I would mutter:

"I give myself to You."

That was all. I don't know where it came from, but it felt right. It felt like what I needed to say to God.

I did it everywhere: On the school bus. During recess or lunch. In class. In the backyard. In my room. At the mall. I would sit quietly with my eyes closed, and mutter to myself: "I give myself to You." At times, I emerged from this prayer feeling something—a warmth, a light—I could tell others noticed in my eyes. I relished knowing that they hadn't the slightest idea what it was, or how it got there. No one knew what I was doing.

As for my goal of becoming a *hafiz*, I not only persevered, I worked even harder than I had before, the dawning certainty of Mina's eventual departure fueling a new kind of fervor in me, as I sought now in faith what I was losing in her. The school library had its own copy of the Quran, a small red tome translated by one Ronald McGhee. The edition had a preface that should have troubled me more than it did, outlining the necessity for an "unbiased version of the Bible of the Moslems" that would help Westerners to understand once and for all how "truly barbaric, even animal," these "Moslems" were, and why "Christendom needed to prepare for a renewed crusade." Perhaps I should have been bothered by this, but I wasn't. As I saw it, beggars couldn't be choosers, and McGhee's renditions of verses I already knew were recognizable enough for me not to care about his opinions. I just needed the words. I checked it out and kept it in my desk at school, renewing it every three weeks on the due date stamped on the slip affixed to the inside of the back cover (which slip, incidentally, showed that the last time the book had been checked out before me was twenty years earlier). I spent many a recess sitting in a corner of the playground quietly working my way through new *surah*s. My classmates teased me at first, but after a few weeks—my

Quranic half hour by then a mainstay—I ended up no more conspicuous to them than any of the new-planted maples in the school courtyard. Of course, there were times I didn't feel like going on, times when I longed to join the midday games of kickball or football. But I knew what I was doing was more important than any game. If the Quran was clear on one thing it was that life on earth was passing, and that to pretend otherwise was the only lasting mistake one could truly make. This was how I started to think of it: Life was like watching a show you loved. You didn't want it to end. But it *would* end, sooner or later; that's just the way it was. And when the show was over, you had to get on with things. The sooner you started getting yourself ready for what was coming after, the better.

It was early one Sunday morning in mid-October. After waking at sunrise to sit at the edge of my bed and pray in my new way, I went downstairs to the family room with a bowl of cereal to watch TV. At some point, I heard Father grumble a greeting from the top of the steps, disappearing into the kitchen to make himself tea. There was a brief clanging of pots and pouring of liquids, and shortly, Mother joined him. Moments later, Father was shouting:

"I don't care! I don't want to be here for it! And I won't! I have better things to do with my life! If she won't listen to me about that fool, at least I don't have to be a party to it!"

"Calm down, Naveed!"

There was a loud, metallic crash. I looked over at the stairs leading up to the kitchen. Father was standing at the cabinet where he and Mother kept their keys.

"Where do you think you're going?" Mother asked in a pointed tone.

"Fishing. That's where."

Father glanced down into the family room and our eyes met. For a moment, I thought he was going to ask me to go fishing with him. But he didn't.

I would gather what the argument had been about later that morning as I lingered in the kitchen while Mina and Mother took breakfast: Sunil was supposed to be coming over to visit. It wasn't the first time Mina and Imran had seen him; they'd been to visit at the Chathas' with Mother a few times in the past weeks. But this was the first time Sunil would be coming to our home. The real idea had been for Sunil to meet Father, but Father wasn't having any of it. He was still upset over what had happened between Nathan and Mina, and he thought this new development with the "Chatha cousin"—as Father referred to Sunil—was laughable.

Mother didn't care that he wouldn't be around, but Mina was concerned.

"This is not good, *bhaj*," Mina said.

"It doesn't matter."

"It does matter," Mina said, putting her piece of toast down and pushing her plate away.

"You're not finished, are you?"

"I'm not hungry."

"You're not eating anything these days. You're starting to worry me. You don't look good...Isn't that right, Hayat?" Mother asked, turning to me. It was true that Mina looked like she'd been losing weight, and she didn't have much to lose. The skin on her face was starting to look taut and drawn in a way that looked unnatural. But I didn't want to say that and hurt her feelings.

"The tea is enough," Mina replied.

"Hayat, bring her a glass of milk."

"*Bhaj*..."

"Finish your toast," Mother said firmly.

"Fine," Mina muttered, picking up the half-eaten piece of bread to take a bite. I poured a glass of milk and brought it to her. She took a sip.

"You haven't been this bad since we were kids," Mother said.

"It's nothing. It'll pass. There's a lot on my plate."

Mother looked down at Mina's plate. "Not as much as there should be."

Mina laughed. Mother did, too. Then all at once, Mother wasn't laughing anymore. She held Mina's gaze, suddenly grave. "Are we doing the right thing?" she asked.

"The right thing?"

"Do you really want to do this?"

"Muneer. We are doing this."

Mother nodded, her chin dropping to her chest. There was a long pause.

"So what are we going to do about the Chathas?" Mina asked.

"About what?"

"Two women having a strange man over to their house? With no man of the house here? If Najat hears about this..."

Mother looked puzzled. "What?"

"What do you think?"

Mother scrunched her face. She didn't know.

Mina turned away from me, lowering her voice. "They'll say we're *loose*."

"Because Naveed isn't here?" Mother replied, her voice lowered as well.

"Do I really have to explain this to you? This can't really be news to you, *bhaj*?"

Mother rolled her eyes. "I didn't think people could still

think that way. You've been to their house on your own with Imran now, I don't know, a half a dozen times..."

"But Najat is there..."

"So?"

"So, she's the one who would be spreading the tale. I would never think of showing up if she wasn't around. She already has her doubts about me." Mina paused. "She was asking me how I could live so long under one roof with a man like Naveed."

"Not a bad question," Mother joked.

"I'm serious, Muneer. He doesn't have the best reputation with them..."

"Hmm..."

"So I lied. I told them I wore the veil at home and kept to myself. That he never addressed a word to me unless you were present."

Mother recoiled with a frown. She held Mina's gaze for a long, pregnant moment. "What are you getting yourself into?"

For a moment, Mina didn't seem to know how to respond. And then she said: "He loves Imran, *bhaj*. He's a humble man. He's made promises. I can live with the rest. It's not the end of the world."

Apparently Sunil didn't mind that Father wasn't there. He just didn't want Mina to mention it to either Ghaleb or Najat. And so it was that I got to meet him for the first time.

I felt bad for thinking it, but to me he looked like a field rodent. He had a narrow face, a small round nose, and wide cheekbones brushed with fine black hairs, like tiny whiskers. And there was his posture, too: As he sat in our living room that afternoon—on the armchair where, four months earlier, Nathan had been laid out with a bleeding cut along his eye when Imran threw a matchbox car at his face—Sunil's thin wisp of a body slouched and seemed to vanish into the loose beige suit he was wearing; and the suit's beige pattern blended cleanly enough into the armchair's beige shade that he looked engulfed by the fabric that surrounded him, a dark brown head peering out from a swollen swath of beige cloth, not unlike a prairie dog surveying the world from its burrow.

"Hayat," he said to me from across the room. I stood in the living room doorway, no less startled by Sunil's appearance than by what Mina was wearing: a tightly fitted veil, like the ones we were seeing in Iran on the evening news. I had never seen her in anything like it. Whenever she covered her head, it was with an Indic *dupatta,* which never really concealed all that much and, paradoxically, had the effect of rendering a woman's femininity, if anything, even *more* palpable than if she wasn't covered at all. But as for the strict, face-framing navy-blue *hijab* on her head now, there wasn't much allure in it. To me, she looked like a nun.

"This is Sunil, sweetie."

"Behtaaa?" Sunil cooed. I stared back at him, blank. I remembered the brief conversation we'd had on the phone. His lilting intonation and elongation of syllables made no more sense now than when I couldn't see his face. He blinked at me insistently as he gazed, like there was something irritating his eyes. "Hoow are youuu?"

"Fine."

"Meen has been telling me all about your studiees? I'm so prouud to know a young *hafiz*-to-be..."

"Thank you, Uncle."

"How faaar have you gotten, *behta?*"

"Ten *juz.*"

"Ten?!" Mina exclaimed.

"A third of the waaay?" Sunil said, still blinking. He looked over at Mina, impressed.

"How did you already get through ten?" Mina asked, shaking her head.

"At school. I work at it during recess."

"Recess?" Mina looked at Sunil, then back at me. "Your dedication is inspiring, *behta*." She turned again to Sunil. "You remember what I told you about Naveed?"

Sunil nodded, his head bobbing side to side in traditional Indo-Pak style, blinking away as he did. "How impressive. Not only self-motivated? But under such *diiif*-icult conditions." Sunil leaned forward and reached out his hands to me. "Come to Uncle..." I approached, but I could only step so far; Imran and his toys were laid out all around Sunil's feet. Sunil reached both his hands out farther, over Imran's head. I couldn't tell what he wanted me to do.

"Give me your haaands," he said.

I did.

Taking hold, he pressed into my palms with his fingers. It was weird.

"You remind meee of my nephew," he said, still kneading my palms. "Only *fifteeeen* years old and already a complete *hafiz*."

"What's his name?" I asked.

"Farhaz...Maybe you will meet him soon," he said, turning to Mina with a smile.

I looked over at her. She brought her hand to her forehead to push a strand of hair peeking out back beneath the veil. That was when I saw the enormous, glimmering white diamond she was wearing on her left hand's ring finger. She noticed me notice the ring. "Oh...Sunil-Uncle just gave this to me." She held out her hand for me to see. "An engagement ring."

"It's big," I said.

Sunil pressed into my palms again. "So maybe you'll get to meet Farhaz sooner than you think..."

Imran moaned, feeling left out. Sunil dropped my hands and leaned down for the boy, lifting him into his lap. Parted from his toys, Imran now squealed, even though he'd been the one seeking the attention. Sunil ruffled his hair affectionately and kissed him on the cheek, and all at once, Imran softened into Sunil's embrace like there was nowhere else in the world he wished to be.

"I love you, Dad," Imran said quietly.

"I looove you, too, *behta,*" Sunil said, gently caressing him.

Mina was clearly moved.

Sunil turned to me. "This means I will be your real uncle. And I waaant you to think of us as your second parents. If you ever neeeed anything?"

I held his blinking gaze, not sure how to respond. Mother appeared at the entryway with a clap of her hands. "Okay, kids. Time for the adults to have a discussion. Get your coats and go out to play."

Imran squealed and whined some more, but Mother knew exactly what to say: "You love the tree house, don't you?" Imran bit his lip, nodding. Mother smiled, then turned to me with a command: "Hayat. Take him to the tree house." Imran hopped out of Sunil's lap and went bounding off for his coat.

As I walked out into the hall after him, Mother grabbed me by the elbow of my still-plastered arm. "Don't go running your mouth with the boy," she muttered. "We don't need any more trouble."

Outside, it was a wet, gray day. The sky was in turmoil. I was, too. I knew I should have been happy everything was turning out all right, but I wasn't. What Mother said to me in front of the others stung, and there was the pang of envy I'd felt on hearing Sunil talking about his nephew, Farhaz, the *complete hafiz,* as he'd called him. And there was something else as well, something rough and empty, something elusive rattling around inside me.

I followed Imran, trudging through yards of soggy leaves, my head lowered, my fists pushed deep into my pockets. He was taking the usual route, singing to himself as he went. We made our way up the hill toward the Gartners', their single-story box-shaped house appearing from behind the hedges. Imran raced ahead, bolting up the empty driveway, past the tall willows that lined the yard, their weeping branches shuddering with the cold wind.

I stopped and gazed at the trees. *Where was their comfort?* I wondered.

I made my way to the front door. Imran pushed at the doorbell. The curtains were drawn at the front bay windows, and there were no lights on inside. Around back, we peered in at the kitchen window. It was dark there, too. The Gartners' cat—a Persian with marbled lapis lazuli eyes—was poised on the counter, staring back at us, placid, inscrutable.

We went around back to the set of trees whose massive trunks were capped and bridged by the interlocking boxes of the elaborate tree house some twenty feet above us. Imran turned to me for permission. I nodded. He darted forward, taking hold of the ladder with his small hands, and started to climb. I didn't move. I watched him. His small shoes squeaked on the ladder's wet rungs as he rose.

Why had they built a tree house? I wondered. *What did they need it for?*

Imran disappeared into the entrance cut into the tree house's floor, his head then appearing through one of the window openings.

"Come on, Hayat," he said, waving me up.

I lifted my arm, showing him my cast.

"When do you take it off?" he asked with a grimace.

"Day after tomorrow," I said.

He shrugged and disappeared inside.

I looked about. Trees on the surrounding lawns didn't look like trees at all. Mostly bare, trunks wet and black in the slate-gray light, they looked like they were made of stone. Even the houses seemed hardened in the chilly drizzle. It was a cold, callous, slippery world, and I was losing the only thing I'd ever loved to it.

15

The Farewell Begins

The wedding was set for the day after Thanksgiving. Mina had been insistent that she wanted a small, discreet ceremony, but Chatha was sparing no expense in marrying his cousin: He and Najat invited more than two hundred and fifty people; he'd booked the opulent chandelier ballroom at the posh Atwater Hotel downtown for the reception; he even flew in a cook from their local village in Pakistan to prepare the meal. When Mina found out about the cook, she and Sunil had their first argument.

She complained to Mother over dinner one night about all the money Ghaleb was spending, and was visibly surprised by Mother's response.

"Ghaleb and Najat know what he's been through... You're a catch. Look at you. They want to show you off. Heal his wounded pride after what that last wife of his did to him... Maybe there's more wisdom in it than you realize. If it makes him feel stronger to have a big wedding, what's the problem? They're footing the bill! Live it up!"

"I don't want them to think I'm after his money."

"But you are." Mother laughed.

"*Bhaj.* Please. It's not even *his* money..."

Mother scrunched up her face. "Have you *completely* lost your sense of humor?"

Mina shrugged. "You *know* why I'm doing this. For Imran."

"Then *bite the bullet.* It's not the end of the world." After a pause, Mother added: "Could be worse. You could be one of *four.*"

Mina chuckled. "You don't realize how unbearable Najat really is..."

"The in-laws are always unbearable."

"But they're even terrible with Sunil. He's always complaining about how Ghaleb bosses him around."

"Ghaleb is paying the bills."

"Which is nothing to say about what they think of Naveed and you."

"What do they say about me?"

"That you're harebrained."

"Harebrained?" Mother repeated. "What does that mean?"

"Nothing. It doesn't mean a thing."

"Hare as in *rabbit?*"

"I think."

"Najat's the rabbit. Not me."

"She won't leave me alone about my skin."

"Well, there *is* something wrong with your skin. You're not eating properly."

Mina sighed. "I just want to get this all over with and behind me."

"Harebrained?" Mother repeated again.

"It's nonsense, *bhaj.* They can't understand a woman like you."

"Like *us.* You're the same as me. Probably worse."

There was a long pause. "You're right," Mina finally replied.

* * *

I stopped by Mina's room that night, hoping for a story. I found her sitting in her bed, a book open in her lap, her eyes red and swollen.

"Are you okay, Auntie?"

"Fine, *behta*," she replied with a weary shake of the head. "Can you get your auntie some water, please?"

"Mmm-hmm."

I went down into the kitchen, filled a glass with tap water, then brought it back to her room. She blew her nose into a tissue, tossing it to the floor. I handed her the glass.

"Thank you," she said quietly. Imran was sleeping in his bed.

"You're welcome, Auntie. Are you okay?"

Almost at once, tears appeared in her eyes. She reached for another tissue, bringing it to her face. "It's nothing," she said. "Just something I'm reading."

"What is it?" I asked, looking down at the open book. It wasn't in English—it looked like Arabic to me—but it wasn't the Quran either.

"Jami's *Nafahat*."

"What's that?"

"It's about the lives of the great Sufis. I was reading about Kharaqani, and ..." She stopped suddenly, choking up again.

"It's okay, Auntie. You don't have to tell me."

"No," she said, shaking her head. "I want to ... Here. Sit down next to me." I took a place beside her. "I'm going to translate it for you."

"What language is it, Auntie?"

"Persian."

"Persian? I didn't know you could read that."

"There's lots of things you don't know about me, sweetie."

I was quiet. It had never occurred to me that there might be something more about my beloved Mina than what I already knew of her. That there were things I didn't know—and might never know—made my heart ache.

"So this is a story about Ansari," she said, pointing at the page. I noticed she wasn't wearing the ring she'd had on during Sunil's visit. "Ansari was one of the great Sufi poets, Hayat. When he was a young man, he had a teacher, a wise old man named Kharaqani. And Ansari learned all about what it meant to be a Sufi from Kharaqani." She started to translate from the text, slowly: "'If I had never met Kharaqani,' he says, 'I would never know God. From Kharaqani I learned that you can't judge a Sufi by what he wears. One is not a Sufi because he wears broken clothes, or has a beard or because he carries a prayer mat.

"'To be a Sufi,'" she continued, "'means to give up the world and everything in it. To be a Sufi means to depend on nothing, to want nothing, to be nothing. A Sufi is a day that needs no sun, a night that needs no moon, no stars. A Sufi is like the dust on the ground, not the stones that hurt people's feet when they walk, but the dust that no one knows is even there.'"

Mina started to cry, and this time she didn't try to stop herself. I reached out and held her. Her bones were hard, with little flesh to pad them. She sobbed quietly into another tissue. "This is what life does to us, *behta*. It grinds us. Grinds us to dust. The Sufi is just someone who doesn't fight it. He knows that being ground to nothing is not bad. It's the way to God."

I didn't really understand what she was saying. But as with the tale of the dervish and his orange peels, I wouldn't soon forget the bizarre pairings of images, days without sun, nights without a moon, God and dust, and, of course, the startling notion that being ground to nothing was the true way to our Lord.

* * *

Mina wasn't eating. For weeks it seemed she subsisted almost entirely on a diet of tea alone. Mother did what she could, often forcing Mina to linger at the dining table once everyone else had finished, trying to get her to nibble a little more at meals she would barely touch anymore. I saw Mother sit beside her, putting forkfuls of rice and curry into her best friend's mouth. But even when Mina took in the nourishment, her body would reject it. More than once, I heard her in the bathroom after dinner, retching. My parents were terribly worried. Father brought home powdered glucose from the lab for her to mix into her tea; Mother took her around to a host of specialists. All the doctors thought Mina's problem was psychological, and that she needed therapy. Mina didn't agree.

"Therapy is not the solution, *bhaj*," she told Mother. "It's getting the marriage done and behind me. I'll be fine once this is over."

"If you make it that long," Mother joked, blackly.

It was true that one had to wonder if she could make it that long. By mid-November, some ten days before the wedding, Mina really started to look strange. The flesh on her face had ebbed to reveal the outlines of the forbidding, boxlike structure of her skull underneath, its flattish planes covered with skin drawn like a sickly, matted yellow membrane across the bony surface. Even her once-bright gaze had a jaundiced hue. She looked more and more unreal, and this transformation of her features endowed her face with something uncanny, something which held my attention as avidly as her once-vital and devastating beauty used to. Perhaps I was just stunned at the erosion taking place before my eyes—the change in her appearance was so startling that even her parents wouldn't recognize her at the airport when she picked them up—or maybe there was truly something newly bewitching about her, something at once desperate and alive, a woman who sensed defeat approaching, but whose glow only brightened at the prospect, an incandescence quickened to its brief, brilliant zenith, a prelude to the decline she must have sensed was ahead.

On the Saturday before the wedding, Mina's parents arrived. I was struck as I stood at the living room window, watching two small, slight men at the trunk pulling out bags, both with narrow shoulders and thick heads of bushy black hair; I knew one of them was Sunil and the other was Mina's father, Rafiq, but at first, I couldn't tell which one was which. And the similarities didn't end there. Over tea at the kitchen table, I was surprised to discover that both of them had the same annoying habit of blinking a lot. No doubt it was a meaningless coincidence, but it left a troubling impression: as if the most important men in Mina's life were somehow similarly distracted, unreliable, unsteady.

Tea that Saturday afternoon was a lively affair. Rafiq was worked up about the trip he and Rabia had just completed, which, already a strain at over twenty hours, had been truly insufferable with an eight-hour layover—due to the airplane's mechanical problems—in Paris. He was still seething over a meal at the airport cafeteria that the airline had served a flight full of mostly Muslim passengers. "It's the middle of the night. Everything is closed. They had to make us *something*...So they throw together some soup of green peas with pieces of meat in it." Rafiq was a natural entertainer, and his expressions and tone were as animated as his hands, which didn't stop moving as he spoke: "*Arey*...at *that* point everyone is *starving*. We've been sitting there five hours. Five hours! The people are hungry. So they start eating. Children are eating. Parents are eating. Old people are eating...But *what* are they eating? I'm the only one with a brain to ask the woman: *'What are you serving?'* No English. Not a word. She gives me my food, and I see something floating in the soup. *'What are these pieces?'* I ask her. 'Lardo,' she says. 'Lardo.'" Rafiq repeated the words a few times with a blank face, imitating the waitress's expression. Spying the amusement on my face, he turned to me: "Lardo? What is lardo? And then I realize: Maybe it's *lard.* 'Is it a pig?' I ask her. No concept. She couldn't be bothered. Looking at me like: *Be happy and eat what you're given, you dog.*" I was having difficulty squaring my initial impression of Mina's father as a man who wanted to break all his daughter's bones with the very likable and gregarious fellow seated before me. I kept looking over at Mina to see how she was feeling. As far as I could tell, she appeared to be enjoying Rafiq as much as I was. He went on with his story, pointing to his wife now, a plumper, older, less arresting version of her daughter: "But then *this one* has the brilliant idea of making *mooing* sounds. The waitress shakes her head and makes some other sounds. 'Oink, oink,' she makes. 'What is oink, oink?' I ask. And then somebody's child, born here in the States, says 'That's the sound of a pig!' Can you believe it? They're serving peas with pork to a full flight of Pakistanis!? When people found that out, it was a riot. Running to the bathroom to wash their mouths. Others trying to throw up. A real zoo!" He was laughing. We all were, except Father, who looked like he wanted to be elsewhere. "The airport staff sees all these *jungli*s running around. They're terrified. So they lock us into the gate. Won't let us out. Throwing us bits of bread and cheese like people in jail. *That* for another two hours! Three hundred people, coughing, passing gas. I'm a sixty-year-old man. She's a sixty-year-old woman. It was a nightmare!"

Rafiq settled back into his chair and looked at Mina, the mood at the table shifting. His eyes slimmed as he considered his daughter. "And after all of that, to get off the plane and ..."

"Please, Rafiq," Rabia interjected. "Don't start."

"Don't start? Our daughter looks like a bag of bones!"

"*Abu,*" Mina said. "I'm fine."

"You're *not* fine. You look like a bag of bones."

Mina picked up a tea biscuit from the plate at the center of the table and took a bite. "See. I'm eating."

Rafiq shook his head, blinking now—if at all possible—with even more frequency as he looked over at Sunil, and then at my parents. "I have to thank you, Naveed and Muneer, for everything you've done. God only know she's not easy to deal with ... but honestly, you could have taken better care of her ..."

Father didn't respond. Not even with a nod. He'd retreated completely, ceding the table and the afternoon to the elder Rafiq.

"*Abu,* it has nothing to do with them," Mina said. "It's me. I've not been feeling well."

"And why is that?" Rafiq asked.

Mother jumped in: "Rafiq-Uncle, she's been through a lot."

"Really?" Rafiq asked, his voice thick with sarcasm. "Like what? She meets a nice man ...," he began, looking over and trading a smile with Sunil, "who accepts her for who she is and wants to give her a new life? What is so difficult about that?"

"Stop it," Mina said to her father, firmly.

Rafiq turned to her, shocked.

Sunil spoke up now, addressing Mina sharply: "He's concerned for you. And I am too."

Mina's gaze darted back and forth between them. "Fine," she said, taking a sip of her tea.

Rafiq continued to stare at her.

"I said fine, *Abu*," Mina repeated.

Rafiq seemed to let it go. He turned to Sunil, blinking briskly. "I'm expecting you to fatten her up, *behta*."

Sunil smiled, blinking back.

"First class, *Abujee*. First class," he replied with sudden, unaccountable glee. "Don't you worry about it one bit, Ali-*sahib*." Sunil reached out for the tray, picked up a biscuit, and laid it on Mina's plate. "Have another," Sunil said to her.

Rafiq smiled widely, baring a top row of thick, yellowing teeth. He looked back at Mina, waiting to see what his daughter would do.

Mina stared at her father, the tension palpable between them.

"Do as your husband-to-be says," Rafiq said quietly. "Eat it."

Mother stole a glance at me. Father was looking down at the table.

Finally, Mina looked down, picked up the biscuit, and put it in her mouth.

"What a tyrant," Mother complained once tea was over and the Ali parents had gone upstairs to my room to rest. (I was to sleep in the family room during their two-week stay.) "Forcing her to eat that biscuit! He used to do things to her like that *all the time*. Never to his boys, but always to her. And did you see Sunil sitting there? Enjoying every second of it? I wanted to reach over and smack that grin off his face."

We were standing at the sink. I was drying the porcelain; she was scrubbing the inside of the teapot. Through the kitchen window before us, I could see Sunil and Father in the backyard, talking. Sunil was holding Imran's hand as he spoke.

"Rafiq has a Napoleon complex," Mother said. "You know Napoleon, don't you?"

I knew enough to see in my mind's eye the image of a military man from another century with a hand pushed into his coat. But that was about it.

"A tiny man. Just this high," Mother indicated, her hand showing a height not much taller than mine. "And this *midget* takes over Europe. He could have been the *ruler of the world*. Do you know why? Because a man like that, who thinks the world looks down on him—and let's be honest, it *does*—a man like that stops at nothing to make the world respect him. He'll take it over just to prove a point! So you see, you have to be careful with these small men! They're all trying to take something over!" She handed me the teapot to dry. "That's a Napoleon complex, *kurban*. Put it into a Muslim man, and you have *complete* disaster! I hope to *God* Sunil will at least be a good father to the boy...and there's no reason to think he won't. He has been tender with him."

She looked out the window. The discussion between Sunil and Father seemed tense, heated. Father didn't look pleased.

"What could they be talking about?" Mother muttered. "I hope your Father doesn't say anything we'll all regret." She turned to me, suddenly worried. "Don't mention anything about Nathan. Under *any* circumstances. His name doesn't need to come up. Her parents don't know anything about him. Neither does Sunil..."

"You already told me," I said.

Just then, the patio door flew open. It was Father.

"What a nonentity!" he fumed.

"Naveed. I asked you to bear with him. *Please.*"

"Bearing with him is one thing. Being *abused* is another."

"Abused?" Mother said with a smile. "How is *that* possible?"

Father shot her an intense look. "If you're looking for trouble with me, Muneer... trust me, you'll find it."

"I just asked what he said to you."

"If you had any idea what he really thinks of you, you wouldn't be so sympathetic to that *idiot.*"

"What did he say about me?"

"That I don't keep you in check. That I'm setting a bad example. That he won't let Mina have anything to do with you if I don't stop you from putting ideas in her head."

"What?!"

"You still want me to bear with the idiot?"

Mother looked over at the window. Sunil was headed up to the house.

"He's coming," she said.

"And I'm going," Father said, leaving.

The patio door opened, this time gently, and Sunil walked in holding Imran. "Where's Naveed?" he asked in his usual unctuous tone. I was surprised Sunil was so calm, given how irritated Father had been by their conversation.

"He went out...," Mother replied, hesitating before she added: "For groceries."

Sunil smiled. Mother smiled weakly back, chewing on the inside of her cheek.

"Is there something you want to discuss with me, *bhai-jaan?*" she asked.

"Discuss? Like whaaat, *bhaaji?*"

"Is there something on your mind? About me, maybe?" Mother's voice was tense.

"Absolutely not," he said with a smile. "But if there's anything *you* wish to discuss, pleeease let me know. You're like her sister. So you're like my own sister, too. I don't have any sisters."

Mother didn't seem in the least bit appeased. "I *am* her sister, Sunil," Mother announced. "Her sister *in spirit*. Which is stronger than blood."

"Of course you are," Sunil affirmed, with a bobbing nod.

Mother held his gaze. "Don't forget it," she warned.

"Forget?" Sunil asked, blinking. "How could I ever *forget?*"

Mina's father was ecstatic to find himself in America. Up early every morning, he went for long walks. He visited the post office, the grocery store, city hall, the library, the local high school. For breakfast, he had pancakes—American-style *paratha*s, he called them—at a local diner, and then made his way to the mall across the road to wander for hours in the shops. "Everything is so *big*," he kept remarking. "The roads, the cars, the trees, the houses, the people. Even the children are huge. I saw a group of boys with arms thicker than my legs. From a distance I thought they were men. But when I came up close, they had faces of babies. I asked one of them how old he was: 'Sixteen,' he said. Sixteen! And already as big as a monster!" America's size impressed him, and so did its cleanliness. He remarked one night at dinner: "There's no garbage anywhere. No dust. The roads are so clean, you could eat a meal on them. How do they do it?"

"They take care of things," Father replied, gruff. He was spending even less time than usual at home now. It was clear enough he didn't like Rafiq. And it was clear Rafiq felt the same way about him. "Unlike us Pakistanis," Father added, "Americans know how to make the world a better place."

Rafiq didn't reply to Father's provocation. At least not until dinner the following night, when he broke into a colorful tale of how, that afternoon, he'd wandered into a funeral home and found himself in an empty room with an open coffin. Rafiq described his shock at stepping up to the coffin and discovering inside it a dead young woman in a tight-fitting dress, her face covered with mounds of makeup, and reeking of perfume that couldn't quite mask the unpleasant odor her body was giving off.

"Like she was getting ready to go out!" Rafiq mocked. "Who is she going to meet? She's dead!"

"It's for the family and friends," Mother explained. "They have a party for everyone to see the body one last time before they bury it. It's their ritual."

"Party?"

"It's not a party," Father corrected. "It's called a *wake*."

Rafiq frowned. "Well, Naveed-*behta*. As you said, they do know how to take care of things—but do the dead need this kind of *taking care?*" Rafiq's tone was a challenge. Father met it with silence. Finally, he shrugged and looked away.

Rafiq looked pleased. He turned to Mina. "She happened to look a little like you, *behti*. Dark hair...but not *such* a bag of bones."

Rabia looked up from her meal with surprise. "What a terrible thing to say, Rafiq!"

Rafiq now shrugged.

"And look at her," Rabia continued, pointing at her daughter, "she's eating."

It was true. Mina was working her way through her meal, and already half-finished.

"Awake," Rafiq said to himself after a pause. "What a strange thing to call it. The person is not *awake*. She's dead. But they still want to pretend that she's *awake*."

"It's not one word, *sahib*," Father said. "It's two words."

Rafiq looked confused.

"Not *awake*," Father explained. "But *a wake*."

Rafiq waved his hand dismissively at Father. "One word or two, it doesn't matter. Nothing will change the surprise in store for that poor woman when she finds out where she's really headed once the party is over!"

Mother was depressed. Mina's stay with us had been her lifeline, not only a healthy distraction from her *bête noire*— Father's affairs—but also a sustaining reprieve from the punishing loneliness she felt living in America. She didn't speak about it much, but she suffered terribly from homesickness— a conclusion I would draw once Mina was long gone and Mother populated her life with reminders of her homeland: shelves filled and walls covered with Pakistani arts and crafts; *ghazal*s lightly playing on the stereo all day long; and the Indian films into which she would disappear, it seemed, for days.

Mother's doleful, grieving mood that autumn was only compounded by the fact that she'd been completely excluded from the wedding preparations. To some extent, so had Mina. And though Mother had been advising her best friend to let the Chathas handle things as they saw fit, when Ghaleb and Sunil stopped making any attempt to hide their blatant disregard for our family, Mother had difficulty taking her own advice. She realized somewhat too late that her earlier attempt to draw the line with Sunil was backfiring. Sunil's counter to her claim of centrality in Mina's life came in the form of the very sort of interdiction Mother feared: He told his fiancée he didn't want to hear Mother's name spoken in his presence. When Mother heard this, she humbled herself. She called Sunil to apologize. But his response was less than gracious: He told Mother that while he wouldn't stand in the way of her friendship with Mina, he himself didn't see any reason for him and Mother to have anything more to do with each other.

Mother's difficulties with Sunil turned Najat against her as well. Mina had wanted to reach out to the Buledis in the wake of what had happened. Father had convinced her that Sonny couldn't have had anything to do with the telegram—being a supposed *kafr* himself—and Mina concluded it would be appropriate to extend to the Buledis the goodwill gesture of an invitation to the wedding. The only thing was: She didn't want to broach the matter herself with her in-laws. So she asked Mother to do it.

When Mother phoned the Chathas and left a message on their machine making the suggestion, Najat didn't call back. Mina brought up the matter with Najat a day later, and Najat used the opportunity to make a point: Unbelievers like the Buledis had no place at the wedding (it was bad enough Naveed would have to be there), and if Mina's "friend"—by which she meant Mother—didn't like it, "no one was forcing her to come either." Mina was shocked. And it took every ounce of her will not to give Najat a piece of her mind.

Mother, too, was shocked on hearing what Najat had said—and more than a little dismayed—but she remained adamant that Mina was doing the right thing by keeping quiet. There was no use, she kept repeating, in fighting a battle one could only lose. And so, practicing what she preached, Mother decided she was going to stay home on Thanksgiving Day, when the Chathas had planned a party at their house, an all-day function for Mina and her mother to try on the clothes and jewelry Najat was having made for the *nikah*. Mina was to get her hands covered with patterns of henna, and the Alis would meet for the first time much of the extended Chatha family that had come from out of town to attend the ceremony. Mina didn't want Mother to stay home, but Mother had made up her mind.

"It's what's best," she insisted. "I'll be fine."

But at breakfast on Thanksgiving Day, Mother wasn't fine. She looked utterly defeated. And as we all munched on Rabia's supremely buttered and inimitably tasty *parathas*—Mother's were good, but these were stupendous—Mina wanted to revisit the question.

"Reconsider, *bhaj*. I know you want to be there. I want you there. As long as no one gets into *discussions*—and you don't even have to worry about Sunil. He's not going to be there. He's going with Ghaleb to the hotel to check on things..."

"Why not, Muneer?" Rabia said brightly as she returned from the stove with a new plate of steaming, buttered bread. "It's only right. You *should* be there."

"Not a good idea," Rafiq announced as he reached across to grab a fresh *paratha*. "Not a good idea at all."

"Why not?" Mina asked.

"Yes. Why not?" Rabia added.

"He's right," Mother mumbled before Rafiq could reply.

Rafiq turned to Mother. *"Behti,"* he began, gently, "I know it bothers you. It bothers me, too. My own sons are not here. How do you think that makes me feel? These are the kinds of things that arise in life. The *situations*. And what matters is not so much *what* these situations are, but *how* we deal with them." Rafiq paused. He was gazing at Mother warmly. "You know Rabia and I love you like a daughter. You're like my own daughter. You are family. You know that." Mother's eyes were filling with tears. "I don't need to tell *you* these things are complicated. You know that from your own experience. Let's do what's best. Let's be sure our dear child is settled and happy. And when we've accomplished that, then we attend to the politics. Hmm?"

Mother nodded, still fighting her emotions. But across from her, Mina was crying. *"Bhaj,"* she keened, reaching out and pressing her hand into Mother's.

Their eyes met, and Mother crumpled.

"Ladies, please," Rafiq said. "We should be celebrating. Laughing, not crying." His comment went unheeded, as his own wife was now tearing up.

Mina got up and went to hold Mother. Rabia did the same. And now, enclosed in the women's embrace, Mother released her pain. The sounds she made were round and deep, full of sorrow. Imran, alarmed, started to cry, too. Rafiq reached across and caressed his grandson. "Your Muneer-auntie is just a little sad," he said, sounding a little choked up himself.

I watched it all with the only dry eyes in the house.

I didn't cry, but maybe I should have.

That afternoon was the first time I got a sense of what life would be like with Mina gone. Mother had locked herself in her room, buried beneath the covers. Father had returned from a morning at the hospital, but he didn't linger long inside. He went out to the yard to rake leaves in the rain. I tried to join him, but he didn't want me. "You're going to get sick and then I won't hear the end of it with your mother. Don't you have any homework to do?" he asked with that familiar light lisp in his speech—and that subtle blur in his gaze—that implied he'd been drinking.

I did have homework. I went inside to the kitchen table, pulled out my math book, and got to work. I started in on the next day's assignment, but I couldn't concentrate. A thick, insistent silence pressed in, demanding to be heard. I kept trying

AYAD AKHTAR

to work, but even the scratching of my pencil's lead tip seemed like an unwelcome affront.

I put the pencil down and I listened.

I heard a baseboard creak. I heard a clock ticking in the next room. I heard a car drive by the front yard. And when the refrigerator's electric hum came to a sudden stop, and when I noticed there was no more rain tickling at the windows, I heard the silence itself. A cold, dead, bone-still quiet.

What it would sound like once Mina was gone.

16

Nikah

The afternoon of the wedding, Father and I were standing in the splendid lobby of the Atwater Hotel when a short man in a red suit and wavy salt-and-pepper hair came through the revolving front door, a boy about his size by his side. The man noticed us and approached. "You're here for the wedding?" he inquired with a thick Pakistani accent.

Father nodded. The man reached out his hand: "Mirza. Mirza Hassan."

"Naveed Shah," Father said, shaking his hand. "Nice to meet you."

"This is my son, Farhaz..."

The boy reached out his hand to Father. Then to me.

"Farhaz?" I asked, surprised. "The *hafiz?*"

"Yep," he replied, coolly. He was nothing like what I'd imagined: I'd been seeing him in my mind's eye as tall, much taller than me. With a wide, strong face. And piercing eyes that gazed down on me, now with compassion, now with contempt, but always bright with glory. I'd even pictured him, like the Prophet in my dream, with a gap between his teeth. But here he was, not much taller than me, his eyes small and lackluster, his teeth covered with silver braces. And he was losing his hair: His scalp clearly showed beneath the sparsely growing, oily strands that barely covered the top of his head. Had it not been for the braces and the red splotches of blooming acne across his face, I would have guessed he was at least five years older than he was.

"What's your son's name?" Mirza asked Father.

"Hayat," Father replied. He turned to me. "Don't be rude."

I held out my hand to Mirza, then to Farhaz.

"So you're a *hafiz?*" I asked again. I was having a tough time believing it.

"I already said I was."

"Indeed." Mirza turned to Father and added proudly: "The first in our family."

Father ignored the comment.

"So what do you do, Naveed?"

"I'm a physician."

"Fantastic! I'm in medical sales!" Mirza said enthusiastically, pulling out his wallet. "What specialty?"

"Neurology."

"Aha! Great stuff, great stuff." Mirza removed a business card and handed it to Father. "Mostly cardiac equipment. But you never know, Dr. Shah..."

Father gazed at the card blankly, then shoved it in his pocket.

"What a place this is!" Mirza remarked as he peered about the lobby atrium. It was three stories high, with two sets of dark, mahogany balconies held up by ornately carved columns. Along the lobby's walls, paintings hung neatly side by side. Mirza pointed at the canvases. "Someone was telling me this is all *real* Victorian art. Worth hundreds of thousands."

Father feigned interest, his gaze drifting to the glass and latticework skylight above, which showed a gray-white, overcast November day.

At the revolving doors, Sunil appeared, unwrapping a new pack of cigarettes.

"There's the man of the hour!" Mirza exclaimed. "Ready for the big day?"

"Now I am," Sunil joked, holding up a cigarette as he approached. "Naveed? You waaant one?"

Father shook his head.

Sunil nodded, lighting up. "Naveed Shah, Mirza Hassan."

"We've met," Mirza said.

Sunil looked over at the reception desk, exhaling smoke. Imam Souhef and Ghaleb Chatha were standing there, watching us, Souhef in a resplendent *jalabiyah* that ballooned around his impressive girth, Chatha in a tailored Nehru.

Sunil held up his finger to indicate he would be right there. "Sooo...the young scholars have met?" he asked, turning to Farhaz and me.

Farhaz stared blankly back at him, not seeming to understand.

Sunil explained, smoke pouring from his mouth: "I told you about Hayat, *behta*. He's studying to be a *haaafiz* like you."

I could feel Father seize up beside me. I stole a glance at him. He was eyeing Sunil with contempt.

"Better Muslims than we'll ever be," Mirza joked.

"You're mistaken," Father said abruptly. "The boy has given up his studies." Father turned to me. I winced, suddenly afraid he was going to hit me. Sunil noticed.

"Better Muslims than we will ever be, indeed," Sunil said softly, still holding Father's gaze. "They're waiting for me," he finally added, blowing smoke. "Have to prepare the room for the *nikah*."

"Oh! Good luck!" Mirza said, excited.

"Next time you see me, I'll be *marrieeed*," Sunil said as

he turned and headed for the reception desk to join up with Ghaleb and Souhef.

"It warms the heart to think that such things are possible," Mirza said, watching Sunil go. "It's a miracle after what he's been through...just a miracle. *Mashallah! Mashallah!*"

Father was looking off now, simmering.

"So what's your relation to the family?" Mirza asked.

Father made no attempt to hide his disgust. "Friends of the bride."

"I see." I couldn't tell if Mirza was doing his best to ignore Father's behavior or just didn't notice it. But whatever it was made him seem like a good man. "What a wonderful story *that* is. After what she went through. And now the boy has found himself a magnificent father!"

Father shrugged, grunting a reply.

"Excuse me, gentlemen," we heard, looking over to find a young blond man in white gloves and a tuxedo addressing us. "We're expecting quite a few of you people, and we'd like to keep the lobby clear. The reception area is this way."

Father didn't move. He just held the young man's gaze. "A few of us *people?* What *people,* if you don't mind my asking?"

"Sir, correct me if I'm wrong...you're with the Chatha–Ali wedding, no?"

"That's right."

"The reception area is this way, sir," the young man said curtly. The defiance in his tone was unmistakable. He lifted his arm and pointed down the hall. "Allow me to show you the way."

"Go ahead, young man!" Mirza offered, warmly, stepping forward to stand between Father and the tuxedoed man.

"Will you take Hayat with you?" Father said to Mirza. "I'm stepping out."

"Very good, Doctor-*sahib*."

Father turned to me. "If your Mother asks where I am, tell her I had to make some calls."

"Okay," I said.

I looked over at Farhaz. He was staring at me. I tried to keep staring back, but I couldn't.

"Let's go, boys," Mirza said, patting me on the back as he led us off.

The Atwater's chandelier ballroom was impressive. As you walked in through the twenty-foot-high mahogany double doors, it hung there before you: the enormous glittering chandelier—easily the size of a small elephant—for which the room was named. It sparkled, like a diamond in the sun, filling the room with white light.

The room's paneling was—like the doors and much of the hotel's woodwork—a deep mahogany hue. The flooring was a lighter, elm shade. Two sets of a dozen tables each had been set up—tables for the men on one side, for the women on the other—each covered with a green tablecloth and a light blue vase at the center, filled with fresh white peonies. Along a wall of windows to the left, a dais had been raised, on which three chairs and a table stood, all draped with golden fabric. We were not the first ones there: Caterers were setting up trays and stacks of plates along the far end of the room; a young man was standing behind the dais at a mixing board, testing the PA system; and there was a heavy-shouldered woman in a head scarf wandering among the tables and placing tiny cards before the chairs, with a girl who must have been her daughter—also in a head scarf—walking along in tow.

Mirza led us to a table, but he looked unsure. He turned to

his son. "Go find out from your auntie Neema where we're supposed to sit."

Farhaz lumbered off toward the woman and her daughter.

"Where are you from, *behta?*" Mirza asked me.

"We live here."

"That's convenient. We just drove in from Michigan. Seven hours' drive and not a scenic minute. Seven hours! My back is *killing* me." Mirza looked over at his son, who was consulting a sheet of paper the large woman was holding. "Oh, all this fuss for nothing. I'm just going to sit...So what's your name, again, *behta?*"

"Hayat."

"Hayat. What a nice name. You are a *hafiz*, too, *behta?*"

"Not yet."

"But you're on your way, no?"

I nodded.

Mirza looked over at his son again, who was now making his way back toward us. "It took him three years. He had a very good teacher...But don't get the wrong idea. I *paid* for every minute of that man's time. It cost me a *fortune*." Mirza paused, considering. "But it's worth it. Heaven is worth every penny and a hundred million more."

"Dad, we're at table fifteen," Farhaz said, approaching.

"Which one is that?"

"Says by the bouquet. This is table twelve. Fifteen's over there," Farhaz said, pointing.

"What a lot of fuss," Mirza complained as he rose.

"I don't know what table you're at, though," Farhaz said to me.

"I'll just sit with you."

He shrugged. I followed them to the new table, where we all settled in.

"So, Farhaz," Mirza said. "Our young friend here is studying to be a *hafiz*."

"I know, Dad. Uncle Sunil told us. I'm not deaf." The boy's tone was surprisingly dismissive. His father didn't look pleased, but instead of saying anything, Mirza just looked away.

People were appearing at the double doors. "There's Salman!" Mirza exclaimed. He got up and went over to embrace a man with a thick handlebar mustache and a beige Afghan hat.

"So how far are you?" Farhaz asked me. His expression was as blank as his tone.

"Huh?"

"How many *juz* have you got through?"

"Eleven."

"Just nineteen more, huh? That's pretty cool."

I nodded.

"Boy, am I fucking relieved *that's* over. What a fucking nightmare."

"What?"

He looked at me, confused. "Memorizing that stuff. Like drinking castor oil every day for three years. *Jeez-fucking-Louise*."

For a second, what he was saying just didn't compute. And once I realized he was talking about the Quran, I didn't know what to say.

"What do you say we hit this shit hole?"

"We do what?"

"You're a little wet behind the ears, aren't you? I said: Let's check out the hotel, see what they got goin' on."

"Oh—okay," I said.

We got up from our places, but before we left, Farhaz went

over to the girl laying out the place cards, said something to her, then pointed at the double doors. She nodded.

Farhaz looked pleased as he returned. "She's gonna meet us when she's done," he said. "I told her we'd be scopin' out the joint. Let's go."

The long, mirrored hall was filling with guests, men in *shalwar*s or suits, women in long, loose-fitting clothes, almost all of them with head scarves and holding or corralling young children. We passed an adolescent in a white skullcap. "What's up, Hamza?" Farhaz called out.

The boy looked over. His eyes sparkled with recognition. "Farhaz!"

They greeted each other with high-fives. To me, the boy looked a little like Farhaz, the same wide jaw and small eyes. But he wasn't losing his hair.

Farhaz turned to me. "This is Hamza, my cousin. Hamza, this is Hayat."

"Hey, Hayat, what's up?"

"Nothing," I replied.

"So what're you guys doing?" Hamza asked.

"We're gonna check out this hole in the wall," Farhaz said. "See if this place's got any action. Wanna come?"

Hamza looked back at his father, another wide-jawed man with tiny eyes, who was in the midst of a conversation with an elderly man in a gray Nehru jacket. "I'munna go with Farhaz, *Abu.*"

"Farhaz, *behta,*" said Hamza's father. "Nice to see you. How are you?"

"Fine, Uncle Imtiaz. How are you?"

"Good, good. So where are you boys going?"

"We were just going to take a look around."

"Okay—but don't get into any trouble."

"We won't. Don't worry."

Hamza's father nodded and returned to his conversation.

Farhaz led us both to a large, sweeping marble staircase at the end of the hall, and we sat down at the first turn of the steps, where we had a clear view of the guests filing into the reception room.

"Let's wait for Zakiya," Farhaz said. "She said she'd meet us."

"Zakiya, huh?"

"I haven't seen her in like two years. The rack she grew on her!"

"She's got tits. That's for sure. But she's our cousin."

"So what? We can marry our cousins in Islam."

Hamza shrugged. "You don't have to spend time around her. She's annoying. And I don't like her face."

"Hate to break it to you, Hamz. But you don't fuck a face."

"True."

Hamza looked at me. "You know what fucking is, right?"

"Huh?"

"Fucking. Do you know what it is?"

"Sure," I said. I didn't have a clue.

Hamza shook his head, turning back to Farhaz. "He doesn't know. Should we tell him?"

"Let's do him the favor."

"He may get pissed off at us, like what's-his-face."

"That guy's a fucking moron."

"What was his name?"

"I don't even fucking care." Farhaz turned to me. "You're not gonna be a moron if we tell you what fucking is, right?"

"What do you mean?"

"You're not gonna go tattling to your mommy and daddy that the boys you met were talking dirty to you, are you?"

"No."

No sooner had I replied than Farhaz had already started in: "So *fucking* is how *you* got here. It's when your dad put his dick in your mom."

I didn't know what he was talking about.

"You do know what a dick is, right?"

"Yeah?"

"And you do know that girls don't have dicks, right?"

"Yeah, of course."

Farhaz studied me for a moment. If my reply had sounded less than confident, it wasn't because I wasn't aware that girls didn't have dicks, but because I wasn't sure what they had instead. Aside from that night more than a year prior when I spied the dark triangle between Mina's legs in the bathroom mirror, I'd never seen a naked woman.

Farhaz was looking at me closely. "You know that's what makes them girls, right? That they don't have dicks. You know that, right?" he asked, insistent.

"Yeah. Of course."

Farhaz kept staring at me, then turned to Hamza, exasperated. "He doesn't know that they don't have dicks. What is wrong with this kid?"

Hamza explained, more gently: "Girls have a slit. Like someone came and cut off their dicks and cut them open between the legs. That's all they've got. That slit. And that's where you put it in."

What he was saying didn't square with what I remembered between Mina's legs. I didn't recall a cut or a slit. Just that dark, triangular patch. I was confused.

"Right," Farhaz went on. "So when your dick gets hard, you put it inside a girl's slit, that's what *sex* is. And it's fucking killer."

Sex. I'd heard the word so many times. They were both nodding like they knew what they were talking about, but what they were describing sounded so improbable, so unnecessary. It didn't make any sense.

"Why would you ever do that?" I asked.

"You have to. That's how you make a baby. You put your dick in a girl's slit and squirt your *sperm* in there. That's *fucking*." Farhaz turned to Hamza. "That's what *nikah* means in Arabic, by the way."

"What?" Hamza asked.

"Fucking. My buddy told me. He's an Arab. I told him I was going to a *nikah*, and he told me it means 'fucking.' "

They both laughed.

I wasn't really listening to them anymore. My mind was clearing with a sudden, alarming thought.

"Sperm?" I asked. "What does it look like?"

"White and sticky," Farhaz answered. "Like Elmer's Glue."

"But it smells more like bleach," Hamza added.

They laughed again.

All at once, I realized that the white milky fluid that came out of my penis that afternoon I touched myself was sperm. He wasn't lying. And the dawning truth that I could not escape whatever they were describing dislodged a torrent of unease inside me.

"It all sounds disgusting," I replied, angry.

Farhaz held my gaze for a moment, then shook his head. "What's wrong with this kid?" he said to Hamza.

"He thinks *that's* disgusting. Wait'll he hears about blow jobs."

Farhaz looked at me and laughed. "That's when you put your dick in a girl's mouth and she sucks on it."

Now I was sure they were making fun of me.

"Did you ever have a dream with the Prophet, Farhaz?" I asked, defiant.

"Did I what?"

"Did you have a dream with the Prophet, *peace be upon him?*"

Farhaz frowned, looking confused and not a little annoyed. "No. What's your point?"

I shrugged. "I did."

"So what?" Farhaz asked.

I shrugged again, feeling inwardly triumphant.

Hamza was looking at me, his gaze newly glistening with interest.

Farhaz snickered, turning away. "There she is," he said getting up. Zakiya was standing at the bottom of the staircase.

"Hey, guys," Zakiya offered cutely as she made her way up toward us. Sensitized to the matter, I had to admit her chest was big. Very big. "So what are you guys doing?"

Farhaz was smiling. "Just having a little discussion. Little Hayat here was ignorant about the birds and the bees..."

Zakiya smiled. "And is he still?"

"We did our best. Gotta hope for the rest... What d'you say we split up and go exploring?"

Zakiya smiled, nodding eagerly.

Farhaz turned to Hamza. "You take the kid and scope out the downstairs, Zakiya and I'll take the upstairs. Meet back here"—he looked at his watch—"in half an hour."

"The *walima*'s going to start," Zakiya objected.

"They can stick their *walima* in the shitter."

Zakiya giggled.

(After the official ceremony, called the *nikah*—and which took place in private with only two witnesses and an imam—the *walima,* or reception, followed. It was the guests' first opportunity to see the new groom and bride.)

"So what d'you say, Hamz?" Farhaz asked, gazing down at us.

"Fine," Hamza said.

"Let's go," Farhaz said to Zakiya, moving up the steps and gesturing her on. She giggled some more as she hopped up the stairs after him.

Hamza turned to me. "You ever go down to the lake?"

I nodded. I was having a difficult time looking him in the eye. I felt troubled, exposed. I didn't know how to shake the discomfort Farhaz had awakened in me.

"Hey, Hayat," Hamza prompted, briskly. "What's up?"

"Nothing."

"Don't worry about Farhaz," Hamza said, patting me on the back. "My mom says he's like that 'cause his mom died."

"His mom died?"

"Yeah. When he was like nine."

"That's sad."

"Yeah, it is...How about we head out to see the lake? Looks pretty cool."

"Okay."

The hall was filled with folks like us, and so was the lobby: Our various hues of brown, our baggy clothes, our skullcaps and beards, our shawls and head scarves on full display. If the help behind the desks and at the doors hadn't been white, one could have imagined being in Cairo or Delhi or Baghdad: some architectural remnant of colonial times repossessed by the natives for their own inscrutable purposes. The young man in the tuxedo was looking on unhappily. "Keep! It! Moving! People!" he shouted as if addressing a crowd he wasn't sure understood what he was saying. "To! The! Back!" he yelled again, exasperated. But the crowd paid him no mind. It was a growing, unruly mass, jabbering and moving about aimlessly. The young man finally gave up and returned to his perch beside the concierge's podium, where he buried his head in his hands.

Outside, Hamza and I made our way along the sidewalk lined with shops and bars and restaurants leading down to the lakeshore. Above us, the cloud-swept sky was grim, dark—night was falling—but along the lake, the warm yellow lights in the windows and the muffled sounds of patrons dining and enjoying the evening offered a picture of life as warm, inviting. As Hamza and I walked, I noticed a woman with sandy-blond hair move past us quickly. She was wearing a thin, black over-coat, which her fingers—painted bright red—clutched at the lapels. As she hurried along, I caught the faint trace of a famil-iar lilac scent. The woman stopped at the door of a restaurant, and as she turned to pull it open, I realized I knew her face. I wasn't sure why.

She disappeared inside.

"You cold?" Hamza asked.

It was chilly, but I was wearing a heavy sweater. I shook my head. We walked on, now passing the windows of the restau-rant into which the woman had disappeared. I glanced inside. I didn't see her.

"So what's the deal with this dream? You really saw the Prophet?"

"Peace be upon him," I added.

"Right. Peace be upon him."

"I had a dream he saved me from this crazy woman who was chasing me. He took me to a mosque and then we led the prayer together."

"You led prayer with the Prophet? Jeez. That is so cool... I heard that if you see the Prophet in a dream you're gonna go to heaven."

The conversation was only making me more uneasy. More than ever, I wanted the dream to mean what Hamza was saying, but I knew it didn't.

We wandered farther on, toward the railing along the lakefront. "So what'd he look like?"

"Who?"

"Who do you think? The Prophet."

I waited.

"Sorry," Hamza said, adding, "*Peace be upon him.*"

"I don't know. He looked good." Then I added: "He had a gap between his front teeth."

"I'll bet he was a *badass,*" Hamza said, nodding. "That's what my dad always says. That if the Prophet was still around, *we'd* be running the show. Like Bo Svenson on *Walking Tall.* You ever see that show?"

I shook my head.

"He's this sheriff and all he has to do is carry a stick and everybody listens to him. My dad says that if the Prophet was alive today—sorry, *peace be upon him*—then we wouldn't have any problems in Israel. He says Palestinians are babies. They want someone to take care of them. The Prophet would never let anybody—sorry, *peace be upon him*—the Prophet would never let *anyone* treat him that way. He would have taken over Israel by now if he was around."

I heard what he was saying, but I wasn't really listening. We were looking out at the lake now. Its surface rose and fell gently, like a slow steady breath. It was beautiful.

"Pretty cool," Hamza said. "It's one big lake. Sure looks like an ocean to me."

"I guess."

"You cold?" Hamza asked.

"Kind of."

"We should go back. My dad's gonna be pissed if I'm gone too long."

"Hold on," I said as he pulled away. "Is it true what he was saying about putting your dick in a girl's mouth?"

Hamza nodded. "Sounds weird, doesn't it? What's even weirder is some guys put their mouth in a girl's slit. They stick their tongue in there."

"They what?"

"I saw it in a magazine."

I shook my head. I didn't want to hear any more.

We made our way back, approaching the restaurant into which the blond woman in the overcoat had disappeared. I stopped at the window and looked inside. There she was, standing at the bar. Beside her, a man was seated, his arm around her waist.

It took me a moment to recognize it was Father.

He was listening as she talked, every part of him leaned in toward her. He sipped at a drink, nodding. He looked happy. They both did.

And then he kissed her.

As if sensing something, Father stopped. His gaze turned to the window. Our eyes met. He froze. Then the woman turned to look. I recognized her now. It was the nurse from the hospital room. Julie.

"What are you doing, Hayat?" Hamza asked. "Why are you standing there?"

"Let's go," I shouted, starting briskly back toward the hotel.

"What's going on? Are you okay?" Hamza asked as he scurried after me.

I charged ahead, my heart darkly drumming in my ears. We were already most of the way back to the Atwater when I heard Father's voice behind me: "Hayat!"

Hamza slowed and turned.

"Let's go," I said.

"Who's that?"

"Who cares!?" I yelled, marching ahead.

"Hayat! Come back!" Father's voice cried out again.

I didn't stop. "Go to hell," I muttered to myself as I went through the hotel's revolving door.

As all of this was happening, Mina was being married in a hotel room on the tenth floor. The tale of her dramatic afternoon nuptials would become part of her legend, an episode Mother would recall and recount for years to come.

It began with a headache.

Shortly after getting to her hotel suite that afternoon, Mina started to complain she wasn't well. Her head was hurting. She was feeling dizzy and light-headed. At some point, she asked Mother to open a window. Mother did. Then Mina asked her for a glass of water: "But cold, *bhaj*. Very cold."

Mother took the ice bucket from the bathroom and headed out into the hall to the ice machine. On her way, Najat's door opened abruptly, and Najat appeared in the doorway, completely covered in her black *burqa*.

For a second, Mother was startled.

"Which room is it, Muneer?" Najat asked. She was holding a bag filled with Mina's bridal jewelry.

"Ten fourteen," Mother told her, "halfway down the hall."

Mother watched as Najat glided down the hall, her billowing *chador* shawl trailing behind her as she went. Najat stopped at the door and knocked. She disappeared inside.

When Mother returned with the bucket of ice, Mina was in the midst of a full-blown panic attack. She was sitting on the couch, heaving as she tried to stand. Rabia, her mother, was holding her in place.

"But where do you want to go, *behti?*"

"I just need to leave," Mina kept repeating. "I need to get out."

"But to go where?"

"Anywhere...*Bhaj!*" she screamed suddenly when she saw Mother.

"What's going on?"

"I need to get out."

"Rabia, let her go," Mother said sharply.

Rabia looked at Najat—who'd now removed her *burqa*—and Najat nodded. Rabia released her daughter, who then dashed to the window.

She stood against the sill, taking quick, deep breaths. Then she started to pull the window farther open.

Rabia shouted: "What are you doing?"

"Getting some air!" Mina shouted back. "I need more air."

It wasn't until Mina threw one leg onto the air-conditioning unit that Mother realized what she was doing. "Stop it!" Mother yelled, rushing to the window to take hold of her friend.

By now, Najat and Mother were both pulling Mina inside.

"I need to go out. I need to get out," Mina kept repeating through her wheezing, labored breath.

She didn't fight long. Najat led her back to the couch and Mother went to the bathroom to get Mina that glass of water. When she returned, Najat was already holding out a tiny, round powder-blue tablet on her open palm.

"What is it?" Mother asked.

"Valium."

Mother offered Mina the water; Najat pushed the pill closer. "Take it. You'll feel better."

Rabia, who had taken a seat next to her daughter, picked the pill from Najat's palm and brought it to Mina's mouth.

Mina gazed at her mother, her chest heaving. Then she closed her eyes and parted her lips. Rabia inserted the pill between her daughter's teeth. Mina closed her mouth. Mother held the glass of water to her lips.

Mina sipped and swallowed.

"Give it ten minutes," Najat said. "And you'll be just fine. You'll see."

Mother turned to Najat and asked: "Where did you get that?"

"I always have it with me," Najat said quietly. "I've been suffering panic attacks for years. I don't know what I would do without it."

Najat was right. It took ten minutes for Mina's breathing to ease, and as it did, she started to feel better. She smiled as the women dressed her, and even smiled when, after a knock at the door—and after Najat stopped Mother from answering it long enough to disappear again beneath her *burqa*—Mother opened it to find the lanky, gray-clad Ghaleb Chatha standing there before her with his cadaverous gaze.

"Is she ready?" he asked.

"She may need a few minutes," Mother replied.

"No, *bhaj*," Mina said lazily from her place at the couch. "I'm ready."

"Take your time," Chatha said. "Just to let you know Adnan is ready for the *nikah*. We'll need the witnesses, too."

"Thank you, *bhai-jaan*," Mina offered in a singsong tone.

Chatha stared at her for a moment, sensing something. "Is she all right?" he asked.

"Everything's fine, Ghaleb," Najat said. "We'll be right there."

Fifteen minutes later, in room 1058, the short, unceremonious *nikah* took place. The participants gathered around the living room set: a couch, two armchairs, and a coffee table covered with a white cloth, on which a contract and two pens sat, as well as a copy of the Quran. Imam Souhef sat on a chair before the table. Sunil was on the couch beside him, Imran on his knee. Mina sat across from them, in an armchair. She wasn't wearing a *hijab,* but a white silk *chador* shawl, which covered most of her body, leaving only her face and hands exposed. There were supposed to be two official witnesses, but since Ghaleb was the only male witness, it would take—according to Islamic law—two women witnesses to equal one male witness, so Mother and Najat were also huddled behind the couch. Just behind Souhef, Rafiq stood, watching nervously. Beside him, Rabia cried softly into a handkerchief.

Imam Souhef began the proceedings by holding his palms up before him and reciting the short Arabic text that composed the traditional Islamic marriage sermon. He offered this *nikah khutbah* to a group of Pakistanis—all listening with their eyes lowered—in its original language, which none of them understood. With his brief address finished, Souhef turned to Rafiq.

"Since this is the second marriage of your daughter, I am not required by Sharia to ask your permission to wed your daughter, Amina Ali, to this man, Sunil Chatha."

Rafiq nodded. Souhef turned to Sunil.

"Have you brought with you the *mahr?*"

"I have, Imam."

Sunil pulled out a thick, brick-shaped envelope and laid it on the coffee table before them all. The envelope wasn't sealed, and the open flap revealed that it was filled with hundreds.

Souhef turned to Mina. "Are you satisfied with your choice?" This was the cue for Mina to address Sunil with the

Arabic formulation she'd last spoken six years prior, to her first husband, Hamed.

"*An Kah'tu nafsaka a'lal mah'ril ma'loom,*" she said, the words lightly slurring on her lips.

Souhef then glanced at Sunil, his attention prompting the groom's response to his bride:

"*Qabiltun nakaha.*"

Souhef nodded. He reached out, picked up both pens, handing one each to Sunil and Mina. "With witnesses present, the bride has given herself in marriage and accepted the *mahr,* and the groom has accepted the bride. Please sign the contract."

Sunil scratched his signature across the bottom of the papers, then pushed them across the table to Mina. She took a moment before setting her name—with a loopy scrawl—under his.

"You are husband and wife," Souhef said, standing. "We will now give the new husband and wife a moment of privacy."

With that, Sunil set Imran down beside him and stood. He reached his hand out to Mina. She rose and he led her into the bedroom.

Imran whined as they walked off. Sunil stopped in the doorway and addressed his new son in a firm tone: "Give your mother and father a moment to be alone, *behta.*"

"Okay, Dad," Imran replied, quietly.

Once they were gone, Rafiq stepped in and sat beside his grandson on the couch. The envelope of money—twenty-five thousand dollars in cash—was still sitting on the coffee table. He reached out and stuffed it into a pocket in his coat. Then he looked over at Ghaleb—who was watching him—and offered a grateful nod.

* * *

When I returned, the ballroom was abuzz. On the dais to the left, Sunil and Mina sat side by side, dressed in crisp, shimmering white *shalwar* suits. Sunil was wearing a tall golden triangular hat. Mina was wearing a gilded scarf, and her arms and ankles were covered with golden bangles. Beside the two of them sat Imran, dressed in the same shiny white fabric, and wearing a small golden *topi* of his own. Imran was eagerly watching as the wedding guests approached the bride and groom, rolled bills in hand, circling the couple as they twirled the money and muttered blessings, finally handing the cash to the groom. Sunil met each offering with a smile. Mina's eyes had an odd, lackluster look.

"There you are!"

It was Mother. She was wearing a pale-yellow *shalwar-kameez* and a brown shawl across her shoulders. She looked exhausted. "Where were you?"

I hesitated for a moment. "With Hamza," I finally said.

"Hamza?"

I looked around. Hamza had drifted off and was now standing beside his father at one of the tables. I pointed. "Over there."

Mother looked confused. "Where is your father?"

I didn't reply.

"Weren't you with him?"

"He left. He said he had to make some calls."

"*Calls?* What kind of calls?"

"I don't know."

"We've been to hell and back the last hour and he's making *calls?* Who is he calling? Hayat, where *is* he?!"

"I don't know."

"You don't know? Well, go find him! And get him back here!"

I wasn't going to go back and get him. And I wasn't about to tell Mother where he was. So I just stood there with her, the hordes of well-wishers twirling money at the couple on the dais gathered before us.

"Go on! Go! What are you waiting for? Go find him!" she said, pushing me away. "Calls...," she muttered to herself as she walked back to the women's side of the room.

I went out into the hall. I thought about sitting on a couch in the lobby, but then I remembered the young man in the tuxedo. So I headed for the back of the hallway, to the marble steps where Farhaz, Hamza, and I had sat earlier.

After a few minutes, I heard something behind me. I turned and saw Farhaz and Zakiya coming downstairs from the floor above, holding hands. The smile on Zakiya's face vanished the second she saw me. She snatched her hand away from Farhaz's.

"Where's Hamz?" Farhaz asked.

"Inside," I replied, curt.

"I have to go back," Zakiya said. "My parents are gonna kill me."

"Suit yourself," Farhaz said.

Zakiya hurried down the steps.

"So what's the word?" Farhaz asked, taking his time to descend the staircase.

"Huh?"

"What's goin' on?"

"Nothing."

He shrugged and walked past me.

The room was filled with the smells of *biryani* and curries. Caterers stood along the back, ready to serve the meal. At the other end of the room, up on the dais, hefty Souhef stood with a microphone to his mouth, reading from a piece of paper.

"The Prophet, peace be upon him, said that among the most perfect believers are those who are best and kindest to their wives." Souhef looked up with a smile. Gentle laughter passed through the crowd. He pointed his finger, playfully. "Yes, brothers. It's true. Even lifting a morsel of food to the mouth of the wife grants the husband a reward in the Hereafter. According to the Prophet, peace be upon him, the mercy of Allah Ta'ala flows down from heaven when a husband looks at his wife with love and pleasure."

I was making my way across the room to the ladies' side, where the women were sitting, children in their laps or at their sides, in *chador* shawls, head scarves, *dupatta*s. Mother was the only woman not wearing something on her head, and with no trace of a smile on her lips.

Souhef turned to address Sunil directly now.

"When a husband takes his wife's hand with love..."

Souhef stopped and waited. Then he repeated it:

"I said, when a husband takes his wife's hand with love..."

This time Sunil picked up on the cue. There was more laughter—mostly from the women's side—as Sunil reached out to take hold of his wife's hand.

"When a husband takes his wife's hand with love...," Souhef said now for a third time as he resumed his address to the crowd, "a couple's sins fall from the gaps between their fingers. Love between a husband and his wife is a great purification."

Mother eyed me as I approached her table. She wasn't paying any attention to Souhef. "Where's your father?" she asked.

"I don't know. I looked everywhere."

"Bastard," she muttered under her breath. "That bastard...Fine. Go sit with your Rafiq-uncle," she said, waving me away.

From the dais, Souhef continued: "Our Prophet—peace be upon him—once said that when a man enters his home *cheerfully,* Allah creates, as a result of his happy attitude, an angel who says prayers of forgiveness on behalf of the man until the Day of Judgment. That's the truth, brothers! May we love our wives. And may love prevail between our happy bride and groom."

There was hearty applause.

As I made my way back to the men's side, I noticed Sunil watching me. He leaned over and spoke something into Souhef's ear. Now Souhef looked over at me as well. He stepped forward again, his lips to the microphone.

"Brother Sunil reminds me that we are honored by the presence of a couple of very special young men here today: Farhaz Hassan and Hayat Shah."

Hearing my name, I stopped.

"Both young men are very dedicated young Muslims and I think we should honor their commitment to our *din* by bringing them up here for a moment. Farhaz? Hayat?"

Again, there was applause. Farhaz stood up at his table—he had been sitting next to Hamza—and started to weave his way to the front of the room.

"You, too, Hayat," Souhef encouraged, waving me forward. "Come on up."

I followed Farhaz to the steps along the edge of the dais, stumbling up nervously behind him. I looked down at Mother. She was staring off vacantly, muttering to herself. I looked over at Mina. She was watching me, blank. I smiled, but her expression didn't change.

Up on the dais, Farhaz took a place at Souhef's side, and I took a place at Farhaz's. "These young men are truly better than us. Young Farhaz is only fifteen, and he's already a complete *hafiz*. And Hayat here...How old are you, Hayat?"

"Twelve," I offered, my voice quavering.

"Twelve. And how far have you gotten in the Holy Quran?"

"Eleven *juz*."

"*Mashallah*," Souhef said.

There was a smattering of applause.

"In the *nikah khutbah*, there is a passage from *Surah An-Nisa*, and our groom had the wonderful idea for these young men to recite a bit of it for us here. How does that sound to you boys?"

"Fine," Farhaz replied with a shrug.

I turned to Farhaz, nervous. "*An-Nisa*? Which one is that?"

"Starts at the end of the fourth *juz*."

I didn't know where the official *juz* breaks were. To keep track of my progress, I'd come up with my own system of dividing the number of pages I'd memorized by thirty to have an idea.

"Which number *surah* is it?" I whispered.

Farhaz looked annoyed. "It's the fourth *surah*. Do you know it or not?"

I nodded, relieved. I did know it. But only by its translated title, "The Women."

Souhef handed the microphone to Farhaz. He cleared his throat and closed his eyes. After a short silence, he brought the mike to his mouth:

> *Ya 'ayyuha an-nasu attaqu rabbakumu al-ladhi*
> *khalaqakum...*

I was stunned. I had no idea he knew the Quran in Arabic. The sounds he made—the shifts and turns of phrase, the elon-

gated vowels, the shocking breaks and swallowed conso-
nants—came through the speakers with clarion authority.

> *...min nafsin wa idatin wa khalaqa minh zawjah*
> *wa baththa minhum rijl an kathr an wa nis'an*
> *wa attaq...*

I felt myself shrink. *You were wrong about him,* I thought as
I listened in awe. *This is better than your dumb dream with the
Prophet.* I looked over at Imam Souhef. He was smiling. Behind him, Sunil beamed with pride. Mina, too, was watching,
but with a vague expression. Farhaz paused. I looked away, my
gaze wandering to the entrance.

There, leaned against the double doors, was Father. His
arms were crossed. He was staring right at me.

Souhef stepped forward and took the microphone from
Farhaz. "Wonderful," he commented to the room. "Just
wonderful." The applause was swift and strong. Farhaz was
glowing.

Souhef turned to me, still speaking into the microphone:
"Hayat? Do you know *An-Nisa*?"

I could feel my heart beating through my entire body, down
into my toes and fingertips. I nodded. The imam smiled and
handed me the microphone, but it slipped from my grip,
screeching. I wiped my sweat-drenched palms on my pants and
reached down to pick it up. The room full of faces was watching. I looked over at Father again, surprised at his expression.
It wasn't angry. It looked helpless.

"*Surah An-Nisa.* 'The Women,'" I began.

> In the name of God, the Benevolent, the Merci-
> ful...

Mankind! Do not forget your Lord, who made
    you from a single soul,
And from it, carved its mate,
And brought forth the many men and women.

The sound of my own voice coming through the speakers
gave me confidence. I closed my eyes to shut the thought of
Father out. I went on:

Fear God, in whose name you make demands
    upon each other.
Honor your ties of kinship.
Truly, God watches over you!

I felt a gentle touch on my shoulder. I looked up. It was
Souhef. "In Arabic, son," he said quietly, correcting.

"I don't know the Arabic. I only know the English," I answered. My mouth was close enough to the microphone for
everyone to hear.

"You only know it in English?" Souhef seemed confused.
"Who's teaching you?"

"I'm teaching myself," I replied.

"Really?" Souhef asked, surprised.

I nodded. Beside me, Farhaz snickered.

"*Mashallah,*" Souhef said now as he patted my head. He took
the microphone from me. "We have a very original young man
here," he said to the crowd, "memorizing the Quran in English.
He will be our first English *hafiz,* brothers and sisters."

Souhef paused. Hushed whispers rippled through the crowd.

"Let's give these holy boys another round of applause."

I looked over at Father. He was still standing by the double
doors, watching.

"You're a *moron*," Farhaz said to me as we moved to the steps. "Didn't anybody ever tell you it doesn't count if it's not in Arabic?"

"That's not true."

"You don't believe me? Ask him." Farhaz looked back, pointing at Souhef.

I turned to the imam.

"What is it, son?"

"Farhaz says it doesn't count if I didn't memorize the Quran in Arabic."

"Arabic is our holy language, young man."

"Does it count in English?"

"Count for what?"

"To get me and my parents into heaven."

Souhef looked at me, a gentle light in his eyes. He smiled, shaking his head. "No. You have to learn the holy book in our *holy* language for that. But don't be discouraged. You have all the time in the world."

I made my way down the steps and walked to the men's side, my eyes to the ground. But what I didn't see, I heard: There was laughter in everything. In the chatter, in the shifting of bodies in their seats, in the sounds of the caterers preparing to serve the meal; even the distant static hiss coming over the PA speakers mocked me. I was burning up inside.

I passed the table where Rafiq and Ghaleb were sitting. Rafiq reached out to stop me. He held my hand, offering me a kind smile.

"Nicely done, *behta*," he said, encouragingly. "Very impressive."

I didn't believe him. To me, there was more pity in his voice than praise. Sitting beside him, Ghaleb made no gesture toward me at all. He simply stared at me with his silent, gray gaze. Rafiq pointed at one of the two empty chairs at their table. I shook my head and moved on, passing Hamza and Farhaz. Hamza reached out his hand for a high-five. I ignored it. I didn't dare look at Farhaz, but I heard him mock me as I passed: "What a dork! He actually believed all that stuff!"

In back, I found an empty table. I heard Souhef announce into the microphone that it was time to eat, and that the men should begin to serve themselves. There was a sudden bustle: chairs moving, men rising. I noticed Mother was up, too, rushing across the room for the double doors where Father had been standing. But he was gone.

17

The Long Unraveling

Father walked out of the *walima* and was not to be found. He left us—Mother, me, Rafiq, Rabia, and Imran—to find our way home on our own. Mother stewed in the cab the whole way back, and stewed through the evening. She didn't once mention the recitation. It was as if it hadn't happened.

Once everyone was in bed, I curled up on the family room couch, where I'd been sleeping for days. I tried not to think of my humiliation at the *walima,* but I kept hearing Farhaz's voice in my mind:

What a waste of time! What a dork you are! You actually believed all that stuff!

At some point, I must have fallen asleep. I roused to find Father sitting next to me in the darkness, his hand on my shoulder.

"*Behta,* wake up," he said in a hushed voice. He looked exhausted, his egg-shaped eyes webbed with crisscrossing red lines. "Are you okay?"

"Mmm-hmm." I nodded.

There was a long silence as he stared at me. "I want you to know something. I left because I was so disgusted. I was disgusted by what they're doing to your auntie, and what they did to you. Those people are idiots. *Idiots.* And she's letting herself become one of them." He spoke slowly, trying to enunciate. But the words were slurred. "I know it's a question of *credibility*. I know I don't have *credibility* with you. I know that."

I was confused. I didn't understand what he was talking about.

After a pause he went on: "I know what you and your mother think of me. But I want you to understand something. I'm a successful man. And that is not an easy thing to become. There is no guarantee for success. And that means that whatever you may think of me, I still know a few things. And whatever *she* thinks of me, the truth is: I can't be the complete *fool* you people think I am…If anything I say has *any* meaning for you, you have to trust me. *I'm* not the fool. *They* are. Those people tonight. *Those* are the fools. Not me. And *not you*. I want you to understand, Hayat, no matter what they made you feel tonight, *you* are not the fool. Those people are like sheep, following each other around, always waiting for someone else to lead them. All of them. They're all the same. Even Souhef."

He paused again. He was getting emotional. As he leaned closer, I could clearly smell the alcohol on his breath.

"I saw you talking to him at the end of your recitation," he said. "What did he say?"

"He said it didn't count if I knew the Quran in English."

"*That's* why I hate these people, Hayat," Father said angrily. He was squinting at me in the darkness now. "I know that you won't understand what I'm going to say to you now…You're not one of them. You're not. That's the truth. I know you don't understand why I burned your Quran, but there was a reason. It's because you're different. You can't live life by rules others give you. In that way, you and I are the same. You have to find *your own* rules. All my life I've been running away from their rules, Hayat. All my life. You will be the same. Don't ask me how I know it, but I do."

As he spoke, I remembered my dream with the Prophet, how I had been running, and how I had then left Muhammad in the mosque. For a second I thought I understood not only what Father was saying, but the dream as well. And then the clarity faded.

"That's why I hate these people, Hayat," he said. "They don't understand why they came here, or what they came here for. They don't know *who* they are, or what *life* is. *They* are the *fools*." He was spitting words now, disgusted. "Don't listen to them. Their mindlessness. Their stupidity. Now do you see why I hate them so much? Hmm? Do you?" He had taken hold of me, and was squinting harder now, as if having trouble seeing me, though I was just inches from his face. "Do you see why now?" he repeated, his voice breaking. He sounded like a child. "Don't you see what they are doing to her?"

And then he started to cry.

I held him against me. As close as I could. In my arms, he shuddered and moaned. He pressed himself tighter against me. I tried to do the same, to close all the distance between us. Soon, I felt his tears against my neck.

"Don't you see?" he cried. "Don't you see? Don't you see?" he kept repeating.

I didn't answer. I just held him. It was all he seemed to need.

Mina and Sunil showed up the morning after the wedding to finish packing up her room for the movers. She looked unhappy. Her face was framed with a tightly tied *hijab,* her eyes lowered, as if she were reluctant to see or be seen. We all took tea together, after which Sunil and Mina disappeared into her room upstairs and shut the door behind them.

Rabia and Rafiq went to my room to pack their things. They were going to be joining their daughter and new son-in-law at the Chathas' for the rest of their stay in America. I took Imran and went down into the family room to watch television. We sat side by side on the couch, Imran snuggled up against me as we watched *The Flintstones*, then *Scooby-Doo*. At some point, Mina came down to see us.

"Imran? Are you enjoying your big *bhaiya?*"

Imran nodded vigorously, pushing up against me, taking hold of my waist.

I held him tight, a flood of emotion filling me. I started to cry.

"Why are you crying, *bhai-jaan?*" he asked.

"I wasn't a good big brother to you," I said.

"Yes you are. You're my big brother," he said, cheerily, pressing even closer.

Mina put her arms around me as well. "It's okay, Hayat. We all make mistakes."

"I don't want you to go," I pleaded.

"I know, *behta,*" she said calmly. She held me. "Be good to your mother," she whispered into my ear. "You're all she has. Take care of her."

"Okay," I said, still crying. We held each other for a long moment.

She pulled away, her eyes wet at the corners with tears of her own. "I was so proud of you yesterday."

"Of what?"

"Your recitation."

I looked away. Mina took hold of my chin and led my gaze back to hers.

"What is it, *behta?*"

"Why didn't you tell me I had to know it in Arabic?"

She looked confused. "You don't..."

"But that's what the imam told me."

Mina shook her head. "Remember what I always told you. *Intention.* That's all Allah cares about. Not what language you speak."

"But the imam said if it's not in Arabic then I'm not a *hafiz.*"

She smiled. "Being a *hafiz* is not what matters. It's the quality of your faith. Not the name you put on it."

I didn't know what to make of what she was saying. She was the one who'd said becoming a *hafiz* was the greatest thing a person could do. I looked away, dismayed.

She led my chin back to her gaze again. "Come say good-bye to your uncle," she said with a smile.

Mina led Imran and me upstairs into the living room, where Rafiq and Rabia were saying their good-byes to my parents. Imran leapt up into Father's arms. Sunil saw me and smiled. "I'm proud of you, *beehhta.* Keep up the goood work."

Mina went over to Mother. There was a sudden, thick silence in the room as they hugged. We watched them hug and sniffle and whisper pleas for forgiveness into each other's ears. They must have kissed each other a dozen times. Rabia was moved. So was Father.

Sunil looked on, annoyed.

"Come on, girls. Not the last time you'll see each other," Rafiq said after glancing at Sunil. "Let's go."

"Don't rush them, Rafiq," Rabia snapped.

Rafiq looked away, turning to me. "Okay, *behta!*" Rafiq said with enthusiasm, reaching his hand out for me to shake. "You're a sensible young man. I look forward to hearing great things about you someday."

I wasn't sure what he was talking about. "Okay," I said, shaking his hand.

Mina and Mother finally parted, and Mina turned to Father—who was still holding Imran—to say her good-bye. She didn't dare touch Father; Sunil was present. Instead, she put her hand on her heart and offered him a gentle bow of the head.

"Thank you for everything, Naveed-*bhai*."

Sunil stepped forward and reached out to take Imran into his arms. During the transfer, Imran leaned out and kissed Father on the cheek. "I love you, Uncle," he said, endearingly. Hearing this, the women cooed. Mother bit her lip to stanch a new impulse to start crying. The boy in his arms, Sunil stepped over to Mother.

"Say good-bye to your auntie," Sunil said.

"'Bye, Auntie."

"'Bye, *kurban*," Mother replied, choked up. "Be a good boy."

"I will." They kissed.

And then Sunil brought Imran over to me.

"'Bye, Hayat."

"'Bye, Imran."

All at once, Imran's eyes brightened. "*Bhai-jaan?* Remember in the castle keep when we played chess? Remember when you told me don't forget? Remember?"

It took me a moment, and then I did. I nodded.

"I'll never forget it," he said.

"Promise?" I asked.

He reached out and took hold of my neck. "I promise!" he sang.

Mina looked at me again. I felt a sickening pain in my stomach. "I love you, Hayat," she said.

"I love you, too," I replied.

* * *

When I got to school on Monday morning, I opened my desk and saw the red library copy of the Quran sitting atop my books. I felt the fresh shame of my recital at the *walima*, but then I heard Father's voice inside me, reassuring me:

You are not like them, it said. *You are not a follower.*

At recess, instead of resuming my usual daily memorization of holy verses, I took the Quran and walked down the empty hall toward the library. I passed the bald old janitor, Gurvitz, pushing his trash can along on its wheels. He nodded at me. I nodded back. "How's things?" he asked flatly.

"Fine," I said, surprised. It was the first time he'd ever spoken to me.

"Thing is, I see you around, and I have this feeling about you. Like you're a good kid."

"Thanks," I said.

"Don't let it go to your head," he offered—suddenly brusque—as he doddered off.

Inside the library, the return bin was filled with books. I didn't give the moment much thought. I didn't kiss the cover as I usually did. I just put the Quran down on top of the other books and watched it slide to one side, tumbling out of view. It was the last Quran I would touch for almost ten years.

Mother and Mina spoke on the phone daily for the next three weeks, and then, one day, Mother called and Mina didn't call her back. Mother made nothing of it at first. But then two days passed. And then a third. And now, when Mother called the Chathas', no one was picking up.

On the morning of the fourth day—it was a Saturday— Mother got in her car and drove to the Chatha house to find out what was going on. She was gone ten hours. When she got home that night, she was seething. "He's a savage!" she shouted, tossing her keys in the cabinet. "I knew something was wrong with that man. I just knew it." When I asked her what happened, she exploded again: "Hayat! Her face is swollen. Completely black and blue. She's been lying in her room for three days. And you know why that bastard did that to her? Hmm? Do you know why?"

I shook my head, my blood suddenly hot and rushing to my face.

"Because she *questioned* him. He wanted to tell his cousin that he doesn't just want a job working for Ghaleb. He wants to be an equal partner. Ghaleb has built up his pharmacies for I don't know how many years, and this *idiot* comes along and says he wants to be an equal partner? All because he has a doctor's degree and he thinks that makes him more special than his cousin, who is just a pharmacist? Can you believe it? Napoleon complex, *behta*. Just like I told you. Just like her father. But this one is a true *savage*."

Mother sat down. She was shaking. I thought she was about to cry, until she spoke again and I realized she was trembling with anger.

"Hayat! All she said to him was, *Do you think it's such a good idea to say something like that to your cousin?* That's all! She's trying to give that *fool* some good advice! And what does he do? You should have seen her face, Hayat! Thank God he wasn't home when I got there. Thank God! Because if he was, I would have *broken* his head open! I *hate* these Muslim men. I *hate* them!... Not that Najat is any better. Do you know what she said to your Mina-auntie?"

I shook my head again.

"In front of your Mina-auntie and me, she tells us that the

Quran says it's all right for husbands to beat their wives. '*Bull-shit! Bloody bullshit!*' I said." Such language on Mother's lips was surprising. Her anger made her seem strong and alive. "So you know what Najat does? She goes and gets the Quran and opens it and shows me some verse in the fourth *surah*. About beating your wife? ..."

I nodded. The fourth *surah* was one from which I'd recited at the *walima*. I spoke the verse:

> Men are in charge of women for He has endowed
> them with greater resources.
> Good women will obey and guard what He or-
> dains.
> Those whose rebellion you fear, reprove them;
> then leave them alone in bed; then beat them.
> If they obey, do not harm them.

Mother stared at me for a long moment, a puzzled look on her face. It was as if she was noticing something about me she had never seen before.

"That was the one," she finally said. "I didn't know it, but there it was right in front of my eyes, written to give every Muslim man ideas... And then Najat says to me something you will never believe: '*Ghaleb beats me, too,*' she says. Almost like she's proud! Can you believe it?"

I didn't know what to say. But Mother wasn't waiting for me to say anything.

"So what do I do? I ask her, like any normal person would, '*Why, Najat, does your husband beat you? Hmm?*'"

Mother was absorbed in the moment, as if reliving it.

"'*Because we need it,*' she says. '*Because it's something about our nature. Something that needs to know its limits.*' My jaw hit the floor, Hayat. I looked at her and thought to myself, this is an *insane* asylum..."

Mother paused. And then she added, her chin slightly raised, her tone hushed and heavy with a sudden philosophical cast: "It was the first time I realized maybe I don't have it so bad with your father. Maybe, all these years, I haven't had it so bad, after all..."

For the next two days, I tried not to think about Sunil beating Mina, but it didn't work. In my mind's eye, I saw that small rodent of a man repeatedly hitting her with his closed fists. I tossed under the covers at night trying to forget what Mother said about Mina's face being swollen, but I couldn't. It made me angry. But not only angry. I felt responsible. I hadn't had any reason to think about what I had done since Sunil entered the picture. Everything was supposed to turn out for the best. But that wasn't happening. And if it hadn't been for me and that afternoon in the Western Union office, she never would have ended up with this man.

But what could I do now?

All I could think of was either crank-calling the Chatha house—which I did more than a dozen times—or praying. So I prayed. I prayed that her husband wouldn't beat her. I prayed that she not suffer. But with time, my prayers would prove as ineffectual as the crank-calling. As the bad news continued to pour in about Mina's new husband, my doubts about the power of my prayer began to grow.

A month later, Mother had another alarming development to relay: She'd been trying to get Mina to leave Sunil and come back to live with us. But Mina wasn't going to do it. The thought of another divorce made her want to die. She'd made her choice and that was that; now she had to live with it. What-ever the consequences. Which meant (and this was the bad news): She was moving to Kansas City.

Sunil had gone ahead and imprudently demanded the equal business partnership from his cousin, and now Ghaleb was no longer speaking to him. So Sunil decided to pack up the family, to go back to being an eye doctor, and to move the family back into the house he still owned in Kansas City. Mother didn't like it. "She thinks it will get better. That once he's out of his cousin's house and back home, he will feel more like a man. Like he's *in charge*. What is it about these Muslim men that they need to feel *in charge* all the time?! What is the *big deal?* My God!" She looked up at the kitchen ceiling, as if hoping for a response from the Lord Himself. She shook her head and went on: "Your auntie keeps talking about how good he is with Imran. That he's taken to him like his own son. But how happy can the boy be if he sees his mother getting beaten by his father? Hmm? How happy can he be? *Behta,* I have a *terri-ble* feeling about them moving back to Kansas. That's where he had another wife who left him. God only knows why. I mean, who knows if he didn't beat *her* to shreds? After all, Muslim women are not like white women. They don't *run away* for nothing."

About Sunil's first wife, Mother's intuition would turn out to be right.

Upon Mina's arrival in Kansas City, she received an af-ternoon visit from one of Sunil's first wife's friends. The woman—a local Pakistani—came by when she was sure Sunil wouldn't be home to alert the new wife about what had hap-pened. His first wife had indeed left him because of the abuse. And Sunil's history of domestic violence was well documented enough that a court had denied him any meaningful custody rights regarding his son. This, of course, was not the tale Sunil had told Mina. According to him, his ex-wife's exposure to the American lifestyle had turned her into a sex-crazed maniac, and her conscience could no longer handle life with a God-fearing man like himself. When Mother found out about all this, her worry started to eat away at her stomach lining. For months, she complained about Sunil and about the pain in her belly. When she was diagnosed with an ulcer, all she kept saying was: "At least I can take medicine for this. But what medicine can they give Mina for a man who's going to make her life a living hell?"

For a time, Mother continued to speak on the phone with Mina daily, learning each new alarming detail of Sunil's bizarre behavior almost as soon as it surfaced. As Mother had suspected, rather than stabilizing him, Sunil's return to his former haunts only fueled a paranoid fear that Mina would leave him just as his first wife had. So he took precautions. He had Mina dispense with the *hijab* and take up the full-body *chador*. Now she was forbidden to address a man, even at the local mosque, which the family started to frequent every weekend. Mina didn't fight him, but despite her compliance, Sunil's jealousy only grew more unruly: Mina's passing look at a male driver stopped at a traffic light in the car adjacent was enough for Sunil to lose his temper. On one occasion, an argument in the car escalated to the point that Sunil, in his howling rage, shouted—as he recklessly pulled at the steering wheel, and swerved the car toward the highway's concrete median—that he would kill all three of them before ever losing her to another man.

Mother's support was untiring, but so was Mina's resolve to stick it out. She claimed Sunil was no longer beating her, and she was quick to make excuses for him: His professional life back in Kansas City was not going well. He was having more difficulty rebuilding his practice than he'd expected. Never particularly good with finances, he'd mismanaged his seed capital, and was steadily inching toward insolvency. Then Mina got pregnant. She and Mother both hoped this good news would soften Sunil. It didn't. In fact, Mina's pregnancy only made him more paranoid. Now, Mina had to wear the full, face-covering *burqa*. She was forbidden from leaving the house unless she was accompanied by him, even for groceries. And he didn't even want her answering the door, an injunction he would test by having male friends come by and ring the bell to see if she would answer. "He's got her under house arrest," Mother moaned after getting off the phone with her dearest friend. "He's going to drive her into the ground."

Herself poisoned by the latest toxic twists in Mina's life, Mother became sicker. Now her stomach ached constantly. For hours at a time, she would hold her gut, doubled over in pain. Father suspected another ulcer, and he was right. But it wasn't just that, for even once Mother made the necessary adjustments to her diet and her pain subsided, she still wasn't well. She never spent all that much time out of the house, but now she really never left. She was so depressed. And seeing Mother's anguish—just the echo of Mina's own—solidified my certainty that I was to blame: Had I not said those things about Jews to Imran on that fateful night, had I not sent that telegram, Mina would likely have married Nathan. I couldn't understand anymore what I thought would have been so wrong with it. At least she and Mother would have been happy now. And even if Mina's father had broken her bones over such a marriage, wouldn't this have been better than the soul breaking she was getting from Sunil on a regular basis?

I suffered my blame in silence. I still had told no one about the telegram. And there was some solace, I found, in keeping my secret. This, at least, was something I could control. It made my pain somehow fully my own, a pain that now began to inform my choices. My first year of middle school, I overheard someone in the hall mentioning that Simon Felsenthal, the shy boy with thick glasses in the back of social studies class, was Jewish. Though I'd barely noticed Simon before, I now worked to make him my best friend, but only to discover that I was actually more preoccupied by his faith than he was. Simon was all about the video games. He weaned me off Atari and introduced me to the subtler pleasures of Intellivision. Simon's was the first house I ever slept over in, and I remember thinking that his parents—vital and bickering—weren't all that different from mine. I thought back to the morning I'd awoken from my dream about the Prophet in the hospital room, confused over why Allah hated the Jews so much. It made even less sense to me now.

With the passing years, Mina's situation only worsened, and by the end of high school—some five years into her marriage to Sunil—the simple mention of her name would be enough to send me into a depression that could last for days. And it was no longer just Mina. My soul was outgrowing the childsized raiment with which my Islamic childhood had outfitted me. But I wasn't ready for the terror of nakedness. Out at an ice cream shop one night with my friends, I noticed that the woman serving ice cream was wearing a thick layer of foundation, and that the area around her eye was swollen. My gaze lingered there, and I could tell the skin was black and blue underneath. *Someone is beating her,* I thought. It made me sick. I took the ice cream and went out to the parking lot with my friends. My sickness turned to nausea and then to grief. Before long, I had wandered off, leaving everyone behind. I sat by a dumpster behind the local grocery store, where I cried and cried. When my tears had run their course, I looked up into a dark, still sky, stippled with tiny, twinkling lights—like the fireflies that so delighted Father. My heart yearned to pray. I put my hands out before me in the Muslim style and tried to conjure the heartfelt fire I knew so well from back when Mina lived with us. But my words rang hollow. Like sounds spoken to the deaf, or worse, to no one at all.

Now, when Mina called, I left the house. I couldn't bear her increasingly wan, fragile voice, in which all I heard was my own blame. I had tried countless times to apologize to her on the phone for what I'd said about Nathan—I never mentioned the telegram—but Mina was insistent. It was all behind us, she would say. I should move on. So I tried. I asked Mother not to tell me any more about what was happening to her best friend. "It's too painful," I confessed. Mother seemed to understand. And for a time, I didn't have to think about my aunt Mina or be reminded of what I'd done. I could merrily play at becoming the sort of American boy—embracing a bright future, unhampered by his Muslim apprenticeship in the necessity of pain— that my childhood would not have promised. I worried about my brand of jeans and my style of hair. I listened to the latest by U2 and R.E.M. on my Walkman as I sat on the bus to school. But the shadow of Mina's misfortunes always loomed. I may have hoped for a reprieve, but I didn't have to have read Emerson to know that I'd done nothing to deserve such mercy. Indeed, what I had done bound me to her in a way I couldn't simply leave behind. And what's more, Mother's life was completely enmeshed in Mina's. When Mother moped about the house, weighed down by the latest unfolding horror in her best friend's life, of course she couldn't turn to Father. She had only me. I had no choice but to listen.

* * *

After a second financial collapse, Sunil sold his professional assets to cover the debts, and he was forced to take the only offer he could find: a junior partnership at a local practice. Unable to adjust to the office hierarchy and its frustrations, Sunil became suicidal. One night, he emptied into his mouth Mina's bottle of Valium—which she'd been using to manage her anxiety ever since the day of her *nikah*—and would have ended up dead had he not confessed to his wife what he'd done as he drifted off to sleep. Mina called an ambulance, and for once she didn't bother with the *burqa* as she left the house to accompany him to the hospital, where he had his stomach pumped. Mina and Mother couldn't agree about what the meaning of Sunil's attempted suicide was. Mina thought it was a cry for attention. Mother told her it was just another, even more pernicious attempt to terrify her into further submission. What Sunil did next would prove they were both right.

He bought a gun, which—Mother suggested—had the advantage over pills that it got him the sort of frightened, all-consuming attention he sought without a trip to the emergency room. Now, all he had to do was brandish the pistol and put it to his head for Mina to get down on her knees and tell him—which she did, on more than one occasion—that he was her master.

Sunil started bringing the gun downstairs to dinner. He laid it by his plate, alongside the silverware. Having it there calmed him, he said. It kept her "fast mouth" in check. If he didn't like something she said, all he had to do was raise the gun and point it at himself, or—increasingly—at her. This kept her quiet. But even with his wife's silence at dinner ensured, Sunil would find new uses for his weapon. Too much turmeric in the ground beef curry was a reason to aim the revolver at her face. So was an empty pitcher of water that needed filling. Training the gun on his wife became the way Sunil prefaced whatever orders he had for what should be done at the table, or in the house. More than once, Imran himself closed his fist and extended his thumb and index finger to form a pistol with his hand, pointing it at his mother to make a demand or complaint.

When Mother told Father about Sunil's shenanigans with the gun, he was outraged. He picked up the phone and called Ghaleb Chatha to tell him what was going on. For once, the two men were in agreement on something: Sunil had gone too far. Ghaleb promised Father to put pressure where it counted. He called his cousin and told him to get rid of the firearm. If he didn't, Ghaleb said, the monthly checks that now composed a significant portion of Sunil's modest income would stop coming. So Sunil had no choice. He sold the gun. But not before forbidding his wife from ever speaking to Mother again.

Mother did her best to circumvent the interdiction, but soon enough, there was another reason they stopped talking. They got into a series of arguments—Mother growing more and more strident about pushing Mina to leave Sunil; after all, now she was a legal resident, and there was no chance she was going to lose Imran anymore—and Mina retaliating by saying the sorts of nasty things only one's best friend could.

One day, I found Mother at the kitchen table looking out at the smooth blanket of glowing snow covering our backyard. She wasn't moving. It didn't even seem like she was breathing. I asked her what was wrong.

"Your auntie and I got into a fight," she said quietly.

"Again?"

"I told her to leave him. She doesn't need the bloody man anymore. She has her permanent green card. But she doesn't want to hear it. She's had his child now, she says, and she's not leaving..."

"*Ammi.* This isn't new."

Mother paused. "She said something else, too. She said I've been miserable most of my life." She paused again. "And that I've made everyone around me miserable, too...Is it true?" Mother asked, weakly. She looked like she was going to cry.

"Mom. Of course it's not true."

"Maybe it is."

"You made her happy, didn't you? You helped her when she needed help, right?"

She nodded, unconvinced. "But what about you?" she asked. "Did I make you happy? You know what Freud says about—"

"I don't care what Freud says," I replied, interrupting.

"I make you happy?" she asked, her voice cracking.

A sudden knot was forming in my throat. "Of course you do, *Ammi.* Of course you do."

"Oh, Hayat," she keened, reaching out to me.

The next day Mina called to apologize. But almost immediately, the two of them got into yet another argument, and this just as Sunil was getting home from an uncharacteristically early day. When he realized Mina was on the phone with Mother, he flew into a rage and ripped the phone from the wall.

And so it was that Mina and Mother lost contact for three years...

Of all the stories that Mina told me as a young boy, the ones that stayed with me most were the ones about dervishes: the first, in which a dervish sitting by the side of a road has orange peels tossed on him by a couple of passersby and, in that moment of ill-usage, awakens to the fiction of the personal self that imagines it is any different from the peels or the passersby, or God Himself; and the tale that suggested being ground to dust was the way to our Lord.

Whether Mina, like one of her dervishes, found God, I can't say, but in marrying Sunil I certainly believe she found someone to ill-use her, someone who would eventually grind her to dust.

After eight years of marriage, the stress and strain would finally end when she was diagnosed with a terminal case of uterine cancer that had metastasized to the bone. Mina's illness would make Sunil repent his ways. He called Mother to deliver the news himself. He confided that he felt he was responsible for her sickness. Mother agreed—she was to give Sunil a great deal of grief during Mina's last months—but Mina herself didn't. Though she appreciated Sunil's change of heart—and probably didn't mind him bearing the brunt of Mother's outrage—to Mina, her own illness could only be Allah's doing, another *station on the path,* as she called it.

During the last eight months of her life, Mina and I spoke on the phone at least a dozen times. And I saw her two months before she died.

Mother had already been to visit her once, and as she planned her second trip, I told her I wanted to go as well. At that point, there was little doubt Mina was dying, and I knew I had to see her.

Mother and I took a plane to Kansas City, where Sunil picked us up from the airport in the late afternoon. It had barely been eight years, but he seemed to have aged at least twenty. His small face was covered with wrinkles, and his head with white hair, and I'm not sure I would have thought it was the same person if he hadn't taken my hands and pressed his fingers into my palms the way he had when we first met, speaking with the same distinctive, distracting drawl which, once heard, was difficult to forget: "Your Mina-auntie will be so haappy to see yoou, *behta*. She always looved you so much."

We sped along the freeway to the hospital, Mother in front with Sunil, me in back watching the houses and businesses pass outside the window. Quranic tapes quietly played over the car speakers as Sunil spoke, mostly about Mina's imminent passing. He seemed to be working himself up into a state, repeatedly saying that his wife was the only person he was one hundred percent certain was headed directly for Paradise. At one point—as we pulled into the hospital lot and parked—he broke down. Mother put her hand on his shoulder. "What I put her through, *bhaji*," he repeated through his tears. "I don't know how she can forgive what I put her through..."

Upstairs, on the eighth floor, at the end of the hall, was Mina's room. She was awake, propped up on pillows, machines humming quietly around her. Her skin was ashen and she was thin, as thin as I'd ever seen her, even at her worst. But her eyes sparkled when she saw us. However sick she appeared, she looked no less alive. When she saw me, a wry smile came across her face. "My goodness, Hayat."

"What?"

"A heartbreaker. I've seen pictures...But in person, you're even better..."

I couldn't help but laugh. "I don't know if you remember...that's the first thing you ever said to me."

"And it might be the last," she joked, wincing from the pain her laughter caused her.

338

"Stop it," Mother said.

Mina ignored her. "Eyelashes like that?" she coughed, lifting the arm from which an IV drip snaked to point at me. "Wasted on a man! Just look at those!"

Mother sat down beside her, taking Mina's other hand. "Man? I don't know about that yet."

"He's a man, *bhaj*. He's a man, all right."

Mina looked over at Sunil, who was watching from the corner. To me, he looked sheepish, even cowed. Seeing the two of them together now—after all this time, after all the tales—was strange. It was difficult to imagine that the man had ever had any power over her.

Sunil left the three of us to be together. Mina was eager for details of my life at college: my classes, what I was reading, and then—when Mother got up to go to the bathroom—she wanted to know about girls.

"None yet," I told her.

"Just as well. Because when you get started..." She laughed again, wincing. When Mother returned, Mina said she was getting tired and needed to sleep. Mother leaned in to kiss her. I got up and did the same. But as we were about to leave, Mina put out her hand to stop me. "Hayat. You can stay. If you want. *Bhaj,* if it's okay, do you mind if he stays while I sleep? I don't want him to go yet..."

"If he wants to, it's fine with me," Mother said.

"I'd love to," I said.

I would end up spending the night, much of it watching her sleep from the armchair beside her bed, thinking about what I had come to say. (Mother had gone back to Sunil and Mina's home for the night, and planned on returning in the morning with both Imran and Imran's younger sister, Nasreen.) At daybreak, she roused and looked over, clearly in pain. "You're still here?" she asked.

"I didn't want to leave."

She smiled through her pain.

The nurses came in, and I stepped out. I went down to the canteen to get a cup of coffee. When I returned to the room, she was sitting up in bed, a small plastic cup of apple juice before her. She looked better, and she was eager to talk. We chatted more about books. She showed me a quote from what she was then reading, a collection of Fitzgerald's letters:

> The test of a first-rate intelligence is the ability to hold two opposing ideas in the mind at the same time and still retain the ability to function.

She seemed so pleased to share it with me, and so interested in what I thought of it. I remember not telling her what I was really thinking: that she herself was a paradox I couldn't resolve, my opposing ideas of her—enlightened and devout; intrepid and passive—only ever colliding, and never sitting comfortably enough for me to hold them at all, let alone function.

At some point, she said she could tell I had something on my mind. I told her I did, and then I mentioned my regret over the things I had said about Nathan to Imran that night.

"How many times have we talked about this, Hayat? It's okay. You did it. You learned from it. That's life."

I was quiet.

She went on: "I've told you. You're not responsible for what happened to me. It was my own choice. And it was all for a reason, *behta*. You need to accept that."

There was another silence. And then I said: "There's something you don't know, Auntie. Something I never told you."

"What is that?"

"The telegram? To Hamed? That was me. I sent it."

"What?" Her eyes widened with surprise. There was silence. The answer to her long-unresolved question was taking some time to make sense. "But how did you..."

I completed her thought. "You had a book. It had your address from when you were in Karachi. I went to the mall and sent it."

"Enterprising," she said after a brief moment.

"I don't know about that."

Again there was silence. Mina took a deep breath. "So that's why you won't let this thing go."

"If I hadn't sent it, you might still..."

She lifted her hand to stop me.

"It doesn't change anything, *behta*. It was my choice. I made that choice. If I was going to make a different choice, I would have made it anyway."

"But why?"

"Why what?"

"Why didn't you make a different choice?"

"You could say it's who I am, Hayat. What I experienced in my life, and that made me what I am. Or you could say it was Allah's will for me." She paused. "In the end, both ways of looking amount to the same thing..."

"They're not the same thing," I began. I wanted to tell her that I had been giving up on Islam little by little for years, and that now there was barely anything left.

But somehow, it didn't seem like this was what needed saying.

"You say Allah's will. Fine. But why follow His will? So you can go to heaven or something like that? I mean, isn't it all a little silly? Isn't it more moral to be good and to do the right thing for its own sake? Isn't that really the sign of the good?"

She smiled. I thought she almost looked proud of me. "Absolutely," she said.

"Then I don't understand."

"Faith has never been about an afterlife for me, Hayat. It's about finding God *now*. In the everyday. Here. With you. Whether I'm living in a prison or in a castle. Sick or healthy. It's all the same. That's what the Sufis teach. What comes our way, whatever it is, *that* is the vehicle. Every single life, no matter how big or small, how happy or how sad, it can be a path to Him."

What are all these Sufi tales, I thought, *but fictions she's using to shed a redeeming glow on a life scored with pain, pain I caused her, pain Sunil caused her, and that she should have sought not simply to bear, but escape?*

She could tell I didn't agree. She wanted me to speak my mind.

So I did. I made my point with all the force I could muster. Humiliation, I told her, was not a vehicle to anything but senseless injury. And to say otherwise was to let a world filled with pain go its own way, unchecked, unredeemed.

As I spoke, I had the distinct feeling she was relishing every moment of what was happening, the discussion, my turmoil and passion, the apple juice she was slowly sipping.

I finally put the question to her as directly as I could:

What did the suffering she had gone through over the past eight years at her husband's hands—and for that matter the suffering she was experiencing now, as she lay dying—what did any of this have to do with finding God?

I should have expected she would reply with another anecdote pulled from a dervish's life.

"When Chishti was dying," she began, "he was in pain all over his body. His followers didn't understand how a man who Allah loved so much could be put through so much pain...Do you know what he told them when they asked him why Allah was making him suffer so?"

"What?"

"'*This is how the divine is choosing to express Himself through me.*'" Her eyes glistened with eagerness to make the point that was—I would later come to see—something like the boiled-down essence of her life. "What he meant is that everything, *everything,* is an expression of Allah's will. It is all His glory. Even the pain..." She paused. "That is the *real* truth about life."

Epilogue: 1995

This story ends in Boston.

I ended up dating Rachel my junior and senior years, and after college we moved to Boston together, into an apartment in Kenmore Square. Our wonderful and troubled interfaith romance is a tale for another time, but there's still something that needs to be said to finish this one: It was in Rachel's arms—and it was with her love—that I finally discovered myself not only as a man, but as an American.

She was working at a clinic in Brookline; I was interning at the *Atlantic* on North Washington Street. On Saturdays, I would take the Green Line to the Red Line, and the Red Line to Harvard Square, where it was my habit to spend the afternoon and evening at the Algiers Coffee House, writing. There was something about the place—its oriental woodwork, its mirrored ceiling dome, the mint tea and the Arabic music—that put me in the frame of mind to set words to paper. It was on the Algiers's second floor that I would write my first short story. And it was on that same second floor that I would run into Nathan.

I was sitting at a corner booth when a short, striking man came up the stairs, coffee in one hand, a plate of baklava in the other. I recognized Nathan almost immediately. It had been more than a decade since I'd last seen him, and aside from looking a little more weathered—his head of woolly hair was finely shorn and peppered generously with dashes of gray—he looked the same. He was standing at the top of the stairs, surveying the cramped room for a place to sit, when he noticed me looking right at him.

"Dr. Wolfsohn?" I asked, standing. Nathan's brow crinkled and his eyes narrowed as recognition seemed to dance across his gaze. "It's Hayat Shah," I said.

"Hayat...My God," he said, a hint of wonder in his voice as he approached. "How you've grown. You're a man."

"Not quite," I joked. "But it sure has been a while."

"What are you doing here?" he asked.

"I come here a lot on the weekends. I'm interning at the *Atlantic*."

"Good for you," he said with an abundant smile. He kept looking at me, shaking his head gently in disbelief. My limbs were weak. My heart was racing. I was completely disarmed by how happy he was to see me. And all at once, it occurred to me for the first time that the apology I'd been trying to make to Mina all of these years was really one intended for him.

"Listen, Dr. Wolfsohn...," I began, hesitant.

"Call me Nathan, Hayat."

"Right. Nathan. Do you—uh—wanna sit for a second?"

"Sure," he said, putting his cup of coffee and his plate of dessert down on the table between us. He pulled out a chair and sat. I sat down, too.

"I'm not sure how to say this exactly..."

"Just go ahead, Hayat," Nathan said. He was looking directly at me, something grave—even stern—in his gaze.

"I never got a chance to talk to you after what happened...I mean, I was pretty young and..." I stopped myself. My words somehow didn't seem right. I looked up at him. He was still listening.

"I guess what I wanted to say was...I'm sorry for what happened. I didn't exactly understand what I was doing, and...I can't believe that I said those things."

Nathan held my gaze for a moment, then gently nodded. He shifted in place, softly clearing his throat. "You know...I always knew that you would say that to me. One day. I always knew it...Thank you."

"You're welcome," I quietly replied.

There was a long silence between us. I was about to say more—to tell him about the telegram—when he asked me about my parents.

"My dad's not so great. I don't think he ever got over going into private practice. He drinks a lot. More than he should. Not that he admits it...My mom suffers, not quite in silence, as I'm sure you can imagine."

"She has her hands full with him," he said with a smile. "Naveed is a stubborn man."

"Indeed."

"But a good one. I owe him a call."

"Do you still speak?"

"From time to time."

"I think a call from you would be great. He still talks about you..."

"Does he?" Nathan asked, a sudden brightness in his tone. "What does he say?"

"You know—remembering the good times you used to have at the lab together. He still laughs about you not being able to tell a joke...or eat spicy food."

"Well, that's changed. At least the spicy food. He got me hooked. He...and Mina, of course."

"She died," I said. I don't even think I realized I had spoken until I heard my voice say the words.

But there was no surprise. Nathan nodded, quietly affirming that he knew.

There was another long silence.

Until he finally spoke: "There's something you should know, Hayat. It might make you feel better."

"What's that?"

"Mina and I were in touch."

I was shocked. "You were?"

Nathan nodded. "I got a letter from her a year after everything that happened between us. Sent to my parents' house. She still had their address from a letter I'd written her from their place." He smiled to himself, remembering. "Getting that letter was, I think, the biggest surprise of my life."

"What did she say, if it's okay for me to ask?"

"It was basically her version of what had happened. Her explanation. I mean, I think the real meaning of it was to let me know she regretted the decision she made... but she wasn't going to come out and say it... Though she did later."

"She did," I said, meaning to ask a question, though it didn't come out that way. And the clear relief in my reply was as much a surprise to Nathan as it was to me.

He held my gaze for a long moment, nodding. "That man she was married to was insane," he added with visible anger.

"He got sick, did you know?"

"No, I didn't. What happened?"

"Something with his lungs. He's out of breath all the time. Has to carry oxygen around with him wherever he goes. It happened right after Mina died. Imran takes care of him."

"How is Imran?"

"Fine. I saw him a few years ago. I mean, his mom was dying, so he wasn't too talkative. But I think he's okay. He's in high school. He and his sister are both going to an Islamic school in Kansas City. The girl looks just like her mother. Her name is Nasreen."

I paused.

Nathan shook his head. "You have no idea how many times I told her to leave him, Hayat."

"Why didn't she?"

Nathan shrugged. "You probably understand that better than I do. It has to be a cultural thing...My own feeling was that she knew if she wasn't with him, she'd come back to me. And she knew I would take her back..." He stopped for a moment. "I never got over your aunt. She was, and always will be, the love of my life."

Nathan held my gaze a moment longer before looking away. I suddenly felt close to him. I wanted to tell him that my girl-friend, Rachel, was Jewish. But I didn't. His eyes were full, alive with memory. I didn't want to interrupt.

Nathan cleared his throat. "We were lucky. The postal worker who delivered her mail was a black woman named Sheniqua. Somehow, she and your aunt got to be good friends. Mina would make that famous tea for her, and they would talk. Your aunt must have told her all about Sunil, and I guess at some point she told her about me as well..."

Nathan paused, remembering.

"So when Sheniqua found out about me, she offered to be the go-between for our letters to each other. I would send them to her, and Sheniqua would send Mina's letters to me. And she would only bring them over when Sunil and the boys weren't around. Mina would read them and give them back to Sheni-qua. Sheniqua held on to them. All of them."

"That's amazing."

"I don't know how she kept it from her husband all those years, but she did..."

"Did you ever see each other?" I asked, not realizing—until Nathan didn't reply—that the question might have been a delicate one.

He stared at me for a long moment, his eyes full, still, unblinking.

Just then, the Arabic music playing over the speakers stopped, revealing a mosaic of sounds underneath: spoons stirring porcelain mugs, the quiet talk between patrons, the beeping of the cash register downstairs. The sudden absence of the music felt naked, revealing. Nathan looked away, taking a sip of his coffee. His gaze was covered with a thin, wet film of what seemed to me like longing and regret. I wanted to ask him again if they had seen each other, but I didn't.

All at once, the music returned.

"I should get going, Hayat," he said, checking his watch. "I'm glad we ran into each other."

"Me, too."

"You want this?" he asked, indicating the piece of baklava before him. "It's great. They make it with orange blossom water here."

"You don't want it?"

"Kind of lost my appetite." Nathan got up and reached his hand out toward me. I got up as well. "Good luck with everything. And you know, if you want to get in touch with me sometime, I'm at Mass. General. In the radiology department now."

"Okay. Thanks...Um, Nathan, you know...There's something else I should tell you ..."

He held up his hand, looking at me with what felt like knowing tenderness. "Whatever it is, Hayat, don't worry about it. It's okay." He smiled. "Good luck at the *Atlantic*. I'll be looking out for your name."

"Don't hold your breath," I replied.

He turned and walked to the railing. After a last, lingering look, he went down the steps.

I sat upstairs at the coffeehouse a little while longer, finishing the baklava Nathan had left me. I was stunned that he and Mina had stayed in touch. And I sat there revisiting Nathan's pregnant silence around whether he'd ever seen Mina again. I wanted desperately to think that he had.

I packed my pad and pens into my bag and got up. As I made my way down the steps to the street, I felt awake. Outside, a brisk March breeze blew, sharp against my face. Instead of heading for the subway to return home, I turned to walk toward the river. I wove my way through the campus buildings and the old homes lining Brattle Street and Mount Auburn, an ease in my body as I moved. The alertness I was feeling tingled even along my limbs, and the ground itself—strong and solid beneath my feet—seemed different to me.

As I walked with the wind, verses from the Quran I'd not recalled or thought about for more than ten years echoed inside me, unbidden:

> Have We not opened your heart
> And removed your burden?
> Have We not remembered you?
> Truly, with hardship comes ease,
> With hardship comes ease!
> And so when you are finished, do not rest,
> But return to your Lord with love…

I crossed the road at the river's edge and found a bench along the joggers' path. The Charles River was thick and brown, full from days of rain, its surface rolling and choppy in the breezy day. The trees across the river were bare. The ground around me was covered with brown grass only recently showing from beneath a winter of heavy snow. Joggers came and went in both directions, the shuffle of their sneakers on the wet pavement sounding an even pulse. I sat down. Behind me, a bare linden tree reached out and over the bench, its bud-covered branches defining the form of a canopy that, in a couple of months' time, would provide ample shade from the summer sun. But for now, that sun was nowhere to be seen, hidden as it was behind the sheetlike gray of an overcast sky. Low against the horizon, billows of slow-moving dark blue clouds drifted, pregnant with rain. It was a picture of power and grace, and it filled me with quiet wonder.

All at once, I felt a swell of gratitude.

Gratitude for what? I wondered.

I remembered the afternoon of the ice cream social when Mina first taught me to listen to a still, small voice inside, hidden between and beneath the breath.

I breathed in deeply and exhaled. And into the silence at the end of my breath I quietly intoned my question.

Gratitude for what?

I listened for a reply.

I heard a passing car's wet tires on the road. And then a jogger's rubber soles lightly squeaking on the pavement.

I breathed again and listened more deeply.

The branches lightly creaked and swayed in the breeze. The river softly coursed at the bank's edge.

I kept listening. Another breath. And then another. And then again.

And finally I started to hear it. It was only this:

My heart, silently murmuring its steady beat.

Acknowledgments

I would like to thank: My extraordinary agent, Donna Bagdasarian, for her devotion to this book. The inimitable Judy Clain for her brilliant editing. Arzu Tahsin at Orion for her incisive comments. Marc H. Glick for support that seems to have no limit. Nathan Rostron and the whole team at Little, Brown for their enthusiasm and commitment. Don Shaw and Michael Pollard for more than I could list.

I have had so many important readers: Foremost, my brilliant brother Shazad. Nicole Galland, who helped me to shape this story from earlier drafts. Larry Levine, Jason Shulman, and Seymour Bernstein, who offered sage and illuminating commentary. Marisol Page and Poorna Jagannathan, who asked the questions that helped me find the ending. Martha Harrell, Dan Hancock, Elise Joffe, Ami Dayan, Sean Sullivan, Brett Grabel, Shane Leprevost, Jeremy Xido, and Nadia Malik, all better friends than I deserve. Stuart Rosenthal, Marcia Butler, Aja Nisenson, Barbara Stehle, Oren Moverman, Firdous Bamji, Alexa Fogel, Nicole Laliberte, Amina Chaudhury, Siddhartha Mitter, Andrew Dickson, Aisha Ghani, Kiran Khalid, Faraaz Siddiqi and the Siddiqi family, for their time, energy, and intelligence.

The verses of the Quran cited in the novel are my own personal interpretations as seen through the eyes of the fictional characters I created. I wish to acknowledge the work of Marmaduke Pickthall, Muhammad Asad, Abdullah Yusuf Ali, and Andre Chouraqui, whose interpretations of the Quran were inspirations.

Finally, I would like to thank my remarkable parents for their endless love and limitless support.

Ayad Akhtar is an actor, playwright, and novelist. He lives in New York City.